TERMINUS

LEE HARDEN SERIES

BOOK 6

★

D. J. MOLLES

The characters and events portrayed in this book are fictitious.
Any similarity to real persons, living or dead, is coincidental and
not intended by the author.

Text copyright © 2022 D.J. Molles
All rights reserved.
No part of this book may be reproduced, or stored in a retrieval
system, or transmitted in any form or by any means, electronic,
mechanical, photocopying, recording, or otherwise, without
express written permission of the publisher.

PART 1

Turning and turning in the widening gyre
The falcon cannot hear the falconer;
Things fall apart; the centre cannot hold

—*Second Coming*, William Butler Yeats

PROLOGUE

THE PROBLEM WITH DEMOCRACY

SECRETARY OF STATE ERWIN BRIGGS swirled his tumbler of scotch, and wondered what it was. The man from The Corporation, whose office Briggs now stood in, was much too classy to pour straight from a bottle. He struck Briggs as the type to fill his decanters with top-dollar spirits, and let the enigma of his wealth enhance their flavor even more.

Briggs was always of the opinion that a decanter was for hiding the fact that it *wasn't* top-dollar spirits. But Briggs was ever a pragmatist.

The man from The Corporation seemed a tad more of an idealist. An idealist with big, world-wide ideas. Dangerous ideas, to be sure. But exciting ones. Things that could change the world, if you could stomach the eggs that had to be broken to make the omelet.

Briggs looked out one of the tall windows with its thick, dark drapes pulled aside. It was a chilly, dismal day in Washington, D.C., and he could only just make out the spire of the Capitol Building in the distance.

The clink of a glass, made distinctly rich by the knowledge that it was being set down on hundred-year-old mahogany. A light sigh. The creak of a leather chair behind a desk.

"I've been very pleased with your men's performance in China," the man said.

Briggs turned, taking a sip from his glass. He could taste the money as it slid down his throat. "Security is pretty simple stuff for our operatives."

The man from The Corporation leaned back in his chair, looking so calm and regal. So untouchable. So above it all. The quiet knowledge of knowing that you're so insulated from any accountability that you can do whatever the hell you want and never have to worry about the consequences.

If he were being honest, it made Briggs a little jealous.

"Oh, it's not the security that I'm impressed with," the man said. "Anyone can carry a gun and do sentry duty. I'm impressed with their discretion."

"Well, I'll pass that on to my partner, then," Briggs replied, mildly. "Technically, I'm not the CEO of Cornerstone at this point. But I'm sure he'll be pleased with the compliment."

The man nodded, smiled, then quirked his eyebrows in a way that told Briggs there was another shoe that was about to drop. Possibly a rather nasty shoe.

"Unfortunately, our business arrangement is coming to a close."

Briggs felt the tiny twitch of his facial muscles, but kept them from sinking into a full-blown frown. "You won't be renewing your contract, then?"

The man motioned lazily with his glass. "We're reaching a point in our endeavors where it will no longer be conducive to have any outside ties. Even with a company so discrete as yours. I wanted to personally express my appreciation for their discretion, so that you and your partner understand that I hold your operatives in the highest regard. And

I may have need of your services again in the future. I didn't want you to think that my terminating the contract had anything to do with being unsatisfied."

Briggs took another sip. This one deeper. More for the fortification than for the enjoyment. The Corporation was a whale of a contract, not in the amount of men they were employing, but in the cost of the contract.

After all, discretion came at a high price these days.

Briggs stepped away from the glittering collection of crystal decanters, away from the gloomy view of the capitol, and sat in a plush leather chair across from the man and his mighty desk. He draped his arms on the rests and crossed his legs.

"Again, I'll be happy to pass on this information," Briggs said, with a bit of caution in his tone. "But, I reiterate: My partner is really the one you should be speaking to. My duties on the cabinet preclude me from having any direct dealings with Cornerstone. For now."

"Oh, of course. And I will be notifying your partner as well. And I'll be cutting a bonus to all of your men." A tiny sip from his own glass. The man scooted forward, elbows on his desk. "Fifty percent to each operative."

Briggs kept a good poker face, despite having the urge to drain the rest of his glass in a single gulp. That was in the neighborhood of a hundred grand per operative. And there were thirty operatives working at the facility in China.

Three million dollars was a decent chunk of hush-money. What the hell were they working on there?

For a brief and rather stupid moment, Briggs considered telling him that such exorbitant sums were unnecessary to ensure the discretion of the operatives—Cornerstone prided itself on having the best men, who knew about opsec and could keep their mouths shut...

But he wasn't about to screw those boys out of their payday.

He went with, "That will certainly...ease the sting of the contract termination."

All of the sudden, Briggs found himself intensely curious about what The Corporation was doing. And hiding. Oh, he had some general concept, based on his knowledge of the province where The Corporation had seated itself in China, and the type of facility that it was.

The type of facility that took advantage of a combination of lax laws and easily-bribed officials. The type of facility that went deep underground. The type of facility that was built to keep things from escaping it.

Troublesome, microscopic things.

But Briggs knew something about companies like The Corporation. And how secrets were kept. Which wasn't primarily through money. Money only went so far against people's consciences. It was really only good for getting people to turn a blind eye. Good for keeping people from getting too curious.

The people that actually *knew* the secrets? Well, they fell into two categories: The ones that were running the show, and had a vested interest in keeping their secrets from going public...and the disposable ones.

The very fact that The Corporation was shelling out three million to the Cornerstone operatives that ran their security meant that the operatives really didn't know shit about what they were guarding. The money was to make them happy, and to shush that little angel on their shoulder that told them, "This seems shady as hell."

Pretty easy to stuff that angel down if it meant a paid off mortgage and maybe a pair of nice Harleys for you and the wife. Your conscience tends not to bother you much when you're floating in your brand-new, lagoon-style pool, with your children happily splashing and your wife freshly manicured, a new pair of tits bursting from a bikini top the size of an eye patch.

No, Briggs would not be asking any questions, no matter how curious he was. After all, the contract had come with its own fine dividends for he and his partner.

There was something else that he was curious about, though.

"So." Briggs tilted his head back. "Why am I here? All of this sounds like business between you and my partner."

The man from The Corporation smiled again, leaning comfortably on one elbow now, while considering his glass, running a finger along the rim.

After a few moments, the man raised his eyes and looked out the window, his smile turning sad. "It's all so broken, isn't it?"

Briggs couldn't keep himself from issuing a derisive snort. He had to remember who he was sitting across from: An idealist. A dreamer. Luckily, the man either didn't notice, or didn't much care. He gave no reaction to the rude noise.

"Not just here," the man continued, his voice quiet and pensive. "Everywhere. It's all been built up into this glorified edifice, and everyone stares up at it with wonder in their eyes, but very few pay attention to the fact that the base is rotten. It's moving towards cataclysm. It always has been. It always makes me think of Yeats: 'Turning and turning in the widening gyre, the falcon cannot hear the falconer; things fall apart; the center cannot hold.'" The man's eyes cinched up in the corners as though distressed by something. "The base cannot support the structure. It's doomed to crumble from within." He raised the glass to his lips, his voice hollow inside. "The inevitable implosion of democracy."

The man drained his glass, set it down, his teeth bared for a moment.

Briggs shifted in his seat. The luxurious leather suddenly felt cloying. "A grim outlook for the free world."

"Free world," the man scoffed. "Free of what? Free for whom? Freedom to do…what exactly? While away your pathetic existence, plugged into the system like a drone, fed a constant stream of dopamine-inducing impulses in the form of pleasant pictures and videos and clever jokes? People don't even know what freedom is anymore."

Briggs took the last of his whiskey, glanced at the decanter, feeling like this was a conversation that required a good deal more alcohol. "Do tell."

The man looked at him sharply. "Democracy isn't freedom. That's the crux of the issue. Democracy is a flawed concept, built upon the idea that people aren't idiots. Which we all know to be false. Find me a hundred people, and I'll find you ten that can think for themselves, and ninety that are utterly inept, slaves to their own whims and emotions. In a democracy, the intelligent ten percent are left beholden to the lowest common denominator. Democracy is a shallow, fairy-tale notion that doesn't stand up to the acid test of reality.

It's meant to make all men equal, but all it really does is shackle the worthy few to the impulses of the thoughtless many."

Perhaps the man wasn't as much of an idealist as Briggs thought. Maybe their philosophies were closer than he'd originally assumed.

Still, Briggs maintained a cautious demeanor. "And I suppose you have a solution?"

The man laughed. "A solution? No. There is no solution. That's my point. You can't repair this structure. You know what all the wannabe DIYers say, because they watch too much HGTV: 'the bones are good.' Well, the bones of this house are *not* good."

He sidled forward to the edge of his chair, his fingers interlacing. "Take, for instance, the current state of our democracy. Half the country at the throat of the other half. Not for any real philosophical differences, but because of a bunch of rhetoric. Any Joe Schmoe can simply hop on the internet whenever he pleases and say whatever he pleases, and there will be a mind-boggling swath of people that actually believe him without ever taking the time to consider whether anything he's said is true.

"Now, how would one fix this? Every person in this country believes it's their God-given right to spout whatever bullshit they want without consequence. Do you make the libel and slander laws more stringent? So that people can't simply make things up about whatever politician they don't like? Well, that might Band-Aid the issue, but ultimately, you once again negatively affect the worthy few with lowest-common-denominator legislation. And the problem with the lowest common denominator is that, while they're complete idiots, they're still perfectly capable of rioting. You ever notice how an idiot never doubts their intelligence?"

He laughed again, this time mirthless. "And that's the problem with democracy. It propagates a lie that all men are created equal. A fine lie. The best type of lie, really. Because it makes people feel good about themselves. That's how you get to believing it. But haven't you ever noticed that the things that feel the best to believe in typically end up being false?"

Briggs smiled and nodded. In fact, he *had* noticed that.

"The best system of government is a benevolent dictator," the man from The Corporation concluded. "A wise strongman."

Briggs squinted at him, as though the thoughts pouring out of the man were a sandstorm. "And are you the wise strongman we've all been waiting for?"

"Me?" the man looked genuinely surprised, if not a little flattered. "No, no. I'm an idea man. I'm a fixer. I identify problems and come up with solutions. That's all."

"But," Briggs said, opening his palms. "As you said, this particular problem doesn't have a solution."

The man leaned back in his chair once again. Regarded Briggs for a long moment. Crossed one leg over the other. He laid one hand upon his desk and tapped his fingers thoughtfully.

"I like you, Briggs."

"Well, I'm flattered."

"You're a realist. Which is something that dreamers like me always need. People like me, always with our head in the clouds." A not-quite-self-deprecating smile. He didn't actually believe the nice words he was saying. He took a big breath, the type of sound that seems to change a conversation. "Anyway, I've digressed quite a bit. You were asking why I wanted to meet with you specifically, and all I've done is spout philosophy and Cornerstone business. You'll have to pardon me. Sometimes my thoughts run away with me."

Briggs gave a slow, forgiving nod.

"Something is..." The man looked upwards, selecting his words from an invisible cloud over his head. "Coming this way. Your business dealings have proven that you're a man of discretion, otherwise I would not be telling you this."

Briggs couldn't help but lean forward in his seat. "What type of thing are we talking about?"

A smile that said *my trust doesn't go that far.* "Things will change drastically. Things you might not even believe if I told you. And the only reason I'm telling you this is that I believe—and I have good instincts for these things; I always trust my instincts—I believe you are one of the few. One of the ten out of a hundred."

Briggs felt a flash of heat on his lower back. A chill of newly-sprouted sweat.

Careful here. Proceed with extreme caution.

"Well, I certainly like to think so," Briggs said. "But, as you already observed, maybe I'm an idiot that thinks I have everything figured out."

The man from The Corporation grinned and pointed at Briggs. "Ah, but the idiots never even entertain the possibility that they might be idiots. Which proves you're not one of them." The man pushed himself up, opened a desk drawer, and drew out a small, black object. A thumb drive, it looked like. He walked around the desk, and Briggs stood to meet him.

The man held out the thumb drive.

Briggs stared at it for a moment, then took it. "What's this?"

"It has some useful information on it. Should you see the need for it in the future. Something for a rainy day."

Briggs kept the thumb drive pinched between his fingers, not sure if he wanted to fully accept it by placing it in his pocket. He began to think about federal regulations and wire taps and who might be listening. He'd done enough shady shit in his life to learn that paranoia usually wasn't.

The man seemed to recognize Briggs's thoughts. "Don't worry, it's nothing that will get you in trouble," he said as he crossed back to the mini bar with his empty tumbler. "Consider it a gift. From me to one of the worthy few that…well, who knows." He sloshed a heavy finger of scotch into his glass. "Might be able to do something good with it."

Briggs took a deep breath, wished he'd had that second glass. "I have to ask, in my official capacity as Secretary of State: Is there a threat that I need to know about?"

The man sipped his glass, not turning to look at Briggs. Just staring out the window at the capitol, silhouetted by the diffused light coming through. "Greeley, Colorado," he said, somewhat nonsensically. "Little town. Not much to look at. Fairly private. But just big enough to go unnoticed, if someone like me were to want to stash a little something. A little something that might help a friend though some trying times."

It didn't escape Briggs that he hadn't denied that there was a threat.

But then again, he hadn't admitted to one either. Which meant that Briggs had done his due diligence, as he saw it.

Greeley, Colorado. How odd.

He finally closed his palm around the thumb drive, and slipped it into his pocket.

ONE

INCHES

THERE'S SOMETHING ABOUT AN AMBUSH that feels like murder, Sam thought. It's not the hot-blooded, me-or-them, kill-or-be-killed situation that you might find once the ambush turns into a firefight.

For a few seconds, right at the start of it, it's just you, killing a person that doesn't even realize they're in a fight. Just a tiny difference, a faded gray line between black and white, and Sam knew that he'd stepped over it several times already. But he wasn't entirely sure it was wrong of him to do.

Morality gets slippery when you're surviving.

And really, at that moment, with the gray dawn backlighting the man that had stepped into the dilapidated office building that had become their hideout, Sam didn't really think about any of that. He'd had hours to think about it in the lead up to this moment, watching the teams of newly-conscripted Cornerstone operatives clearing the structures nearby them.

Now, there was no thought. There was just this sliver of time called the present, and everything else fell away. It was just facts at this point.

One man. Four more coming in behind him.

Stillness. Shadowy shapes of rubble and old office equipment. The man's weaponlight spearing the darkness, sweeping back and forth. Sam's heart, pounding in his chest. Just one eye peering around the corner of the crumbling support column that he hid behind. Rifle tucked close to his chest, ready to deploy. Ready to snatch another life from another person. No second thoughts. No going back. He was strapped into this moment, and he couldn't get free of it even if he wanted to.

"Hey, yo! Contact!" a voice shattered the quiet.

Sam didn't move.

Jouncing beams of light. The scuffle of feet.

"You! Hands up!"

Sam didn't move.

He was in darkness, and all the weaponlights of the Cornerstone conscripts were honing in on a lone figure, laying supine on the cold floor. Sam couldn't even see the figure, but he knew it was there.

Pickell's body. Bloody rags all about. Sightless eyes staring up at nothing.

Closer. Let them get closer.

Sam's right leg, tucked in tight to his body, began to cramp up. Still, he didn't move.

"I think he's dead, man," a second voice called.

"We'll see," the first voice said.

Then, a single shot.

Sam winced.

"Well, he is now," the first voice declared with a sort of shaky bravado.

"Who the fuck is it?"

"I don't fucking know. Some guy."

"Well, you blew half his face off." A giggle. "No identifying him now."

Sam slid. Burning. Seething. Shaking. Two eyes clear of the column now. Rifle slowly coming up.

Four of them standing over Pickell's body. A fifth taking up a rearguard position, his back turned to the others.

"You think it was one of them?"

"Well, someone was here. For sure." Lights traced across the floor. "See all these boot prints in the dust?"

Now.

Sam shouldered his rifle, tight and low, coming around the column. Optic up. Red reticle over dark shapes. One was looking right at him. His face was pale and stark. His eyes went wide when he saw Sam. But it was too late for him.

Fire bloomed from Sam's muzzle. Faces vanished. Projectiles slammed, puffing up dust from clothes and blood from bodies. Two more muzzles erupted in the darkness, and then a third, all in a half-circle surrounding the men that stood over Pickell's body, and in just a second or two, they joined Pickell on the ground.

Screaming. Sam didn't know where it was coming from.

He swept left, to the fifth man taking up the rearguard, who had spun around and begun firing wildly. Bullets smashed the column behind which Sam hid, fragments of concrete and bullet jacketing sliced the air, sliced his arm and the side of his face.

Sam yelped, lurched back behind cover.

More screams. More gunshots. All a terrible mix. No logic to anything. Just physics. Just bullets and terminal ballistics. Wound channels. Shattered bones. Dropping blood pressure. Lights out.

One man's screaming ended.

Another man's screaming kept on—short, sharp, barks of fury.

Sam clattered around the other side of his cover, came up low again on his knees, his face on fire, but his eyes still good. Scanning the ground where the bodies lay, all slumped atop each other. Amateurs. Jumbling themselves together like cattle in a slaughter house.

Sam stood up, forced his feet to move. They seemed slow and unwieldy. The cramp was relieved, but he'd been so long in that crouch that now his feet were all pins and needles.

He charged into the middle of the bodies, kicking them, kicking their weapons out of their dead hands.

One hand, not so dead. A groan. Fingers grasping at the rifle Sam had just kicked away.

Is he dead?

Sam slammed his heel savagely down on the man's hand. Bones crunched. The man didn't even cry out. He didn't even have enough life left in him to do that. Sam jammed the muzzle of his rifle down on the man's head. Felt the skull crack. Didn't really matter. He fired.

Well, he is now.

Rifle up again. A quick scan. Shadows moving amongst the rubble.

The man named Evan, standing over the conscript that had taken up the rearguard, the pistol they'd given him pointing at the dead body. Sam didn't think Evan realized the slide was locked back, the pistol empty. He was still cursing.

"Evan!" Sam shouted. "Evan!"

Evan seemed to come out of his rage with a jerk. "What?"

"You good?" Sam lifted a questioning thumbs-up with his support hand.

Evan looked down at himself as though checking for wounds. "Yeah. I'm good."

"Weapons!" Sam shouted, immediately switching gears. "If you don't have a weapon, grab one!" He stooped, grabbed a rifle, found a shadow moving in the gloom, empty, eager hands. One of the squad leaders. Sam chucked the rifle at her and she caught it.

Jones emerged, his rifle ported, still smoking. "Heads up on the perimeter! We're gonna have incoming!"

A radio chirped from somewhere in the pile of bodies: "Squad Two, Squad Two, we heard gunfire from your poz, you okay? Come back."

"Shit." Jones stamped over to the pile of bodies, tripping over dead feet and legs, bent at the waist as he tried to search for the radio.

"Just leave it," Sam snapped. "They're gonna come anyways."

Jones straightened. Huffed. "Fine. Fuck. Whatever." He navigated himself over the bodies. "Alright, Sarge. Can I call you sarge again? Because I'm pretty sure we're not undercover anymore."

Sam pedaled his hand rapidly in the air. "Ask your question."

Jones nodded to the fifteen people now snatching up rifles and ammunition. Still wouldn't be enough to arm them all. "Where you want 'em?"

"We gotta hold out here," Sam said, spinning around, trying to find that battered door through all the visual confusion. "Bottle neck 'em." He found the door. "There. We can hold them off in that stairwell. Keep their attention on us. Cross our fingers and hope the Canucks get here in time."

Jones grimaced. "I'd much rather move to a location with an exfil."

"Well, I'd much rather be anywhere but here," Sam snapped. "And yet here we are. Besides, you can always jump off the second floor."

"You never *go up*. Only dumb bitches in horror movies *go up*."

Sam felt heat rising up his neck. It wasn't that Jones's observations were so infuriating—because they were true—but it was the fact that he acted as though Sam hadn't already considered every other option.

"Jonesy…" Sam held his hand like a claw in front of Jones's face, as though he wanted to rip it off. "We're playing a game of telephone with the Canadians. Me, to Lee, to the colonel, to the operatives. We start moving around they're not gonna know where we are. We need to stay put. And the most defensible position is on the second floor, pinching them at the stairwell."

"Alright, alright, okay." Jones held up a hand in surrender. "God. You don't have to get all salty about it." He spun to the others, several of whom were clumsily checking their rifles, like the weapon was some mystical artifact they'd never seen before. "Everyone! Up the stairs! Now!"

"We're going *up*?" one of them gasped.

"Yes, goddammit!" Jones barked. "We've thought this over and it is the thing to do!"

Marie straggled up as Sam ducked down, peering out into the dim sky outside. Looking for threats. "What about Pickell?"

Sam's throat felt like it was pulling away from his stomach. He forced his eyes to keep scanning. No threats. For now. He straightened, shaking his head. "Gotta leave him, Marie. Nothing we can do about it."

Marie's face flashed as though she'd pricked herself on something. But then came right back to level. "Alright, then. Let's go—Ah!" The column just to her left exploded, shards of concrete tattering the shoulder of her shirt, and the flesh beneath.

Sam snatched her up and started hauling for the stairwell, his eyes skipping to the outside world for just a glimpse—muzzle flashes twinkling out there, four or five dark shapes aggressing up on them.

"Stairs!" Sam shouted, hoping that was all the description necessary. Tucked his rifle in under his armpit as he staggered across rubble and bodies, firing haphazardly in the general direction of their attackers, no idea if he actually hit anything because he wasn't even looking.

He saw Jones ahead of him, rifle up, taking another support column and letting his rifle loose in rapid bursts, all the noise becoming a wash in Sam's ears, his hearing dulled, everything muffled. Jones shouted something at him as he squirted around the back, but Sam didn't catch it. He only had eyes for that door to the stairwell.

Someone let out a yip and crumpled, writhing, right in Sam's path, but he was already pulling Marie along with him and couldn't stop. He jumped over them, lost his grip on Marie, but she was running on her own now, and then he slammed into the door.

"Get in!" he shouted, just a hoarse gasp of air as something mean buzzed right by his ear, and he'd never before wished more that he was wearing armor. He posted on the open door, knowing it wouldn't provide much in the way of cover, but "not much" in that moment was better than "nothing at all."

Marie charged past him, followed by two more bodies, and he fired three bursts before he actually got his eyes down to his optic. He was about to yell at Jones to "Peel!" when he felt the bolt *clunk* back into the stock, that horrific sensation of going empty at the worst possible moment. He cursed, backpedaling into the darkness of the stairwell as he ripped the magazine out and dove into his pocket for his only spare.

"Someone cover me!" Jones screamed, much higher pitched than normal.

Sam seated the fresh mag, sent the bolt forward, and tried to push out to the door again, but now there was a cavalcade of bodies rushing through, a river of panicked faces in the gray gloom.

"Out of the way!" he belted out, swimming against them like a salmon upstream, then going a little rougher and throwing some elbows to punctuate his words. "Outta my fuckin' way!"

He had no idea how many of them had made it into the stairwell. Managed to get himself out the door and thrust his rifle around it, damn near triggered a round right into Evan's face as he came skittering around the door, chased by a dozen bullet impacts to the floor and then to the door, inches from Sam's torso.

One mag. No more blind-firing. Every round counted at this point.

He spotted Jones, still stuck behind that column, less than ten yards away. Jones couldn't even get his rifle around the column, he was getting so much attention, rounds smacking and stabbing at the concrete, chipping it away like jackhammers.

Sam dropped to his knees and leaned out, rifle up, reticle hovering, tried his damndest to find something to shoot at—there! A dark shape—

hunched shoulders, armor, helmet, a professional—laying into the column behind which Jones was trying to be the smallest he could.

Two quick pulls of the trigger—*crack-crack*—and the shape twisted, then crumpled. No clue where he'd hit, only that the threat was down, and he had the tiniest sliver of breathing room to find a new target.

"Jonesy! Peel!" Sam screamed, settling that little red dot on another shape and squeezing three rounds off. The shape dove for cover behind a low pile of rubble. Bastard. Sam's breath seethed out between his clenched teeth. Had to change targets—another shape slipping inside the building, star-like muzzle flashes spitting bullets as it moved.

Sam registered the *thwack* of one of the rounds punching clean through the door and felt a smack on the side of his head—*oh fuck!* Terror and rage all mixed up into the same savage thought process as he centered the dot on the moving shape, leading it just a pinch and firing as he did, firing, firing, firing, until he saw the figure keel over, head-first.

"Jonesy!" and he was about to say "Peel!" again, but caught his friend barreling into his field of vision just to the left, posting on him with a firm thigh in his back and firing his own rifle right over top of Sam's head.

Sam took that as an invitation and sprawled himself back into the stairwell.

Darkness. And boots. Lots of boots, shimmying around, bumping him in the face.

Oh shit, I got shot in the head!

But shouldn't he be dead then?

He straggled upright, sucking in air that smelled of dank and sweat and dust. "Up!" was all he could manage. "Go up!"

"Up the stairs!" Marie shrieked in the darkness. A bloom of white light. For a half-second, Sam thinking he was seeing stars because of his perforated brain, but then realized it was Marie's weaponlight, waving madly to get their little band of rebels up the damned stairs.

Trampling boots. A mad stampede. Someone crushed Sam's support hand heedlessly under their boot. Didn't even have the decency to apologize for it.

"Jonesy?" Sam burbled out, on his hands and knees now, and then up to his feet.

The slam of a door. Sam twisted, saw Jones scrabbling about with the latches.

"This thing got a lock on it?" Jones demanded.

"I don't know!" Sam grabbed him by the shoulder and yanked him for the stairs. "Marie!"

"What?" White light blazing in his eyes, making him squint. Then: "Oh, shit, sorry!"

She averted her light and he saw the worry all over her face, staring at the side of his head.

"How bad is it?" Sam cringed.

It wasn't Marie that answered. He felt a hand grab his head and twist it to the side, Jones's face looming, all stark shadows and pale, sweaty skin. He stared intensely at the side of Sam's face for two heartbeats and then said, "No brains! You're good!"

"I'm good?" Relief, strong enough to make his knees quake.

"You're good!"

The stairwell was a mess of sounds, none of them making much sense. Someone was hyperventilating. Someone else trying to soothe them. Another kept on asking "What happened? Who was that?" And, of course, several people were shouting out suggestions for how they might extricate themselves from this position.

Sam forced his feet to move again, up the stairs to the first landing, his support hand—the squished one—creeping up to his face, fingertips poking at the wound in his head. A big, ragged groove right across his temple that smarted at the salt on his sweaty fingers. But it was shallow, thank God.

An inch to the left and I'd be done. One fucking inch. That's all it takes.

Jones was breathing in his ear: "Those were operatives! How'd they get here so fast?"

"Must've had a squad close," Marie answered, and Sam figured he couldn't add much to that statement, so he didn't.

Halfway up the second set of stairs, Sam stopped. Took a big breath. Had to push down all the crazy thoughts and go with the only thing he knew: They needed to hold their position.

"Evan!" Sam shouted, fumbling for his own light. Flicking it on. Washing out all the faces huddled on the second-story landing. "Evan!"

"Yeah?" The man poked his head up, squinting against the light.

"You and three others, watch that second-story door!" Sam snapped, pointing to the door with the big 2 painted on it. "The rest of you form up right here on me!"

"What are we gonna do?"
"How are we gonna get out of this?"
"Are they gonna keep coming?"
"We're not gonna make it!"

"Has anyone seen Rob? Rob! Rob!"

"Rob's fucking dead!" Sam shouted at them. He had no clue whether Rob was actually dead, but he sure as shit wasn't answering up, and Sam had seen at least one of them go down, so it might as well have been Rob, whoever that was. "Everyone shut the fuck up! If you want to live, then do what I told you and form up on me! Guns on that door! Don't let anything come through!"

Someone was weeping now. Probably the hyperventilator. But Sam didn't have time to comfort every jackass that hadn't known what they were getting into.

He took a position on the stairs that gave him a small sliver of the lobby door. Metal stair rails, painted dark blue. He settled his foregrip on the middle rung and squatted there, Jones just behind him, Marie behind Jones.

"How many we got?" Sam didn't dare take his eyes off the door. "Marie, count heads!"

"Only got one mag left," Jones whispered as Marie counted aloud. Whispering. As though the operatives out in the lobby didn't know exactly where they were.

"Same," Sam returned.

"Fuck."

"Yeah."

Marie: "Ten. Plus us. Thirteen total."

"Anyone swipe any extra mags?" Sam tossed over his shoulder, still not taking his eyes off the door. What was taking the operatives so long to breach? Probably because they were professionals. Probably because they were waiting for backup. Probably because they were assembling a good, solid breaching team and a plan to splatter every one of the idiots now sequestered in the stairwell. Why should they rush? Time was on their side.

"I got one!" Someone answered up.

"I got two!" Another said, a bit overeager, like it was a competition.

"Pass 'em up!" Sam snapped.

"God," Jones prayed. "If you love me, turn this AR into a belt fed weapon."

Silence. Except for the whining and sniveling somewhere behind him.

"Dammit," Jones huffed. "Why is it—"

The lobby door burst open. Sam didn't hesitate—just started firing, as fast as his finger could go. Saw a hand. Saw a leg. Saw a splash of blood. The whole stairwell was thundering now, chewing the door to shreds, and the concrete and steel frame around it.

Something arced in. Sam didn't need to think about what it was. People in a firefight generally only throw one thing, and it wasn't heart-shaped candy.

"Grenade!" Sam yelped, or maybe he just thought about saying it, because he barely had time to flatten himself back against Jones, his arms up over his head, before there was a flash and a pressure wave that hit his whole body at once. Eyes, ears, nose, throat, and lungs, all violently compressed in an instant.

Strangest thing: He heard absolutely nothing.

Dust. Like being caught in a cloud. Couldn't see a damn thing. Maybe his eyes weren't even open. Maybe they'd been turned to jelly. Maybe he was dead. Except that he could feel his rifle in his hands.

"Guh!" Wasn't sure what he was trying to say, or if it was just a grunt of effort. No, it was a gag. He was gagging. Choking. Trying to breath, but either the air was too thick with dust or the wind got knocked out of him.

Fire licked his face, more pressure blasts smacking at his brain. Someone was shoving him, thrusting at him. He realized he could see light—flashes of it right over his shoulder. Jones. Jones was alive and shooting over his shoulder. And in the flashes, a shape looming up through the cloud at the bottom of the stairs, and then immediately falling backwards under the onslaught of fire.

Sam wrangled his rifle upwards. Started firing, right as Jones's rifle went dead over his shoulder and he yanked it back for one last reload.

Where are those extra mags? Sam wondered, completely disassociated with reality and all of its very real concerns. *Did they pass them up? Did I get one?*

Firing into the cloud of dust. It was thinning. He couldn't see any more shapes coming in at them. He was firing at nothing. Wasting ammo. Stupid. He forcibly removed his finger from the trigger, panned to the left, whacked his muzzle against a stair rail, fumbled to right it.

A rifle and a head, leaning through the door at a downright dramatic angle—what kind of body contortion was that?—fire and gunsmoke spitting. No sound, but Sam could swear he felt the rounds buffeting the air.

"Gah!" Still couldn't breathe.

An incoming round punched right through the stair rail, just to the left of his head, a perfect little hole with metal flower petals reaching out. Damn. Another inch to the right…

He fired again. All in silence. All nonsensical. Lungs burning, diaphragm bucking, throwing his aim off, but the contortionist at the door got the idea and ducked back into cover.

Someone thrashed at his back. Sam let off another smattering of rounds through the lobby door and then snapped a look over his shoulder. Saw Marie crouched there over Jones, her own shoulder bleeding, but with her hands pressed to Jones's right trap muscle, blood oozing between her fingers. Jones's legs were kicking, but he still had his rifle up, still firing at the lobby door, slow and deliberate fire, just keeping their heads down.

Everyone's mouths were moving. Cords standing out in their necks, spittle frothing from their lips. Everyone was shouting, but all Sam heard was a dim burble.

Sam twisted, his stomach flip-flopping at the sight of Jones's wound, so damn close to his neck— *an inch to the left*—but Jones just gnashed his teeth and said something inaudible, but his eyes kept slashing back to the lobby door, and Sam got the picture: he couldn't worry over Jones. He had to worry about them surviving.

A rattle of blindfire, skittering up the stairs, just pulses in the air to Sam, more feeling than sound. One of the civilians toppled over, hitting Sam in the shoulder as he fell, head-over-foot down half the flight of stairs and then crumpling dead at the landing. Tangled blonde hair. One of the women.

Sam righted his aim from being shoved by the falling body, snapped off three more rounds at the rifle spitting hate at them. A snap of a spark, one of his rounds slamming into the magwell of the enemy rifle and sending it flying out of the holder's grip.

Sam almost called for them to fall back. Thought about hauling Jones's body up to the next landing. But why? Where would they go from there? All they'd accomplish would be to give up this one, precious bottle-neck. It would only seal their fate, even if it did prolong the fight an extra minute.

This is it. This is your stand. You're going to die in this stairwell.

There's something almost comforting about simply throwing yourself at death. You spend so much of your time trying to avoid it, but when you recognize that it's right there, right in front of you, inevitable, and if you can wrap your brain around your own imminent mortality, then suddenly everything gets really simple.

Rifle on the door. Reticle searching. How many rounds left in his mag? And where was a spare mag? Even if he could ask, he wouldn't be able to hear the answer.

Finger poised on the trigger. Probably no more than ten rounds left, if that. He hadn't really been keeping track.

Down below, the lobby door hung open, dawn light seeping through amid the pall of gunsmoke and dust. The smell of it all. The sharp tang of spent propellant, mixed with the high explosive of the grenade, still clinging to the air. Their sweat, like fear and panic he could taste on his tongue.

Reticle hovering, right in that open space, just to the side of the door frame. Waiting. Waiting for the next rifle to come sticking through. Maybe it would catch him this time. Nothing to be done for it. All he could do was try to kill the other guy first.

So simple.

He realized he was feeling the percussion of rifle reports, but none of his people were shooting, and none of the operatives were breaching. Who the hell was shooting? He snapped his head around for a glimpse, but only confirmed that everyone was huddled there, a mass of doomed faces, bristling with rifles and pistols thrust out through every angle of fire that could be found.

Marie. Yelling something.

Marie, with a look on her face like they weren't actually going to die, which struck Sam as odd. Her words actually came through the piercing shriek of tinnitus, just clear enough that, if he focused on her lips, he could tell what she was saying.

"Cease fire! Cease fire!"

Cease fire? Was he hearing that right? Shouldn't she be...?

She did: She waved her hand in front of her face, palm out.

Cease fire.

Sam swung back to the door, frowning, breathing hard of all that stink caught in the stairwell. Finger really wanting to touch that trigger, but moving off, outside the trigger guard, resting on the magwell.

A hand came sticking out of the doorway, and Sam damn near shot it off, but held back at the last moment because the hand was waving at them, palm out. *Cease fire.*

"Everyone hold your fire!" Sam bellowed, momentarily relieved that he could hear his own voice. Maybe his ears weren't as bad as he thought. Back to the door. "It's clear! You're clear!"

Didn't dare to actually feel hope. It might be a trap. Might be a trick. Might be the operatives just trying to buy themselves some time. What were they going to send in? A hostage negotiator? They didn't even have any hostages…

A man swept through the door wearing fatigues that Sam couldn't place. But he wasn't wearing a black polo shirt, so that was a good reason not to shoot him. Oddly enough, Sam's first emotion was jealousy: The man had a helmet and body armor, and a wealth of magazines. Everything Sam wished he could've had seconds ago.

"Who are you?" Sam shouted, wondering if he was being overly loud, but he could still only barely hear himself. Probably wouldn't be able to hear the response.

The soldier swept his rifle left and right, doing a quick clear of the base of the stairs, then ported it and looked right at Sam. Looked at the rifle pointing at him. Then said something that Sam didn't catch.

"What?" Sam shouted back, craning his neck forward.

Felt a hand on his shoulder. Jones leaning into him and shouting into his ear: "He's Canadian! They're here to exfil us!"

TWO

THE DEPOT

"I CAN'T HEAR TOO GOOD!" Sam shouted as he staggered up to the soldier. God, but his legs felt like rubber. Super-charged with adrenaline, and yet weak and shaky and unwieldy.

"I can see that," the man hollered back, leaning into Sam's half-deaf face. He pointed at Sam's ears. "Your ears are bleeding!"

Sam touched his ear hole, found it sticky with a thin stream of blood. "Shit."

The soldier put a hand on his shoulder and leaned in again. "You can call me Red. We're here to get you out."

"No rank?" Sam wondered.

A grim smile and a shake of the head. "Not today. Are you Sam?"

"Yeah." His hearing was slowly getting to the point that he didn't have to shout to hear himself. "You got a vehicle?"

Red shook his head. "No, but there's two pickups outside, and I'm of a mind to take those." A glance over his shoulder. No—he was listening to his comms. Fancy comms. Fancy headset, attached to his helmet with a boom mike protruding. Red keyed a PTT on his chest rig. "Copy." Back to Sam. "Sam, we gotta roll out before we get any more attention. Switch positions and then we can figure out what we're doing. Are you in charge?"

Sam almost shook his head. Then dumbly nodded.

Red eyed him up and down, very briefly. In that look, Sam could tell he was being measured. And yes, he could tell he was being found a bit wanting. "Alright then," Red said. "We're at your command." He said it like it took a bit of effort to reconcile himself to it.

"We gotta take a weapons depot," Sam said, feeling entirely off-kilter. Unprepared for this. Was he stupid for talking about the weapons depot at this juncture? Or was he right for staying mission-oriented?

"Whatever," Red shot back, pedaling a hand in the air. "But we need to move. Now."

Another soldier in an identical uniform—looked like Marine Corps digis, but not quite—slipped through the lobby door and jacked a thumb over his shoulder. "Vehicles are good to go. We're ready to roll."

Sam turned and found Jones standing there, Marie still holding pressure on the wound to his trap. He looked miserable, but with-it. The rest of the civilians clustered behind them, like kids behind their parents when strangers show up at the door.

"How bad is it?" Sam asked.

Jones shook his head. "Through and through. Just muscle."

Red stalked up to Jones, lifted Marie's hand from the wound. A slow ooze of red slaked down from a wet hole in Jones's shirt. Red hit his PTT again. "Hey, Blue. Need a patch job."

Jones grimaced, quirking his eyebrows. "Red? Blue? What is this? Reservoir Dogs?"

Red just grinned at him. "You'll be alright."

Yet another Canadian soldier swept through the door, this one with a big pack on his back, unlike the others who looked like they were only carrying three-day assault packs. He smoothly sidled up to Jones, shucking his pack off and motioning for Jones to sit on the first step.

"Hey." Red was staring at Sam. Eyebrows up so far that Sam couldn't see them under his helmet.

Right. Exfil. Sam turned to his people. "Marie, get these folks loaded into those pickups. I'll stay with Jones and the medic." He glanced at Red. "You wouldn't happen to have extra mags, would you?"

"Oh, we got a bit of this and that," Red said, edging towards the door and motioning Marie and the others through. He called into the lobby: "White! Get these people some ammo!"

Sam squatted in front of Jones while the rest of the harried civilians-turned-rebels shuffled after Red. The medic was speaking, calm and businesslike: "You're gonna be alright. I'm not giving you anything but ibuprofen, 'cause you still got work to do, eh?"

"Oh yeah," Jones rolled his eyes. "Ibuprofen will do the fucking trick."

The medic sniggered as he seated a bulky dressing over Jones's trap, then repeated, "You're gonna be alright."

***

The worst part about being an old, broken bastard, was that the adrenaline didn't have an outlet.

Lee stood there atop the MATV, staring out at the city in the distance, just a gray disruption of the horizon line with the sky slowly turning pink to the east, and he had to clench the satphone tight to keep his hand from shaking. His belly was taut and empty and rolling over and over on itself. The air was cool, and tinged with the rapidly-fading scent of dew. Then the air would shift, and the smell was of human rankness, and diesel exhaust, and fear-sweat.

If he'd been armored up, leading a squad into a firefight, he'd just breathe deep and sink into it, get lost in the motions that he'd trained into himself for years, and the queasiness and the thoughts and the worries of a thousand different things would dissipate in the flow of *move, shoot, communicate.*

But he couldn't do any of that. Because he was an old, broken bastard.

The better part of having adrenaline that didn't have an outlet, was that it made the aches of his half-healed wounds go away. The stabbing pain in his hip didn't seem so bad. His stiff and mangled left hand didn't throb so much. The incessant itchiness of his missing eye…

Well, that was still there.

"This fucking patch," he grumbled, snaking a trembling finger up underneath it to delicately soothe the itch the only way he could—by lightly brushing his fingernail across the sensitive scar tissue. Then he got pissed and ripped the patch off his head.

Stared at it in his hand. What was the point of it? To pretend to others that he wasn't some scarred-up remnant of what he'd once been? The stupid thing was an affectation. It didn't have any medical purpose. Just made him feel better not to have to see the slight wrinkle in people's noses when they glanced at his ruined eye socket.

So, you're a monster and you make people nervous.

Good. They should be nervous. And if there was ever a time to be a monster, it was now. Right at the threshold of it all, with Sam's last report still ringing in his ears, telling him they were good to go, they were moving on the weapons depot, and now everything was greenlighted.

Go time. Do or die time.

No room for niceness. No room for mercy. No room for fucking pointless eyepatches.

He let the eyepatch fall from his hand. He didn't need to convince anyone of anything, except where to go, and who to kill. And for that, he didn't need them to see him as a human. They needed to see him as he was. Scarred. Battered. Mean.

He took a deep breath. Held it in. Let it out. Time was of the essence, but there's always time to clear your head. Tamp down the anxieties. Think clearly. Think coldly. Take a moment and center yourself. Take a moment to remind yourself of why you are where you are.

Lee was here because the world was broken. And he meant to fix it.

He turned, pocketing the satphone as he did. His good eye ranging across a mass of cars, trucks, vans, and military vehicles. Faces through windshields. Bodies standing outside, some of them in military dress, most of them in worn-out civvies. All of them armed as best they could be. Desperate people, just like him. Pushed to the brink, clawing their way forward, tooth and nail. Knowing they couldn't go back—they had nothing to go back to. The only way out was through.

He didn't say anything to them. They looked like they might've wanted him to, and he was certainly the center of attention, standing there on that leading MATV. But anything worth saying had already been said. The time for words was over. Now it was time to fight.

Lee swore under his breath at all that unwanted attention, and, still grumbling, navigated himself to the rear of the MATV and clambered down with as much grace as he could muster, which wasn't graceful at all, but at least his hip didn't give out.

He landed on the ground. Pain lanced his hip, but it was quick and manageable with a hiss through his teeth. A cold, wet nose immediately greeted his left hand. Deuce, wagging his tail, as he only really did for a select few people. Probably happy that Lee hadn't killed himself climbing down.

"Good boy," Lee murmured, giving the dog a scratch behind the ear. Then he started walking. People watched him pass by, Deuce trotting at his heels. They nodded to him. He nodded to them. All of them tight-lipped and tense. The civilians looking a tad green. The soldiers and Marines with a practiced air of macho boredom that Lee could see right through.

He made his way back to the MATV with the command module. A more familiar collection of faces waited for him there.

"Was that Sam?" Angela asked, pressing forward, Abby glued to her side, as usual. "Is he alright?"

Lee gave her a curt nod. He couldn't exactly say that Sam was alright—he was surrounded by hostiles, low on weapons and ammo, every surviving member of his original squad was banged up in some way, and the rest of his people scared as shit and untrained. So, Lee chose to focus on the silver lining: "Canadian team got to him in time." He glanced over to Marlin and Worley, the two operatives from Canada, standing near their British counterparts, Guidry and Wibberley. He gave them a nod of appreciation. "They're on the move now."

A look of relief passed over Angela's face, but it was gone just as quick. There are always fresh new worries to ponder, after all.

"So." Brinly squinted into the distance, as though the dim dawn was a scorching bright light. "We doing this?"

Abe answered that one: "Best news I've heard all week." He had a look about him. Eyes wild and harsh, lips almost invisible behind his overgrowth of black beard. Nostrils flared out like he was scenting prey. "Been waiting to get back to Briggs since I left the bastard."

"Bird ready?" Lee asked.

"Fueled up and spooled up. Team's waiting for the go."

Lee nodded. "I want Briggs as bad as you do. But—"

"Airfield first." Abe nodded rapidly. "Right. Yeah. I got it."

Lee looked to Brinly again. "You gotta hit that south side of Greeley *hard*. Give 'em everything you got. You got command of ten squads of civilians in reserve, wherever you need to put 'em. You got 'em on comms with you?"

"Can barely get them to shut the fuck up," Brinly griped. "Hogging all my radio waves."

"They're yours now," Lee said. "You tell them whatever you need to tell them to make it work. Only thing that matters is that you raise hell on that south side, get as much aggro as you can handle." Lee tilted his head in Abe's direction. "Hopefully it'll be enough for Abe to slip through to the airfield." Finding Abe's feral eyes again. "I want my FOB on that airfield by sundown."

"I'll find a way to make it happen," Abe grunted.

Guidry flicked a finger at the two Canadian operatives. "Marlin and Worley are staying with you in case you need to make contact with Colonel Donahue again, but Wibberley and I figured we'd be more useful on the ground." He turned his dark eyes on Brinly. "You cool if we tag along with your crew?"

Brinly nodded. "I'll never turn down two good rifles. Glad to have you."

Wibberley smiled at the Marine and gave him a wink. "Don't worry, we won't get in the way."

Brinly gave him a smirk back. "As long as you don't do any weird-ass British shit."

"Wouldn't dream of it."

Lee cast a sidelong glance at Angela, but forced himself to focus on Abe and Brinly. "I need quick, brutal action. Overwhelming violence. Because we don't have time for anything else. We got Griffin's army breathing down our necks, and I don't want my ass hanging out here in the plains after dark." He didn't exactly look at Angela this time, but he could see her out of the corner of his eye. Saw her arms cross over her chest. "There's going to be…a significant amount of collateral damage." By which he meant dead civilians. "There's nothing we can do about it. We can soothe hurt feelings once we own it, but we gotta own it first. So don't stop. Whatever you do, don't fucking stop."

Abe spat. "Don't intend to."

Brinly gave him a sidelong glance. Held it for a moment. Then shrugged. "Nothing to be done for it. I'm with you."

Only then did Lee look directly at Angela. Oh, how he knew that face so well. Could read it just as plain as the letters on a fifty-foot billboard. Eyes slightly pinched at the corners. Lips drawn tight. Jaw muscles clenching and unclenching. A slight curl of the nose, as though she'd smelled something bad.

And she had. She'd smelled the truth behind the words "significant collateral damage."

"You good?" Lee asked, quietly, fully expecting another one of her bleeding-heart tirades, and getting his pulse all ramped up just thinking about it.

But Angela just nodded and looked away. "Yeah, Lee. I'm good. Do what you do. Win."

Win.

No matter the cost.

"That's my intention," Lee husked, throat feeling a bit tight. Maybe from the unresolved tension between the two of them. Or maybe just because this was it. No more planning. No more strategizing. All that was left were a few simple words. A verbal pulling of the trigger.

"Alright." Lee murmured. "Let's get it done."

***

"I don't like it," Red shook his head, frowning down at Sam's makeshift sand table—just a few rocks and some lines gouged into the dirt with Sam's finger.

Sam rose from squatting over the sand table. Glanced around them, feeling that almost-constant, unnerving sensation that they were being watched, being scouted out by enemy forces. But all was still and quiet on this side of Greeley. The two pickup trucks they'd stolen from the Cornerstone operatives sat in the burgeoning daylight, engines still ticking. They'd hightailed it out of the commercial area they'd been holed up in, and fled to the west end of Greeley, where Sam knew there wasn't much going on but city parks turned to crops. They were back behind a stand of chest-high corn now, the better to conceal them with, though if someone had a mind to, they could easily follow the tracks through the corn and find them.

The ten guards-turned-rebels hovered around their pickup, some of them in the bed, some of them clustered around the front end, watching Sam from a short distance away. They seemed nervous and edgy. Shit, they were *all* nervous and edgy. Except for the Canadians. They seemed like this was just another day in the office for them.

"What's the problem with it?" Sam asked, returning his attention to Red.

Red, White, Blue, Black, Green, and Brown. That's the names that Sam had got, and the context of it was "Don't ask," and so he didn't. They were there illegally, Sam surmised, and didn't even have their flag patches on their uniforms. Nothing to identify them by.

Red draped his arms over the buttstock of his slung rifle. Eyed Sam again with that evaluating gaze. "Look, man. I'm not here to bust your balls or step on toes. But you got two elements here—the main push on the weapons depot, which you want to be a feint, and the flankers that you want to actually infiltrate the depot." He glanced discretely up at the civilians around their pickup. "The flanking is the more technical job. It should be us. And you guys." He nodded towards Marie and Jones, standing to either side of Sam.

Sam was already shaking his head by the time Red finished speaking. He wasn't trying to be a dick about it, but they were looking at this from two different perspectives. "That main push is gonna get all the heat that the guards at the depot have to give. I can't ask these people to be cannon fodder. I just barely convinced them to join us."

Red's eyes squinched up. "And yet you trust them to flank and infil?"

"I don't trust anybody." Sam raked a hand through his mess of unwashed hair. He stank, too. Every inch of him covered in a layer of grit and greasy sweat. Felt like his clothes were starting to meld into his skin. "That's not the point. The point is..." Sam struggled for a moment. "The point is, I just can't do it. There. I'm the weak fucking link here, is that what you wanna hear?"

Red raised a hand. "I don't wanna hear shit but a good plan, Bud."

Sam knelt on one knee again, leaning over and jabbing his finger at the rock that represented the weapons depot. "If we hit 'em hard enough, all their attention is gonna be on us. And we can handle that attention. The civilians go in the back while the attention is on us and wipe out any resistance. I get that it's not ideal, but you wanna talk about trust?" Sam lowered his voice. "I don't trust them to lay enough hate to get us in the back. They'll be too cautious, and they're barely equipped to make the ruckus we need. They've got just enough ammo and weapons to get in and mop up. It's the easier job. Therefore, it goes to the people with less training."

White, a big fellow with Nordic features and a giant wad of dip in his mouth, spat off to the side and tilted his head at Red. "Kid's got a plan. Just let him roll with it. We'll figure it out."

Red eyed his comrade. "Oh, it's a plan. I never argued with that."

"We're wasting time," Sam urged, rising again. "This is how we gotta do it. If we need to adjust, we'll adjust. But I'm not putting those ten people in a position where I know they're gonna get wiped out."

"Bud—" Red started.

"It's Sergeant Ryder," Jones corrected, flatly, staring Red right in his face.

"Well, hi-di-fuckin'-ho," Red mumbled. "Fine. Sergeant Ryder. It's on you, alright? This is what you wanna do, then we're gonna do our best to support that. As long as you're prepared to shift strategies when it goes tits up."

"Everything always goes tits up," Sam griped, kicking the sand table clean. "Why do you think we're here in the first place?" He looked at the Canadian operatives. "Y'all in or what?"

Red sighed. Nodded to his men. Then to Sam. "We're in, Sarge."

"Good." Sam swallowed hard, hoped that nobody noticed. "We'll take point and lead the way in to the depot."

Five minutes later, a field of corn, brushed with golden morning light, disgorged two pickups that hit the blacktop and turned north, then hung a right, heading east, straight into the heart of Greeley.

Sam in the front passenger seat. Jones driving. Marie sandwiched between Red and White in the back of the cab, with Blue, Green, Brown, and Black huddled in the back, trying their best not to look like an assault team.

Behind them, the other pickup truck tailed them, bed and cab crammed full of rebels.

Probably nobody would think anything of it, they were so used to seeing civilians and operatives paired up and hauling around the streets, just like this. And by the time anyone thought to be suspicious, Sam hoped to be shooting at them.

His guts were in a knot. Head pounding with his own pulse. He loved Red and his team for pulling their asses out of the fire, but dammit, he hated the bastard for what he'd just done. Sam was barely maintaining himself as it was, and then to have everything he'd planned suddenly shadowed in doubt? Well, shit. Now he wasn't sure of anything.

"How long you been doing this, Sarge?" Red asked.

Sam twisted in his seat and stared at the operator. "I don't think telling you would make you feel any better."

Red shrugged. "Well, at least you're honest."

Jones hung a left, tacking north again. Businesses flew by. Houses and neighborhoods. Lawns turned to gardens. Only a handful of people out, but they seemed normal—just going about their business, like Briggs hadn't pulled the big red handle the night before.

Sam stiffened when he saw the two SUVs come hauling around the corner ahead of them. "Shit, shit, shit," he whispered, bladder suddenly feeling like it was full to bursting, though Sam knew that was bullshit—he'd barely had any water in the last eight hours.

"Be cool," Jones murmured. "Everyone be cool."

"Don't look at them," White grunted. Neither he nor any of the other operatives attempted to squish low in their seats. They tucked weapons down so they wouldn't be so obvious, but otherwise just sat there, as casual as you please.

Sam stared at the two incoming SUVs. Definitely Cornerstone—the red delta symbol emblazoned on the side. Not just civilian guards or new conscripts. These were people that had half a brain and were currently on high alert.

He felt a jab against his arm. Whipped around. White was looking at him sternly. "Don't fucking look at them."

The two SUVs roared past. Sam tried not to look, but he caught a glimpse anyways. Wished he hadn't. The second he let his eyes snap across the sides of those vehicles as they passed, he caught a face looking right back at him.

"Oh, shit." Sam plastered himself back into his seat.

"It's cool, it's cool," Jones yammered on. "Everyone's cool. Nothing to see here." Kept glancing at his sideview mirror. "They're not gonna turn around on us. They're busy men. They've got shit to do."

Sam hazarded a look through the back glass.

The backend of the two SUVs suddenly lit up with red brake lights.

Heart in throat. Stomach in feet.

The two SUVs made sharp turns, one after the other, turning left. "Shit, they're turning around on us!"

But the second he got the words out, he watched the two SUVs just haul their way down another side street as though they had urgent business there, rapidly dwindled, and then were out of sight behind the rows of buildings.

"Itscool-itscool-itscool," Jones breathed, a bit ragged. "See how cool I was?"

"Yeah, you're sweating, you're so cool," Marie observed.

Sam leaned back in his seat again. Hands like vices on his rifle. Teeth clenched to the point of pain. Throat feeling raw and stretched like he'd just screamed his head off.

Jones pressed the brake. An intersection ahead. "Eyes on target."

The intersection was one of those weird jumbles of five different streets, and staring at it for that brief second as they approached the darkened signals, Sam had the strange thought that he'd never really learned to drive in the "real" world, and if he had to now, he wouldn't know what the hell to do with an intersection like this. All his days behind wheels had been spent gunning it through abandoned cities and byways.

He snapped his eyes to the right of the intersection. There it was: AutoZone. Or that's what it used to be before they'd stockpiled weapons and ammo in it. Made sense to him though—a concrete building with only one entrance and exit, and only a few windows. Pretty secure.

Two guards out front. Black polos. Armor and helmets. Cornerstone.

Jones proceeded through the intersection.

Red craned his neck around, looking at the pickup following them. "Don't fuck it up," he muttered at the rebels.

Sam glanced in his sideview, breath all caught up in his chest now, and watched the pickup full of civilians whip a right-hand turn at the intersection, and he knew like having a cinderblock dropped on his chest that there was no going back now. He'd made the call, and Red was absolutely right: It was on him. No matter how this turned out, it would be on him.

"Right there," Sam pointed ahead, past the repurposed AutoZone. It was a tumbledown building that looked like it'd been a restaurant in its past life. No clue what it was now. But for the next however-long-this-took, it was going to be their cover. "Park behind it."

"Behind it?" Jones asked, slowing, eyes darting. "Or with it between us and the weapons depot?"

"Dammit, Jonesy, you know what I mean."

"I don't know what you mean, that's why I'm asking!"

"With the fucking thing between us and the guys with guns!"

"Alright! Alright!" Jones spun the wheel, turning into the parking lot. "Don't yell at me."

The pickup skidded to a stop. Sam heard the rumble of the ABS and the light chirp of the tires and hoped to God that it hadn't alerted the guards. But of course they'd heard. Not like there was tons of traffic around.

"Hold, hold, hold," Sam jabbered, reaching across the center console and grabbing Jones's arm. "The second we get out, the jig is up. Everyone good? Everyone clear on what we're doing? Jonesy?"

Jones gave him a longsuffering look. "Yes, I know what I'm doing, Sarge. Your poorly-worded directions notwithstanding."

Sam craned his neck around to the back. "Marie? Red? White?"

Red simply responded by pounding a fist against the back glass. Blue, Green, and Brown raised their hands, all three giving a thumbs-up. "We're good to go."

"Alright." Sam checked his mag and chamber for the umpteenth time. "Pick your shots. The second we start shooting, the civilians will start moving—"

Pop-pop-pop-pop!

A torrent of curses erupted from everyone in the pickup at the same instant. Sam kicked his door open, the cinderblock on his chest pressing right through him—*Those idiots! They sprung it too quick! They were supposed to wait!*

Nothing to be done for it. They were in it now.

Sam's feet hit blacktop. Barely restrained himself from the urge to simply sprint around the corner and start firing at the first target he saw. Waited the agonizing seconds while the rest of his crew unassed the vehicle.

"Red!" Sam pointed to the far corner of the building. "You go around that side! Marie, Jones, you're with me!"

Red took off at an easy lope, his men forming up behind him, rifles up.

Sam pounded for the side of the building, cold sweat on his hot palms, slicking his grip on his rifle. He hit the corner, brought his rifle up. A clear shot to the front of the AutoZone. The two guards…nope, not two guards anymore, now there were five—all scrambling around to one side of the building. Were the civilians even engaged with anybody or were they just winging shots off? Had

Sam been unclear in his instructions? He thought he'd been pretty damn clear, and yet here they were, shooting at nothing. Unless there'd been guards on the other side of the building that Sam hadn't known about. Unless those rifle shots he was hearing were from those guards and all the civilians were now getting their shit pushed in.

There were two natural areas between him and the AutoZone—one on either side of the street, overgrown with woody brush. Sam tried to angle around the worst of it, tried to find a keyhole to spot the Cornerstone guards through, but they were slipping around the back of the weapons depot now. All but one of them. Taking up a rearguard, scanning the streets.

Sam could only see the top of his head from this vantage point. The rifle fire continued, and Sam stood frozen for a few hammering beats of his heart, trapped in a moment of indecision. Regroup with Red and change the plan? Or push through? What's the best option?

The best option was decided for him when Marie edged low, down on one knee to Sam's right, and fired two rounds.

Sam jerked, not realizing Marie was going to start firing. Snapped his gaze up just in time to see the guard hoof it for the front doors of the AutoZone, yelling into a radio.

A smattering of rounds from the other side of their cover building—Red or one of his men. The guard went down in a heap, two strides from the front door, which burst open just as he hit the ground, another operative watching his comrade drop, and then jolting back inside.

Sam had fancied himself totally prepared—hell, he'd infiltrated Greeley, dealt with mad bastards, took down an entire squad, and then took his revenge on his betrayers—and yet somehow, he still found himself frozen, unable to decide what to do, and the idea that he was choking in that moment only choked him more.

Make a decision and go with it! Any action is better than no action!

"We're goin' in!" Sam belted out. Then leaned around the backend of the building. "Red! Red!"

A head poked out from the opposite side of the building—maybe just Sam's overwrought imagination, but he looked pissed.

"We're moving!"

Red waved a hand at him and brought his rifle up in the same motion. "Move!"

Sam took off, sparing only a single glance over his shoulder to make sure that Jones and Marie were following. The Canadians started a steady, suppressive fire, shattering every bit of glass on the front of the AutoZone by the time Sam wrangled himself through the first natural area and hit the street on the other side.

Shit, it was a long haul across this street—three lanes, two bike lanes, and two sidewalks.

His only mercy was that the overgrowth of the second natural area was still between him and the front of the AutoZone. If he just kept his head down…

Zzzip!

"Fuck!" He almost dropped to the ground—having bullets whiz by your head will have that effect. But there was no cover, and he couldn't just camp his ass in the middle of the damn street.

Two more rounds zipped by. He was so close. He fired through the brush, no clue what he might be hitting on the other side, every mistake now compiling, making him feel smaller and smaller, less and less prepared, more and more Sameer Balawi and less Sam Ryder. His fears were turning to panic and he didn't seem to be able to pull himself back from the brink.

No sleep, no water, no food—yeah, those have effects too.

He hit the ground at the only point of semi-cover: The curb on the other side. Skinned knees. Skinned elbows. Unhelmeted head pressed to the concrete, huffing the smell of it. Jones and Marie went two strides past him, just outside the brush of the natural area.

Couldn't think of anything to say outside of curses. Didn't have a single reasonable command to give. Where the fuck had his brain gone?

Forward. You got to go forward.

He started crawling. Up over the curb. Rifle clenched in his grip, elbows gouging their way across the sidewalk, and then into the brush. Bullets whined, snipping leaves and branches right over his head. Had they seen him? Or were they just shooting? Trying to keep his head down?

Gotta get eyes on. Gotta see something to shoot it.

And now he was getting pissed. And getting pissed helped. Getting pissed elbowed the fear out of the way. Made him just want to see a target, see one of those bastards in the black polos and put him down. And all of the sudden, that was all that mattered to Sam.

He growled like an animal as he thrashed his way through the brush, crawling around thick stands of prickling briars, thorns slashing at his skin, catching his clothing and stalling him like barbed wire. He swore and shoved at the worst of it, kicked it off his legs. He was halfway through. Saw daylight on the other side. Saw the twinkling of shattered glass, and the big, empty darkness of the inside of the weapons depot—muzzle flashes coming from at least four points.

Sometimes you didn't get to see the person you were about to kill. You just saw the muzzle flashes. That makes it easier on you, somehow, not having to see them jerk and jiggle as you pump rounds into them.

Sam's reticle jumped with every pulse. He tried to lay himself flat and steady. Pushed forward just a bit more, lungs burning, but trying to control his breathing. The bumping red dot, right on top of where he'd seen a muzzle flash a microsecond before, and then he fired, one-two-three. Had no clue if he hit anything. Screams from the darkness, but he couldn't tell if they were screams because someone had been hit, or just screaming in general.

More muzzle flashes. The dim perception of movement—shapes inside, the source of those flashes. Sam kept on firing at them, a morbid game of whack-a-mole. A pattern to it, a flow. *Just put them down, put them down!*

He registered Marie and Jones's shots to either side of him. Tried to listen for the crack of the Canadian team's fire, but he couldn't tell in all the chaos. Were they moving up? Or were they still hanging back?

Movement to the right—a Cornerstone operative, leaning out from the side of the building, one of the ones that had disappeared around it moments ago. He was looking right at Sam, rifle already coming up.

Sam twisted, trying to get his rifle turned to the threat, but it hung up on some brush. The dirt in front of his face exploded. He yelped, jerked back, blinking the worst of it out of his eyes, everything foggy and blurred now. He could barely see the man shooting at him.

A single crack from his right—Marie or Jones? He had no idea. Then three more shots.

By the time Sam cleared the dirt out of his eyes, all he saw of the operative at the corner was his boots, shimmying about on the concrete. Death throes. Sam was well-acquainted with what that looked like.

Screeching tires.

A burst of gunfire to his left—more than just Marie or Jones. The Canadians were in the brush with them, pounding the front of the AutoZone.

More movement, this time from the street. Sam barely recognized it until it cleared the intersection, and he saw the dawn sun glint off the side of a white pickup, saw three desperate figures clinging to the bed of the truck as it rocketed through the intersection, jerked out a chittering turn, tires spraying gray smoke, and roared away.

Sam swore viciously at them.

His civilians—the people he'd tried to keep from the worst of it—had cut and run.

The next thing Sam perceived was a rapid chattering—one, prolonged burst of muzzle flashes from inside, all coming from the same point, raking back and forth through the brush, tracers glinting every five rounds.

Belt-fed weapon.

"They got a SAW!" he heard Jones shout.

Someone crashed through the brush. "Ryder! Ryder!"

The fusillade didn't let up. Started coming back towards Sam, like it was chasing whoever was running towards him. A big, camouflaged shape came hurtling through a stand of briars and slid, boots-first, right into Sam's side. The machine gun fire whipped over their heads, splinters and twigs showering him. White's big, angry face right there, nose almost touching Sam's.

"Your boys ran!" White bellowed into his face. "We gotta pull back!"

Pull back? *Not* take the weapons depot? Abject failure?

It's all on you.

Something snapped across the dome of White's helmet, jerking his head. He flattened out, mushing Sam down with him. "Fuck!"

"You good?" Sam managed, with his face half in the dirt and leaves. Spotted the gouge in the Kevlar—no penetration.

"Just rang my fuckin' bell—we gotta roll out!" He keyed his comms. "Gimme some breathing room! We're falling back to the vehicle!"

All of Red's men opened up at once, the second White's finger released the PTT. The machine gun inside the AutoZone kept up for another hellish second, then faltered, and the next thing Sam knew, White was on his feet, dragging Sam up with him and shoving him hard.

"Get out! Move!"

And Sam was running, his vision just green leaves slapping his face, screaming: "Jones! Marie! Fall back!"

Pounding concrete. Pumping arms. He'd never run so fast in his life. Away from the sound of gunfire. Away from the objective.

Painted white lines on the blacktop. Up over the curb. Through the crowds of brush on the other side, and only then did he stop, drop to a knee, and spin around, knowing that he had to post, had to return fire so the others could get out.

"Peel!" Sam shouted. White was yelling something else into his comms, coming down prone five yards from Sam and firing as he did.

Marie and Jones, faces ghastly, mouths gaping for air, halfway across the road. Bullets chased them, keening through the air, scattering concrete and spall at their feet.

Clunk—bolt locked back, mushy trigger.

"Reloading!" Sam wheezed out. Fumbled for the extra mag that White had given him. Fingers didn't seem to be working like they should. All shaky and numb, like a nightmare where you can't get your body to work properly even in the direst of circumstances.

Footfalls all around him—Marie and Jones, racing past, then spinning, firing over the top of Sam and White. Sam finally got the magazine seated just as White yelled "Down!" hands flashing so rapidly across his rig it seemed like a magician's trick when his rifle was suddenly hot again and he called "Up!"

Sam fired again—that's all he could do. Point in the general direction of the bad guys and fire away. Movement to his left—Red, Blue, Green, and Brown, tearing up to the opposite corner of the building from Sam, right where they'd started, the whole damn thing just a big reversal, one step forward and ten steps back.

It's all on you. You stupid, ignorant fuck!

One of the Canadians yelled something, and a second later, White was on his feet, hollering at Sam and Jones and Marie: "Peel! Peel!"

Sam staggered to his feet. Something snapped at his hip, but it didn't stop him from running. Pain came a moment later—sharp and hot as a branding iron. His pace flagged. He goggled down at his right hip, still running, saw the tattered fabric, blood coming through.

Around the corner of the building—*safety!*—and straight into the side of the waiting pickup, like he intended to run through it. He bounced off with a metallic *clang*, then staggered for the door, the Canadian team hauling ass around the other side.

Sam slammed into the passenger side door and spun, holding his rifle up in a shaky grip, covering the side of the building as Marie and Jones skittered around it. He had to be the last boots off the ground—that's what a good sergeant would do. He had to hold until everyone else got in the truck. He had to prove that he wasn't a complete idiot.

Then White smacked him hard in the shoulder, damn near knocking him over. "What're you waiting for? Get in the fucking truck!"

And Sam obeyed, without even thinking about it. Wrenched the door open and threw himself into the seat, smearing blood across the door and the fabric. Never feeling smaller or more useless. Never feeling so inept. Never feeling so far out of his depth than he was right at that moment.

The pickup rocked violently as seven other bodies piled in, Marie not even wasting the time to get in the back, but just hurling herself into the bed, and then the engine was roaring to life and Jones was yanking it into drive, and Sam was pressed back into his seat with the sudden acceleration, all the doors slamming at once, steering wheel spinning, the whole world spinning, everything gone off the rails.

And all Sam could say, little more than a hoarse gasp, sounded more like a kid than a soldier, even to his own ears: "I'm sorry. I'm sorry."

THREE

THE ASSAULT

Brinly rolled into LaSalle expecting a fight, but not entirely surprised that they didn't get one. He stared out his window at the passing buildings, wondering the same thing that he'd wondered for the last three damn years.

What the hell is broken in me?

He glanced down at his hand, and it was stone-still. It always was. That wasn't the issue. Nerves were never the issue. The issue was their complete, and very conspicuous absence. For three years now, he'd watched hard men fall apart. Good warriors, beaten down to dust. Consumed by their own rages. Or their own depressions. Or anxieties. The off-kilter, helter-skelter, hyper-violent world they lived in twisting them up in different ways, but twisting them all the same.

But not Brinly. No, never him. What quintessential element of humanity was missing in him, he wondered? It almost gave him a laugh, how often he thought of this shit. You'd think a fifty-year-old Marine Corps First Sergeant-turned-Major (erroneously, but it happened all the same) would have a better handle on who he was. And it seemed that he gave that impression to others, simply by virtue of the fact that he was so rock-steady all the time.

Was it ironic that the one thing that caused him to worry was his complete lack of worry?

He was never quite sure of what ironic really meant, but felt pretty strong this was an example of it.

Did everyone else have something he didn't? Or did he have something no one else did? Was it a blessing or a curse? Seemed like a blessing. Except for the fact that, if he wasn't diving head-first into the shit, he was bored out of his mind. The only time he felt like he was actually alive was when the bullets were flying, and those had been rare opportunities since Angela shoved these fucking oak leaves at him. The rest of the time it was like he was on standby. Just floating. Waiting. Hibernation mode.

Like now, for instance: A tiny, solitary note of discomfort that they weren't getting any resistance as his column of Marines pushed through to the northern edge of LaSalle. Not worry that it was some sort of trap—oh, no. An ambush would be just the thing. But it made perfect sense that Briggs had pulled his troops out of LaSalle. Which was why he wasn't entirely surprised to find it completely abandoned. He was just discomfited because now there was another chunk of doing officer shit before he could actually start living again.

The radio fizzled at his side, and he cringed before he even heard the voice on it, because he somehow knew it wasn't going to be one of his Marines: "Uh, comm check? Anyone else not seeing anything at all?"

Brinly raised his eyebrows. "Anyone else not seeing anything at all?" he echoed to the captain in the driver's seat. "The fuck does that even mean?" He shook his head, still staring out the window. He wasn't that pissed about it—Brinly didn't really get pissed—but sometimes he acted pissed because that's what folks expected of a grizzled Marine Corps Major. "Tell that idiot to shut up and keep the radio clear."

Captain Gosling obediently nabbed up the radio handset and transmitted a slightly edited version: "Drifter Actual, keep the radio clear. Out."

"And tell them to use their callsigns," Brinly gruffed. "Gave 'em fucking squad numbers for a reason."

In the process of setting the handset down, the captain obediently brought it back to his face. "Drifter Actual, all units, observe proper radio protocol and identify yourself at the start of your transmission. Out."

Brake lights bloomed down the column of fighting vehicles—five MATV's, including Brinly's all the way in the rear, five Humvees, and two cargo vans that weren't exactly fighting vehicles, but they didn't have any APCs, so what the hell.

Brinly pushed his door open and slid out of the MATV, followed by the captain and the two corporals in the back. He looked behind him at the line of civilian vehicles pulling to a stop right there in the middle of LaSalle. Twenty of them, just a mashup of different makes and models, and the lumbering hulk of a single tanker truck, all the way in the rear.

Frankly, it should've scared the piss out of him. Any sane officer would piss. Or at least have knots in his stomach about what he was getting into and how little he had to get into it with. Or maybe a shaky hand. But Brinly had none of that. Just a quiet, sardonic impression of the universe's very morbid sense of humor.

The first vehicle behind his MATV was a little coupe that might've been gold in another life, but was now a flat beige with all the dust it had gathered on it. Inside, Guidry and Wibberley's faces were barely visible through a glint of sunlight across the windshield. He hadn't lied when he'd said he was glad to have them—they were well-trained operatives, and that's always useful—but he still had a vague sense of misgivings about them. Like they were watching him. Grading him.

"Right," Brinly mumbled, then turned away from them. Stalked up the line of military vehicles. Right up to the front, to the guntruck at the very tip of the column. A Marine in the turret, with no shirt beneath his flak, like he thought he was in a Vietnam war movie. Whatever. Not the time. So, he just stared at the kid until he shuffled and nodded and said, "Major," and Brinly let him go with a deathly glare and called it good enough.

Around to the front of the vehicle. He stopped. Stretched his back. Planted his hands on his hips. A spear of sunlight was escaping a thin blanketing of gray clouds in the east, and casting the scene in pale yellow. The river was a slow mover, and he couldn't hear it, but he could smell it. That slightly swampy, wild smell of muddy water.

Here was the problem with assaulting the south side of Greeley: There was really only one way in, and he was standing on it. Highway 85, heading north. The only bridge within miles that crossed the South Platte River.

"Quite a fucking bottleneck," Gosling observed.

"Can't see shit from here," Brinly remarked. He scanned the land around him, hoping for a high point, a hill, a tall building, even a radio tower—

something he could put snipers on. But it was all flat and there wasn't a building in sight more than two stories tall, and that wasn't enough to clear the trees.

Brinly sighed. "Alright, fuck it. Up the gut it is. Why make fancy plans when brute force will do just fine?" Brinly turned and started back. He'd seen what he needed to see. No nice intel, no satellite pictures for planning. Nope. This was old school shit. Put your eye on the field and call an audible.

"Gosling," Brinly spoke as he stalked back to the vehicle. "Keep the civvies here as reserve. I want a wall of guntrucks up front—as many as we can get abreast on this road. Which I think would be all of them. We're gonna roll in guns blazing. Get to the other side of the river and find a place to set up shop."

He reached his MATV and climbed in. Settled himself into the seat. Keyed his own radio—this one on the command frequency straight to Lee. "Drifter Actual to Marshal Actual, we are in position and ready to roll."

Just a moment. Was that hesitation, or was Lee just busy with something else?

"I copy," Lee's voice was subdued on the radio. "It's on you, Old Boy."

"Roger. We're moving." Brinly flicked his fingers forward, and Captain Gosling, who'd already been chattering away on the task force channel, concluded his list of commands with, "Lago, Lago, Lago. Take it to 'em, gents."

The brake lights disappeared, and they were rolling forward.

Brinly took a deep breath—not to calm himself, because he was already calm. Just a breath to take it in. He was alive again. And what a time it was to be alive.

***

Lee couldn't stand being in the box. "Command Module" is what it was called. But you could pin a nice name on something, and that doesn't change it from being a damn box.

So, he stood outside the backend of it, a radio in each hand, and his satphone in his pocket. Pacing out around the side of the MATV to look out at the city in the distance, and then back to the open doors of the command module, where two former Air Force specialists sat inside, monitoring the radios, ready to delegate Lee's orders.

Orders. Shit. When had it come to this?

Oh, yes. He recalled. It had come to this when Angela had shoved these damn oak leaves at him. Forced him into a position he was entirely unqualified for. But, ah, he couldn't go down that road right now. Everyone had a roll to fill, and he'd already—kind of—made his peace with it.

He stood there, staring into the command module, tapping the antenna of one radio against his thigh. Radio discipline was great. But since he was leashed to the rear in a command roll, he found the long empty silences unnerving.

When was Brinly going to hit? He kept straining to hear the distant gunfire that would mark the beginning of their invasion of Greeley. But until Lee heard the Marines start shooting, it still felt unreal. Until he heard those first shots, this was all still a strange fever dream.

Three years he'd been fighting this bastard, this "acting president" that had no right to the title he'd taken. Three years of trying to survive. Three years of wanting this moment, right now, when he was pounding down Briggs's doorstep, the wannabe-dictator's chickens coming home to roost. He could hardly believe it was happening.

Deuce was channeling Lee's anxiety in the back of the MATV. Pacing just as much as Lee was. Pacing to the front with a low whine, then sticking his head in Specialist Lopez's lap, then, unsatisfied with the lack of attention, went to Hurst, who gave him a distracted pat on the top of his head, and then, grumbling softly with his head and his tail hung low, he ambled to the back and sat with a huff, and started panting nervously.

I get it, Buddy, Lee thought.

The radio chirped in his hand. Brinly's voice, as calm and level as ever: "Drifter Actual, we're crossing the South Platte River now."

"Marshal copies," Lee said. Stared into the back of the command module again. Then, unable to restrain himself, hobbled sideways on his bum leg and stared in the direction of La Salle, and the south side of Greeley.

Where was the gunfire? Why wasn't there any? Maybe his busted-up eardrums just weren't hearing it. Could anyone else hear it? He almost asked one of the specialists, but didn't want to sound too desperate or nervous. Even though he was both.

Was this some sort of trick? Did Briggs intentionally leave the door open for Brinly because he had something up his sleeve? Nightmare scenarios started rampaging through Lee's head— all the reasons why this moment wouldn't be the moment he'd wanted for three years. The bridge would blow with the entire convoy on it. Or Briggs would have fuel that they didn't know about and the Marines would get shredded by attack helicopters that Lee had assumed were grounded. Or—

Gunfire.

Lee half-raised the radio in his right hand. No. Had to restrain himself. Sitreps would come when sitreps came. Brinly was a professional. He'd keep Lee in the loop.

Dammit! What's happening?

The heavy chug of .50 caliber M2 machine guns. The guntrucks? Or Cornerstone defenses?

Dammit, Lee wished he was there, instead of here. Cursed the bastards that had taken his eye, taken his hip. Cursed the primal that had mangled his left hand. Trapping him in the shell of his body, when all he wanted was to charge out in full battle rattle and get into it.

He half-raised the radio again, and again, with teeth clenched, lowered it.

Agonizing.

More chattering guns. And then a slowing of the rate of fire. And then silence for a long, painful moment. Tap-tap-tap-tap went the radio antenna against his leg. Why the silence? Why the pause? Had something happened?

Then it suddenly exploded. All the guns going off at once. And answering fire now, Lee was positive. That hectic, chaotic, back and forth of a firefight. A furious rhythm to it that sent Lee's already elevated pulse into high gear.

"Drifter Actual," Brinly's voice, raised now to be heard over the thundering of guns in the background. "We've made contact. Heavy fire coming from the east and west. We got a toehold on the north side of the bridge, but not much further. I'll update you when the situation clarifies."

Immediately after the transmission, Lee heard another voice, emanating from inside the command module, coming from the squad comms.

Not Brinly's voice, but his captain, and significantly more stressed than the major: "Actual to Two-Six and Two-Seven! Guide right! Hit that flank!"

Lee jerked back to the command module, almost clambered up inside, but still didn't want to be in the box. Specialist Lopez hunched in her seat, frowning at the radio.

"Two-Six..." a pause, the line still open, crackling rifle fire—but no heavy machine guns. Why no heavy machine guns? "Two-Six, Two-Seven, pull your ass to the left! Behind that building!"

Silence then, save for the distant drumming of the guns.

"Two-Seven, there's three...three fortified houses. Right flank. Can't maneuver past them. Two-Six, can you get a line on 'em?"

"Two-Six, I got eyes on, but...standby."

"What the fuck is the problem?" Lee hissed under his breath.

Brinly's voice: "Actual, Two-Six, I need that right flank shut down. We can't get off this bridge until you shut it down."

"Two-Six, Actual, there's civilians all up in that shit! Unarmed civilians, all around those fortified positions!"

Lee felt his spine stiffen. A skitter of cold electricity all the way up. He glanced over his shoulder, guilty as a caught man, but Angela wasn't standing where she'd been a few moments before—she was back a ways, immersed in some conversation with a handful of civilian squad leaders.

Brinly's voice brought Lee's attention back: "Actual to all units—if they're not fleeing the combat, then they're combatants. Two-Six and

Two-Seven, clear out that flank so I can get off this fucking bridge."

For a third time, Lee raised the radio in his right hand, but this time for entirely different reasons. But for a third time, he stopped himself. No mercy. That was the only way success was even in the universe of possibility. They had to be meaner, and harder, and nastier than their opponent, because the odds were stacked against them.

He lowered the radio.

Lopez glanced at him, then looked away.

Brinly was right, wasn't he? If they hadn't fled the combat, then they were combatants. No room for moral dilemmas. Acting President Briggs would take advantage of that, and Lee's invasion would be over before it even got off the starting block.

He swallowed. Raised the radio in his other hand, this one tied to Abe's task force. "Marshal Actual, Stranger Actual. Drifter is engaged. Standby for 'go.'"

Abe's voice came back, hard and merciless. He sounded like Mr. No One again: "Stranger Actual, we copy. Ready to roll on your word."

***

Abe Darabie had changed. Not in any earth-shattering way, because people really never change like that until their earth gets shattered. Abe's earth had been shattered much too long ago to even remember what he'd been like before.

He had changed, but in a smaller, subtler way.

Have you ever come back to place after years away from it? And all of the sudden, just by seeing it, just by smelling it, just by *knowing you're there*, you're pulled back across all of those intervening years. You're yanked into the past again.

Sometimes that's a pleasant thing. Oftentimes it's not.

It wasn't for Abe. And it made him mean.

Three years he'd been a fugitive from this place. Three years he'd been Briggs's prodigal son, except that now that he was back, he wasn't falling on his knees and begging forgiveness. No, he was back for blood, and he meant to take it.

Change. Switch flipped.

It'd happened to Lee. Abe had witnessed it—right after Julia had died and they'd rampaged all through Texas, slaughtering the people that they hated. Except, that had been Lee's hate. Lee's vengeance ride. Abe had just gone along because…well, that's what friends do.

This was *Abe's* vengeance ride. His homecoming, in all its grim and bloody glory, that'd been relegated to the desperate yearnings of his subconscious, all made manifest before him now. And all he had to do was reach out and take it.

Snatch it up with iron fingers. Rip its fucking throat out.

"Yo." A hand slapped his back. "We good?"

Abe let out a breath he'd been holding in his chest like a pressure cooker. Turned to find Sergeant Menendez and his boys, heads ducked from the rotors splitting the air over their heads, eyes squinted against the rotor wash.

Abe leaned in so he wouldn't have to shout so loud to be heard. "Brinly's engaged. We're waiting for the go ahead."

Menendez nodded and smashed his helmet down over his head, buckling the strap. The squad behind him did the same. They were good dudes. Abe had gotten to know them pretty damn well, and he liked the way they worked. Called dibs on them the second Lee laid out his plans and Abe knew he'd need a solid crew of people he trusted.

Because they were only twelve guys, heading in to take over an entire airfield. Plus the Blackhawk, which could give a pounding from the air with its M240. But still—only twelve guys. But they looked about as hungry as Abe felt. They had their own bones to pick with Acting President Briggs—codenamed Outlaw for this operation. And that was good. That's what Abe was counting on.

A little hatred goes a long way.

Abe held the command-net radio up to his ear so he could hear it over the rotors, ears primed, so he didn't miss a single word of it when Lee's voice came over the airwaves again.

"Marshal Actual, Stranger Actual, you're a go. You're a go. Get me what I want."

And what he wanted was an airfield.

And that was just fine with Abe. Because the airfield was just an obstacle that he needed to navigate on his way to FOB Hampton and putting a bullet through Acting President Briggs's brain.

"Stranger copies. We're rolling." Abe snugged the radio into a pouch on his rig, and didn't even bother signaling to Menendez and the crew—they knew from the look in his eyes that the command had been given, and they fell in behind him as he stalked under the rotors, and hauled himself up onto the deck of the Blackhawk.

Tucked his lid under his arm and seated the helicopter's bulky intercom headset over his ears.

Adjusted the boom mic. Waited for the last of Menendez's men to pull their boots off the ground. "We're in," he said to the pilots. "Greeley-Weld County Airport, please."

The pilot offered him a wry smirk—just the smirk, because the rest of his head was covered up by flight helmet and tinted visor. Offered a thumbs-up. And then they were lifting off.

FOUR

THE AIRFIELD

"Ryder. Ryder. Hey! Ryder!"

Sam jerked, blinked, twisted rapidly in his seat. Everything was all crossed wires and confusion. Where the hell was he? He hadn't been asleep, had he? No, he was almost certain that his eyes had been open, but everything was swimming as though he was in a dream.

He moved his hands, which were clutched at his right hip. A stab of pain shot through him. His fingers were sticky. He let out a little noise of surprise and looked down to find blood coating his hands.

Oh, shit. He'd been shot.

"Sergeant Fucking Ryder," a voice boomed from behind him.

Made him jerk again. Jones was staring at him like he'd just done something terrible. What? What had he done wrong? He looked further in the back and saw a bunch of strangers...

Canadian Special Forces. Right. And they were pissed.

Red. That was his name. Shit, why was everything so upside down right now?

Red leaned forward, glaring. "What the fuck are you doing, man?"

"Ease up," Marie snapped, shouldering herself up to Red. "He's been awake for..." she trailed off, glancing at Sam as though looking for an answer.

"Was I asleep?" Sam murmured.

"No," Jones said. "You were just staring with your mouth open like a vegetable."

Sam guiltily looked back to Red, but found that the man's anger had simmered down a bit. Now he had a circumspective look. "Shit, Ryder. When'd you sleep last?"

When had he slept last? He remembered going to sleep in that flat, but couldn't place the day. How many hours had passed since then? Forty-eight? Less? More?

"I'm fine," Sam mumbled, and only then realized that they were parked. He twitched around, looking out the windows. Didn't recognize the spot. Houses, all around them, but they were all burned out. An abandoned section of Greeley that had been turned to cinders long enough ago that nature was growing up from the ashes and twining in with the blackened bones of old homes.

"You're not fine," Red said. "You can't operate on no sleep."

"Well, what the fuck do you want me to do about it?" Sam snapped, suddenly and irrationally furious. He felt the heat tingling through his scalp, felt his veins and arteries distending with the pressure of rage.

"How long?" Red insisted.

"Forty-eight hours, alright?" Sam growled, rubbing his bloody hand across his face before he remembered it was bloody. "Or somewhere in there. But I'm fine."

"Forty-eight hours since you slept," Marie said, a bit exasperated. "But it was shit sleep, and you know it. You haven't had real sleep since we fucking got here."

Red shook his head. "After twenty-four hours you're basically drunk." He tilted his head. "You think that might've had anything to do with your shit decisions?"

"You think you can get off my fucking back?" Sam nearly shouted, lurching about in his seat, sending stabs of pain through his wound. Pulse in his head smarting where the bullet had grazed his skull. He fully intended to be all high and mighty for a moment, but he suddenly felt faint and wilted back against his own door. "Shit."

"Alright," Red grunted. "You're done."

"I'm not done."

"You're done for right now. You can't keep going."

"Don't tell me…" Another wave of faintness hit him. The edges of his vision sparkled with encroaching darkness. Everything swam in his vision. Everything felt off. Nightmarish. Suddenly the whole world was a predator looming over him. Scaring the shit out of him.

Red turned to Marie. "He needs sleep. And medical attention." Red pounded the back glass. "Yo! Blue! Medic up here."

Jones looked aghast. "Sleep? We can't just sleep! There's an invasion going on!"

"No time to sleep," Sam groaned. He was hunched over, as though against a gale of wind. Trying to keep himself conscious. He clamped his eyes shut. That seemed to help for an instant, but then he got scared he might pass out.

Sam felt the door open behind him. It gave him a jolt, but it was weak, like his adrenaline was all spent.

"Ryder. Look at me."

Sam stretched his eyes wide. Red, and Marie, and White on the other side of her, and Jones in the driver's seat, all staring at him with knit brows. Except for White. He seemed kind of amused by the whole thing.

Blue, standing outside the door with his medical pack hoisted around so it sat on his belly. Waiting for his patient to settle down.

"What?" Sam slurred. God, he could hardly make words. Maybe Red was onto something with this whole sleep thing.

"Blue is going to patch that wound in your side. And then you're going to sleep."

"Can't sleep—"

"Shut up." Red pointed at him. "You're a liability right now, not an asset."

Well, that cut right through the proverbial crap cake of Sam's wonky logic. Now the tingling heat he felt wasn't anger—it was shame.

"You wanna be able to actually do some good here?" Red demanded. "Then you need to grab some shut eye before you lose touch with reality. I've seen it happen. Shit, I've had it happen to me."

"But…" Sam struggled mightily to come up with something. Maybe there really wasn't a good excuse, or maybe he just couldn't dredge it up right now.

"Two hours," Red said. "Two hours won't change the course of the invasion. We need to regroup anyways." He pressed forward and frowned at Sam, whose focus was guttering out. "You with me so far?"

Sam bobbled his head. "Two hours." Sweet Lord, that sounded like heaven, even if a small part of him was still throwing a tantrum about it. But Red was either right, or Sam was too tired to see it differently: He was a liability right now. He wasn't doing anyone any favors in his current state.

That didn't mean he liked it. Oh, no. He resented the hell out of it and felt weak and helpless. But what are you gonna do? Humans have this fantastic organ swimming around in their skull, and if you don't let it shut down every once in a while, it makes you crazy and you eventually die. That was just the unfortunate fact of it.

"You wanna turn that busted hip towards me so I can work on it?" Blue asked, laying a gentle hand on Sam's shoulder.

Sam looked at him, already feeling that thready disconnection of sleep coming at him hard. Now that he wasn't fighting it so much, it was sucking him out like a rip current. "Yeah, okay, whatever," he mumbled.

He thrashed himself back into a sitting position on the passenger seat. Let his head fall back. Eyes flickering. The sound of zippers as Blue opened his med-bag. The tearing open of a package. Pressure on his wound that hurt for a second, but not quite enough to keep him awake, and then Sam was gone.

***

Abe already knew that the Greeley-Weld County Airfield was a mess of buildings, and that every one of those damn things would need to be cleared, but he still felt his stomach drop a bit when he looked at it from the air, their Blackhawk coming in towards the southeastern corner.

Well over twenty buildings. If Abe had organized this op in ideal conditions, he wouldn't have gone in with less than a battalion, and plenty of ass to back it up. But he didn't have a battalion, and they didn't have any ass, so here he was with twelve rifles, and they'd just have to make up the difference of *several hundred troops* by being meaner, faster, and more determined than whoever the hell Briggs had stationed here to protect it.

He fervently hoped that Lee's plan had worked and the airfield had been emptied out to help defend against Brinly's assault in the south. But you know what they say about plans.

He smushed himself up between the pilot and copilot. Thrust a hand out to the main hangar. "Set us down right over there and then circle for air support."

The pilot just nodded. The aircraft banked, angling for the main structure.

"I'm off the intercom," Abe said, shucking the big headphones off and slapping them on their hanger. He turned back to the twelve men in his team, keying his comms so they could hear him a bit better through their earpieces. "We don't gotta own the whole field, we just gotta get a foothold. We're setting down on the eastern side, right next to the main hangar. Watch your backdrops and do your best not to shoot up the aircraft—Lee wants those. Other than that? Kill all the bad guys."

Abe felt the altitude drop in his gut as the Blackhawk slowed, coming in low. He wrangled himself to the open door on the left side of the aircraft, where Breckenridge and his fire team sat. Menendez and his fire team were posted on the right side, just now hauling their door open.

The wind outside blasted his face, whipped his fatigues against his legs as he settled onto the deck, legs hanging out. He looked over his shoulder at his fire team and gave them a nod. They nodded back. Breck gave him a thumbs-up.

The nose of the Blackhawk lifted as it came into a hover. Abe peered over his legs, cinching the rifle tight into his chest pocket. The ground rose to meet him. He checked the brightness on his reticle. Dialed it up two notches.

The door gunner beside Abe slapped him on the back and held up all five fingers, then started retracting them one by one. The ground continued to come up at him. His eyes flicked from one thing to another—three fingers, the distance to the ground, scan for threats, one finger, no threats. And then it was a fist.

Abe thrust himself off the deck. Hit the dirt and immediately dropped onto a knee, rifle up. Rotor wash tore at him, filling his ears and thrumming through his chest. He took in his surroundings in one rapid circle. The main hangar stood about a hundred yards off. Beyond it, he could just make out the edges of a jumble of helicopter tails. Those were the aircraft they wanted. Now all they had to do was make it happen.

The sound of the rotors got louder—thundering, pressing him down. And then the pressure lifted, and the noise began to abate, as the Blackhawk took to the sky again.

"Menendez!" Abe transmitted. "Take your team to the north side of that hangar. We'll go south."

Up and running. Gear rattling. Armor bouncing, constricting his diaphragm. Grip already sweaty on his rifle. He kept expecting to see tracers coming in, or hear the pop of gunfire and the buzz of projectiles skimming past him. It was almost eerie to be running with no one shooting at him. Just the sound of his breath and his gear and his boots stamping across the scrubby grass. Then concrete. Angling around a truck that looked like it'd been pirated for parts. He slowed and cleared it anyways. It was a flatbed, so just the cab. And then Abe was running again, this time towards the middle of Breck's fire team.

They hit the wall of the hangar, just a few feet from the corner. Rifles out, covering all directions. Abe thumbed a drop of sweat off his eyebrow and sidled towards the corner. Backed off the wall just a bit. Leaned until he had a good angle on the rest of the field beyond the hangar.

More buildings. A few vehicles. Nothing moving. All quiet.

His lips pressed together as he slipped back into cover.

Sure, everyone likes an easy op. But shouldn't *someone* have been shooting at them at this point? Made his guts get all tangled, doubt and hesitation whispering down the back of his neck. He poked at his PTT.

"Hey, Menendez, what you got over there?"

"I can see the tail end of six helos. Looks like two Blackhawks and maybe four Little Birds?"

Sounded about right, if Abe's memory served correctly. Hell, he'd probably ridden on those very same helos back when he'd been under Briggs's thumb. Back when he'd followed Briggs's orders. Back when he'd killed people just for wanting food.

"Copy," Abe responded. "Hold tight." Then he switched to his command-net radio and called up the Blackhawk. "Stranger to White Horse, we need eyes on those—"

A blat of heavy gunfire sent electrical sparks down his spine.

He snapped his head to the right to see if Menendez was taking fire, but he wasn't acting like it—still hovering around the corner just like Abe. Then the noise of their Blackhawk in the air changed—a rapid maneuver.

"White Horse, Stranger," the pilot said, sounding strained. "We're taking fire from a nest right in the middle of those grounded birds!"

Abe's eyes snapped skyward just in time to see the Blackhawk roll sharply over the top of the hangar, the door gunner on the right side ripping his M240 around and firing a long string of tracers down at the ground.

"White Horse, get outta range and hold what you got! We gotta clear this hangar!" Abe fumbled for his other radio. "Menendez, you got a man door on that side. Pop in and see if there's anything we need to worry about."

Abe heard Menendez's response, but he was already angling out around the corner again. With every little shuffle away from the building, the sound of that enemy machine gun got clearer, until all the sudden it went silent again.

Squeezing breath out through pursed lip. A little more. A little more. A swath of blacktop. A smattering of buildings—there.

He barely had time to lay his eyes on the sandbag machine gun nest before something bloomed yellow and angry and Abe jolted back into cover, big bullets splitting the air where he'd just been.

"Fuck! That was close!" he yipped, smashing himself back against the hangar. He jammed a finger in the direction he'd spotted the nest. "They got at least one M240 in that nest, and they know we're here."

Breckenridge spun and slapped the back of their grenadier, Gordon. "Get in there, you wily sonofabitch."

"How far?" Gordon demanded as he scooched up to the corner with Abe, hefting his launcher.

"Three hundred yards, give or take," Abe answered, heart still hammering. "Hold up a sec." Then he transmitted to Menendez: "What you got in the hangar?"

"I got big empty space in the hangar," Menendez said.

"I got you," Abe said. "Come on back and take up that position. Gordon's gonna lob a few shots and see what we can't make happen."

"Roger, we're coming out."

Abe looked at Gordon. "You ready?"

He fiddled with the iron sights on it. "Yuh."

The man door over on the other end opened up and Menendez and his team spilled out, hustling for the corner again. Abe tracked his eyes across the sky, spotted their Blackhawk skimming low, well out of range of the enemy machine gun.

"Stranger to White Horse, can you spot anything else we need to be aware of? We're about to make a move on that nest—I don't want any surprises."

"White Horse, I got nothin'. Just that nest. Place looks dead everywhere else."

"I copy. Be ready to come swooping into my rescue, you hear?"

"We're ready."

Juggling radios again. "Menendez, on my mark, I need you to lay some hate on—"

The ground shuddered under his feet, ears suddenly blasted by a roar, the whole of the massive hangar they were huddled against vibrating like a steel drum.

"What the hell was that?" Abe snapped to no one in particular. Didn't dare lean out of cover. When you hear big booms, you get your head down and get your bearings first before you go popping up to solve your curiosity.

"White Horse to Stranger!" The pilot's voice was not happy, and Abe felt his stomach plummet. "They just blew the birds!"

"Are you fucking serious?" Abe didn't transmit that part. "Copy! Standby! Gordon, get ready!" He grabbed the man by the shoulder, shoved him into position, Abe's own rifle hovering over his shoulder. "Menendez! Fire on that nest! Now!"

Menendez and three others leaned out of cover, rifles cracking rapidly.

"Send it!" Abe snapped, following Gordon out of cover, two steps to the right, Gordon going low on one knee, Abe staying high, just above him, firing fast at the sandbags, watching the rounds send up gouts of tan dust.

Thoonk! Thoonk!

Gordon sent two 40mm grenades out, then Abe grabbed his drag strap and hauled for cover again. He'd barely made it four steps before the two rounds struck, *BOOM! BOOM!*

"Right on!" Menendez called over the comms. "Hell yeah, Gordon!"

"Menendez, cover!" Abe ordered. "We're moving!"

Around the corner, Abe first, followed by Breck, then Gordon, then the rest of the fire team. Someone on Menendez's team fired off a smattering of rounds just as Abe laid eyes on the decimated machine gun nest: sandbags ripped from the topmost layers, shredded and toppled, a cloud of whitish smoke drifting lazily away from it.

No movement from the nest. Abe decided to push his luck and bound straight for it, this time hazarding a glance at the aircraft that Lee had wanted so bad.

Shit. Lee was gonna be pissed.

They hadn't just taken out a few of the birds, they'd taken out every fucking one of them. Looked like they'd placed the charges right on the tail boom and sheared the tails right off.

Abe started yelling when he was within fifty yards of the nest: "Get your fuckin' hands up! Hands up!" He had no intention of giving quarter, even if they did raise their hands—they were way beyond that now.

No one took the bait. Either smart or dead. Hopefully the latter.

He thought about telling Gordon to hit it again, but they didn't have the ammunition to waste. God, but how nice would it be to be working for the good ol' US government again, where cost was no object and accuracy by volume was still a viable strategy. Not the first time he'd had that wishful thinking.

They slowed as they got nearer. Abe waved his hands for them to spread out. There hadn't been a peep of movement from inside the nest since Gordon had hit it. And he'd scored two straight hits right in the middle, so if there was anyone in there, they were either made of steel, or they'd be unidentifiable as human.

The barrel of an M240 lay there, nestled in the crook of two shrapnel-tattered sandbags. It didn't move. Neither did anything else.

Abe went in low, practically duck walking, and then jolted upright, thrusting his rifle at…

Nothing.

Not even splatter.

"The hell?" he demanded of the nothingness.

"Shit," Breck spat. "Fuckers must've ghosted us."

Abe immediately snapped his rifle up, stomach roiling. Couldn't figure out if it was rage or dread. "Gimme three-sixty. I gotta call this in."

FIVE

ABBY

ABBY STOOD WATCHING everyone else run around, and she felt like a tree. Trees just stood there, never moving, never feeling. Just still and silent in the river of life while all the other animals and birds and squirrels and whatever climbed around, always stressed, always in a tizzy about something or other.

By standing still, it seemed like the grown-ups always forgot that she was there. And by being silent, it seemed they thought she wasn't listening. But she was taking it all in. Absorbing everything that everyone did. Listening to the words they said, as though she couldn't hear. Maybe it was because they thought she couldn't understand. Maybe because she never seemed to react to any of it.

Not anymore anyways.

Her mother stood at the back of the big, tan, Army vehicle—they called it a MATV, she knew, though she didn't know what it stood for. Lee stood beside her mother, the two of them so close that if they wanted to, they could've held each other's hands. But they probably didn't want to. Grown-ups always waited until things were absolutely terrible to do anything like that.

Was this absolutely terrible? Well, it sure sounded like it.

She heard Abe's voice coming over the radio: "They blew the birds in half. We got nothing. They didn't even have any intention of holding the airfield—they just didn't want us to have the aircraft."

Abby watched her mother's face. Her lips turned down at the corners and flattened out. She didn't used to have those wrinkles at the sides of her mouth. From frowning all the time, Abby guessed.

Her mother's eyes flitted sideways to Lee, and Abby looked too, supposing she was as curious as her mother to see how Lee was going to handle this development.

Lee. Standing with that slightly-off posture that he'd had since getting shot in the hip. Abby could only see the side of his face. It was the left side—the side with no eye. The side with all the marks on it from bits and pieces of things that had blown up in his face. Mostly the scabs had fallen off now. But under the scraggly growth of Lee's short beard, she could see the pale marks where they'd been.

Lee's mouth was all tense and frowning too. But that wasn't anything unusual. That's just kind of how he looked. He looked that way for as long as Abby could remember. Used to scare her because he looked so damn mean all the time. But that was when she'd been a little girl. She knew she wasn't grown-up yet, but she'd grown up enough. Enough to see the sadness and the desperation in all that kind-of-scary anger. Enough to appreciate that all those scars on him weren't because he was so damn mean, but because he cared. Maybe a little too much?

He raised his left hand—the one with the mottled scars all over the wrist and the fingers that didn't work right anymore. Seemed like his thumb was okay, and his pointer finger. But all the other ones just kind of hung there and didn't do much. He raked that hand through his hair, a sheen of sweat coming with it. Then dragged that hand across his scarred face.

"Goddammit," he whispered.

Hm. Must've been bad.

Lee keyed his radio, head hanging a bit. "Marshal copies. How much of the airfield were you able to clear?"

"The main hangar is clear, and a handful of buildings around the lot where the helicopters were parked. That's all clear. There's about a dozen other buildings we haven't got to yet."

"Roger. Hold what you got. Assholes might've taken my birds, but I'm still gonna take their airfield. We're on the move to your location in five."

"Stranger copies. We'll be waiting."

Abby leaned back against the open door of the MATV. Looked down at the dust under her feet. Everything was so dry here. She poked the toe of her old sneakers into it. Drew a smiley face. Then scuffed it out.

More voices on the radio. Brinly this time. She liked Brinly. He was kind of like a weird uncle. "Drifter Actual to Marshal Actual, I gotta commit my civvies." For once, Brinly sounded ever-so-slightly stressed-out. That was odd. Abby had never heard him sound like that before. "We're taking way too much heat trying to push into the city. Requesting additional reserves to get on standby in La Salle. Over."

"Shit," Lee murmured. "Marshal copies, standby, Drifter." Lee turned to Mom. "How many civvies we got ready to roll right now?"

Mom considered this, still with that sullen frowny face. "They should all be ready, but how many do you want to commit to Brinly? We still gotta push into Greeley from the airfield."

"Well, I ain't gonna act like we're flush with troops, but I want Brinly to keep pushing. I can't afford to have him bog down." A moment of silent consideration. "Send five squads. That should leave us plenty to take the airfield and push in." An exasperated chuff. "As if 'plenty' means a fucking thing right now."

"It's all relative," Mom observed. She took a step back and finally looked at Abby, almost like she was surprised to find her there. "Abby, I want you to stay with Lee. I'm going to go get some squads moving."

Abby just nodded. *Yeah, okay. No problem, Mom. You go get your squads moving.* The thought of saying it all casual like that gave Abby a tiny little shred of humor that tickled the sides of her mouth and almost made her giggle, but not quite. Still, it was nice. She hadn't almost-giggled in a while. Hadn't really felt *anything* in a while.

As Mom went hustling off, Lee turned and stared at Abby. Again, with that expression like he'd forgotten she was there. That was the funny thing about grown-ups. It's not like they were dumb, but geez, all you had to do was sit still and be quiet and they forgot you were there?

"Abby," Lee said, his voice weirdly chill after all that rapid-fire cussing.

"Yeah?" Abby raised an eyebrow.

Lee shook his head, his one good eye fixed on her. "Nothing. I was just saying hi."

"Oh. Hi."

He blinked a few times. Like he wanted to say something else, but couldn't quite settle on what. Then he just turned away from her. Looking all stiff and awkward.

"Things going bad?" Abby asked.

He snapped back to her. There was that little glimmer of fire in his eye that used to scare her—used to make her think he wanted to hurt her. But he would never hurt her. Only other people. He hurt them plenty. But never her. He opened his mouth and seemed to gnaw on the words.

Abby sniffed. Waited for him. Sometimes you have to let grown-ups take their time. They're super sensitive about what they say in front of kids. Thought they were doing the kids a favor by putting everything in nice, G-rated terminology for them. But Abby could always tell there were things left unsaid. And then she would wonder about those things. She would think they must be pretty awful if the grown-ups couldn't just tell the truth. And then sometimes she'd find out the truth later on, and realize that it wasn't as bad as she was imagining, and that would kind of piss her off, because she'd spent all that time worrying about it and imagining something far worse than the truth, and the grown-ups could've prevented that if they'd just been honest from the start.

Finally, as though Lee had read those very thoughts, he just snorted and shook his head. "Yeah, it's all fucked up. But I'll tell you something, Abby—I've never seen it *not* be all fucked up. So, I guess everything's going as expected."

She smiled at him. "Yeah. Seems that way."

He nodded and looked into the back of the MATV. "Seems that way because it is that way. All we can do is keep pushing. Sometimes you catch a break, sometimes you get broken. Won't know until you get out there and do it." He shook his head again. "Sorry. I should have something more…inspirational for you. But there it is."

"I don't mind," Abby said, looking off to catch the back of her mother's blonde hair bobbing through the crowd of terrified-looking civilians, all of them staring out towards Greeley where the distant sound of gunfire kept rolling towards them in constant waves. "Wish my mom would tell it like that every once in a while."

"She's just…" He faltered. "Aw, hell, I don't even know, Abby. I don't have kids. Don't know what it's like. Cut her some slack."

Abby looked off at the people and their cars and trucks and vans. She was thinking hard about something, and she kind of wanted to get Lee's opinion on it. Always some hesitation about what to say to a grown-up, but hadn't she just been thinking it would be better if everyone was honest with each other?

So, she just blurted it out: "You ever feel absolutely nothing at all?"

His mouth opened, but he didn't say anything. Had a look on his face that Abby couldn't quite decipher. And before he could unstick his brain into responding, the phone in his back pocket started going off.

He snatched it up like it was saving him. "Abby, this might not be the best time."

And Abby was already backpedaling anyways. She'd shot it out there, seen it fall flat, and now all she wanted to do was get distance. "No, yeah, it's cool." He was bringing the satphone to his face, still looking a little worried with that one eye. "I gotta pee." That was always a good excuse to get gone.

"Yeah, okay," he said, distractedly, as he answered the phone.

***

Lee watched her march off as he pressed the call button and put it to his ear. She was a weird little girl, but what did he expect? A normal, well-adjusted kid? Shit, none of them were normal at this point in time. The kids least of all.

"Sam, that you?" Lee asked into the phone.

"No, it's me." Marie's voice.

Lee's breath caught. "What happened?"

"We're still alive," Marie said quickly. "Sam got a little banged up, but he'll make it. Look, Lee...the civvies we had with us went and poofed the second shit went hot. Useless bastards."

Lee's breath came out. He was getting used to the sensation of his stomach sinking, but still didn't care for it. Felt like it was trying to find its way to his feet. He swore a good streak and only cut himself off because he was only succeeding in making himself angrier, and that wasn't going to do him any favors at this point.

He closed his eye, already knowing the answer, but needing to hear it confirmed: "And the weapons depot?"

"Not taken. And now they're on high alert."

"Motherfuck."

"My thoughts exactly."

"Where are you now, and who do you have backing you up?"

"We pulled back to a burned-out neighborhood, maybe five miles west of the weapons depot. We got the..."—hesitation—"...the *other* team?"

The Canadians, she means. She was just being cautious about what she said. That was good.

"But that's it," she concluded. "Sam's bombed out, Lee. We forced him to grab a couple hours of sleep."

Lee opened his eye wide and almost asked her why in the hell they were sleeping during the first hours of the invasion…but…

"Dammit, Marie."

"I know, but what do you want me to do? His brain's done, Lee. He's been up trying to prep for this thing for two days straight."

"Alright, alright." Lee squeezed the bridge of his nose. There wasn't anything he could do about it. It's not like they were going to win in twelve hours, and he couldn't expect his troops to stay awake for the duration of the fighting. That would only weaken them and lead to mistakes. "Are you secure where you're at?"

"As much as we can be."

"Hold what you got. You might as well get some rest while you're at it. I'll be in contact."

When Lee hung up the satphone, he turned, casting his eye about for Abby, but she'd gone and disappeared on him. A little thorn of worry pricked at him. But what was he going to do? Watch her take a piss?

Besides, Abby had a good head on her shoulders. She wouldn't go wandering off.

***

Abby was really thinking about how nice it might be to just…wander off.

No, she didn't need to pee. Yes, she'd lied to get free of adult eyes. Or in the case of Lee, eye, singular. And now she was just staring out at the big endless plains to the south of them, and wondering what it would be like to just start walking and not stop.

Abby didn't care for whatever was happening in her brain. She couldn't really make sense of it. Didn't have the words to put it into. It was like...she'd lost her sense of taste. If life could have a taste. Sometimes it was bitter, and sometimes it was sweet, and sometimes it was salty and puckering like vinegar. But lately it hadn't been anything at all.

Life had become a cold bowl of oatmeal.

What had happened to her?

Well. She'd watched her father get killed right in front of her. Watched her mom develop some sort of weird feelings for the guy that had killed him. Watched a bunch of other people get killed. Almost been killed several times. Had any sense of security she might've tricked herself into feeling ripped away when her home in Fort Bragg got overrun by primals. Been bitten by one of them. Had someone else try to poison her with FURY-infected stuff, since the primal bite didn't seem to do the trick...

Oh, the list goes on.

Maybe a better question would be what *hadn't* happened to her?

Her brain had been pressed and shaken and scraped and pummeled and abraded and sandblasted. Her defenses had been torn down, then rebuilt stronger, then torn down again, and rebuilt stronger yet, until she'd managed to build them up so tall and thick that nothing could get through them at all, not even anything good.

So, yeah, walking out into the plains seemed like it might be a pretty good idea. But what she really wanted was to *feel* something again. What did she have to do to make that happen? Would walking out into the plains help? Would being *alone* help?

She didn't think so.

Couldn't say why, but being alone just sounded like the worst possible thing. The more she was alone, the thicker and higher her walls became. And she was trying to let something through them! No, she needed to stay around people.

How did other people deal with this? She knew they had to. Because she could see the looks in some of their eyes. She could see that they'd gotten hard too. Like calluses. Like the really thick one on your heel. Or maybe the one on the side of your big toe.

She put her hands on her hips and frowned around at all the callused people. What were they doing to figure this out? Well, for one thing, they all had guns, and they were all staring at Greeley, and even though they looked pretty scared, they also looked kind of eager.

She tilted her head. Gave one of the nearest women a good, hard look. She was far enough away that the woman hadn't really noticed her staring—staring was rude, apparently, though rudeness seemed like a really silly thing to care about. The woman looked…well, what was the word for that?

Hungry?

Yeah. Kinda hungry. Or starving. But more like if you were starving, but the only thing to eat was an alligator and you had to wrestle it first. Kill it with your own two hands. Then you could eat. If you didn't die.

That's what it looked like.

Was she hungry for the same thing as Abby? Did the woman just want to feel something? And what was she going to do about it? How was she going to solve that hunger?

It sure looked like she was going to go shoot at people.

Maybe that's the only way you get to feel anything when you're all callused up.

Maybe killing is the only thing that gets through.

And it just so happened that right at the moment that Abby was thinking those thoughts, staring at the hungry woman, and wondering what it might feel like to fire a weapon in anger, a car came hurtling up next to the woman. A battered, silver four-door. A man hopped out, obviously excited, and he yammered some things at the woman, that Abby didn't really listen to, even if she heard him clear enough. Then he said something she *did* listen to.

"She says we're going into the south side of Greeley, where Major Brinly's at! We're moving in five minutes!"

Five minutes.

The woman scooped up an old backpack at her feet. "Pop the trunk, will ya?"

The man popped the trunk, and the woman jogged to the back, tossed in the backpack, and slammed the trunk shut.

And that might've been it. That might have terminated this particular line of thinking, even as Abby was feeling her way along it. She'd read about when they used to send scientists up into the arctic, and the snow was so thick there, that even to get from building to building, they had to follow a rope.

You just grabbed onto the rope and followed it until it led you to where you were going.

Abby was holding onto a rope of her own thoughts, following it wherever it might lead.

Might've led to nothing, if it weren't for one inch of wayward nylon strap from the backpack. But there *was* a wayward nylon strap, and it happened to lay itself right across the latch of the trunk so that when the hungry woman slammed it, it popped back up about an inch and didn't quite latch. The woman was too jittery to notice. She'd already gone and sat in the passenger's seat.

And there it was: the rope of her thoughts actually led to something.

A possibility. A promise of an answer to a question.

She didn't think about it too much. Why would she? You kept your hand on the rope and went where it led you. So, she walked confidently, right up to the back of that car, not even bothering to glance around—she knew glancing around would only make people notice her more. No, she just opened the trunk and slipped inside. Held it closed, but left the nylon strap where it was so it wouldn't latch.

She lay there breathlessly for a moment, her heart beating like she might actually start to get nervous—something she hadn't legitimately felt since the fall of the Butler Safe Zone. Wondering if someone had noticed her. Wondering if the trunk was going to yank open again and her mother was going to drag her out. Probably screaming at her.

Time stretched a bit. Got kind of hard to track. Yes, her heart was definitely beating hard. She was getting nervous. Almost needed to pee for real this time.

And then, apparently, five minutes had gone by, because the car started moving.

Abby was almost shocked when she let the trunk drift open an inch, just enough for her to peer out, and watched the collection of vehicles—and her mother, and Lee—shrinking behind her.

***

They were, quite naturally, the first words out of Angela's mouth: "Where's Abby?"

That was one of the weird things about being a mother: No matter what was going on, the safety of your kid had a way of supplanting everything else. It wasn't a voluntary thing. It just had a way of taking hold, like a sudden mania that won't be denied.

So, while she knew that there was an invasion going on, and she could see that Lee was speaking to Marlin and Worley, and clearly trying to get things moving towards the airfield, all of that was swiftly crushed under the sudden dread of not seeing Abby where she'd left her.

Lee turned from Marlin and Worley and jerked his head in a direction that clearly meant *Somewhere over yonder, but I wasn't really paying attention.* "She went to go take a piss." He stopped. Frowned. "Or maybe a shit?"

Her first, rather unreasonable instinct was to think *Why didn't you go with her?!*

But of course he didn't go with her. Abby was a ten-year-old girl, and while they all had gotten used to relieving themselves more or less in the presence of others, you still didn't want a one-eyed, mid-thirties man hanging over your shoulder while you did it.

And also, Lee had more important things to do than making sure Abby had a safe bathroom session.

Lee started to turn back around. He'd given Marlin one of their command radios and was clearly trying to issue some orders in reference to it, but Angela just couldn't quite squash a feeling of wrongness.

"How long's she been gone?"

Lee turned back to her again, this time with a slightly more dismissive manner. "I dunno. Five minutes?"

Yes, mothers could be a little paranoid about their kids. But men were on the opposite side of that spectrum. Where mothers seemed to believe they could keep their kids safe by swaddling them in their own manic anxiety, men seemed to think that the survivability of kids was just some mystical concept they had no control over.

Lee turned back—a little more decisively this time—and pointed out at the civilian forces ranged out on the plains around them. "I want you two to hang back with the rearguard—I need at least *some* experienced people here watching our backs. I'm taking the majority of them into the airfield with us, but I'm gonna leave ten squads here to keep an eye on things and make sure we don't get any Cornerstone leaking out and trying to test our flanks."

Angela was still standing there with them, so she felt the need to nod along to what Lee was saying, even as she started turning in a slow circle, trying to find Abby's tousled mop of white-blonde hair somewhere in all that mess. Five minutes wasn't so long. And kids—God, they were constantly getting constipated. Especially with the shit they'd been having to survive on.

"Angela."

She jerked. Turned to Lee. "Yeah?"

He hiked his thumb over his shoulder at the MATV. "We gotta roll."

Angela looked at him like he was insane. "I can't leave without Abby."

Lee blinked a few times, which was like some sort of morse code that he did to impress upon her when he felt she was being unreasonable. "The airfield's open, and we need to get on it. We have a very narrow window of operations here, Angela. We don't have time to waste."

Angela shooed him at the MATV. "Go, then. I'll catch up."

More blinking. And a downturn of the mouth to boot, which set the scars on the side of his face into stark lines. "No, you can't just 'catch up.' I need you at the airfield."

"You don't—"

"I *need* you at the airfield," he said, more insistent. "Because you're the one in charge of all these civilian squads, and most of them are coming to the airfield."

"Angela." Marlin scooted around Lee, pocketing the radio he'd been given. "Me and Worley are staying behind with the rearguard. Abby'll be safe with us. Probably safer with us than at the airfield, to be honest. They've still gotta clear out a bunch of buildings there."

Angela's heart was starting to beat faster than it should've been. "No, you don't need to babysit."

Lee was rolling his hands over each other, impatient. "Angela. We gotta *go*."

Marlin put a hand on Angela's shoulder and gave it a gentle squeeze. "You know you can trust me." He smiled, and, in fact, did look very trustworthy. "Let the girl take a shit in peace for once. She'll be safe with us and we'll bring her along when the airfield's cleared."

Lee was already hauling himself up into the back of the MATV, apparently finished with the conversation.

"Okay," Angela found her mouth saying, even as something else far deeper inside of her pulled away. But she was just being paranoid, wasn't she? She needed to be *reasonable*. She needed to have some *perspective*. Abby had grown up a lot recently. She was tough and smart. She'd be fine. And, like Marlin had pointed out, Angela was heading closer to danger, so technically, Abby was safer here.

"Okay." One last blast of motherly paranoia: "You know what she looks like, right?"

Marlin laughed and waved her off. "Yes, I know what Abby looks like. We've met. Several times."

The MATV rumbled. Shifted into gear. Lee, hanging out the back with his one eye wide and exasperated. A line of civilian vehicles trundling forward, ready to follow the MATV into the airfield they'd just claimed.

Strategy. Big picture. That's what Angela needed to focus on. Abby would be fine. And yes, she trusted Marlin. Didn't know Worley that well, but Marlin had earned her trust several times over by then. If he said he'd handle it, she knew that he would.

"Alright," she said, steeling herself against the insanity of her motherly instincts. "Alright, I'm coming."

SIX

PRIORITIES

THE FIRST THING LEE THOUGHT when his MATV roared onto the airfield was, *They didn't destroy all the Blackhawks!* That was just the part of him that was ever-hopeful of things maybe making a turnaround before they really went down the shitter. And he promptly realized it was the Blackhawk he already owned.

"Dammit," he murmured, half to the universe for playing tricks on him, and half to himself for falling for it.

The driver—Specialist Lopez—glanced up at him. "Problem, sir?"

He was straddling the center of the vehicle, quite uncomfortably, one might add, wedged between the two front seats and glaring out the windshield. "Nope. Everything's hunky dory."

Abe was already jogging up to them when the MATV jerked to a halt, just shy of the Blackhawk, its rotors still spinning on standby.

Lee patted the other specialist on the shoulder—Specialist Hurst, in the passenger seat. "Make sure that bird gets topped off." Then he turned and hobbled his way past Angela, who was sitting in one of the jump seats, looking worried. But of course she would look worried. Everyone was worried. He paused before reaching the back doors. "You good?"

Angela jerked her head up, distractedly. "Yeah."

Best to give her something to take her mind off Abby. "Grab five squads and send 'em to secure the rest of these buildings. Tell them to watch out for booby traps. Who knows what other surprises these assholes left."

She nodded, rising from the seat.

The back doors were hauled open, letting in a blast of sunlight and heat. Deuce, who'd been circling around Lee, immediately squirted out with that urgency of pace that told Lee the dog needed to piss on some things.

Abe stood there at the back doors, looking impatient.

"I'm coming," Lee grouched at him, negotiating himself to the back and easing one leg down, then the other, trying to hide the effort. "Any more contact?"

Abe shook his head. "Whoever it was manning the machine gun nest was only there to slow us down. They didn't want to blow the birds unless they had to. After that, they hightailed it."

"Coulda used those birds, Abe," Lee said, squinting his eye against the sun and taking in the airfield.

"Not like I could've done anything about it, Lee."

"I know. I'm just pissed."

"Yeah, well, I'm pissed too. Now how about we ram a stick up their ass?" Abe shucked a bottle of water from a side pouch on his pack, took a big swig, holding Lee's gaze the whole time. Made that little gasp when he was done. Burped. "We can take FOB Hampton."

Lee's face screwed up. "FOB Hampton's in the middle of the city."

"Yeah, and I got a Blackhawk," Abe said, a bit of a challenge in his voice.

"Brinly hasn't even punched through the south side yet. There's no way."

"Perfect," Abe said, stubborn as ever. "He's keeping them busy. We land that Blackhawk right on the top of the hotel—there's a good spot there, I know, I've been there. Briggs stays holed up in his penthouse. We can assault downwards and take him out."

"You can't just go changing the plans all willy-nilly!"

"I can take an opportunity when I see one."

"Abe. Abe." Lee put his hand on his shoulder. "Abe, listen to me."

Abe grimaced. Looked away. "I'm listening."

"We're gonna get him. But he's not the priority right now."

"Head of the snake, bro."

"How many times has that worked in the past?" Lee scoffed. "They should take that phrase out of the lexicon; it's bullshit and you know it. Briggs isn't the priority. Owning Greeley is the priority. And I need the power grid taken down. *That's* what'll be effective—remove his ability to command and control."

"Unless he's got generators."

"If he does, he don't have fuel for them," Lee brushed it aside. "That's the plan, Abe. We're sticking to the plan."

Abe took another long drink of water, and did it in the most rebellious and resentful way that one can possibly drink water.

"The power substation, Abe," Lee was nodding, like he was trying to convince a toddler.

Sometimes pissed off grunts were about the same as pissed off toddlers. But with weapons.

"Right, right, right," Abe grunted, capping his water and squishing it back into the pocket it came from. "The substation. I got it."

"You got everything you need?" Lee asked. "'Cause I want that shit blown up yesterday."

Abe patted his pack. "Yeah, I got it. Blackhawk should get topped off. Just in case."

"Already on it." Lee patted him on the shoulder, glad that yet another head-butting between the two had been put to rest. "Your guys all good? How are you fixed on ammo?"

"Shit, we barely fired a shot. But I'll nab some spare mags if you got 'em."

Lee nodded, pointed back towards one of the fastback Humvees that held their meager stores of ammunition.

"We got any more ammo coming in?" Abe asked, giving Lee a sidelong glance.

Lee shook his head. "Sam wasn't able to take the weapons depot."

"Well, someone needs to. Can't take the city with a bunch of civilians with only two mags apiece."

Lee took a harsh breath. "Abe, I'm working on it. Can you focus on the fucking power grid?"

"I'm focused." Abe hazarded a humorless smile. "Just checking in."

"Well, check in later when I'm not pissed off. Christ."

"Hey."

"What?"

Abe situated his pack on his shoulders. Gave Lee a gentle fist to the chest. "It's still early, man. And it could always be worse."

Lee rolled his eye. "Yeah. We could all be on fire."

"There you go." Abe flicked a salute off his sweaty brow. "Perennial optimist."

Lee watched him hustle off and realized he was feeling marginally better, despite himself. Abe had that effect on him. Like any true friend, Abe knew just the right buttons to push, but he also knew when to back off.

And he was right. It was still early.

Lee put his hands on his hips and looked around him at the gathering vehicles, the specialists getting settled in the command MATV, the tanker pulling up to the Blackhawk, the squads that Angela had just dispatched hustling for the buildings on the outer perimeter, Abe's team swarming the Humvee with the spare ammo despite the fact that he'd claimed they'd barely fired a shot. Greedy bastards—but they were worth the cost in ammo.

It was still early. And now Lee had a Forward Operating Base.

***

Sam thrashed awake to the sound of gunfire.

Well, awake was maybe a strong word. His lizard-brain heard gunfire and dumped whatever adrenaline he'd managed to replenish while he'd been sleeping, and he rolled, came up short and breathless against the door, was utterly confused by its presence in his life, fumbled for the handle and thrust it open, even as someone was hissing at him, "Whoa! Easy! Easy!"

Body not fully capable of operating just yet, Sam's swimming vision caught sight of the ground rushing up at him and he managed to put his hands out just before slamming face first into the concrete. He hit the ground in a great clatter of his rifle banging around and then rolled, trying to figure out which way was up.

Gunfire. Gunfire. Where's it coming from?

"Yo!" a bark blasted the side of his face. Rough hands grabbed him and pinned him—which was good for the owner of those rough hands, since Sam was about to start swinging the second he felt them.

He goggled about, gasping for air, heart beating itself against his rib cage. A stern face glowered down at him, but it had a distinct twinkle of amusement in its eyes that made Sam think maybe he didn't need to try to kill this person.

"It's me, it's Red."

Red? Who the hell…?

Oh. Right.

Reality didn't so much leak back into Sam's mind as it did burst its dam and flood his brain. He went limp under those pressing hands for the sole purpose of letting Red know he wasn't trying to fight anymore. But he was still hearing gunfire.

"Who's shooting?" Sam rasped, mouth all dry and words still hard to make clear.

"Don't know, but it's a good ways from us. Chill out. Take a breath."

"I'm breathing." Sam demonstrated his best combat breathing as a good faith measure. "Has it been two hours?"

"It's been forty-five minutes."

"I can't sleep anymore," Sam pressed his torso up, and Red let him rise into a sitting position. "No way I can sleep now."

Red sat back on his haunches and looked to his left. Sam tracked his gaze and spotted the rest of the crew. White and Blue were seated on the ground, leaning back against the passenger side of the pickup. Marie and Jones, too. White was eating something. The rest looked like they'd just been rudely awakened. Bleary, half-lidded eyes. Marie and Jones significantly more bleary than the others.

Sam frowned. "Where's your others?"

"On overwatch. They're close." Red had pulled his pack around to the front of him and was rummaging around inside the main compartment. He came out with what looked like a bottle of pills and a Powerbar. He handed the Powerbar to Sam. "You should eat something."

Sam didn't need to be told twice. He ripped into the packaging like an animal and crammed it into the dry hole of his mouth. Gummed at it with his pasty tongue for a minute, cringing and wondering about the wisdom of what he'd just done. "Sorry to be needy," he murmured around the wad of sweetness in his mouth. "You got any water?"

"Yeah." Red shook out two pills from the bottle and handed them to Sam, then pulled a tube from his shoulder and shuffled close so Sam could get his lips on it.

Sam eyed the pills. "What's this?" Thinking they were something that would make him sleep again.

"Ripped Fuel, baby," Red said, smirking. "That's how you stay awake in a combat zone."

Sam shrugged, then sucked from the water tube. Warm and plastic-tasting, but still somehow glorious, like he'd never had water in his life. Felt a little guilty at how much he gulped down, but hell, he was dehydrated.

"Damn, son." Red shook his head. "Should've knocked over a Seven-Eleven instead of a weapons depot."

Sam winced. Shame washed over him like a billow of flames. Made it hard to swallow the rest of the Powerbar. "Yeah, well. I didn't do either." He shoved the pills into his mouth and took a more controlled sip of the water to get them down his gullet.

Red didn't respond, which only made Sam feel worse. In the cold light of clarity provided by a whopping forty-five minutes of sleep, he wondered what the hell he'd been thinking. Lee's whole plan was contingent on Sam getting the weapons and ammo locked inside that building, and he'd gone and bungled it like a complete newbie. He should've listened to Red—you know, the guy with all the operational experience? He should've just let those worthless civilian bastards take the brunt of the fire and damn the consequences. Now he'd lost them anyways, and he didn't complete the mission on top of it.

Sam cleared his throat, still hanging his head, staring at his crotch. Felt stupid just sitting there like a punished kid, so he raised his head and looked at the only two people in the world that he actually knew. "Marie. Jones. I can't do this."

They both sat up. Exchanged a glance between them.

"Whaddaya mean?" Jones demanded.

Sam glanced at Red, who stayed silent, but had his eyebrows raised, curious. "I don't have the operational experience for this shit. I shouldn't be in charge. Red knows what he's doing. He should be in charge."

"Uh, Sam..." Jones rose to his feet and shuffled over. "That's not really how this shit works. It's our op. Our invasion. They're here as an assist."

Sam shook his head, his shame turning to resolution now that he really had a chance to tinker with what he'd just declared. "Jones, I've been behind the ball this whole time, man. I fucked it up royally—not just the hit on the depot, but the whole operation to get us in here."

"You didn't fuck it up. Things happened."

"You think Frenchie and Johnson would agree with that?" Sam pulled himself to his feet and was abruptly reminded that he had a wound in his side—shallow, sure, but shallow wounds still hurt. He winced as he dragged himself upright. "I made bad decisions. And it cost lives. And now it's cost us the weapons depot. What am I supposed to do? Just keep banging my head against the wall?" He was getting angry, and mostly it was at himself, but he was still leaning into Jones, feeling his face contort, feeling the veins stand out in his neck. "I'm not prepared for this shit! I can't do it! Red knows what he's doing, and he's gonna be in charge from here on out."

"Or..." Red held up a hand. Sam and Jones both looked at him. "You could just listen to me next time I tell you something's a shit idea."

"Yeah," Jones nodded rapidly, latching onto this possible compromise. "You could just listen to him. Like an advisor."

But Sam was already shaking his head again. "You? Me? Marie? We're all shot. Sleep-deprived. Hungry and dehydrated. We should *not* be making decisions right now. The best we can do is follow orders. Every time we have to sit around and discuss shit in committee so that I can *feel* like I'm in charge is just going to make us that much less effective. There's no point to it, Jones. If we're going to do what Red says anyways, then let's just skip the asinine discussion where I try to make it sound like they're my orders, and we'll just do what he says right when he says it. It makes sense. You *know* it makes sense."

"Sarge," Marie said, sounding a bit stiff. "Can I talk to you privately for a second?"

Sam considered refusing, but that was just being obstinate. Sure, he'd made his decision already, but it didn't hurt to hear her out. In fact, just recently there'd been a time that he'd made his decision, refused to hear someone out, and it had caused some problems. That time being about an hour ago.

He nodded, glanced at Red, who shrugged at him and took a step back.

Marie pulled herself to her feet. It didn't escape Sam that it took a moment and a few winces to accomplish it. And he immediately felt bad for her. Here he was, a young man—he and Jones both in their prime—and yet he was complaining. Marie was a forty-year-old woman. You know, that age when everything apparently starts to hurt. And she'd been just as abused as they had. And yet she hadn't complained once.

Funny how just watching a person get up can suddenly drive home your deep respect for them. Yes, he was going to hear her out. She deserved to be heard.

The three of them walked away from the others. Sam tried to stop about fifteen yards from them, but Marie kept on going. She clearly didn't want the Canadians to hear what she had to say. Sam wasn't sure how to feel about that.

They stopped when they'd crossed the neighborhood street and were standing in the "lawn" of another house-husk. Unlike in the subtropical climate of the Southeast, it seemed around here, stuff didn't grow as crazy. The "lawn" wasn't waste-high shrubs like it would've been in North Carolina or Georgia. Just dry, scrubby grass.

Marie looked around their environment. Glanced over her shoulder at the distance they'd created. Had a look on her face that was all tense and stern. Finally, she met Sam's gaze. Spoke in a low voice. "Look. You do what you think is best for the mission, okay?"

Sam frowned. Did she really need privacy to say that? "Okay."

She leaned into him. "But you need to remember that they're Canadians, not Americans. They're here to assist because they've got some sort of vested interest in *something*, and we don't even know what that is. But we can't just assume that their goals are aligned with Lee's. You want to give command of our little squad over to Red? I get it. But just remember that the onus is on you, Sam, not anyone else. If they divert from the plan? If they put Lee's strategy at risk? You need to be ready to take control again."

Jones was nodding along with everything Marie said. Arms crossed over his chest. The two of them as resolute in this admonishment as Sam had been in his decision.

Sam took a deep breath. "Okay. I got it."

Marie watched him for another few seconds, as though gauging whether he really got it or not. Hard to tell if she was satisfied or doubtful, but she eventually sniffed and jerked her head back towards the pickup truck. "Alright. Let's get on the horn with Lee and see what trouble we can get into."

SEVEN

RULES OF ENGAGEMENT

The bullets were flying, so everything was right as rain.

Brinly stood to the side of the MATV, fixated on how things were developing, and totally fine with the occasional *zip* of a round going by. He was in his element. This was how things should be. Almost made him regret that his whole job was to put an end to it.

"Gosling!" Brinly barked, eyes narrowing as he spotted two of the guntruck Humvees on his left flank, trimming the sides of a few commercial buildings with overlapping arcs of fire. Problem was, they were over-focused on a handful of defenders that were just taking potshots from around the corner. The defenders didn't even look like real soldiers—just civilians who'd had rifles shoved into their hands.

"Sir?" Gosling peered at him over the MATV's hood.

Brinly jabbed a finger at the offending Humvees. "Tell them to push up! They got a clear alley right in front of them! Fuck the handful of militia! Tell them to move around!"

Brinly's MATV, along with a handful of civilian vehicles, were still jammed up on the edge of the bridge. Still too hot to go charging in, but the defenses were breaking, slowly crumbling under the onslaught. But Brinly held no illusions—it wouldn't last forever. He had to assume Briggs would reinforce this area sooner rather than later. And when that happened, Brinly wanted a solid foothold so he couldn't get pushed out the door.

Gosling chattered away on the radio. Brinly stared at the two Humvees, waiting for them to respond. It didn't take them too long—ten seconds after Gosling said "over" the two Humvees jerked forward in unison, taking to the free alley that Brinly had spotted from his vantage point.

"Yes. Get 'em," Brinly murmured to himself. "Gosling! We get those replacement squads into La Salle yet?"

"Yes, sir. Angela sent five. They're there now."

"Good. Have them move up to our rear." Brinly snapped his eyes to his right flank—that troublesome neighborhood with the machine gun nests. Four guntrucks on that side now, some of the Marines on foot, clearing the structures. "Gimme a sitrep on that neighborhood."

Gosling did as requested and Brinly listened to the response on his own radio.

"Neighborhood's mostly cleared," one of the squad leaders transmitted. "You want us to move forward?"

Brinly took the radio for himself. "Drifter Actual, negative, leave that shit pile be. Two-Six and Two-Seven, I want you to hold that perimeter. Two-Four and Two-Five, cross back over to the left flank and reinforce that hole right between those two gray buildings."

He waggled the radio in his hand, thinking at the speed of combat now. The defenses were cracking, and he needed to push and exploit. The biggest hole was over on the left, and that's where

Brinly wanted to smash harder, establish his foothold.

Two MATVs—designated Two-Four and Two-Five—roared across the highway, jumping the curbs and ramming themselves right into the empty spot he needed them to fill. The gunners in the turrets were being more disciplined now. Their bursts were a little shorter, a little more controlled. They were conserving ammo.

He was already aware that Sam's mission to seize the weapons depot had gone tits-up. But they were still going to need it. Hell, they needed it right now. But all things in due course—Brinly couldn't push on the weapons depot like he wanted until he had a secure foothold.

The fighting on the left reached a crescendo and then suddenly bottomed out, and Brinly felt it like you feel the tides changing.

"That's it," he snapped, launching himself into the passenger seat of the MATV. "That's our hole. I want everyone to hit that spot right there on the other side of that junkyard!"

The entire left flank was partially-obscured by some sort of you-pick automotive yard. The defenders had set up in amongst the cars—a "natural" barricade—but they'd been rousted by Brinly's first push and had fallen back to the few commercial buildings behind it. One was called "Cimarron Energy" and that's what Brinly had decided he wanted. Take that building, and he owned this whole intersection. If he owned this whole intersection, then he had his foothold.

"You want me to drive in there?" Gosling asked.

Brinly slapped the dashboard. "Yes, drive in there! Go! Everyone go, now!"

Gosling juggled his radio as he yanked the MATV into gear and hit the gas. "All units behind Drifter Actual, get on our ass and follow us in."

Brinly craned his neck out his open window to see the vehicles behind them following. Looking forward again, he grabbed the rifle stuck in the center console. Looped the sling over his head and his left arm. Checked the mag. Checked the chamber. Shouldered the rifle and stuck it out the window. God, but it felt good to do that again.

Their MATV hit the curb, jangling Brinly about in the passenger seat. He steadied his rifle, peering over the top of the optic, searching for anyone that wasn't one of his Marines. Or his civilians. Dammit, but it was hard to tell the difference between *his* civilians and what he was starting to think of as the Greeley Militia. Had to make decisions based on which way they were pointing their weapons.

Something pinged off the hood of the MATV.

"Shit!" Gosling yelped, jerking the wheel. "Taking fire!"

Brinly leaned out, foregrip of his rifle snugged between the frame of his vehicle and the sideview mirror. Saw a dark shape—Cornerstone black. He sunk into his sights, tried to stabilize his sight-picture as the vehicle moved.

The figure in his sights did a little panic-dance at the sight of all those vehicles charging at him. Then the man fired haphazardly, most of the bullets going high, two of them *pock-pock*-ing across the hood of the charging MATV. A slash of pain across Brinly's knuckles as a bit of spall caught him. Good, clear pain.

Brinly clenched down. Steadied that red dot. Pulled the trigger on burst and watched his target wilt. Felt the immense satisfaction of an accomplishment. Panned right. Humvees. Marines on foot. Two civilian vehicles with their occupants huddled at the trunk.

"Move forward!" Brinly bellowed at them as his MATV whooshed past.

Cimarron Energy. Right there in front of him. A big, white, metal building. Enemy combatants on the other side, seen only by their huddled heads and muzzle flashes.

"Pull up here! Stop!" Brinly barked. He had his door open and was about to get out. Spotted the chainlink fence behind all the mess of defunct infrastructure—concrete and metal culverts, jersey barriers, old cars, spools of cabling. He didn't want to mess with that fence. Ran his gaze along it as the MATV rocked to a halt and spotted an opening a little further down. "Check that! Go forward! You see that opening?"

"I see it." Another jolt on the gas. The tires skidded—they were on a dirt road, or a road that had been covered by years of dust, Brinly wasn't sure.

"Here, here, here!" Brinly ordered, batting a hand at Gosling as they pulled up to a pile of jersey barriers—perfect cover. Brinly hadn't even closed his door, so he just spilled out and grabbed the nearest barrier, squatting behind it. Got a little keyhole between the concrete. Spotted some shapes on the other side that didn't look friendly. They were focused hard to the right. Didn't even see what was coming on their flank.

Tempting to just start shooting—like fish in a barrel. But Brinly forced himself to wait. Gosling scampered over, his own rifle in his hands now.

"Hold fire," Brinly ordered as Gosling grabbed some cover. He looked over his shoulder and spotted the other two squads of Marines that had followed them, as well as the civilians. He waved a hand, motioning them over. Doors flew open and men in fatigues got out. The civilians were a little more confused, but that was to be expected.

The Marines formed up neatly. The civilians jumbled up haphazardly.

Brinly lowered his voice to a normal level, though he doubted the enemy on the other side could hear over all the gunfire. "Got a nest of 'em in there," he said, poking his hand at the holes in the concrete. "Take 'em out and move in. I want that building."

He scooched out of the way, moved back off the jersey barriers as the Marines crowded in, everyone finding a hole to shoot through while the civilians crouched and goggled and were generally useless. Brinly eyed them up. Might as well get *some* sort of use out of them.

"Hey!" He stalked over, keeping his head down. "You three squads! The second my Marines start shooting I want you to hustle through that opening in the fence and take that building, you hear me?"

Wide-eyes and gaping mouths. A few nods. Someone let out an overeager "Yes, sir!"

POGs.

The Marines opened up.

Brinly stood back, letting the gunsmoke and the battering noise wash over him. One of the boys lurched back, grenade in hand, and let it fly over the top of the fence. Brinly waited for the boom. Didn't even flinch when it erupted out a geyser of dirt and smoke.

"Target's down!" one of the Marines yelled.

"That's you!" Brinly shouted at the civilians, started waving them rapidly towards the gate. "Haul ass! Take that building!"

He fell in behind the last of them. Marines coming up from cover, forming into their fire teams and running for the opening.

"Gosling!" Brinly snapped as he marched past. "Get my MATV in there!"

A flood of bodies through the gates. Brinly pulled up short, standing right in the middle of it all, civilians and Marines charging through, running for the building, running for the barricades behind which the defenders had been ousted, the pall of smoke thick in the air, catching the sun in magnificent blazes.

Brinly keyed his squad comms. "Drifter Actual to all units on the south side! If you're not holding perimeter, fall in on my location! The Cimarron Energy building on the southwestern corner of the intersection!"

A smattering of fresh gunfire. Someone screamed, high-pitched. One of the civilians toppled, wailing as they clutched their leg, blood spurting.

Brinly grabbed the nearest Marine by the shoulder. "Put a tourniquet on that motherfucker!" he shouted, shoving the Marine towards the downed civilian.

More shouting. More screaming.

Words coming in through the chaos: "Don't shoot! Don't shoot!"

"Hands up, motherfucker! Lemme see your hands!"

"Get on the fucking ground!"

Brinly scowled as he stamped through the gate, scanning to find where all this kerfuffle was coming from. Spotted it at the right corner of the Cimarron Energy building, right there where the barricades were all draped with lifeless bodies and a few still-squirming ones.

Three people. Two men, and one woman. None of them with weapons. All of them with their hands up, now dropping down to their knees while a fire team of Marines surrounded them, one big, corn-fed bastard grabbing them one by one and face-planting them into the dirt.

"What the fuck is this?" Brinly bawled at them as he approached.

Corn-Fed righted himself, pushing his helmet back on his head so he looked a little dopey. "Prisoners, sir! They were unarmed!"

"Yeah?" Brinly glared at the figures on the ground. "And who do you think was shooting at us?"

"It wasn't us!" One of the men. The other two were just weeping.

Corn-Fed looked confused on the matter, so Brinly clarified it: "We don't have the time or resources for prisoners. And if you let 'em go, they're just gonna go grab another rifle and get back in the fight. You understand what I'm telling you, Marine?"

Corn-Fed looked down at the three captives. The confusion left his face. And it wasn't replaced with anything near to regret. He just shrugged. "Sorry, sir. Old habits die hard."

Brinly nodded to him and continued past. Three shots rocked at his back, but he was looking at the Cimarron Energy building. He finally had his foothold.

***

This was perhaps the only FOB in the history of FOBs that didn't have a map of its Area of Operations. What they did have—and, as crude as they were, Lee thanked his lucky stars for them—were drawings that Abe had rendered to the best of his recollection.

As thankful as he was though, it looked like a third-grade class project. Partially due to Abe's rendering—he was not an artist by any stretch—but mostly due to the fact that it was on fifteen pieces of standard printer paper (the backs filled with typed copy from whatever business they'd yanked it from), all haphazardly taped together. Five rows of three pieces of paper.

And they were delicate. Didn't like a breeze, and certainly not the wind they were getting across the plains, which meant that if Lee wanted to use them he had to clamber up into the damn box, which had now become the *hot* box, and lay them out as best he could on what little space was provided by the tiny "tables" on one side of the vehicle. Which were more like trays.

"Alright, can you get me a better location than 'west side'?" Lee asked the satphone pressed against his sweating ear.

Sam's voice came back: "Ah…shit…"

Lee gritted his teeth, waiting.

Someone said something in the background.

"Okay," Sam said. "We're right off of Tenth Street, about five miles or so west of the weapons depot."

Lee shifted his travesty of a map over. Abe hadn't been too detailed about that section of

Greeley—when he'd left, it'd still been in the untamed "Red Zone." But he had the main thoroughfares marked down, and there was 10th Street, a long, straight road that cut east to west through the northern third of the city.

"I don't think you're far from it," Lee said, frowning down. A drop of sweat detached from his nose and splatted on the paper. He quickly wiped it away. "Abe's enroute to that substation right now in the Blackhawk. I want you to step on it, see if you can't get there and secure it, then hook up with Abe and his team."

"And where's the substation again?"

Right. He hadn't gotten to that part.

Lee traced a finger down the grid of scribbled streets to the point that Abe had scrawled out a box with the words GRID CONTROL. "Greeley gets all its juice from this substation on the west edge of the city, right off of Seventy-First Avenue. I don't know whether Seventy-First is east or west of your current position."

"We can find it," Sam said, sounding like he was already moving. "We'll be there as soon as we can."

"Copy that." A pause. "And Sam?"

"Yeah?"

"You're doing good."

Another pause.

"Roger that. We're enroute."

The second that Lee pulled the satphone away from his ear, Specialist Lopez was waiting to swoop in.

"Major Brinly's on the radio for you, sir," she blurted out.

Lee swore. Shuffled communications devices until he had the right one. Christ, this was the most ad hoc shit he'd ever seen in his life—and he'd done it to himself. He checked the radio screen to make sure it was the right frequency, then transmitted.

"Go for Marshal Actual."

"We got our foot in the door," Brinly declared. "Right at Highway Eighty-Five and Forty-Second. We own the whole intersection and we're pushing northwest to expand."

"Fuck yes," Lee seethed without transmitting. Shuffled his map around to the south, papers crinkling and jumbling. Then he keyed up again. "Excellent work, Brinly. Pull any reserves you got in La Salle up to your location and keep pushing north. But hold back a portion of your Marines—I'm gonna need another push on that weapons depot, and soon."

"I copy. Civvies are already pulled up and distributed. How soon you wanna move on the depot?"

"How soon can you?"

"You give me thirty minutes to get my house in order and scrape up some ammo, I can get you a platoon ready to roll."

Lee rapped his fingers on the paper, thinking furiously. Thirty minutes was a great timeline. Thirty minutes might also be *too* soon. Briggs was still likely in the process of throwing every spare gun he had at Brinly's position. If Lee pulled that platoon before Briggs committed all his forces, Brinly might lose his foothold.

Was thirty minutes going to be too long? Or not long enough?

Impossible to say. It was right smack dab in the middle. Which, to Lee, meant it was a fair average.

"Thirty minutes is good, but wait for my go-ahead before you move on it. I wanna make sure I give you every chance at success."

"Much appreciated." The line stayed open. "Also, I got a change in ROEs."

Lee felt his throat tighten up. "Go with it."

"ID-ing combatants is becoming a serious issue. And we got no way to hold prisoners."

Lee waited for something else, but the transmission ended. It was the strategic equivalent of an elephant in the room. They all knew it when they'd planned this op. It had been in the back of all their minds. And yet they hadn't come right out and said it. Almost like they all were hoping it wouldn't be an issue, even though they all knew it was a ridiculous thing to hope for. Of course it was going to become an issue.

Well, they'd waited to cross the bridge until they'd come to it, and now here they were, and the bridge needed to be crossed.

Lee chose his words carefully. "Is there a request in there somewhere? Or just a statement of fact?"

"That was a statement of fact," Brinly replied. "Here's another: I'm telling my Marines to shoot anyone that isn't straight up running away. There's no other way to do this. This entire city is filled with scared people that don't know what the fuck is going on, and Cornerstone is shoving rifles into their hands and booting them at us. We can't take them in, and if we let them go, Cornerstone is just going to arm them again and send them right back at us. And you know I'm right."

Then why does it feel like you're trying to convince me?

And what the hell was "right" at this point anyways?

"Lee." The voice was sharp—coming from behind him.

He jerked upright and whirled. Angela was standing with one leg up on the deck of the command module, staring at him with that same look she'd got when this topic had been brushed right before they'd started.

"You can't seriously consider this," she said, half-pleading, half-accusing.

Lee held her gaze. Keyed the radio. "Standby a minute." And the second his finger released the PTT: "What do you want me to do about it, Angela?"

She pulled herself up onto the deck, eyes widening. "You can't change the ROEs to *that*!"

Lee's grip tightened on the radio. His head started to ache. "You keep saying I can't. I can't consider it. I can't do it. Well, do you have a better fucking option? Because how I'm looking at it right now, I don't see one."

"Maybe you're not looking hard enough!"

Lee's entire body squished around his lungs and he felt the shout blowing up inside of him and he wanted to scream in her face, but held off at the last second. Swallowed it down. Ears starting that damn ringing again. Brow tingling with flush.

When he opened his mouth to speak, it was cold and hard and slow, like sledgehammer blows: "Do you have…a better option?"

Angela raked frazzled hair out of her face. Looked around desperately as though she was going to find an audience that might support her. But it was just Lee. And the two specialists, but they were doing a mighty fine job staring silently at their radios.

"We can..." he watched her searching and finding nothing. "We can pull them back here! It won't take that many people. We have plenty of buildings on the airfield, and—and they're all empty! We can make a prison in there!"

"And who's going to guard them? Keep them from running around and sabotaging our shit?" The more he spoke, the lower his burst of anger burned. Now just a little spark. Now nothing at all. Smothered by a sickening sadness. "We don't even have restraints to put on them, Angela."

"It won't take that many people!" She insisted, and even her voice was getting quieter now. Like she could feel the righteousness bleeding out of their cause. "A handful of guys with machine guns. They can guard *hundreds* of people. And if anyone gets out of hand...then..."

"Then they mow them all down?" Lee asked.

Angela didn't answer.

Lee took a step towards her, all the tension going out of him. He felt weak now. Spent. Shaky. "Angela, you've been my conscience all along. Since day one. And we've butted heads about it, I know. But I've grown to value the humanity that you try to keep. And try to maintain for everyone else." He shook his head. "But we don't have the manpower to watch prisoners, let alone secure them and transport them in the first place. Every person that we take as a prisoner will take five guns out of the fight. And we're strapped for people as it is. And once the..." he swallowed. "Once the casualty reports start rolling in? It's only gonna get tighter. And tighter. And tighter."

Angela just stared at him, her mouth open but unmoving. There wasn't much fight left in her eyes anymore. Just a gray, hollow sort of depression. "Don't do it."

Lee took a steadying breath. "Hold onto it, Angela. And don't let it go. Because when this is over we're going to need people that give a shit about other people. But until we own this city...we just can't do it."

She said nothing to that, and Lee felt that this might be the only chance he had to shove it through. Make it happen. Give his troops the go-ahead to be as merciless as they needed to be to get the job done.

But did he want to?

Well, sometimes it's not about what you want. A lot of times, actually. We like to believe in higher ideals, but higher ideals tend to go by the wayside when the whole reason you're in a place is to kill the other guy before he kills you. And that's when despicable things like the ends justifying the means become the rule and not the exception.

He keyed his radio. "It's approved, Brinly. Disseminate the change in ROEs. Carry on. Over."

"I copy," Brinly said, like it wasn't terrible at all. "Out."

Someone must've been waiting impatiently for the end of their exchange, because it didn't even sound like the radio cut out. It was immediately filled with another transmission.

"Major Harden...uh...this is Matt. From the rearguard?"

Lee frowned at the radio. Good that "Matt" had the discipline to not interrupt Lee and Brinly. But really, was proper radio procedure *that* difficult to learn? It was unlikely that Briggs had the resources to decrypt their comms, but there was still an outside chance it might happen, and Lee didn't want to give his enemy anything they didn't already know.

"*Marshal Actual*," Lee said, pointedly. "Go ahead, rearguard."

"Oh. Right. Marshal Actual. Sorry..."

Lee clenched his eye shut as though the man's voice was a physical pain.

"...I'm not sure what I'm looking at, sir, but we got eyes to the south and I'm seeing a large dust cloud and some...glimmers? Like sunlight off of windshields?"

"Shit," Lee breathed to himself. It wasn't like he thought he had oodles of time, but dammit, he'd thought he had more time than *that*. Now the entire schedule of events had been mercilessly crunched. He didn't have enough time. He didn't have *any* time. "Marshal Actual, get that entire rearguard out of there and get your asses to the airfield, how copy?"

"Uh. I copy." Matt sounded like he was running now. A little breathless. "Who is it? Do we need to be worried?"

Lee goggled at the radio. Do they need to be worried? Of course they needed to be worried! "That's Griffin's Army coming in on your ass, and you need to get out of there! Do not engage them. No one engage them. Fall back to the airfield. Over."

"Okay. I copy." Barely-bridled panic now. "We're on the way."

Lee set the radio down, swearing under his breath. Turned and looked at Angela, who still had that dead shock across her face. "Griffin's here. Our timeline just got fucked."

Angela's eyes cinched into sharp focus. "Who's got Abby?"

Lee had that urge again to respond sharply. He was fighting a war for chrissake, could she get focused on the strategy and quit worrying about babysitting? But as soon as he thought it, he felt a wave of shame. Angela was a mother, and a mother had a one-track mind when her kid was in danger. He shouldn't expect anything less.

"I'm sure they got her," Lee said, evenly. "And they'll be here in a few minutes. Abby's fine, Angela."

EIGHT

CALLUSES

ABBY FELT THE VERY PRESSING NEED to get out of the trunk when it reverberated with a metallic *thwack!* and a hole appeared, just inches from Abby's head, a spear of daylight coming through.

"Oh, shit!" she uttered, staring at the hole like she couldn't believe it, but what had she expected? She heard the gunfire outside. She'd known she was going into a warzone. And she knew that sheet metal didn't stop bullets.

Only problem was, in all the jostling during the ride in, the nylon strap that had been keeping the trunk from latching had slipped, and then the car had gone over a bump and—whoops!—the trunk slammed shut and latched.

She was already aware of this, but had just been laying there in the darkness, wondering how she was going to get out of the trunk without anyone seeing her—because if they saw her, they'd recognize her as Angela's kid. And then things would get weird.

Or it would be an enemy that saw her and then they might just shoot her dead.

But being locked in a stationary box and having a bullet pass by inches from your face can really re-prioritize your convictions. So, she started kicking and slapping and then pounding at the underside of the trunk with her fists.

"Hey! Hey! Someone let me out of here!"

Right on the other side of that sheet metal, someone fired a gun, very fast. The sound of it slammed at the trunk, making Abby cringe. It felt like she was trapped in a drum and someone was banging on it. Could they even hear her pounding and shouting over the gunfire?

Another bullet ripped through the trunk, this one a little higher than the last. She felt something ping around the interior and strike her in the shin and she screamed, more out of surprise than pain—but was the pain coming? She'd seen people get hurt before and sometimes they didn't know they were hurt for a few seconds—sometimes the pain takes a bit to hit you full-force.

"Oh my God, oh my God," she whimpered, distantly recognizing that she'd got what she'd come for: She was feeling something alright, but panic hadn't been what she'd had in mind.

She twisted and squirmed, hands scrabbling down her leg to the place where whatever-it-was had hit her. She was wearing an old, ill-fitting pair of jeans, two sizes too big on her, and the pants legs were floppy and loose—was there a hole in there? She pressed her hand to the place on her shin that still smarted from being struck. It didn't feel like there was a hole...

Someone screamed. Woman or man, Abby couldn't tell. She'd heard people die before and when people die, they don't sound like themselves.

A fleshy thump against the side of the trunk. The light streaming in through the bullet holes was blotted out. The scream tapered off into a gasping whimper. That squeaky sound of someone's skin dragging across smooth metal. The light bloomed through the bullet holes again. The dull thud of a body falling.

"No," a voice mewled, so close, just inches away on the other side of Abby's prison. "No, no. Someone…" Choking. Gurgling. Gasping.

Abby was hyperventilating. She didn't know that's what it was called, but she felt her brain getting fuzzy and light as she kept gulping in breaths and not expelling them before trying to gulp in more.

"Betsy?" A man's voice. And then pitching up an entire octave: "Betsy! Oh, baby, no!"

Abby couldn't think about the man's grief. All she could think about was getting the hell out of the trunk. And he was right there, whoever he was—right outside the door with his dead girlfriend, or wife, or sister, or whatever she was. She started pounding again, stronger and more rapid than before—the pure desperation of a claustrophobic in a locked coffin.

"Get me out of here!" she screamed, her own voice rattling her ears. "Open the fucking trunk!"

More gunfire. Strangled sobs audible between them. Bullets coming and going—oh my God, she could hear the whine of them when they streaked so close to the trunk. The slam of outgoing rounds sounding like whoever was shooting back was standing right over her.

"Do you hear me?!" Abby screeched. "Open the trunk! Get me out of the trunk!"

Boom-boom-boom right over her head, making her nose feel like someone had thumped it. Then the scrape and rattle of metal-on-metal, and then the thunk of the latch being turned and all of the sudden the roof of her tiny prison cell lifted right off, and all the sounds got ten times more intense, and daylight blinded her.

She lurched for the daylight. A bleary, silhouetted figure jumped back in surprise.

"What the hell?" the man exclaimed, and then his face just sort of fell off, like half of it had been swiped away into nothing and he pitched backward, making noises that no human should make.

Abby gawked at his bisected face for a handful of rupturing heartbeats, then remembered she needed to *get out of the fucking trunk*, and she dove forward, trying to stay as low as possible, swimming and writhing her way out of the trunk, over the back bumper and falling to the ground in a tumble.

A hand batted at her. Seized her shirt in an iron grip. She wailed and tried to recoil, but it was latched on too strong. Then she realized it was the man—he wasn't dead. He held onto her out of some sort of reflex, like she was a bit of floating debris and he was drowning.

He *was* drowning.

She crawled towards him, because she couldn't crawl away from him, and because he was pulling at her. He had one good eye left in his face—kind of like Lee, but unlike Lee, the rest of his face was just a blood-welled mess, and she could see the inside of his nasal passages and they were pulsing and wiggling and every time he made one of those terrible noises it would splatter blood at her, and she felt it speckle her face like someone had sneezed on her.

"Oh God, oh God," Abby gasped, trying to wrestle his hand off of her. She wanted to get away from him. He was terrible. Something in the back of her mind told her to help him, but the fear was too strong and the grip that he had on her made her feel trapped.

She reared back and kicked him in his ruined face. "Let me go!" she shrieked. And he did. Maybe he'd died. Maybe she'd just killed him? Why couldn't she feel anything but fear right now? This wasn't what she wanted.

But she was already moving. Hands and knees, scrabbling through dirt and dried grass. Still couldn't get a breath into her lungs for some reason—why couldn't she just *breathe*?

She was halfway out of the cover of the back tires when a trail of bullets smacked the ground right in front of her, spewing dirt into her face. She yelped and jolted backwards, crab-walking until her back hit the bumper and her hands hit the dead man's leg.

She tucked her feet in. Eyes stretched so wide they hurt.

What was she supposed to do now?

She looked around at absolute chaos. People in civilian clothes running around in all directions. Farther away, a smattering of military vehicles, and Marines in fatigues huddled in fire teams or sprinting in ones and twos from one point of cover to another. There were buildings and cars all around, bullet holes in everything. A handful of bodies strewn about. Some wounded man holding his belly and screaming, blood slaking his chin.

What are you going to do?

What had she come here to do?

Gradually, her breathing came back to her, lungs didn't feel so stretched and thin, like overblown balloons. And as she breathed, her vision started to sharpen, and her brain came along with it, dragging itself out of panic.

Gun. She needed a gun. That was what she'd come here for, wasn't it? To fight, like all the other callused people. Except they didn't seem so callused now. The man with his gut wound didn't seem callused—he just seemed scared and desperate. And the dead people weren't feeling anything at all.

Gun. Get a gun.

She lurched forward on hands and knees towards the dead man with half a face. Disgust roiled uncomfortably through her. She reached out towards his rifle, still strapped to his chest. Then held back, feeling her throat constrict and her mouth water with the threat of vomit. She swallowed hard against it, then forced her hands forward—the man wasn't anything anymore. Nothing to be frightened of. Just a pile of meat. Not a person anymore. Not something to be disgusted about.

Abby was callused, after all. Wasn't she?

She grabbed the rifle and yanked at it, but the strap was tight. So, she had to get more involved. Had to force herself to touch him, wrangle that sling from around his chest and shoulder and over his dead face.

Okay. She had a gun. Now what?

Ammo. She needed ammo. She only had minimal experience with guns, but she'd seen plenty of other people handle them, and she knew this one was called an AR and the basics of how it worked. So, she did what she'd seen everyone else do when they got a weapon—she fumbled around, found the magazine release and pressed it. The magazine dropped out and landed between her knees. She snatched it up. It was still heavy, which made her think it had plenty of bullets in it. But she looked anyways, because that's what you did. And yes, there were bullets in it. So, she stuck it back in.

Twisted the weapon this way and that. Realized what the charging handle was for and pulled at it. Geez, it was tough. Got the bolt back about halfway, and saw the round in the chamber. Then let the bolt go forward again.

She had ammo. Was there more? She looked up at the man's body. Looked at his pants pockets. He was lying on his back, and he didn't seem to have anything in his front pockets, but she'd seen a lot of people put their spare magazines in their back pockets. So, she leaned forward, cringing as she did, and tried to roll him.

Too heavy.

She grunted against his weight. Then sat back on her heels and sucked in some more air. Steeled herself for what was next, and then jammed her little hands under his butt. Felt the magazine in his back pocket. Wrangled it out. It was heavy and full. She twisted around, and pushed the magazine into her own back pocket.

Alright. She was ready.

Ready for what?

She hefted the rifle. It was almost as big as she was. Pulling it to her shoulder took a lot more strength than she'd thought it would. How was she supposed to fight with the thing? Everyone else made it look so easy, but she'd never thought about how small she was and how big these rifles were—they didn't look so big on adults.

"Move-move-move!" someone shouted.

Abby goggled up at someone sprinting towards her, and she almost aimed the rifle and fired at him. He was waving manically at her, and she realized he wanted her to move over so he could get into cover with her, but by the time she made that connection, he was already sliding in like a baseball player—feet first, a cloud of dust pluming up.

"Scoot over!" he shouted, barely even looking at her. Pulled himself into a squatted position and elbowed her, shoving her so hard she toppled backwards into the dirt.

"Hey!" she snapped at him, straining upright again. "Asshole!"

He snapped his eyes to her and seemed to see her for the first time. He was a younger guy himself, but still an adult. Or maybe an older teenager?

"Who the hell are you?" he demanded.

Abby's indignation at being shoved over suddenly dissipated. She couldn't tell him who she was. If he knew who she was, he might—

Realization crashed over his face. "Oh, shit. You're Angela's girl!"

"No!" she snapped, not even convincing to her own ears.

Certainly not convincing to him. It was like he hadn't even heard her denial. His eyes were wide and disbelieving. "What the hell are you doing here right now?" he shouted at her. "Does Angela know where you are? Oh my fuck! How'd you even get here?"

Glass shattered. Bullets whined. Glittering pebbles scattered over their heads as the two of them ducked down against a fresh onslaught of bullets pounding the car.

"Motherfuckers!" the guy growled. Shoved his rifle out and fired a handful of rounds, but it just seemed like he was firing for the sake of doing something and not really aiming at anyone.

Abby decided she'd do the same. It wasn't really a conscious decision. She just started moving, like an element of peer pressure was driving her. She held the rifle up, arms shaking with the strain of it. She knew she was supposed to use the optic on the top of the rifle, but she couldn't seem to get her eye in the right position—wasn't there supposed to be a crosshair or a dot or something?

She pulled the trigger. Nothing happened. Kept on pulling it. Kept on getting the same result. She started to make little panicked noises, like she was trapped in a nightmare. One of those nightmares where you are trying so hard to do something and against all reason it just wouldn't work.

A hand on her shoulder. She was yanked back into cover.

"It won't work!" she screamed at the rifle. "I'm pulling the trigger and it won't work!"

His hands darted out. Seized the rifle, but didn't take it from her. He checked a little switch on the side, but it was apparently in the right position, because he didn't do anything with it. Then he turned it over and looked at the chamber, then jammed his thumb on a little button right on the backend of the place where the brass shells were supposed to come spitting out, and Abby watched the bolt snick forward by a tiny increment.

"Out-of-battery!" he snapped at her.

What the hell was that supposed to mean?

"Oh," was all she could manage to say. She tried to lean out of cover and shoot it again—really wanted to feel it recoil, like if she could just get a round out of the damn thing the nightmare might end. But the guy yanked her back into cover again.

"You're not supposed to be here!" he yelled in her face.

"I don't care!" she yelled back at him.

"You need to get out of here!"

"I'm not going anywhere!"

They stared at each other for what seemed like an overly-long time, the world feeling like it was spinning around her, screams and cries and animal growls and shooting, shooting, shooting, so much shooting, and bullets whining through the air in all directions so it felt like if you stood up, you'd just immediately fall to pieces.

An explosion went off somewhere. Abby felt it punch her in the head, in the chest, felt her ears compress painfully, and then they started ringing, shrill and unstoppable, so that everything else sounded low and muted like her ears were gummed up with something.

The blast jerked the guy into motion. He yelled something Abby couldn't make sense of and then leaned out again, fired off another handful of rounds and then did a weird little maneuver to get his feet under him, still in a deep squatting position, and he reached out with one hand and grabbed her by the back of her shirt, pulling her up.

"Get on your feet!" he screamed at her.

She really didn't want to do that. But the guy was really insistent. And much stronger than Abby, so that she felt herself being hauled up against her will, and then her feet were under her and she was crouched there, much like he was.

He pointed, his arm jutting out right across her face. "You see those cement tubes?"

She stared. Thought she saw what he was talking about—a pile of them, all stacked up on each other. The same concrete tubes that she'd seen running under roads and such so that water could pass through them.

"Yeah."

"We're gonna run for that!"

"Why?" Abby really had no desire to move.

"Because this car's getting shredded!"

As though to drive the point home to Abby, another chain of bullets ripped through the vehicle, more glass scattering, stinging her face, and bullet holes sprouted all across the minimal space between her and the guy. One of the bullets must've caught his arm because there was a fleshy *thwap*, and his outstretched arm kind of jerked, and when the guy yanked it back, it dribbled blood across the thirsty ground.

"God*dammit*!" he bellowed, rifle dropping out of his grip so that he could clamp one hand across his forearm. The other hand just kind of hung there in a weird claw shape, shaking bad.

Abby started shaking her head. "I don't wanna go! I don't wanna go!"

The guy hissed and frothy spittle bubbled out of his clenched teeth, his face gone all flushed with pain. "We stay here, we're gonna die! You ready?"

"No!"

But he wasn't listening. He grabbed his rifle up again, the blood welling out of a hole in his left arm, and he looped that arm around her—couldn't grab her because she guessed his fingers weren't working, so he just kind of hugged her to him, his blood warm and sickening as it coated her chest, and she wasn't strong enough to hold back against him, and then he was running, half-carrying her with him, and there was no way out, so she just started pumping her legs.

They were running. He was keeping his body between her and the bad guys. Had his rifle held at his hip and he started firing as they ran, clumsily, like two people in a three-legged race.

Oh, God, they weren't moving fast enough, it was taking too long, they were too slow, and the cement tubes were too far away, and there were bullets everywhere, keening, seeking, trying to kill him, trying to kill *her*, and then all of the sudden they were diving, hitting the ground in a gout of dust that blew into Abby's mouth so she tasted the dull dryness of it and felt the grit between her teeth, and they were rolling, him over her, then her over him.

Abby screamed something fierce, but it didn't really come out like a scream—sounded more like the groans a dying person would make, and that scared her bad, made her wonder if she actually *was* dying.

The guy's legs thrashed at the dirt and she thought maybe he'd been shot again, someplace much worse than his arm, but then she realized he was just trying to backpedal, because they were right there, right next to the cement tubes.

She leaped for them. Landed a tad short, and then scrambled on hands and knees, but it wasn't very fluid, because she was still clutching the rifle in both hands, and her knuckles were grinding and skinning across the ground.

The guy thrust himself backwards one more time, swearing, and then had his back against one of the tubes. Abby collapsed next to him, heaving and spitting dirt out of her mouth.

For some reason that she could not comprehend, she stood up. Even as she did it, and the top of her head cleared the top of the tubes, she was thinking, *What are you doing, Abby? Stay down!*

She could see the battlefield now. They were at an intersection—the road a big swath of black, shimmering in the heat—and across from it there were more buildings, so many buildings, and there were people running around those too, except they had guns, and they were pointing the guns in *her* direction, and they were shooting at her, oh my God, they were actually shooting at her! Actual people, actually pointing guns and trying to put bullets into her, and she'd never felt so simultaneously terrified and infuriated in her life.

How dare they?!

She screamed at them and hauled that big, heavy rifle up to her shoulder, and the guy beside her was screaming at her, or maybe them—nothing really made sense, because *everyone* was screaming, and a lot of them weren't even screaming words.

She mushed her face down against the buttstock of the rifle, both eyes wide open, and she thought she saw it now—the thing that you were supposed to see through the optic, and it was a big red circle with a little red dot in the center, and it was shaking all around, she could barely keep it still, but she put that red dot on the shape of a person across the road from her and she pulled the trigger.

The rifle barked and jerked in her grip in a terrifying way that made her feel like she was trying to hold onto some sort of animal that didn't want to be held, but she just kept pulling the trigger, because that's what you were supposed to do, wasn't it?

The figure across the road was just standing there while her bullets punched the air all around it, like maybe he or she or whoever it was—*oh my God, it's a person*—didn't even realize she was trying to kill them, and they raised their own rifle and Abby saw the muzzle of it spew gray smoke, right at her, and a section of cement tube went exploding with a terrible noise, but it only scared Abby and made her pull the trigger even faster, wrestling with the crazy beast in her hands, caught up in a logic-less need to get that red dot on that person, because if she could do that she could stop them from shooting at her…

And then the person fell down. And Abby thought, very distinctly, *Did they trip on something?* But the person didn't get up after that, and Abby stopped pulling the trigger, and all the air had been pressed out of her lungs by her screaming, and so she took in a big gulp of air that went down the wrong tube and into her belly, and she choked then let out a sickening burp that tasted of nothing.

Abby dropped back down to her knees, for a moment still confused about what the hell had just happened, and why the person had tripped and not tried to get up again, why hadn't they tried to get up?

Because you shot them.

The realization seemed so impossible.

Because you killed them.

She blinked, her vision filled with nothing but mottled, gray concrete, and she was seeing that, but she was also seeing that moment over and over in her brain, as though she was testing it for reality, as though she thought maybe she'd imagined the whole thing. Over and over, on repeat.

"I just shot someone," she said. Looked at the guy.

He had a tourniquet and was applying it to his arm. Had a strap of it in his teeth, the cords of his neck standing out as he pulled it tight. His eyes hit hers and he didn't seem surprised, or disgusted, or…anything really.

"You alright?" He said, around the strap in his mouth. Not like he actually cared. More like he was just asking because it seemed like something you should ask a ten-year-old who's just declared that she shot someone.

Abby looked away from him and down at the rifle in her trembling hands, and she was suddenly and crushingly…disappointed.

Because she felt…nothing.

"Yeah," she said, surprised and dismayed by how blank her voice came out of her.

The guy yanked the windlass of the tourniquet around and around and around.

Over and over, the picture of that body falling.

Over and over, she felt absolutely nothing. Shouldn't she feel something? Wasn't that what happened? You killed another human being and you got all torn up about it? You were supposed to *feel* something about it! Why couldn't *she* feel anything about it?

"I'm Ryan," the guy declared.

Abby blinked at him. Why was he telling her his name? What was that supposed to mean?

She had no clue. Nothing made any sense.

So, she smiled at him, because that's what you do when you introduce yourself, and he frowned at her like that was weird, but she didn't know what else to do, so she just kept on doing it. "I'm Abby."

NINE

MISSING

FOUR LITTLE WORDS, and all of the sudden, Lee's extremities felt cold. He could actually feel the blood being pulled out of them, all of it sucking into his heart and lungs and setting both of them to working overtime.

We can't find Abby.

Lee nearly dropped the radio. His fingers felt like they'd been sitting in ice water. He had to mentally make the command for his thumb to press the PTT, at which point he said the only thing he could come up with: "What do you mean you can't find her?"

Marlin's voice came back with a clip in it. "I mean we can't fucking find her! She's not here! We checked every damn vehicle in the rearguard as they were heading out. She's not here. I have no clue where she is. Shit." A few huffs of breath, and then the line went dead.

Lee turned away from the MATV, searching for Angela, and finding her standing a dozen yards off, fixated on the line of incoming vehicles from the rearguard. Expecting her daughter to be among them.

Bad. This was bad. On so many different levels.

First and foremost, obviously: Where was Abby? Was she okay? Who the hell was she with? Surely she hadn't just run off into the wilderness? Dammit, but she'd said something weird to him, hadn't she? She'd said she couldn't feel anything. In the moment, trying to organize five hundred people into doing one, sensitive task, Lee hadn't paid attention to it, but now it rammed right back into his brain with a strange sort of clarity, and he knew in an instant that he could have kept this from happening.

But he hadn't.

Angela was going to lose her shit. And what did that mean for the rest of them? Damn him for being a callused asshole, but when you're invading a city, you have to think pragmatically, and while the man in him wanted to find Abby right-fucking-now, the commander in him was trying to suss out how badly this was going to bone his plans.

"Did you ask anyone if they'd seen her?" Lee husked into the radio, praying that there was some lead, something he could latch onto so that he could tell Angela it was under control, they were in the process of getting Abby back.

"Yes, I asked everyone," Marlin snapped. "There was a lady said she saw her hanging out near those five squads Angela dispatched to La Salle. No one else saw shit."

"Fuckfuckfuckfuck," Lee whispered to himself. Okay. At least someone had seen her. But what the hell did that mean? She was hanging around the squads that had gone into La Salle? It wasn't much, but it was better than nothing. "Marlin, gimme a description of this woman."

"I already told her to get up with Angela the second she gets there. She's a black lady in a silver minivan." A pause. "Do you want us to head your way, or keep looking?"

Keep looking? Marlin and Worley were in the middle of a big, flat plain. Where the hell would they "keep looking"? And yet, as logical as that sounded, Lee already knew he couldn't tell them to come back. "Marlin, sit tight as long as you can before Griffin's army gets in range of you. Just in case she wanders back."

"Roger that. We'll keep our eyes peeled and I'll let you know the second we catch sight of her."

Lee realized he was already moving. Towards Angela. Felt almost like he was walking towards his own gallows. "I copy. Out."

The vehicles from the rearguard were closing in on the airfield now. Amid the clouds of dust they spewed up, Lee searched for that silver minivan. There were a lot of vehicles in that mix, but there only seemed to be one silver minivan, and it was towards the end of the column.

Angela turned to look around right at that moment. Lee's body rocked to a halt, all on its own, like it couldn't even take another step towards her. They were only a few paces from each other, but Lee felt like the distance was awkward. Forced himself to shuffle forward a bit more.

There must've been something in his face. He wasn't taking pains to hide it.

Angela's expression went from latent curiosity to bottomed out dread in an instant. "What?" she said, thickly.

This is your fault, you know. You fucked this one up good.

She'll be fine, Angela. Abby's safe. Marlin's got this. She's just taking a shit. You shouldn't worry so much. Everything's under control.

Bullshit.

It's awful hard to just come out and say you lost someone's kid. Harder still when you'd promised you'd take care of it. Harder still when the kid…shit…when the kid is someone you care about too.

"Angela," Lee said, his voice blank in an effort to keep calm.

And that was it. That was all he needed to say.

Angela's hand went to her mouth. Then both of them. Then they plastered the skin of her face back, stretching her eyes wide and strange. She seemed to be holding onto her own ears. "Where's my fucking daughter, Lee?"

"I just got off the radio with Marlin…"

Angela took a step towards him, fists clenching on her ears. "Where is she?"

"…He said they checked everywhere—checked every single vehicle. There was a lady that said she saw her hanging around those five squads right before they left for La Salle, but that's the only person that noticed her."

Angela was already shaking her head before he finished. She looked almost offended. "You said she was fine! Marlin said he would get her! You both said you would handle it!" She lurched away from him, and then surged back forward. "They lost my little girl? They lost my little girl in a fucking war zone? No."

"No one *lost* Abby," Lee grated. "If she wandered off, then she did it on her own."

"How the fuck do you know that?" Angela screamed in his face. "You don't know that! You don't know if someone grabbed her, or a primal did, or what! You don't know shit! You don't even know what happened to her after *you were supposed to be watching her!*"

"Angela!" Lee barked, his instincts going the entirely wrong direction, thinking he could military-man this situation back into some semblance of control. But that was just dumb fantasy.

Angela thrust a palm at him, almost like she wanted to claw his face. "You shut the fuck up! Where's the woman that saw her?" She spun away. "Where is she?"

No need for Lee to answer: the silver minivan was already rocketing towards them, the rest of the convoy left behind as they ground to a halt in the airfield. Lee didn't bother saying anything else—didn't really have anything, and he knew that Angela wouldn't listen even if he had some grand words. There was no reason that could be spoken into this situation, no calls for calm or logic. All that was acceptable was a plan of action, and Lee didn't even know where to start.

The minivan skidded to a stop just a handful of paces from them, a wash of dust billowing over it as the passenger's door opened and a tall, brown-skinned woman came bursting out of it, her face almost as stricken as Angela's.

Angela wasted no time on niceness: "Where is she? Where's my daughter?"

The woman didn't react to the sudden aggression—almost like she understood it. "I don't know where she is, Angela. I was just the last person to see her."

Angela grabbed her hard enough that Lee took a step forward, not sure what was going to happen next, it all just seemed like it had the potential to go a million different bad directions, but Angela just clung to the woman's shoulders with what looked like a painfully hard grip. "Where did you see her? What was she doing?"

"She was standing around those five squads you sent to La Salle!" The woman's voice pitched upwards. "That's all I saw—I didn't think much about it! I'm so sorry!"

"Well what was she doing?" Angela demanded, her volume way more than necessary, given the fact that the two women were face to face with each other. "Was she just watching? Was she talking to someone? Did she do anything?"

"I don't know!" the woman belted out, then shook Angela's hands off her. "Look! I know how it is! I understand. But I was thinking about other things, alright? I recognized her as your daughter, and that was it. She was just standing there and watching the other squads get ready. She wasn't talking to anyone or doing anything else."

Angela spun around and suddenly Lee was on the hot seat again. "Where'd she go, Lee?"

And his first thought was *How the hell am I supposed to know?*

But then the second thought was a little echo of Abby's voice, ringing through his head: *You ever feel absolutely nothing at all?*

"Lee!"

"I'm thinking!" he snarled.

His brain, manically trying to piece something together that showed some integral pattern to it. Flashes of Abby. In the MATV. Reading that tattered paperback. Those calm, blue eyes looking up at him. How she was just so different than the scared girl she'd been before. How it just seemed like none of it affected her anymore.

You ever feel absolutely nothing at all?

And what had he said to that? What had he said to the ten-year-old girl who didn't seem to mind all the death and destruction that had swallowed up the years of her childhood, and then asked him whether he ever felt nothing?

Maybe now's not the best time.

That's what he'd said.

And then she'd said she needed to pee, and walked away. And the last anyone had seen her, she'd been hovering around a handful of civilian squads about to head for the front lines in Greeley.

Shit. Lee raised the command frequency radio. "Marshal Actual to Drifter Actual, come back."

Agonizing seconds. Angela's face cycling rapidly between disbelief, horror, rage, and some sort of desperate pleading that made him, out of all the other expressions, want to turn away from her.

"You got Drifter Actual, go ahead."

No time for obfuscated terms—they didn't even have a codeword for Abby. "Have you seen Abby?"

There was a pause and Lee imagined Brinly looking at the radio like he'd just spoken Chinese.

"Uh, that's negative. If I'd've seen her, I'd've said something."

Angela moved towards him again. "What's going on? What do you have?"

Lee hissed through his teeth and turned violently away. "Drifter Actual, have you used those five extra squads we sent your way? Have you deployed them?"

"Affirmative. They're pushing on the northern side of our intersection. What's going on?"

"Lee!" Angela shrieked behind him. "Tell me what you're doing!"

Lee spun and spoke into the radio, but stared at Angela while he did. "Drifter, Abby might've snuck in with one of those squads. Do you have comms with any of them?"

"Well, shit! I *had* comms, but things are bit heady right now, and I think the squad leader with the radio might've gone down. What do you want me to do?"

"Have him pull them back!" Angela shouted at Lee.

"I can't have him pull them back! He doesn't have comms with them right now!" *And I can't lose that foothold.* He keyed up again. "I want you to send a squad of Marines to wherever those civvies are and see if they can secure Abby. If they get her I want you to notify me immediately. You copy that?"

"Drifter Actual copies. I'll have 'em on the way right now."

But Lee wasn't even listening anymore. Angela had spun away and started marching towards the silver minivan, the other woman in tow.

"Angela! Stop!"

She didn't even bother to look around. Lee charged after her—or at least he tried to, momentarily forgetting himself and nearly tripping over his bum leg. He swore and hobbled as fast as he could.

"Where the fuck do you think you're going?" he demanded, though that had become pretty apparent by now.

Angela ripped open the driver side door. "Out!"

A very confused middle-aged man came out with his hands up like he was being carjacked.

Angela started pointing to things strapped to him. "Gimme that rifle! And your magazines! Now!"

Lee finally caught up, breathing hard through gritted teeth. "You can't go racing off in there, Angela!"

"The hell I can't," she bit back, snatching the rifle from the man's hands the second he had it unslung.

"Brinly's got his Marines looking for her."

"Brinly's handful of twenty-year-olds aren't going to care like I do!"

"Caring's not gonna bring her back!" He jammed his finger into the side of his head. "Using your fucking head is going to bring her back!"

Angela stared at him for the span of a few seconds, chest heaving. Then she snatched the guy's magazine from his hand and stuffed it in her back pocket. "I'm going, Lee."

Lee reached out to take the rifle, but Angela jerked it away. He fixed her with a mean look. "Gimme the rifle, Angela. I'll go get her. I screwed it up, I'll fix it."

And for just a second there, Lee thought that she was going to relent. Thought it was going to be good enough for Angela. And he fully intended to do it, too, despite the fact that it was a horrible idea—was he really going to run off in the middle of his invasion? Just let everything fall to pieces to save Abby?

Yes. It didn't feel like he really had a choice at that moment.

But then Angela did a weird thing. Her eyes clouded with what Lee could only perceive as doubt, and then they flicked down—oh, so briefly—to his bum leg, and then back up to his eye, and she shook her head.

"She's my daughter. I'm going to go find her."

Then, before Lee could get his gummed up throat to say anything, she swooped into the driver's seat and slammed the door. And Lee just stared at the ghostly image of her through the glass, and couldn't quite get that look out of his head, trying to figure out if it really meant what it had felt like it meant.

"Should I stay?" the woman asked, standing there, shell-shocked. "Or...?"

Lee snapped back into real time. "Go with her. Here." He shoved the command-net radio into her hand. "Keep that." He held up a finger. "Do *not* let her get herself killed."

The woman backpedaled towards the passenger door, the radio cradled in her hands. "I don't think I can keep her from doing shit at this point, but I'll try."

Angela hit the gas the second the woman's ass hit the seat. The door slammed as the van lurched forward, skidding dust and gravel over Lee's legs.

Dear God. What the hell had just happened? What had he *allowed* to happen?

And then the satphone chimed in his pocket.

TEN

BELLRINGER

SAM CROUCHED at the corner of a building, overlooking a small field that looked like it'd been planted with soybeans. He was sweating something fierce, but he took that as a good sign that his dehydration was cured—White had stuck him with a pint of IV fluids on their way over because he looked "ashy." The satphone was pressed to Sam's ear as he looked out across the soybeans and counted heads and weapons one more time.

What was taking so long for Lee to—

"What do you have, Sam?"

Immediately apparent: Something was off.

Sam actually glanced in the direction of the phone, like Lee was right there and he could somehow get a reading from his expression. Then remembered that he was about a hundred yards from a whole lot of bad guys, and figured how-ya-beens could wait.

"Lee, we got eyes on that power substation. Need you to tell Abe to hold off for just a sec. You tell him and then I'll explain."

"I need that substation taken out, Sam," Lee growled.

"I know that. We're gonna take it. Tell him to hold off."

Mumbling from the other line. Didn't sound particularly flattering to Sam. He heard Lee key up on the radio and issue the command for Abe's helo to back off for a minute. He couldn't hear Abe's response.

"Alright, they're in a holding pattern just north of your position. Explain."

Sam craned his neck around to look north. Jones and Marie were huddled right beside him, the Canadian operatives strung out along the side of the building, rifles pointing in all directions. He couldn't see the Blackhawk, but that was a good thing, considering what was waiting at the substation.

He turned back around. "Right. Substation is guarded pretty good. We got eyes on what looks like one squad of Cornerstone operatives, but they got two Ma Deuces. I didn't want our bird to get shredded before it could land."

An intake of breath. "Good call. Can you handle them?"

"Yeah, we can handle them." *Provided nothing goes terribly wrong, like it always does.* Sam looked back north. "Can I get an estimate on how long it's gonna take Abe to land and blow the substation? We can take out the fifty-cals, but there's a couple of the guys that are bedded down behind some sandbags. Chances are they're gonna call for backup the second we start shooting."

"Standby." Lee checked in with Abe again. Luckily, helicopter pilots are whizzes when it comes to estimated time of arrival, and it didn't take long to get an answer. "They can be right on your position in three minutes."

"Copy that. I'm gonna keep you on the line, is that cool?" Sam didn't want the Blackhawk to get chewed up, but he also didn't want his ass hanging in the wind waiting for them when there might be a platoon of Cornerstone heading his way. It would take a bit of timing.

"That's fine. You gimme the word when you're ready, I'll have them roll in hot."

"Alright. Standby." Sam set the phone on the ground and brought his rifle up. Sidled over a bit and rolled onto his side. "Red!" he hissed, waving at him.

The Canadian operative slid low through the dirt and came up between Sam and Jones. "What's the plan?"

Sam shook his head with a grim smirk. "You tell me."

Red sighed through his nose. "Alright then." He peered across the distance, over the tops of the soybeans. "Six bad guys. Eight of us. We got that." A sidelong glance at Sam. "You cool with us taking the shots?"

Which was a very nice way of saying, *I think your ragtag team is gonna miss and fuck it up.*

Luckily, Sam had already had any semblance of pride beaten out of him, so he just nodded. "You take 'em down, we'll move in on point."

"I'm good with that."

"Can you get the dudes behind the sandbags?"

Red looked again, eyes narrowed. "We can certainly try. Just be ready to finish 'em off if we can't."

Sam nodded. "We're ready. Do your thing."

Red keyed his comms so he wouldn't have to raise his voice. "On me, gents."

The others snaked their way across the dirt, staying low behind the field of soybeans. They had no cover. If one of the guys in the substation started firing at them, they'd get chewed up for sure. Their only advantage was surprise.

Red rapidly assigned targets to his team. "Get your sight pictures. Lemme know when you're ready."

Slowly, ever so slowly, the operatives rose. Sam watched them as though he should be taking notes. Just the very tops of their heads and their rifles peeking up over the crops. Luckily for them, they were north of the position, and the Cornerstone operatives were more concerned with the constant thundering of guns coming from the southeast.

Down the line, they checked off in whispers.

Red got himself situated last, in a seated position with his rifle strap wound around one forearm and his elbows tucked into his knees. He spoke without transmitting now. "Fire. Fire. Fire."

Six shots—one rolling peel, like a vicious lightning bolt.

Sam didn't wait for confirmation. He snatched up the satphone and started hauling through the soybeans, having to high-knees it the whole way, huffing into the phone while he did. "Send 'em in, Lee! We're moving!"

Sam was halfway across the field when he saw one of the M2s move. The barrel lifted as someone grabbed the handles, and then a head appeared behind it, and the barrel came swinging around—right at Sam.

He didn't have a choice. He had to slam himself to a stop, his own rifle coming up, all the breath whooshing out of his chest. If there was any other way he could have put that man down without having to come to a stop himself, he would've done it, but he knew in an instant that he couldn't let that M2 start firing on them.

He let out a low wheeze of effort as his lungs bucked for air, but he was trying to get that red dot settled on the tiny outline of the Cornerstone operative's head, just behind that big, nasty gun that was pointing right at him.

Sam squeezed his trigger.

And then the muzzle of the M2 flashed, and Sam went out like a light.

***

Lee heard the booming and knew what it was, even amid the background rustle of Sam running and breathing. There's only one thing that sounds like a .50 BMG chugging away, and that's a .50 BMG.

"Shit," he breathed into the phone, knowing Sam couldn't hear him.

Then there came a tumble. A rattling. The sound of the phone dropping. People's voices screaming. The sound of rifle fire, more like popcorn compared to the M2. Every possible outcome was suddenly made real in Lee's brain—and yet the images that stuck in his head were all the bad ones.

Someone was screaming Sam's name. It sounded like Marie.

"No." Lee said to the phone, as though he had any power at all. And everything went topsy-turvy in his mind, in his chest, like all his organs had up and decided to rearrange themselves, and his brain felt like someone had crammed it full of fire. "Sam!" Lee said, sternly, but there was a shake to it. "Sam!"

It bled in with Marie's cries, and no one answered.

***

Dirt. Plant stems. Leaves shuffling in the breeze. Immature seed pods, like squat green-beans. Slightly fuzzy. And above that, sky. Clear, blue sky, and white clouds tracing through it. And below, on the dirt, a lump of black plastic that was squawking his name in a weird electronic tone.

"Sam! Sam, talk to me!"

The hell? How was the little black box talking to him?

"Sam!" That was a real voice, not the fake, electronic one coming from the mystery box. And now he was feeling something, but dimly. His perspective changed. The ground swept away, and then it was just sky above him, except it was all blotted out by a dark, blurry shape that was screaming at him. "Sam! You with me? You there?"

"Yeah, I'm here!"

At least, that's what he tried to say. But what actually came out was "Ungh?"

"Hey! Hey!" Something patted the side of his face. Nope—they were slapping him. And it set his head to throbbing. He tried to tell them to stop, but again, all he got out of his throat was a weird, semi-conscious groan. "Look at me! Can you see me?"

Of course he could see. He just couldn't see *well*.

He tried to focus, but it felt like his eyes were spinning in different directions. Couldn't quite bring them together on the face hovering over him. The face was too close to him. So, he tried to pull his head back, but that only made it hurt worse. God, the pounding was terrible.

There came a crackling noise that Sam couldn't quite place for a second, and then realized he was hearing automatic rifle fire. Was it close or far away? Did he need to be concerned? Why was he here? Why was he laying down? Had he fallen asleep again? Seemed like a shitty place to do it and—*Oh my God, I got shot by a .50 cal!*

"Wamuhdead?" he wondered aloud.

The face was slightly less blurry now—just enough that Sam saw the crease in the brow. Short-cut hair. Familiar features, even if they were fuzzy. He was pretty sure it was Jonesy.

"What?" Jones husked. "What'd you say? I can't hear you, buddy!"

"Amuhdead?" Sam tried again.

"Are you dead?" Jones let out an insane-sounding titter. "No, you're not dead!"

"Th-fuck-happ'n?"

Another smattering of rifle fire. Jones twisted around, his rifle coming up for a second. He looked like a meerkat, Sam thought. Neck all stretched out, trying to see. Tense and ready to start shooting. Not that meerkats had guns...

He swiveled back around. "They took the substation. We're clear. You with me?"

"The fuck happened?" Sam said, with monumental effort in trying to speak clearly. Words were exhausting.

"What's your name?" Jones replied, which seemed like the dumbest question Sam had ever heard in his life. And then Jones didn't even wait for him to answer—he poked his head up and shouted, "Blue! Blue! Medic!" Then back around. A pause. And then he shook Sam, making him wince at the explosions in his head. "What's your name, man!"

That again? What a dumb...

And yet saying his name was suddenly very difficult. He *knew* his name. Of course he did. He just couldn't quite make it go from his brain to his tongue. He frowned up at Jones, eyes slowly bringing more and more focus into the world.

"Alright, alright," Jones yammered on, sounding worried. "Shit. I don't know what else to ask you! That's, like, the most basic question I can think of!"

"Sam!" He suddenly managed to muscle the constipated word out of his mouth. "I'm Sam!"

Jones nearly wilted with relief. "Oh, thank God! You're not retarded. You know where you are?"

"Greg," Sam said. "Fuckin' Greg." No, that wasn't right. Jones had tilted his head to the side like a dog that's heard a strange noise. "Fuckin' Colorado!"

"Good enough," Jones said, though his expression was a bit dubious.

Someone else came sliding in. Took Sam a moment to place his name, but the pathways in his brain were getting a bit more lubed up now, and he remembered he went by "Blue."

Blue started poking and prodding and asking him all kinds of questions. Sam could hardly tell if he was just making small talk—"You ever play sports?"—or if these questions were somehow diagnostic in nature—"What's the last thing you remember?"

"Getting shot with a .50 caliber." Except it sounded more like, "Getta-shah-widda-fiffy-calber."

Blue gave him a distracted smile as he started rummaging around in his medical pack.

"Don't think you'd be with us if it'd actually hit you."

"Why'ma all fucked up then?"

"Shockwave from the near miss," Blue said, all matter-of-fact, though it made absolutely no sense to Sam at that moment. "Rang your bell something good. Think you got a bad concussion, but you'll live. Probably."

Oh. Probably. Well, that's good.

Blue rumpled something around in his hand and then pressed it to the back of Sam's head. Felt searing hot for a moment until Sam realized it was ice-cold. Blue grabbed Sam's hand and placed it on the ice pack. "Hold that there. Think you can stand?"

"No."

"We should try."

"Okay."

Jones on one side, Blue on the other, hauling him upright—oh, hey, there was Marie, looking pale and wrung out, like she'd thought he was dead for sure and was now looking at his ghost. The second he was upright his head started beating, a very real, physical sensation that seemed to be pulsing all the way through him, like someone was playing drums on his skull.

He winced, swooned a bit, held up by the other two. "My head's pounding. Sounds like a helicopter."

"That's 'cause it's a helicopter," Blue said, pointing one finger up as they started walking. At least walking came easy enough, so that was good.

Sam tilted his head back—which hurt like the dickens—and saw the underside of the Blackhawk, straight over top of him. He had to squint against the downdraft as the bird passed over, then tilted into a hover and started to descend.

"Is my brain gonna be fucked forever?" Sam wondered.

"Uh…" A dubious amount of hesitation, Sam thought, but then Blue put on a confident smile. "Nah, man. If you're walking you're good. Just keep that ice pack on your skull."

"Why?"

"Keep the swelling down."

"Swelling?"

"Your brain might be swelling. Which isn't great, since it doesn't have anywhere to go."

"Could it kill me?"

Blue just shrugged. "If it does, you'll be the first to know."

"Okay." Sam focused forward and watched the helicopter stir up a whirlwind of dust. Figures appeared through the cloud and for a second Sam felt his adrenaline kick again—a nauseas sort of hopeless dread—until he realized that it was Abe and his boys.

Then he leaned forward and puked all over his feet.

"Is that normal?" Jones cried out, still pulling Sam along with them, Sam still retching.

"More or less," came Blue's response.

The heaving made his head feel like it was going to split open, right down the middle. Made him think of cantaloupes. How it looked when his mom used to cut them open and scoop out the brains…Seeds. Scoop out the *seeds*.

"Phone," Sam gurgled on his way up for some air, snot hanging from his nose, watery eyes making everything shifty and indistinct.

"What?"

"Fuckin' phone!" Sam belted, tried to dig in his heels—he needed to get the satphone.

And then it was magically right there in front of his face. Attached to Marie's arm.

"I got it!" she said.

"Lee!" Sam shouted at the phone. "I'm not dead!"

Marie shoved the phone up to Sam's ear and he took it in a trembling hand. Heard Lee's voice on the other end: "Jesus Christ! What the hell happened?"

"I don't know. Talk to Blue. He knows." Sam tried to offer the phone to Blue but the medic just shook his head, mildly annoyed. "Huh. He doesn't wanna talk."

"Are you okay?" Lee sounded like he was asking if Sam was drunk.

"Just got my bell rung," Sam repeated what he'd heard Blue say, though it still wasn't quite connected in his head just yet. "My brain might swell and kill me, but I'll know when it happens."

"Shit," Lee said. "Give me to Marie."

"Alright." Sam passed the phone off, and then they were there at the substation, hunkered against the buffeting rotorwash as the Blackhawk dusted off again. Sam pinched the snot out of his nose and flicked it away. It landed on Marie's leg. She didn't seem to notice, and he decided not to tell her. Hocked up the worst of the slime in the back of his throat and spat, this time taking care not to hit anyone.

"Can you stand on your own?" Jones asked.

"Maybe he should sit down," Blue suggested.

Sam pulled his arms away from them, shaking his head, even though it made his headache worse. "I'm fine. Fuckin' fine. We needa blow the substation. Where's Abe?"

Jones and Blue took a step away from him, still holding their hands out as though to catch him. He swayed a bit, but maintained his balance. Excellent. He was already back on his feet after a .50-caliber round had somehow not hit him but still turned his brains to mush. Life's crazy sometimes.

Sam peered through the diminishing dust and spotted Abe trotting up to them, followed by a guy that Sam knew but took a second to place.

"You alright, Ryder?" Abe asked him.

Sam was looking at the other guy. Waggled a finger at him. "Martinez."

The guy glanced at Abe. Then back to Sam. "Menendez."

Sam clumsily snapped his finger. "Dammit. Menendez. I was close."

"The hell happened to him?" Abe asked Jones.

Sam leaned in. "Got my bell rung. I'm fine."

Jones nodded. "He'll be alright."

Abe seemed to take that as good enough. "Gate to the substation is padlocked. Someone happen to have a pair of bolt cutters?"

"Shoot it," Sam replied, grabbing at his rifle, as though he thought he was the man for the job.

Abe held out a staying hand. "Don't work like that, Ryder."

"Ram it," Sam decided, pointing to the Humvee the dead Cornerstone boys had left them.

"We don't have any breaching equipment," Blue said.

Abe shrugged. "Fuck it. Guess we're gonna ram it."

Sam smiled at Jones. "I knew it."

Jones just looked worried.

Blue shoved a bottle of water at Sam. "Take a knee. Drink some water."

Sam fumbled with the cap. God, but he really was thirsty. "Doctor's orders?" he murmured as he raised the bottle to his lips.

"Yeah, doctor's orders."

Sam shrugged and sank to the ground, decided to just sit on his rump like a kid, with his legs kicked out in front of him. It felt nice. The water was warm, but it washed the taste of vomit away and seemed to bring him back a few more degrees.

There was all kinds of bustling going on. Sam felt like he should probably be doing something. But...doctor's orders and all. He sucked at the water bottle and watched as Menendez and his guys set up a hasty perimeter, some of them hunkering behind the sandbags, pitching dead bodies out of the way so they could take the M2s, others moving amongst the dead and picking them clean of anything useful.

Sam pointed to the nearest one. "Hey! Hey!"

The soldier stood up, having just pulled a set of armor off a dead body.

Sam waggled his fingers. "Armor. I need armor. And a helmet."

The soldier frowned at him. Then shrugged, stooped, grabbed the helmet from the body. Sam noticed that the dead man had been shot in the face. The soldier turned the helmet over and shook it like a stubborn jar of ketchup, and a bit of nastiness plopped out onto the ground. Then he jogged over and dropped the kit unceremoniously at Sam's side.

"There you go, partner."

"Preesh," Sam slurred, clicking his tongue and giving the man finger guns.

The sound of the Humvee starting up. A big diesel rumble. Sam watched over the top of his water bottle as it backed up, angled itself, and then roared forward and with a massive crash, battered down the gates of the substation.

Abe and a handful of others came swarming in after that. Looked like they had their demo gear out and immediately set to rigging it up.

Marie crouched down in front of him, still with that worried-mother expression.

"You know something?" Sam said.

She raised her eyebrows. "What?"

"You really are like my mom. Team mom."

She rolled her eyes. "You want this back?" She was holding the satphone out.

Sam considered it, but shook his head. "Nah. You keep it for now. I can't think straight."

But hey, at least he *knew* he couldn't think straight.

Marie tucked it into her back pocket, still watching him carefully.

Panic suddenly struck him. He started breathing hard. "Am I gonna be like this forever?"

Marie shook her head. "No, you're gonna be fine. Might just be a little confused for a bit."

"How long?" he blubbered. "Can I still operate?"

She chuckled mirthlessly. "At this point, I don't think you have much of a choice. And for all of our sakes, I hope you clear up sooner rather than later."

For some reason, he felt immensely better. Like having your booboo kissed by mom. Man, she really was the team mom. He smiled warmly at her. "Thanks, Marie. You're the best."

Jones again: "Can you get up?"

"Yeah, sure." Sam leaned forward. Got on his hands and knees. Then onto one knee. Then eased his way into standing. The world got a little off-kilter but a few blinks and a deep breath set it right again.

Jones hiked a thumb over his shoulder. "We gotta move out. They're gonna blow it."

Sam drank the last of the water bottle, crumpled it and tossed it. Maybe he should've hung onto it? Whatever. It was way too far away now. He followed Marie and Jones. They seemed to want to run, but were walking for his sake.

The soldiers from Abe's crew were hauling the M2s out, lugging them along, looking pleased about it. Brown, Green, and Blue ran past, cutting back across the field. Going to go fetch the pickup truck, Sam assumed, and congratulated himself for that astute observation.

"That was a helluva shot, though," Jones said over his shoulder

Sam frowned at him. "What was?"

Jones looked at him. "You still hit the gunner. Took him down. Woulda shredded us if you hadn't."

"Really? Well shit."

Sam felt better about the whole thing.

Someone yelled "Fire in the hole!"

Sam hunched and the blast rocked at his back, but wasn't near as bad as he thought it would be. He twisted and saw the cloud of smoke billowing into the sky, debris raining down, a massive shower of sparks from some electrical component, and one of the steel towers tilted with a depressed groan and sagged, but didn't quite fall.

The leftover Humvee sped past them and came to a halt on the road. Abe and a few of his crew were jogging to catch up. Another engine noise growled from behind Sam, and when he looked he saw the pickup truck tearing through the soybeans to join them.

"Got any way to confirm the power's down?" Sam asked as Abe trotted up.

Abe shrugged. "No way to know. But we'll find out soon enough. We're heading to FOB Hampton." He nodded at Sam. "You guys coming? Got the bird inbound."

Sam just kind of froze, thinking, *Is it really time to go to FOB Hampton already?* And then, *I can't make that type of decision. Where's Red?*

But then he said, "Fuck yeah, we're comin'." A glance at Jones and Marie, who were exchanging their own guarded look. "Right?"

"Yeah, okay." Jones nodded hastily.

Marie seemed a bit more reticent, but didn't object.

Sam found Red and waved him over. "Red! We're going to FOB Hampton." Then, after a moment's consideration. "That cool?"

Red traded quick intros with Abe and Menendez. Then looked at Sam. "Sarge, we're here to assist. If that's the next objective, then let's go."

"Alright." Sam clapped his hands together, unexplainably giddy. "Let's do it then!"

Shit. What was wrong with him?

ELEVEN

GRIFFIN

"LEE, WE CAN'T STAY HERE," Marlin's voice shook on the radio. Sounded like he was running.

"I understand," Lee transmitted. It didn't matter much now, did it? Abby wasn't coming back to their location. Lee didn't know for sure, but in a strange way he trusted Angela's instincts, even if they had led her to run off. Abby was in Greeley.

And Griffin was pushing towards them. Marlin and Worley had confirmed it only seconds ago: A big, nasty column of fighting vehicles, heading straight for them. Conservative troop estimate: three to four hundred. All of them soldiers and operatives.

"Get back here ASAP," Lee finished. "Over."

"We're on the way. Out."

Shit. What now? He'd known he was going to wind up crushed between Greeley and Griffin's army, but he'd thought he had a little more time. Thought he would have been able to get himself more secure, but he was still at the airfield with minimal defenses, and if Griffin chose to press him there, Lee knew he wouldn't be able to hold.

Where would they go?

Well, there was really only one option: Into Greeley.

"Major Harden."

Lee turned and looked into the backend of the command module. Lopez was holding up one of the radios. "Major Darabie just called in on a separate channel…"

Lee frowned—why hadn't he done it on the command frequency?

"…he says they've hooked up with Sam's team and our friends from out of state, and they're moving on FOB Hampton."

Sonofabitch. That's why he hadn't called in on the command frequency: He was jumping the gun. Didn't want to speak directly to Lee because he knew that Lee was going to tell him to wait.

Lee put one leg up onto the backend of the MATV and was about to haul himself up and snatch that radio out of Lopez's hand, and give Abe the order to pull back from that objective...

But he stopped himself.

A dull heat kindled in his chest, making him want to lash out. First, Angela runs off into Greeley, and now Abe was charging into FOB Hampton without proper backup to get it done.

And then he realized that he wasn't angry at them—he was angry at himself. Because he was losing fucking control.

He removed his foot from the back of the MATV, Lopez still staring at him apologetically, as though she shared in Abe's borderline insubordination simply by notifying Lee of it.

Their backs were up against the wall. Any moment now, Griffin was going to start pushing them around, and Lee knew he couldn't handle a pitched battle with Griffin's army. Which meant their only other option was to push into Greeley—to push on FOB Hampton.

And if they could take FOB Hampton, they could take Briggs. And if they could take Briggs, they'd have a hostage. Something to negotiate with. Something that might put the brakes on Griffin.

"Fine," Lee husked. Raised a finger and pointed it at Lopez. "But you get on the horn with him and tell him that they're going to take Outlaw *alive*."

Lopez looked moderately relieved and nodded.

Lee turned his attention to Specialist Hurst. "You. Angela's run off to find her daughter. You're my new POC for the civilian troops."

Hurst blinked a few times, but nodded shakily. "Uh, yes, sir."

Lee motioned him hastily out of the MATV. "I want all the civilians rounded up and consolidated for a push into Greeley—and I want it done ten minutes ago."

The specialist clambered out of the MATV. "Yes, sir. I'm on it."

Lee bared his teeth as he turned and stared southward, wondering when Griffin was going to rear his head and start really pushing his shit in.

***

"Answer the fucking phone," Lieutenant Ron Paige seethed at the satphone as he strangled it in both hands. Then he glanced up at Griffin and shook his head. "Nobody's answering."

Captain Perry Griffin was only partially paying attention. He stood in a place that he suspected had been occupied until very recently, if the trampling of the ground and the immeasurable cross-hatching of tire tracks and footprints were any indicator. Not to mention the bits of trash that caught up into swirls and eddies by the taunting breeze.

And, of course, the stink of a few hastily-dug latrine pits.

Griffin sucked his teeth and then bit them together, glaring northward. He heard the hammering of gunfire coming from the city of Greeley. It seemed to be centered around the south end, only a couple miles from Griffin's current location.

Seems he'd been chasing Lee Harden for quite a while, and always winding up just smelling his shit and looking at the detritus left in the wake of his band of rebels. Now he had him cornered.

He should've felt more victorious, but he found himself quietly concerned. Why wasn't Briggs—or anyone for that matter—answering up? Was FOB Hampton even operational still? Or was it that some asshat had simply forgotten the *one form of communication* that Griffin still had with them?

That made him a little hot under the collar, imagining some idiot leaving the satphone languishing in a desk drawer with no one paying attention to it.

Or had Lee already overrun FOB Hampton?

And where was Griffin supposed to go from here? Straight into the south side of Greeley to disrupt whatever fighting was going on there? Or was that a trap? It would've been real handy if someone had answered up from inside Greeley and told him what the hell was happening.

The tactician in him wanted to get down and dirty, and quick. Move to the sound of the guns and figure it out later. But the sense of this moment being an inscrutable tipping point haunted his thoughts, and made the strategist in him say *Wait. Be patient. Figure out what's happening first.*

He would have loved to still have those Predator drones still operational, but fuel had been their biggest constraint. They'd barely had enough to get their ground forces to this point, and they had zero aviation fuel with which to get those birds in the air.

What they did have was the reconnaissance drone, which had no armaments, but at least was battery powered. They'd managed to get a full charge on it through some creative rigging off of one of their MATV's alternators, and Griffin had deployed it ahead of their arrival. If real-time intel from Greeley's forces wasn't possible, he would at least have a bird's eye view of what the hell was going on over there.

Knowing that was all he had to work with, Griffin turned away from the city in the distance and marched around to the back of the Tahoe. The stupid SUVs reminded him of the stupid man that had insisted on their use—Mr. Smith, God rest his soul. It wasn't that the vehicles were so bad, but simply that Griffin knew that Mr. Smith had picked them simply because he liked the way the black SUVs looked.

What an idiot.

Griffin thought once again of the moment that he'd put a bullet through that man's head, and once again he tested himself to see if he would feel anything about it. Once again, he felt nothing but a dim satisfaction. The type of satisfaction you might feel after cleaning up an unsightly mess that'd been irritating you.

Griffin stopped at the open back door on the passenger side. Inside, one of Paige's men sat huddled over the recon drone's controls, frowning into the screen.

"What do you have?" Griffin asked, leaning on the open door.

The operator fiddled a hand at the screen, which Griffin couldn't quite see from his angle. "Fighting on the south side, just inside Greeley. Looks like a sizeable force—mostly military, but some civilians too." The operative shook his head. "But it's still not enough to account for what we think Lee has. So, I spun the drone off towards the airfield."

Griffin nodded. The airfield was a logical place to check. He knew Lee had fuel tankers, and Greeley's grounded aircraft would be a big temptation for someone with enough fuel to get them running. It's exactly what he would have tried to do.

"And?" Griffin prompted.

The operator nodded. "Well, there's someone there, for sure. Got a handful of military vehicles, but mostly cars and trucks—civilians. Just can't tell who they belong to—us or them." He leaned back and looked at Griffin. "That said, I'm thinking they're Lee's people."

"Any reason why?"

A shrug. "They're all facing Greeley."

Griffin smirked. "Well, that's a good indicator."

"You think Lee's there at the airfield or in the fighting in the south side?"

Griffin pondered it for a moment, rubbing one finger over his upper lip. "Doesn't really matter whether it's Lee or not. Someone is at that airfield, and if logic holds up, that's where they'd be commanding from—a relatively safe distance, not right in the thick of it. So, whoever's running the show, they're there."

Griffin, of course, didn't know that for sure. But sometimes you just have to go with the most logical guess.

He turned to find Paige standing at the front quarter-panel of the Tahoe. "Paige, I want you to pick one guy." Griffin held up a single finger for emphasis. "Give him one of our vehicles—one of the civilian cars, something small and non-threatening."

Paige raised his eyebrows. "You tryna send a messenger?"

Griffin eyed his second-in-command. "Why wouldn't I?"

"Why *would* you? Let's just roll in and wipe their shit out. They can't stop us."

"Probably not," Griffin admitted. "But sometimes discretion is the better part of valor."

Paige made a face. "Hm. And sometimes tired old idioms are just tired old idioms."

Griffin sighed. "Until we know what the hell is going on in there—specifically why we're getting no contact from FOB Hampton, and where President Briggs is located and what situation he is in—I'm not just gonna ram my whole army in there. We got one shot to put this shit to bed, and I'm not gonna fuck it up by being too gung-ho. If I can make contact with Lee, or whoever else is running this assault on our city, we can start negotiations."

Paige looked like Griffin had just said something mildly gross. "Didn't realize we were negotiating with terrorists now."

"We don't know what we're doing until we know the situation in there. Besides, if we can open a dialogue, we might learn something." He shrugged. "It can't hurt."

"What if they take my guy captive? Or just kill him?"

Griffin had already considered it, and decided it was an acceptable risk. "You got a better idea of how to open a dialogue with the enemy?"

"Yeah," Paige quipped. "Don't. We can dialogue with them after they throw down their weapons and surrender in nice, orderly lines."

Griffin lowered his chin and gave Paige an earnest, tired look. "And what if we have a chance to end this without committing ourselves to a slugfest? Because I have this sneaking suspicion that if we put Lee in that situation—if we don't give him an out—he's going to fight it out to the last bullet. And yes, we'll eventually beat him down. But how long? And how many are we gonna lose in the process?" He shook his head. "I don't want to sound utilitarian, but the risk of sending one man under flag of truce is a helluva lot better than going toe to toe with Lee in a battle of attrition."

Paige raised his hands in surrender. "I get it. Chess, not checkers."

Griffin reached out towards the operative at the drone controls and snapped his finger. "Hand me that satphone, will you?"

The operator grabbed one of their spare satphones from the center console of the vehicle and handed it to Griffin, who then handed it to Paige. "All your guy has to do is deliver this."

Paige took a deep breath. "Alright. I'll get it done." He looked up at Griffin again, a warning in his eyes. "Just remember who you're dealing with. You don't open dialogues with rabid dogs. You just put 'em down."

Griffin pursed his lips, an unpleasant feeling of misgivings curdling in his guts. "Honestly, Paige?

I have no idea who I'm dealing with anymore. Maybe that's why I wanna talk to him. Maybe I wanna figure out how mad this mad dog really is."

***

"Sir!"

Lee snapped around and saw Specialist Hurst jogging towards him. "Are they formed up and ready?"

Hurst blinked, and in it, Lee detected that maybe there was something else he had on his mind, and that only irritated Lee, because he'd been delegated one damn job. Lee didn't want to hear about anything else—

"They're forming up now, sir, but..." A breath of hesitation.

Lee widened his one eye and pedaled his hand in the air. "Yes? But what?"

Hurst thrust a finger out towards the south. "Perimeter guards have eyes on a sedan approaching."

"Is it Marlin and Worley?"

"They've already checked in," Hurst replied. "I think the sedan is from Griffin's army, sir."

"Shit! How many incoming?"

Hurst faltered for a moment. "Uh. Just the one?"

Lee frowned. "Just the one sedan?"

Hurst nodded. "It's flying a white flag?" He seemed flustered. "What should we do with it?"

Lee's first instinct was to tell Hurst to shred the car to scrap metal and mulch whoever was inside. Hell, they'd already violated a half-dozen rules of war, why would Lee worry about taking someone out under a flag of truce?

But he didn't give the command. Maybe it was pure, morbid curiosity. Who was in the approaching sedan? It wouldn't be Griffin himself, would it? No, that would be ridiculous. Griffin wasn't an idiot, Lee knew, and he wouldn't risk exposing himself to Lee. And for good reason—if it was Griffin, Lee would snatch him up and hold him as a hostage, flag of truce or no.

A messenger, perhaps? But what on earth would Griffin have to say to Lee at this point in time?

Or maybe it was a lone operative on a suicide mission. Get close to Lee and take him out. Shit, the sedan could be stuffed full of explosives for all he knew.

"Sir?"

Lee sucked in a breath. "Hold it at the perimeter—don't let that car get inside. If there's someone inside, they can disarm themselves and approach on foot."

Hurst nodded and raised the radio in his hand. "Units on perimeter, hold that incoming vehicle. Do not let it breach the perimeter, but don't fire on it unless it disobeys your orders."

Lee crossed his arms over his chest and glowered at the radio as the perimeter units sounded back: "Yes, sir, it's already pulled to a stop about fifty yards from our checkpoint. There appears…uh…appears to be only one occupant. Standby."

Just before the transmission cut off there was the sound of yelling.

Lee's eye snatched up, scanning their perimeter to the south. He sidestepped around the back of the MATV to get a better view, and spotted a cluster of his own civilian troops, maybe a quarter mile away, and just beyond them, a white sedan. It's driver's door opened and a figure stepped out, hands raised, a white piece of cloth clutched in one of them.

Lee had the urge to micromanage them from afar—order them to lay the man out, search him for weapons. But he held his silence and just watched. They weren't trained soldiers, but they'd been told how to handle these situations. Lee watched as three of his civvy troops approached the man. The figure under the white flag kept his hands up and sank to his knees. The three civilian troops bounded up, two holding rifles on him while the third swooped in, laid the figure out on the road and proceeded to search him.

Good. No micromanaging necessary.

And now Lee's brain was rolling over and over on itself, trying to figure out how this was going to shape up.

After a moment, the radio crackled again, and a voice came over: "He says he's not willing to approach. He's got a satphone that he says needs to be delivered to Major Harden?" A pause. "Do you want it?"

Hurst looked at Lee, and Lee nodded. "That's affirmative," Hurst transmitted back. "Bring us the satphone."

"I copy. What do you want us to do with him?"

Hurst looked to Lee again.

Lee rubbed a finger over his jawline. Then shrugged. "Let him go, then. If he makes any weird moves, kill him."

Hurst nodded and relayed the order.

From his distant vantage, Lee watched as the three civilians backed away from the man in OCPs, who then slowly rose up, still holding his hands over his head with that white flag, then he backed towards his open vehicle door, settled in, closed the door behind him, and, still holding the flag out the window, backed rapidly away.

It took two minutes for one of the civilians to run across the quarter mile between them and arrive at Lee's MATV, huffing and sweating and holding out a satphone like he couldn't wait to get it out of his hands.

"Sir," the civilian guard said between gasps. "The phone's already on. Someone's on the other line."

Lee stared at it for a moment, hanging there at arm's length. A satphone, huh? So, Griffin wanted to talk. But what in the hell did he want to talk about? And did Lee even want to talk to him?

Lee shuffled forward and reached out. Took the satphone from the civilian, who quickly backed away, but not *all* the way, kind of hovering around at a distance like he wanted to hear what might happen next.

Hurst glared at him and shooed him away. "That'll be all."

The man looked a bit crestfallen, but nodded and turned away, jogging back towards his checkpoint.

Lee looked down at the phone in his hand. The screen was lit up. The call was active. Did he want to talk? Should he just hang up? Why allow Griffin to dictate the terms of communication?

But he was just so damn curious. And really, what would hanging up earn Lee? Pretty much just piss Griffin off. Not that Lee cared about his feelings so much, but why start things off on a negative foot?

They were already destined to try to kill each other. No reason to be a dick about it.

He raised the satphone to his ear. "This is Lee Harden."

TWELVE

OUTLAW

"This is Captain Griffin, and I'm demanding the immediate and unconditional surrender of yourself and every individual under your command."

It was strange, through and through. To hear that voice—a voice that was still connected in Lee's brain with memories of friendship and camaraderie—now coming at him as though they'd never laughed or had a beer together. Not harsh or angry or accusing. Just dead cold and calm.

Lee realized his mouth was smiling even as he registered a miniscule stab of melancholy. Well, shit, what had he expected? Small talk? Even when they'd been friends, Griffin had never been a big gabber. But there was also a flavor of the absolutely ridiculous to it all. And that's what brought out the involuntary smile.

"What, are you serious with that, Perry?" Lee asked, eyes on the retreating dust cloud of Griffin's messenger. "Did you really think you were just gonna drop me a line, demand surrender, and call it a day?" Lee scoffed. "You didn't even ask me how I've been."

"Lee, I'm not gonna prattle on with you," Griffin sighed. "I'm not on the phone with you to catch up. I wanted to give you a chance to surrender before I have to kill you and everyone under your command. Now, once you're disarmed and handcuffed and all your rebels have disengaged and removed themselves from Greeley, and formed up into columns five-abreast with their hands above their heads, then maybe we can sit down and talk about the old days and how sad it is that it all went down like this."

Lee grunted, shaking his head. "You gotta know that ain't gonna happen."

"Why not?" Griffin asked, and his voice sounded genuinely curious. Like he couldn't imagine why Lee wouldn't jump at the chance to lay down his arms.

"You know why, Perry."

"No. I don't."

"Well, hell," Lee chuckled. "If you haven't figured out why I'm fighting, maybe that's why you're fighting me. But let's not pretend like either of us is going to change the other's mind on this. If minds could be changed, they would've been changed before we were pointing guns at each other." The smile was quickly curdling off of Lee's face. "You asked for my surrender. You don't have it. You come to this city, you're coming for a fight. Not how I would have wanted us to wind up, but you've picked your side, and I've picked mine, and I'm pretty sure we're both convinced we're right. Aren't we?"

"I know that I am," Griffin replied, evenly.

"Well, there you have it. There's only one way this ends."

"That's your choice, Lee. Just remember that."

"Trust me, I always do."

And then the line went dead.

Lee didn't wait, didn't hesitate. He took two, big steps to the back of the MATV, tossed Griffin's satphone on the deck and snatched up his command radio. "Marshal Actual to Stranger Actual, come back." And then juggling a different radio: "Marshal Actual to Specialist Hurst—I need you at the command truck."

Abe's voice was dimmed by the background roar of helicopter rotors, coming from the radio in Lee's left hand. "Go ahead, Marshal." Was it Lee's imagination or was there a modicum of guilt in that voice, like a kid caught sneaking candy?

Well, if he thought Lee was about to chew his ass for going after FOB Hampton, he had another think coming.

"Stranger, I need Outlaw in hand and alive, A-S-A-fucking-P, you copy me?"

Gone was any note of guilt. Replaced with an immense satisfaction. "Oh, I copy, five by five."

"You tell me what you need, and I'll get it to you."

"Roger that. Another Blackhawk-load of fighters wouldn't hurt."

Lee nodded to the radio. "Send the helo back to the airfield immediately after it drops you guys. What's your ETA?"

"We're coming up on the target in two mikes."

"Marshal copies. Out." Lee gave the radio a painful three second rest to make sure no one else had anything urgent to say, then transmitted again. "Marshal Actual to Drifter Actual, come back."

Brinly's response was slower coming. Ten agonizing seconds. Lee fidgeted as he watched Hurst jogging towards him.

"This is Drifter Actual, go ahead, Marshal."

"Drifter, you got those squads ready to push on the weapons depot?"

A long pause. "Well, I had a few of them scouring for a certain missing child. But I can recall them."

Shit and fuck. Lee bared his teeth at the sky. Pressed the PTT. "I copy. Do what you gotta do. But I need that weapons depot taken out immediately and the goods delivered to FOB Hampton, how copy?"

"Drifter copies. We're gonna have to deal with more collateral on the way."

Lee shook his head. "I don't care what you have to do. Just get it done."

"Roger that. We'll get it done."

"Marshal out."

Hurst came stamping breathlessly up. "You called, sir?"

Lee pointed to the southern perimeter. "Griffin's army is going to start pushing on us at any second. I need you to think of ten squads that are worth a shit." God, but he wished Angela was still here—she was way better versed on the civilian squads than either he or Hurst. She would know who was capable. But she wasn't here, so Lee had to make do.

"Uh…" Hurst frowned around him, like they might pop up out of the dirt.

"Don't gimme that shit," Lee snapped. "Ten squads that know what the fuck they're doing—do you have them?"

A shaky nod. "Yes, sir."

Lee waved his hand again at their southern perimeter. "I want them on rearguard action right fucking now. The rest of the civilian troops you got formed up? I need them on the road, pushing straight into Greeley, and heading for FOB Hampton."

Hurst started to turn away, but Lee caught his arm. "Wait. Four of those squads..." No. He needed more, just in case they took casualties during the rearguard action. "No, six—have six squads ready to pull back and mount up on the Blackhawk when it returns. It'll have to take two trips, so put your best three in first. They're going straight into FOB Hampton to back up Sam and Abe's crew. You got all that?"

Hurst nodded as though it was all he could manage.

Lee gave him a little push. "Get it done."

Hurst ran off, and Lee grabbed the backend of the MATV and hauled himself inside. On the right side, near the little "tables" where the makeshift map was still jumbled, lay Lee's old, torn up and stained armor, and his rifle. He hissed uncomfortably as he manhandled it over his head and shoulders and started strapping into it.

"Specialist Lopez," he said, cinching the cummerbund around his waist.

Lopez looked up at him.

Lee nodded to the rifle beside her station. "You're gonna wanna get suited up. Shit's about to go sideways for a bit."

Lopez swallowed, then nodded and grabbed her rifle.

***

"Hey!" Sam shouted across the deck of the Blackhawk. "Blue!"

The Canadian medic, his legs hanging out of the helicopter, craned his neck to look at Sam.

Sam held up the ice pack he'd been pressing to the base of his skull. "Do I still need to hold this on my brain?"

Blue leaned back into something of a reclined repose and shouted back: "How's your head?"

How was his head? Well, he still felt like his wires were a little crossed, but the headache was gone. Either from the pounding adrenaline or because it was actually feeling better, he had no idea.

"Yeah, head's fine!"

Blue nodded. "Then you might do your noggin a bigger favor by putting that helmet on it."

Sam smiled as though it was all a merry joke, gave Blue a wink, and then dropped the ice pack and crammed the stolen helmet down over his head. Chin strap was a bit loose for him, but he really didn't feel like messing with it. And he wasn't sure they had time anyways. He felt the Blackhawk beginning to drop altitude, and that only meant one thing.

Sam leaned forward, his own feet dangling out over a thousand feet of air. Looking along the riveted sides of the aircraft, Sam squinted against the wash of air and pounding rotors and spotted a big building dead ahead—a hotel. With sandbag bunkers on the ground level. Men inside, like little action figures. Machine gun nests on the roof.

Oh, hell, this is gonna get spicy.

Abe was shouting to the pilots: "Circle the building! We gotta clear those defenders off! Gunner! Gunner, start taking them—"

The aircraft banked suddenly, forcing Abe to cling to a strap of webbing. Bright little tracers suddenly filled the air around the helicopter, a worrisome *ping-ponk-punk* as a few rounds skittered off the barely-armored hull in bright flashes of sparks.

"Taking fire!" someone yelled, as though it needed to be stated.

The door gunner ripped his M240 around and angled it downwards, the muzzle blooming with angry yellow.

Sam cinched tight into his rifle, and wanted badly to find something to shoot at, but the Blackhawk had angled around so that the defending forces were on the right, and Sam was hanging out the left. He caught a glimpse of the wide, flat top of the hotel roof as the helicopter roared around it at a distance of maybe five hundred yards. The Blackhawk was tilted as it looped around the hotel, and below Sam's feet was only dizzying sky, centrifugal force the only thing keeping his rear fixed to the deck.

Sam grunted against the forces pressing him down. Heard someone yell something, followed by the distinctive *thoonk* of a 40mm grenade, and then five more. Sam craned his neck around to see one of Abe's guys—Gordon—breaking open his smoking MGL and snagging fresh grenades from his webbing as the fired rounds impacted on the roof of FOB Hampton, scattering sandbags and body parts.

The door gunner chattered away at the pieces of defenders still left, while Abe staggered to the center of the deck, still holding onto a strap for stability.

"Roof's clear! Roof's clear!" Abe shouted, first to the men on the right, then to the men on the left. "We're bringing it down! Get ready!"

The Blackhawk swerved around another smattering of fire coming in from the defensive positions on the street, then drifted sideways, now over top of the roof, using the bulk of the hotel as cover from the defenders below.

Abe grabbed at Gordon as he got his last 40mm seated and snapped his MGL closed. "I want you to hit those bunkers on the street so this bird can exfil without getting its tail chewed off!"

Gordon tossed a thumbs-up and hunkered down as the Blackhawk began to lower itself to the smoking rooftop, right near the northeast corner.

Sam felt an elbow in his ribs. Turned and looked at Jones.

"You good?" Jones asked. "You ready?"

Sam patted his stolen helmet, then his stolen chest rig. Which had handily come with six extra rifle mags. Sam felt rich. "Good to go, brother."

Jones offered him a shaky smile. "Let's do it, then."

They both leaned forward—them and Marie and a handful of Abe's guys. Looked up at the white-coated rooftop now lumbering up towards their feet. Rotorwash caught the smoking ruins of the defensive positions, curling them into artful forms before they were batted away in the wind, leaving nothing but the human wreckage beneath, blood made black across the white.

The roof stopped coming up at them when they were still six feet off the ground, and Abe shouted, "Move! Move!"

Sam slid out and fell the six feet to the rooftop. Legs buckled underneath him. A tumble of gear and weapons. Felt his helmet knock around on the ground as he rolled, then came up on his ass and scrambled for his feet, rifle up, looking for anything that might be moving.

One guy—Cornerstone black—with both his legs missing, crawling away from the Blackhawk. Sam's reticle swam unsteadily over the man's prone torso. The stranger looked over his shoulder right at the last second, and his eyes connected with Sam's and there was all kinds of fear and pain in them, and then Sam squeezed his trigger, thinking, *Well, he's gonna bleed out anyways.*

The shot took the man in the side of the chest.

But he didn't die. His mouth opened, his teeth showing. Maybe he'd screamed, but Sam couldn't hear beyond the rotors. The guy writhed for a single second, then started dragging himself along even faster.

"Motherfucker," Sam snapped, his own voice barely audible, and rose up, firing again and again at the crawling man. It took four more shots to the chest to finally make him stop.

Strange how some men took one shot to put down and others needed a grenade and six shots to convince them.

The rotors changed pitch—a harsh, stabbing, slapping noise as the Blackhawk lifted into the air again. Gordon streaked to the side of the rooftop, accompanied by two others. Posted over the side and let his MGL spit out its payload, choosing his shots between the explosions below.

"Ryder!"

Sam jerked, swung around, saw Abe pointing past him.

"Secure that roof access!"

"Roger 'at!" Sam belted out, spinning back around and scanning the rooftop—there it was. A single structure poking up out of the top, right smack dab between two of the sandbag positions,

Cornerstone operatives draped over the tumbled walls, dribbling red in pools and rivulets.

Sam started towards the door, hazarding a glance behind him and spotting Marie and Jones right on his tail, along with Red, White, and Green.

He swung left around the two sandbag walls, muzzle dipping low to address the bodies inside. One shredded all up his torso and hanging over the sandbags, the other curled up like a pill bug around the ammo can that still fed the M240 with a glittering chain of brass.

Neither body moved. Sightless eyes. Sam pulled his muzzle back to the door and wrangled his way over the perforated sandbags, grit crunching under his boots.

Sam took the left side of the door—the side with the doorknob. Jones and Marie stacked up behind him, while Red, White, and Green took the hinge side. Red kept his rifle on the door, but Green had let his sling take his rifle and now had two grenades in his hands, peering over Red's shoulder, while White kept his rifle up and outwards, presumably keeping an eye on the ductwork and air-conditioning units that populated the roof. Anyone could be hiding there.

Menendez's men were taking care of that—rapidly sweeping the entire rooftop in an arc, checking anywhere that a body might be hiding. Sam didn't see it, but he heard someone shout, followed by a burp of automatic fire, and then nothing.

Somebody must've been hiding.

Abe and the rest of his crew came trooping up, Gordon and his two squadmates rejoining them as they swept nimbly over the detritus on the rooftop and formed up on Sam's side of the door.

"Hit it," Abe grunted, nodding at the door.

Sam, in turn, nodded at Jones, who snagged the doorknob and yanked the door open wide. Sam took a half step to the side, angling the muzzle of his rifle into a dark stairwell, thumbing his light on and producing a mishmash of hectic shadows—

A man's head ducked away from the light.

"Whoop," Sam cringed, sidestepping just as the stairwell exploded in gunfire.

Green didn't hesitate. Red caught the door as it swung and pinned it open with his shoulder while Green stepped around, spoons spinning off the grenades, letting them cook in his hand, then going low and lobbing both grenades into the dark. Screams of alarm from inside and, as though it could save them, the defenders let out a last fusillade of shots before the two grenades went off.

The whole roof shook with the explosions. Gray dust and smoke billowed out of the open door along with a clatter of debris.

"Move!" Abe shouted.

And Sam moved. Through the door with Jones right on his ass and everyone else piling in behind. Sam flicked his light to constant-on and peeled to the left, muzzle following the spiral of the staircase down. Shadows leaped and squiggled, light blazing in the smoke like high-beams in a fog. On the next landing down, bodies, and movement. Sam fired at them from between the rungs of the safety rails until he couldn't see movement anymore. A few other rifles joined him, and then it was deafening, ear-ringing silence as Menendez and a stream of his soldiers clattered down the steps.

Calls of "clear" came up to Sam as Menendez and his boys on point reached the first level—the penthouse where Abe had told them Briggs stayed.

The reality of it hit Sam all at once. He was in the same building, on the same level—hell, just a handful of yards away—from the man that had been their enemy from the very beginning.

Acting President Erwin Briggs. Codenamed Outlaw. Just a few walls between him and justice.

"Hold up!" Abe hissed, stepping over a tangle of three enemy soldiers that had died on the stairs.

Menendez posted on the door, slightly to the side, while his men hugged the walls. Abe put a hand on Menendez, but addressed them all, his voice quiet, little more than a whisper, and barely clear beyond the ringing in Sam's ears.

"No frags. ID your targets. We need Outlaw *alive*."

Sam nodded along with the others, feeling his pulse ramp up, some heady mix of excitement and dread. They were *so close*. And yet there were so many ways they could be denied what they wanted. So many ways for it to go wrong.

What was on the other side of the door? A hotel hallway, filled with Cornerstone operatives ready to fight to the death for the man they viewed as their president? How would they be armed? Would there be barricades? Machine guns? Was the door itself barricaded? Would they have to breach it explosively? Were they about to be ground to hamburger trying to infiltrate the penthouse?

Menendez swung around to the hinge side of the door, reaching across and laying his hand on the doorknob. He looked at the others stacked up along the wall. Everyone was ready. He twisted it all the way until it stopped. Then seemed to steel himself. Then pulled.

Sam was almost surprised when the door opened.

Menendez's fire team immediately spilled through the opening.

And into an empty hotel hallway, shrouded in darkness.

That's right—they'd killed the power grid, and interior hallways don't have windows.

Weaponlights shot through the darkness, illuminating carpeted floors. And nothing else.

The column moved. Eerily quiet. No commands given. No vocalizations. Just boots padding across the soft carpet, taking up positions in the hallway.

A sidelong glance at Abe revealed to Sam that he didn't like the quiet any more than Sam did. His beard seemed to have swallowed his face, so that it was just two angry eyes peering suspiciously out, never resting on anything for more than a second.

The hallway was a straight shot, about twenty yards long. A pair of elevator doors on the other end. Another door with a sign on it denoting it as another stairwell. And there to the left side of the hallway, one more door. The door to the penthouse.

Nobody needed to be told what to do. They knew what they'd come for and Abe had briefed them on the flight over.

Again, Menendez and his fireteam took up the point position on the penthouse door. The Canadian team immediately moved to the far side of the door and kept their rifles on the elevator and stairwell doors at the end of the hall. Abe and his fireteam stacked up behind Menendez; Sam, Jones, and Marie behind them.

Menendez tested the penthouse door. This time, no joy. He leaned back and hissed, "Breacher up!"

Gordon slung his bulky MGL and negotiated his pack from his shoulders. Took a knee just to the side of the door, Menendez hovering over him, keeping coverage on the door. Gordon produced a pre-wired breaching charge. He unspooled the wires with practiced hands and then squished the little clay-like squares into position around the door frame.

Menendez shuffled back. The Canadians moved further down the hall, hunkering down.

"Standby for breach," Gordon whispered into the dim quiet.

Everyone turned away from the door, shoulders scrunched up tight, fingers in ears, eyes closed, mouths open. Sam did the same.

BOOM!

The whole hallway rocked and heaved. A mean pressure wave slammed into Sam's chest, expelling the air from his lungs in a big *whoof!*

Hands batting at shoulders. Sam swung, blinking against a harsh gout of daylight now pouring out of the smoking hole where the penthouse door used to be. The smoke stung his eyes like cutting onions. He squinted through tears, Abe moving ahead of him, and Sam following along like a coupled train car. Daylight and smoke. Shapes moving through it, peeling through the breach.

No gunfire. No shouts.

What the hell?

Through the breach, Abe split left, so Sam split right.

The penthouse.

Not a soul inside of it, except for the men that had just infiltrated it.

Sam was in—one step in, one step over, and trying to find work to do, trying to find a corner to cover, but everything was already populated by a pissed off looking soldier. Doors were kicked. Glass was shattered. The bathroom was cleared by no less than three soldiers. The bedroom area of the suite battered by another five.

Calls began to come in, all semblance of stealth now given way to a panicked sort of rage.

"Clear!"

"Bathroom's clear!"

"Bedroom's clear!"

"Shit!"

Abe marched into the center of the main room that they had entered. A large dining table stood there, and beyond it, a bank of windows overlooking Greeley. A few papers lilted desultorily on the table as Abe swept a hand across them.

"No contact," Menendez said, like he couldn't quite believe it.

Abe shook his head at the table. "He's not here."

THIRTEEN

MOTHERS AND DAUGHTERS

SICK TO HER STOMACH AND SLICK WITH SWEAT, Angela hunched over the wheel of the van, the chatter of the command radio distant and disassociated from her. They were taking FOB Hampton. They hadn't found Briggs. Griffin was breathing down Lee's neck.

Angela didn't give a shit.

Her thoughts were just a tight, obsessive loop: *Where's Abby? She went in with Brinly. Into the south side. Is she still there? Is she dead—oh, God, no, don't even think it! Where is she? Where's Abby?*

"Whoa!" someone in the back belted out as Angela yanked the wheel to avoid two hapless figures trying to dart across the road. She didn't even touch the brakes. The eyes of those two people blazed in her consciousness for the bare second that she locked onto them. Terror. Desperation. And then she was past them.

The van shot over the end of the bridge, the two civilians just loping shapes in the sideview mirror, trying to flee southward. And they weren't the only ones. The roadway was lined with them, all of them trying to get out of the city, and choosing perhaps the worst route to do it.

Angela laid on the horn as a man went doddering into the street, blood-streaked and mad, waving a pistol, and yelling. He didn't point the pistol at Angela—held it up in the air in one hand, the other thrust out in front of him like he was going to palm the grill of the van.

Briefly she considered running him over, but what stopped her wasn't the idea of murder—just that the ground clearance on the van wasn't great and she could imagine his corpse getting caught underneath it. So she swerved at the last second.

A loud bang on the passenger side panel.

"Shit!" the same voice from the back—one of the guys that hadn't shut the fuck up the entire time Angela had been driving.

Angela spared a glance for her right sideview mirror and saw the man pirouette and fall in the roadway.

"Did you kill him?" the back-seat driver shrieked.

"You shut the fuck up!" Angela snarled over her shoulder.

Ahead, a pair of Marines sprinting across the road told Angela she'd found the front lines. Or at least the *back* of the front lines? Bubbling clouds of smoke and seeking streams of tracer rounds arcing deeper into Greeley marked a place a few blocks ahead where the fighting seemed hottest.

Angela slowed as she approached a large intersection. Another pack of fleeing civilians. A woman with a bloody child in her arms screamed at Angela, but she just goosed the gas to get by her. She couldn't worry about that woman and her child. She had her own child to save.

She spun the wheel to the left, angling the van through the intersection and then stomped on the brake. The entire way ahead was clogged with vehicles that had been left abandoned while the fighters inside surged forward.

The van rocked to a stop. Angela puffed some stray hair out of her face, looking left and right, hoping against hope to catch a sight—just a glimpse—of her daughter's frizzy blonde head. But this area seemed emptied of humanity, save for a handful of fleeing refugees picking through the vehicles, glancing up at Angela's van with fear in their eyes, as though Angela might hop out and gun them down in cold blood.

"Angela." This time the voice was from the passenger seat.

Angela wrung the steering wheel in her hands, still searching fruitlessly through the wreckage for any sign of her daughter.

"Angela."

"What?" Angela snapped, finally looking right.

The woman that had started this all was looking at her like she'd lost her mind. And Angela supposed that wasn't too far from the truth. She wasn't precisely illogical, but she wasn't exactly what you would call reasonable.

"Where are we going?" the woman asked in a dead-level voice. Not an accusation. An attempt to cut through Angela's panic and get her to think about her next step.

Angela realized she didn't even know the woman's name. "I don't know."

"Where would Abby be?" the woman tried.

Angela slammed the steering wheel with the heel of her palm. "I don't fucking know! If I knew, I'd fucking go there!"

"Well, we can't go this way!" the man said from the back.

The woman twisted in her seat and fixed the man with a baleful look. Angela had the impression that he was the woman's husband or boyfriend. "Jace, you are not helping this situation."

Jace shuffled madly about in the back seat but didn't say anything else.

The woman turned back to Angela. "We're not gonna get much farther in this thing, and it's a tin can coffin. I wouldn't suggest we stay in it much longer."

Angela seized that tiny thread of reason and pulled on it like it might save her from herself. "You think we should go in on foot?" She didn't even wait for an answer. She thrust the shifter into park. "I'm going in on foot."

"I'm going with you."

Angela shook her head. "Just gimme that radio. I'll handle it. No reason for you to get caught up in this."

The woman scoffed. "I think I'm already caught up in this, Angela. You caught me up in it when you took my van."

Angela glared at her. "I'm not asking you to risk your life for me."

The woman shook her head. "I'm really not *trying* to risk my life for you. But Lee told me I had to keep you safe, and I sure as shit ain't going back to him to tell him I let you wander off into Greeley on your own." She undid her seatbelt—why the hell had she worn it in the first place? Oh, yeah. Because Angela had driven like a mad woman.

From the back, Jace murmured something unintelligible and pulled his sliding door open.

The woman twisted in her seat again. "No, Jace. I need you to stay with the vehicle."

"The fuck I am," Jace said back, like he couldn't imagine a more nonsensical thing to say. "If you're going, I'm going."

The woman shook her head irritably, kicking her own door open. "No, you're staying here! Who's the squad leader, huh?"

"I don't care if you're the squad leader!" Jace roared. "You're my wife!"

"Not today I'm not," the woman said, sliding out of her seat, but still leaning into the vehicle to speak to him. "You're going to sit your ass right here at this intersection and guard this vehicle. And you're not going to move from this spot. Because you're our exfil, and if we come back with Abby, I wanna know that I got a vehicle to get me out of here. You understand me?"

Jace flopped his hands around. "This is ridiculous."

The woman apparently took that to mean she'd won. She gave a nod to Angela and then slammed her door shut.

Angela glanced back and, predictably, found Jace glaring at her. She considered apologizing, but then figured *fuck him*, and lurched out of the vehicle.

She met the woman at the front of the van. At first she couldn't keep up with every new bit of information assaulting her senses. The thump of automatic weapons. The hellish shriek of wounded people. The clamoring of the masses of civilians one block back. The stuttering sounds of rifles spitting and being answered by others. The clatter of projectiles over concrete. The dim yell of commands.

Her eyes ranged over the situation ahead of them. Smoke, and tracers arcing out, like chains of glowing beads that seemed to slow drastically the farther they got before they landed on some building or other in a spray of dust. A handful of Marines huddled at the corner of a building, maybe a half mile from where Angela was standing, taking potshots. A gaggle of civilian fighters leap-frogged their way northwards down street, then scattered for cover as someone even farther down leaned out and sprayed the street with a flicker of automatic fire. All of it happening far enough away from Angela that she knew she wasn't in danger, but the cavalcade of sensory input made her adrenaline surge and tingle in her extremities.

"We should get out of the middle of the street," the woman said, inching closer to Angela, as though she thought to shield Angela with her own body.

Angela didn't move. She hefted the rifle she'd taken. She looked at the woman at her side and felt a sudden welling of emotion that threatened to choke her.

"I didn't get your name," Angela managed, after a thick swallow.

"It's Nia," the woman said without looking at her. Eyes downrange. And for just a moment, her expression reminded Angela of the bodyguard she'd lost when Butler had fallen. He'd had that same look to him—determined to protect Angela, always looking for a threat.

And look what had happened to him.

Was the same in store for Nia?

"I don't want you to die because of me," Angela croaked.

Nia finally cast her gaze onto Angela. A flash of pity. Followed by a forced smile. "Yeah, I'm not keen on that idea either. So, let's get your girl and get the hell outta here."

"Alright." Angela took a breath, and, without signaling anything, took off running for the nearest building. Running, further into Greeley, where it seemed there were no rules but the rule of chaos.

***

Ryan was not a good fighter, Abby had realized. Not that she was any expert herself. But she'd been around enough fighting and heard enough of the talk from professionals that she'd absorbed some basic principles. Like how you had to have the guts to push your advantage, and you had to be clearheaded enough to see that opportunity when it arose.

Ryan was just a bit too scared of catching a round, and so he wound up spending a lot of time hunkering behind bits of cover and breathing heavily and mumbling to himself and generally seeming like he was trying to calm himself down. Even when there weren't rounds coming at them.

Abby stared at him now, watching the sweat gather at the tip of his nose and drip down between his legs. He squatted at a corner of a building, head hanging, staring at the concrete between his feet, his rifle hugged to his chest, less like an offensive weapon, and more like a defensive talisman. His lips were moving, but he wasn't actually speaking.

Abby stood next to him with her back against the wall. She wasn't immune to the fear—God, no. But her perception of it just seemed a little different than his. He was afraid for his life, and didn't want to move into situations where it might be put in danger. Abby was also afraid for her life, but wasn't putting herself in danger the whole point of being here?

"We should move forward," she said.

Ryan huffed and shook his head. "We should move forward," he mocked. "You don't know what you're talking about."

"We haven't been shot at it in, like, five minutes."

"Yeah!" Ryan snapped his head up to look at her, disbelief and anger in his eyes. "And that's a bad thing?"

She frowned at him. "We're supposed to be fighting."

"You're not even supposed to be here!"

"Well I am!"

"Could you shut the fuck up for a minute and let me think?"

"What do you need to think about?" Abby said, getting mad. She kicked at his leg.

"Hey! Stop!"

"We're supposed to be—" kick "—fucking fighting!"

"Stop it!" he yelled at her, coming upright and shoving her away with a hand to her chest. "What the hell's wrong with you, kid?"

Abby scowled, then brushed past him and posted on the corner of the building. She didn't just go poking her head out like an idiot—no, she knew better than that. She wasn't stupid. She just wasn't a fucking coward.

So she eased one eye out and peered down the side of the building.

It was a long, straight road that speared north—at least, she thought it was north—into the heart of Greeley. And there wasn't a single soul on it. Far ahead, down that road a good ways, she could *hear* the fighting—chattering guns, distant screams, an occasional explosion. But it had to be, like, a mile away or something.

"It's clear," Abby declared.

"Oh, it's clear," he mocked again.

"I'm going."

"No. You're not supposed to be here. I need to get you to...back to..."

Abby huffed. "Cover me."

"What?"

But she was already running.

"Abby!" he shouted from behind her.

She ignored him and charged down the sidewalk, spotting a little inlet in the buildings—a shop door inset into the concrete walls. She skittered into cover there, went down to a knee—which hurt, because she'd skinned the heck out of both knees earlier—and raised her bulky rifle in trembling, fatigued arms, scanning the world around her through the optic. She felt pretty good about her performance.

Satisfied that she was relatively secure, she looked back over her shoulder. "It's clear!" she shouted. "I got you covered! Come on!"

Ryan's seemingly disembodied head, peering from around the corner back there. He bared his teeth and said something she didn't catch, then looked all around, and sprinted down the sidewalk towards her. He tumbled into cover right behind her, gasping.

"That was stupid!" he snapped.

Abby frowned at him, nose curling in something like disgust. "Stupid? You know what's stupid?"

"What?" he seethed, flecking her face with spittle.

Abby ignored it. Jabbed a hand further down the road. "You're supposed to run *past* me. Not get into cover *with* me. *That's* stupid."

"You think this is a fucking game?" he hissed at her. "You got bored hanging around with your mom and Lee and decided to come see what all the fun was about? Well guess what, bitch, it's not fun! People are dying! Does that look like fun to you? Does this seem like a fucking game for little kids?"

"Why are you so scared?"

He slapped her. The pain of it was so sharp and clear, like a blast of fire on her cheek, the sound of it singing in her ears. She gasped and reached a hand up to touch her face. Goggled up at Ryan in pure shock. And then she started to laugh.

For a second there, Ryan looked mortified with himself. But as Abby began to laugh, his expression became one of nervous confusion.

It was a mad rush of adrenaline that had done it to her. She couldn't hold it back. It was a momentous surge of *feeling*, the shock and momentary indignation at being struck across the face, very suddenly melting into a sort of endorphin dump that set her brain to sparkling in a way that wasn't entirely unpleasant. It was almost…thrilling.

Then, just as rapidly, she got pissed. The laughter died to a husk in her throat, and she looked up at Ryan, a man nearly twice her size, and the sting in her cheek felt like a branding iron.

She pointed to the spare magazine sticking out of his back pocket. "Gimme your extra mag."

Ryan's face went from confusion to incredulity. "What? No."

Abby jutted her chin out. "What are you gonna do with it? If you're gonna be a piece of shit and hang around where there's no fighting, then give it me so I can use it."

Ryan looked like he was sorely tempted to hit her again. Then he did a funny little squirm of shame, his expression pained. "Look, I'm sorry I slapped you."

"I don't give a shit," Abby snapped back. "You gonna give me your magazine or are you going to come along?"

He squinted down at her. "You're insane, you know that?"

Abby didn't respond. What was she supposed to say to that? Ryan didn't even know what insane was. And was she insane? What do you call it when you don't feel like a human anymore because you don't *feel*? Except, of course, when a grown-ass man slaps you and you feel hilarious, and then enraged about it. But those weren't exactly the feelings she'd set out to try to feel. Then again, she hadn't really felt much when she'd done what she'd come to do and killed someone. It hadn't fulfilled her need to feel at all. Left her even more hollowed out than before. Numb.

Yes, maybe she was insane.

But it was better to be insane than a coward, wasn't it?

"Alright," Ryan growled. His shoulders worked up and down a few times. "Fine. Let's go. You wanna get involved in the fighting? After all that you've already seen? Fine. Come on. Let's get involved."

Abby nodded curtly and then marched out of cover.

"Aren't you going to bound?" Ryan said, almost mocking, but not quite—like maybe he thought it was a better idea than just strolling down the street as casual as you please.

"There's no one shooting at us yet," Abby tossed over her shoulder.

And continued on, deeper into Greeley, towards the sounds of the guns.

FOURTEEN

CRIMES AGAINST HUMANITY

Nearly a mile north of where Abby was marching towards the fighting, Wibberley and Guidry had come to a full, shell-shocked stop.

They'd gotten themselves separated from Brinly's main push to the weapons depot. A troublesome section, about two blocks back, had hung up the entire column as they routed some defenders out of an apartment complex.

Routed them out by damn near leveling the complex with a rain of 40mm grenades from no less than four Mark 19 launchers on their guntrucks. Wibberley and Guidry, in a little black hatchback that they'd commandeered, had been forced to go around the fighting, then got hung up by a series of abandoned roadblocks, and by the time they found their way back to the main route north, Brinly's forces had moved on.

And they'd left *this* in their wake.

Wibberley had rolled the four-banger hatchback to a stop, his mouth gaping, Wibberley silent in the seat next to him. And then, just a whisper: "Holy fuck. What happened?"

Wibberley had no answer. At least, no answer he felt like speaking. There was a part of him that wanted to deny it. Wanted to say that this must've been Cornerstone's doing. Couldn't have possibly been done by Brinly. Couldn't have possibly been done by the *good guys*.

Are you really that naïve? Wibberley wondered. *Do you really believe there's any good guys at this point?*

He pushed the shifter into park and opened his door, and the sounds of it hit him like a battering wave. Men and women shouting in cracked voices. Children shrieking hysterically. Wounded of all kinds moaning and pleading at the skies and anyone that passed close by to them.

Wibberley's legs felt weak as he stood up. A ball of ice had formed in his chest, in his throat, in the back of his head—like brain freeze. Like he'd just sucked down a mass of slush made of bitter gall.

It had *been* a suburban neighborhood. Small houses—what would've been called "low income" in times past—cramming both sides of the street.

Bodies everywhere. Lying in patches of lawn little more than dusty scrub. Draped over curbs and sidewalks. Blown to pieces around small craters. Riddled with bullets. No quarter given to the young, the children, the women, or the unarmed. Dark patches of blood on the blacktop. Neon steaks of arterial bleeding, coagulating in the gutters.

Fire. A row of three houses to the right, the middle one fully ablaze, its neighbors catching. Dark black billows of smoke pouring into the sky, making an acrid haze of the air. A handful of people were rushing into the nearest house as its roof began to shudder and cave in, flames leaping high amid volcanic explosions of embers. Soot-stained men and women with their shirts up over their mouths and noses, tears streaming from their smoke-blinded eyes, hauling bodies out, limp and blackened and singed.

Wibberley wasn't quite sure what possessed him, but he started moving towards that house, first at a stumbling walk, and then at a run, as the screaming from inside seemed to carry across all the other sounds of human misery and began to pierce him, driving straight through the hard-fought calluses of a dozen theaters of war, and spearing him straight in the vestiges of his humanity.

"Wibberley!" Guidry called out from behind him. "Wait!"

"We gotta help!" Wibberley shouted back, now in a run, now leaping over a dead child with no head on their shoulders, and onto the lawn adjacent to the burning house. That's how far he got before people began to notice him.

And they screamed.

A woman, standing there in the lawn over an inert form—too blackened and charred to make out if it was man or woman, adult or child—pointing at him as though he was a demon, sheer panic in her eyes.

"No!" she screamed at him, froth catching the corners of her mouth, snot and drool slaking her chin. "You stay back!"

She thought he was one of them.

Wasn't he one of them?

Wibberley shied around her as you might a snapping dog, feeling a leaden pull in the center of him, and it was attached to that quiet background fear—the same fear he'd had from day one, all the way back in the Butler Safe Zone: That Marlin had made the wrong choice in backing these people.

He made it up the shallow, crumbling concrete steps at the front of the house, but before he could plunge into the murk of smoke inside, a dark figure loomed out of it and he stopped, backpedaling off the stoop as the huge figure became three—a man and a woman, and an older man between them, his head lolling, mouth gaping, black spit bubbling out of his mouth, his tongue sharply pink as it flopped around inside like an unearthed worm.

They clattered down the steps, heedless of Wibberley, and he reached out and grabbed the old man in the middle, trying to do something—anything—to help. The man's skin and clothes were hot to the touch, smoke and steam rising from black-crackled flesh. Wibberley realized his error too late—his fingers crunched through a thin layer of crisp skin, and liquid burst over his hand, and the old man came upright with a weak, hacking cough, eyes goggling red and watery in his face.

Guidry was there. "Set him down! Set him down!"

The woman was still screaming at them, "You get away from him!"

A few hostile shouts, Wibberley realized, coming from a crowd of survivors. His eyes swept up and caught theirs—glaring at him as though he were a savage beast in the middle of them. He raised the hand with the old man's juices and flecks of burned skin still clinging to his fingers. "It's okay!" he tried to soothe them, but the words didn't seem to have much effect.

Pop!

Wibberley's core went rigid. Hand scrambling his rifle up from where it was hanging. Someone was shouting. Guidry spun to the left, his rifle shouldered. A man stood about ten yards from them, a pistol in his hand, pointing. He looked more aggrieved than enraged. Like he felt that killing them was an unfortunate duty that had fallen on his shoulders.

Three blasts from Guidry's rifle and the man crumpled, looking mournful.

"Shit!" Guidry spat out. "What the fuck were you thinking?"

As though it were a conversation that could be had with the man at this point.

"Stop!" someone's hoarse cry. Voice shredded and gagged by smoke. The woman that had been helping the old man out of the house now stood, the old man in the dirt at her feet, the other man crouched low over him with his hands up as though he could ward off bullets and hostilities.

"He shot at us!" Guidry said, his voice defensive.

The woman looked at him with both of her palms facing. "Please. Stop."

The old man on the ground squirmed weakly, trying to breathe and failing.

"He's dying!" the man crouching over him said.

Wibberley wanted to look down at the old man, but threats were buzzing, rippling at the edges of his vision. Every civilian that looked at him had hatred or fear in their eyes, and either could flick over to violence at the slightest notion.

"He can't breathe!" the man wailed.

The woman turned away from Guidry. "Do CPR!"

That won't help, Wibberley thought, but didn't say. Didn't think his advice would be welcome at this point. Maybe they should back off...

"Are you with them?" a voice snapped from behind Wibberley.

He spun, thinking about bringing up his rifle just a second after he saw the muzzle of the shotgun pointing at his face. A middle-aged man with a shock of bristly gray hair stared at him from the other side of that barrel.

Too late to scoop for his rifle. Guidry turned and came to the same conclusion. Neither of them released their grips on their rifles, though. The man with the shotgun could only get one of them, after all.

"We're British," Wibberley spat out. An untruth that wasn't really a lie.

The man's eyes crinkled up, but the shotgun sagged a hair. "British? What the fuck are you doing here? Are you on their side?"

Wibberley couldn't answer that question—knew somehow that if he did, the next thing would be a flash and a load of buckshot to his head. "What the hell happened here? Tell me what happened!"

The man's face contorted. The shotgun trembled in his grip. "There were only five of them! The fucking bastards!"

Wibberley tried to make sense of that, and couldn't. Five Marines did all this?

The man nodded to the house that was fully ablaze. "That was all there were! Just five in that house! We begged them not to set up their machine gun there, but they shot at us and we had to back off." The man blinked rapidly, the bottoms of his eyelids looking chapped and wet. "Only the five of them," he strangled out. "But they blew up the whole fucking block!"

The pieces connected. Wibberley gaped at the burning house. Then caught Guidry's stone-faced glare. Then looked back to the man with the shotgun, which had dipped even more now. "Five Cornerstone, you mean?"

The shotgun wilted. The man's support hand came off of it and swept across the scene of destruction. "All of this! For five of them! They didn't need to do all of this!" His mouth worked silently for a moment. Then his hand returned to the pump-action. He fixed Wibberley with a narrow look. "Are you with them?"

"No," Guidry growled.

"We're here," Wibberley added, haltingly. "On behalf of the United Kingdom. To observe…" he trailed off, not even wanting to admit who he was "observing." Again, more half-truths.

"Observe?" the man said, as though it was some archaic word that he couldn't fathom the meaning of. "Observe?" he shook the shotgun violently. "Have you seen enough, then? Who the fuck are these people? They didn't have to do this! They didn't have to do it!"

"He's dead," the woman's voice quavered.

"We should go," Guidry hissed at him.

The man with the shotgun watched Wibberley. Never took his eyes off of him. Never raised the shotgun again, but didn't let it go either. Tracked with Wibberley and Guidry as they backed off the dirt lawn, his eyes full of a trip-wire intensity.

When their feet hit concrete again, they snugged their rifles up and spun away. The streets were choked with people now, standing among the dead, carrying or dragging them and the wounded, or sometimes just stumbling about like they still couldn't figure out what was happening to them.

All of this for a single house? How many dead to neutralize five enemy combatants?

Collateral.

Oh, Wibberley was no stranger to collateral. And he knew the cold logic that went into it. Knew that those Marines hadn't started this day intending to be murderers. But then they'd hit this narrow street, and they weren't supposed to stop for anything, those were their orders. And they took fire and they couldn't figure out where it was coming from, so they raked the whole damn street as they hauled through it. Turned an entire neighborhood block into rubble.

No one ever goes into these hellscapes intending to slaughter civilians.

Was it too weak to simply say that "these things happen"?

It felt too weak.

Wibberley stumbled into his car door. Ripped it open and sat hastily inside. No one pursued them—just the man with the shotgun, still staring at them with that look like he might shoot or might just turn away at any moment. But Wibberley *felt* pursued.

The second Guidry had his ass in his seat, Wibberley slapped the shifter into drive and spun tires accelerating forward. He didn't want to go forward, but that's the direction they were facing. And as they sped along the streets, haggard civilians lurching out of their way, he wondered why it was that he didn't want to go deeper into Greeley, didn't want to keep following this trail of destruction, and it didn't take a trained head doctor to figure out why.

The second they were free of the civilians and their ruined block of houses, Wibberley yanked the car into a sharp left turn onto a side street.

Guidry looked at him. "Where are we going?"

Wibberley just shook his head. "We're getting the fuck out of here."

TERMINUS

***

The chatter of the Blackhawk faded into the distance, and Lee turned away from the view of the bird, shrinking as it flew towards FOB Hampton with the first load of three civilian squads. Hurst and Lopez were now outside of the MATV, both of them having donned their armor and a rifle.

Lee's own rig sat heavy on his chest. He felt his heart beating against the chest plate, felt the weight of it with every breath he took. And he liked it. Even the stale-sweat-smell of it. The stippled grip of his own rifle against the palm of his hand felt good. Right. If he'd known that just being in combat gear would make him feel less like everything was falling apart, he would have put it on earlier.

Lee spared a glance up to the south. Still no sign of Griffin's army, but that didn't mean they weren't coming. There was no doubt in his mind that they'd be there at any time, and when they did arrive, they'd hit hard. Griffin wouldn't leave anything up to chance. He'd encircle and break them to pieces.

Now, if they could only get their asses mobilized in time, they might have a chance to fall back into Greeley before they were taken apart by Griffin's better-trained and better-equipped force.

"Tell me something good, Hurst," Lee said, staring down at the hand-drawn map that now occupied the edge of the MATV's deck.

"Twenty squads, four and five fighters apiece," Hurst said. "They're loaded as best we can make them with what we have."

"How long until they're ready to push?"

"They're formed up," Hurst said, nodding towards where the line of civilian vehicles had made a column, two abreast, just a few hundred yards behind Lee. "They'll be ready as soon as I can give them a route and a target."

Lee nodded, putting the index finger of his unwieldy left hand on the map. "Our road out is Eighth Street, west. They need to haul straight down to Twenty-Third Avenue." He traced his finger until he found the street amidst Abe's grid-like drawing. "Then they head south on Twenty-Third. FOB Hampton is right on the southwestern corner of Twenty-Third and Highway Thirty-Four." He tapped the mark on the map where Abe had drawn a big square and labeled it FOB H. "Their objective is to take the entire two-block radius around FOB Hampton. Secure it and hold it and wait for additional orders."

"Will they be assaulting FOB Hampton?"

"I don't know yet," Lee admitted. "Abe's crew just landed. I haven't got a sitrep from them. We may need the civilians to push on the ground floor, but I don't want them to make that move until I hear from Abe." Lee shook his head and gave Hurst a severe look. "That's for your recognizance—don't even tell that to them. I don't want anyone jumping the gun and creating a blue-on-blue situation."

Hurst nodded hastily. "Roger that, sir."

Lopez lifted one of the radios. "You want me to request a sitrep from them, sir?"

Lee chewed on his lower lip. It was best to just let your troops report in when they could. But he hadn't heard a peep since the Blackhawk had dropped them on the roof, and things were starting to constrict tighter and tighter. Lee's tolerance for strategic patience was fraying to nothing.

"Fuck it. Call them up." He turned to Hurst. "Go ahead and relay those commands."

"Sir." Hurst snatched his rifle—a tad awkwardly—and hustled off, his gait making Lee think he'd never before worn armor. It wasn't a winning recommendation, but what did Lee expect? The guy was trained for desk duty, not warfighting.

Lee turned and focused on Lopez. Her eyes were squinted at nothing in particular, straining to hear the voice in the transmission over the sound of gunfire behind it.

"—breaching to the second floor," Abe shouted over the din of gunfire. He didn't sound panicked—just loud. "Penthouse was empty. Negative on Outlaw. Any word on reinforcements? 'Cause I sure could use some help right now."

Lopez's eyes flicked to Lee's, a question in them, but Lee didn't move to take the radio, so she keyed up. "The Blackhawk is inbound to your location with fifteen civilian troops. You want 'em on the roof or the ground?"

"Not the roof!" Abe said sharply. "I need them on the ground floor to take some of this heat off of us, or we're not going to be able to get out of these damn stairwells."

Another glance between Lee and Lopez. He nodded and snatched up another radio. "Marshal Actual to White Horse, you copy the chatter on command-net?"

The drone of the helicopter buzzed in the background. "White Horse, negative, we did not copy."

"Do *not* drop on the roof. Drifter needs those reinforcements on the ground floor."

The next thing Lee heard was blaring alarms and a single syllable: "Shit!"

The transmission clicked out for a second, as Lee's skin tingled unpleasantly. Then it came back.

"Mayday, mayday," the pilot said, almost grossly calm about it, though his voice strained like he was pulling against a weight. "Ground fire…shit…no rudder, we gotta put her down. Brace! Brace! Brace!"

Lee whirled, looking to the west. Couldn't see the bird from this vantage point.

"Did the Blackhawk just go down?" Lopez squeaked.

Lee didn't answer. He reached out and took the radio from her hand. "Marshal Actual to Drifter Actual. White Horse is going down."

FIFTEEN

WHITE HORSE DOWN

"Ryder!"

Sam skittered back from the stairwell door, gunsmoke filling his mouth, pouring out of his rifle barrel. He'd been a tad liberal with that last mag. He slammed his armored back against the concrete wall of the stairwell, just gloom and smoke, perforated with lances of sunlight coming through twenty or thirty bullet holes in the door.

Sam swore and used the heel of his boot to kick the door shut until it latched. A few more bullets poked holes in the door, chipping the concrete stairs across from it.

"What?" Sam yelled, searching through the weird lighting. "Someone call me?"

"Ryder!" It was Abe, standing on the first landing up. "On me!"

Sam took a breath, waited until he felt that another fusillade of incoming rounds wasn't going to slam through the door, and then hurled himself up the stairs three at a time to where Abe was huddled with the others.

Sam slumped against the stair rail. "Maybe a half a dozen Cornerstone in there. No barricades. They're just hiding behind corners. We can take them if—"

"Hey!" Abe snapped a finger in front of Sam's face. "You let me worry about taking them. Listen to me."

Sam nodded, licking a dry tongue over dry lips and focusing in on Abe's hard eyes.

Abe jammed a finger up the stairs. "White Horse just went down. Take your crew and the Canadians up to the second level. Find a room with an east facing window and try to get eyes on that downed bird. Got it?"

"Got it," Sam huffed, pushing himself off the rail and swapping his mostly-empty magazine with a fresh one. He caught Marie and Jones, mixed in with Menendez's guys, and jerked his head. "We're heading up." He spun around the turn in the stairs, spotted the Canadians in a line, and found Red. "Need your help with something. Blackhawk went down. We need to put eyes on."

"Roger that."

They climbed the stairwell rapidly back the way they'd come only moments before. They reached the door to the second level, and, out of an abundance of caution, Sam eased the door open and cleared the hallway beyond—just in case. It was still empty and lightless. He pushed through the door, spun in a quick circle to get his bearings, and selected one of the hotel room doors, just to his right.

"If it's got a window, it'll be east facing, yeah?" Sam said, testing the handle, though he knew it would be locked. All the doors were electronic locks, and, according to Abe, that was one of the reasons the rooms weren't used—the only way in was to breach the door.

"Green," Red called, waving his hand. "You're up."

Green was already moving towards the door, his pack slung onto his side as he unearthed a breaching charge from inside. Green glanced at Red and then Sam. "I only got two more of these. You sure this is the one you wanna breach?"

Sam wasn't sure at all. But he wasn't sure about any of the other rooms either. Sam looked briefly to Red, but the Canadian team lead deferred with a small shrug. Sam nodded to the door and started backing away. "Blow it."

Thirty seconds and one big boom later, they were moving through the smoky breach.

The first thing Sam noticed as he slid through the door and pivoted to the left—right into the bathroom—was a musty, organic smell. Not the smell of rot, but something that had rotted a long, long time ago.

"Small room," Sam called out, as he splashed his light over the dark bathroom. Spotted himself in the mirror and almost did a double take. Christ, he looked like shit. Chose not to look too closely, but in that little glimpse he'd had he looked drawn and emaciated.

He emerged back into the main portion of the room. Daylight shimmered from between drawn blackout curtains. A thin rectangle of light illuminated the queen-sized bed, and the brownish mound that lay on it, vaguely in the shape of a body.

A flick of his weaponlight gave him all the details he cared to have—a mummified body, splayed out spread-eagle on the bed. The blanket and sheets stained a dark brown all around the body, as though they had turned to dirt over the years. Where the skeletal hands lay, great swaths of black had spilled out. Whoever it was, they'd slit their wrists, Sam thought. Probably did it right at the beginning of the outbreak, so many years before.

"Jesus," Jones remarked, his nose curled though the stench was long past being actually offensive—more of just a cave smell now. "How many other rooms you think have dead bodies in them?"

Sam ignored him and moved around the bed to the window, using his rifle barrel to sweep the blackout curtains to the side. Pure sunlight splashed over his face, blinding him for a moment, until the image beyond the glass began to take form.

It was indeed east facing. A view over the tops of a handful of smallish trees, and then a big, four-lane highway, and a wide intersection with another road, and just north of that, the smoking ruins of the Blackhawk, right in the center lane. The helicopter was tilted onto its side, its rotors bent and shredded, its tail boom hanging at a sharp angle.

"Got eyes on the bird," Sam called out. "Maybe two hundred yards away."

The others gathered rapidly at the window.

"Any movement?" Marie asked, her head protruding over Sam's shoulder.

Sam squinted into the bright distance. There were flames coming from the cockpit, blowing black smoke out of the shattered side windows. He couldn't see inside. The side doors were open. A handful of bodies were scattered about the roadway, having been ejected from the helicopter during the crash. None of them moved.

"I don't…"

A ripple of movement, coming from behind the bulk of the helicopter. Little puffs of gray, and then Sam saw what he'd missed before—bullet impacts, striking the concrete around the side of the craft and sparking off the hull. Someone on the ground level of FOB Hampton was shooting at the helicopter, and someone in the wreckage was shooting back.

"Shit!" Sam jerked out. "Someone's alive in there!" He immediately backed away from the window, looking to see if it had an opening, but there didn't seem to be one.

"What're you doing?" Red growled from behind him.

"We gotta get them out of there!" Sam said, taking a step back and raising his rifle, intending to shoot the glass out.

"Whoa!" Red laid a hand on his muzzle.

Sam ripped his gaze angrily to the Canadian. "We gotta help!"

"Well, don't waste your ammo!" Red snapped back. Then he lunged forward and muzzle-thumped the window, a quick spearing motion right to the corner of the glass. A spiderweb of cracks spread through it. He gave it another thrust, and this time Sam leapt forward and did the same on the opposite corner. A few hits more and the glass exploded all at once, raining the room and the outside with glass shards.

"What're you gonna do?" Jones demanded, as a gust of wind blew in and whipped the curtains around, the sound of gunfire now coming in clear and sharp. "Jump?"

Sam raked the bottom of the window with his rifle barrel and then leaned out. "It ain't that far."

"Goddammit," Jones griped. "We're gonna break our ankles."

"Hold up!" Marie called out. "You're not gonna tell Abe?"

"I don't have comms!" Sam retorted.

"Blue!" Red grabbed his comrade by the shoulder and bodily pointed him for the door. "Go back down to Abe so we can communicate!"

"On it." Blue dashed back through the breached door.

A second later, Red listened to something on his comms, then transmitted back. "Copy that, we're moving." He turned to Sam. "Abe said to haul ass."

"Of course he did," Sam muttered, taking in the drop to the ground again. They were only on the second level. Couldn't be more than fifteen feet. But no one really loved jumping out of windows.

"Tuck and roll when you hit," Jones said, clambering up onto the air conditioner under the window. "I'm right behind you."

"Fuck, I hate heights," Sam said, his boots crunching in glass as he ducked under the top of the window and leaned out.

"You want a push?"

Sam did *not* want a push, so he grit his teeth and jumped, hoping it wasn't nearly as far to the ground as it looked as he hung in the air for a moment. Then came the descent, which felt rapid enough that he should be catching fire, and before he could really register just how fast that ground was moving up at him, his boots hit and he tried to remember to roll, albeit a half-second too late, and crumpled to the concrete, sharp pain lancing up from the balls of his feet to his hips.

He scrambled back to his feet, hissing the whole time and hoping to God nothing was broken but his pride. Swept right with his rifle as another body came plummeting out of the sky like a fleshy meteor, and Jones didn't have much better luck with his own recommendation to tuck and roll—though he did manage to go forward onto his face rather than back onto his ass.

"Aw, fuck!" Jones winced upright, chin already welling with blood. "Right in the face."

The side of the hotel was clear, save for a single barricade on the corner—a V made by two jersey barriers—dead bodies seen through the crack between the concrete sections. They'd already got a gift from Green's MKL. Turned out to be a bad day for them. But there was still plenty of fire pouring at the downed Blackhawk from around the other side of the hotel.

More bodies hit the ground. Marie managed it with impressive grace, as well as all the Canadians, except for Red, who flopped to his left side and came up swearing with a bit of a limp.

But Sam was still focused on that barricade—well, not the barricade itself, but the abandoned M240 sitting just behind it. His eyes flicked back and forth between the barricade and the Blackhawk, ears now picking out the slightly-sharper sound of whoever was inside, firing back.

"Got an idea," Sam belted out, and started running for the barricade before anyone could stop him. He did, however, twist as he ran and tossed over his shoulder. "Be ready to run!"

By the time he reached the barricade, he realized Jones was with him.

"Well, I wasn't going to let you die by yourself, asshat," Jones snapped.

Marie and the Canadians had eased forward a bit to the minimal cover provided by a handful of trees growing in a little section of empty dirt that one might be tempted to call a field. Red watched Sam like a hawk. Probably wondering what harebrained scheme the nut with the concussion had just come up with.

Sam squirted through the gap in the barriers, kicked the arm of one dead body from the stock of the M240, slung his own rifle to his side, and hefted the machine gun. A mostly-eaten belt of 7.62 dangled out of the feed tray, but there was another ammo box lying near the empty one. Jones caught his drift and yanked the lid open. Happy, eager brass glinted up at them.

"Oh, yes," Jones hissed, as a fresh hammering of rounds came from around the corner—sounding closer now, like the defenders were trying to push towards the Blackhawk.

Sam had minimal training with M240's, but he *had* been trained on them. So, it took a second for the memory of those long-lost training sessions as a half-boot to resurface through a pond scum of anxiety, and he fumbled his fingers along the top until he found the pinch point, and yanked up the cover assembly. Swept out the handful of cartridges still seated in the tray. Jones was on the spot with the fresh belt, sliding the first rounds into the tray, then whipping up with his rifle to cover that corner, as Sam slapped the cover assembly down again.

No sooner had Sam racked the bolt, than a tumult of bodies came hauling around the corner, all eyes on the Blackhawk—at least for the single second before Jones opened up with an inhuman shriek of surprise, and Sam yanked back on the machine gun's trigger, firing from the hip.

Rounds went everywhere. Bodies spilled and yelped and tripped, chunks flying off in gristly sprays. The M240 rocked in Sam's hands, but it was so damn heavy his point of aim barely even rose. The belt of ammunition clattered and swayed beneath him as he sidestepped to the right, closer to the building, a weird groan escaping his lips as the last man to come around the corner did so with his rifle up, screaming words Sam couldn't understand.

But Sam had never even let up on the trigger. And a single sweep of his arms cut the man down, curling him up in a fit of puffing red and jiggling meat.

Only when that body hit the ground did Sam detach his finger from the trigger. A waft of gunsmoke poured over him, stinging his eyes. His right shoulder hit the concrete wall of the hotel and he shouted in the general direction of Marie and the Canadians, "Move! Move! Move!"

Jones had launched himself over to the other side of the jersey barrier and was inching along it with his rifle tight, getting a wider and wider angle on the corner of the building. "Get that corner, Sarge! Get it!"

Sam slogged forward, ammunition belt whipping at his legs, threatening to tangle him as it raked out of the ammo can. He hit the corner.

"You're clear!" Jones called.

Sam dropped to his belly and shuffled his way around the corner so it was just the gun and his head and shoulders poking out. A straight shot down the shallow south side of the building. A handful of bodies milling about the far corner, seeming shocked that the last fire team got chewed up. Sam sent a chatter of rounds their way, taking one in the leg even as they lurched for cover. The man went down, mewling, and Sam finished him off with a quick burst to the chest, his breath ripping through his throat, every inhale dry and scratchy and smoke-stinking, and every exhale rattling out a strange animal wheeze from his voice box.

Suppressive fire, Sam remembered. *Steady, three to five round bursts.*

He squeezed the trigger in a slow, controlled rhythm. Far more controlled than he actually felt.

And it was pretty effective—except for one little arm that came whipping around the corner on the far side, and the little metal ball that went arcing through the air, straight at Sam's face.

"Grenade!" he screamed, and never before had he moved so fast. In the span of a single second, while the grenade was still in the air, he contorted his body, scrunched up tight, and rolled in a little ball until his body stopped against the wall of the building, the machine gun cradled in front of his face.

Then came a stretch of time that Sam knew couldn't have been more than three seconds, but in it he began to wonder, was it a dud? Is it actually going to go off? Was it going to kill him when it did? Had he ducked far enough around the corner?

It was not a dud.

The pressure wave blotted out all perception of sound so that the whole world became a silent earthquake. He felt it in his teeth. A jamming, slashing, penetrating power, and his vision was nothing but gray dust and acrid smoke.

He leered like a mad devil, coughing and hacking, blinking dust and debris out of his eyes, wiping it off of his face. A thousand stinging sensations all across his exposed skin. He was terrified that he might be blind, but then he managed to clear the worst of his watering eyes. Spotted Jones coming up from behind the jersey barrier, rifle spitting for a few rounds before he ducked back into a cover, chased by impacts that chipped away at the top of the concrete.

Almost as an afterthought, Sam glanced between the gap in the barriers and saw Marie and the Canadians sprinting for the Blackhawk, their backs exposed, trusting in Sam and Jones to keep the defenders pinned down long enough for them to stretch the two hundred yard distance to the downed helicopter.

Sam thrust the M240 out again. A clatter of metal. He wasn't holding it right—had it at arm's length so it protruded from around the smoky corner, and jammed his finger into the trigger, blind firing like an amateur, but sometimes amateur moves were called for. Would have felt less like an amateur if he'd managed to get the weapon to fire more than five rounds before it stopped dead with a sad little *clunk*.

"What the fuck?" Sam roared at it, as though the machine had a mind of its own and was being petulant about the whole debacle. The ammo belt had caught up in the stock when he'd thrust it around the corner, and the tension had caused a misfire.

"I'm down!" Sam shouted, hoping that Jones could hear him. He ripped the weapon back towards him and started to fumble his way through clearing the jam before recalling that he had a rifle still strapped to his side.

Jones came up firing again. Let out a full auto burst, then shouted, "Incoming!" and disappeared back below the barricade.

Incoming? Incoming *people*? Incoming *grenade*?

Sam froze for a single beat of his heart, until he caught the sound of boots.

Incoming *people* then. Shit and fuck.

Sam heaved his rifle around to his front, caught Jones out of his peripheral, coming low around the side of the barricade, rifle blasting away, the noise of each report like a slap in Sam's face, making his nose tingle and his eyes water all over again.

"Got 'em!" Jones screeched with a savage sort of terror. "Clear that jam!" And, as he said it, he came scrambling around the barricade on one hand and two knees, rifle with an empty magwell. He tucked into the corner beside Sam, scrunched tight on his heels, and slapped a fresh mag in.

"What are you doing here?" Sam shouted at him, snagging the carrying handle of the M240 and hauling it back into cover with him. "You were better over there!"

"I didn't know if you knew how to clear the jam!"

"I know how to clear the jam!"

Did he know how to clear the jam?

"Well, fucking clear it, then!" Jones leaned around the corner, popped off a single round, and then posted, waiting like a spider for some unlucky bastard to show a bit of meat.

Right. Clear it.

He could almost hear his old instructor's voice, bawling at him, and he found his lips moving to the words, as his hands followed his brain's sluggish instructions: *POPS, half-boot!*

Pull the cocking handle to the rear!
Observe the ejection port!
Push the cocking handle forward!
Squeeze the trigger and fire!

Sam held off on that last one, thinking, *So, basically just rack the bolt?* Leave it to the Army to overcomplicate everything. "I think it's clear," he called up to Jones.

"Get on the corner!" Jones shuffled out of the way as Sam squirmed forward to take the corner again, snugging the buttstock into his shoulder. "Did you fire it?"

Sam fired it. "It works!"

"You're a fucking phenom," Jones huffed, as sarcastically as one could manage when their life was on the line.

Down the side of the building, a few corpses that hadn't been there before. The side of the building speckled with red. Concrete soaked with it.

"Did they get to the Blackhawk?" Sam wheezed against the buttstock. He didn't dare take his eyes off the corner of the building opposite from him. They weren't shooting, and he couldn't hear them talking either. What did that mean? Were they maneuvering? Had Abe breached the ground floor successfully and drawn them off? Were they about to charge around the corner en masse?

"They're at the bird now," Jones said, sounding a little distracted. "They're pulling someone out. Looks like...a few someones."

A face at the far corner—just a quick peek.

Sam spasmed and fired two rounds—just a twitch of the finger, but the face had already disappeared. "Shit. He just looked at me."

"Who looked at you?"

"The guy over there."

"Did you shoot him?"

"Missed."

"Next time, shoot him."

"We should move. Can't just stay in this same position."

"Where?"

"I don't know. Can you see a good spot of cover?"

"No."

"Shit."

"Just hold on, they're running back now."

Sam's finger clenched a bit tighter on the trigger. He felt it twitch backward by a tiny increment. Were they going to try another grenade? He'd been lucky the first time—the toss hadn't cleared the corner. If it had, the shrapnel would've got him.

Interminable seconds passed. The sound of boots again, and Sam almost fired reflexively, until he realized that the noise was coming from behind him. A wash of relief. Heavy breathing now accompanied the stamp of feet.

Jones nudged him with his foot. "Here. Switch up."

Sam waited for Jones to lower himself to the ground, and then the two of them did a little maneuver, rolling over each other so that there was only a second or so when the machine gun didn't have someone's finger on the trigger. Sam surged up to his feet as Marie pounded up to the wall next to him, face flushed, heaving for air. The Canadians followed, White with his arms around a limping man with blood cascading down his shocked face. Four more of the civilian troops hustled up behind, all of them looking dazed from the crash and the ensuing firefight. One of the pilots was struggling along at the back of the pack, a squat little carbine in his hands, his bulky flight helmet still on his head.

"Six survivors," Marie huffed. "No one else made it."

Red came up next, keying his comms. "Green, we've extracted five survivors from the wreck, and one pilot. Tell Abe we're on the southeastern corner of the building, ready to push on the main entrance."

The rest of them came piling in. As Red waited for the response, he moved quickly down the line of them, looking each of the civilian troops in the eyes and touching them on the shoulder, asking them if they were good, if they were ready. Most of them just nodded, having that look about them like they'd just run all but the final mile of a marathon and were now being asked to sprint the rest of the way.

Red held up at the end of the line, listening to his earpiece.

Sam watched his brows sink into a frown. Watched the determination bleed out of his expression. His eyes hit Sam's and held them, and Sam felt his stomach cinch up tight. There was something in Red's face that looked like pain. Or guilt.

Red's eyes flicked away. He stabbed at his PTT. "Yeah, I copy." His mouth worked like he wanted to say something else, but he just issued a low growl and released the PTT. His shoulders slumped. Then he took a deep breath, straightened, and looked at Sam again.

"We got a problem," he said.

Sam took a step towards him. "What kind of problem?"

Took him a moment to glance to the side and see that the rest of the Canadian team had that same guilty look on their faces. They'd heard the transmission too. And they liked it no more than their squad leader. White, his back against the wall, let out a swear and rapped the back of his helmet into the concrete, gritting his teeth and looking pissed.

"What happened?" Marie pressed.

Red grimaced. "We've been ordered out. Immediately."

SIXTEEN

ALLIES

"Guys," Jones called out, voice straining to stay low. "What's going on over there? What's everyone mumbling about? Why does everyone sound so angry?"

Sam couldn't rip his eyes away from Red. He'd heard the words perfectly fine, he was just struggling to make them fit into his reality. "Ordered out? Like, immediately after we take the FOB?"

"No," Red shook his head. "Immediately, like right now."

Sam's eyes widened. "What are you talking about?"

"I don't know. I wish I did. Blue got the call when we were extracting from the Blackhawk. Our command just ordered us to exfil immediately and to…" he let out a ragged breath. "…to cease all hostilities."

"The fuck's that supposed to mean?" Sam demanded. "Why?"

Red's face flashed with anger, and Sam wasn't sure whether it was directed at him or just at the circumstances. "It means they don't want us fighting with you anymore! Something spooked them. But those are my orders."

"Well, fuck your orders!"

Red brushed Sam off with a shake of the head. "That's not how it works."

"Heads up!" A voice from above.

Sam jerked. Looked up. Blue was hanging in the broken window over their heads, then jumped and landed with a great clatter of gear and a whoosh of breath. Came up hopping on one leg and swearing.

"Wait!" Sam held up his hands. "We don't even have comms with Abe now! You can't just—"

Blue slid in beside Red and thrust a radio at Sam. "That's from Abe. There's nothing we can do about this." He turned to Red, like Sam wasn't even there. "Boss, we gotta roll. They were not happy, and they were not kidding. Some serious shit just descended from on high and it's rolling downhill right for us."

"This can't be happening," Sam seethed. "You can't just leave us right now!"

Red whirled on him. "Not up for debate, Sarge. I got people in charge of me, just like you got people in charge of you."

"Fuck you," Sam spat, and immediately turned away. His face was burning, his chest all hot and cold at once. All of the sudden everything was landing right on his concussion-stunted brain and it was only his anger that kept him from wilting under the weight of it. Sam began batting the civilian troops on the chest as he passed them, stalking back to the corner. "Stack up! Get ready to move!"

It was only once he reached the corner, standing over Jones and beside Marie, that he glanced over his shoulder. Wasn't sure what he expected, but still managed to feel disappointed when he saw nothing but the armored backs of the Canadians. They'd wasted no time moving out. Were already halfway down the hotel, heading north towards some unknown extraction point.

"Ryder to Abe," Sam said over the radio. "We're ready to assault the front."

Abe's voice was like a knife. "Bastards already leave?"

"They're gone," Sam confirmed, grinding his teeth together. How the hell was he going to manage this? He'd already ruined the assault on the weapons depot because of his inexperience. Now he was supposed to help get Abe out of a tight spot? How many different pitfalls lay ahead of him, and how many of them was he going to fall into before he got everyone killed?

And yet, he found himself saying into the radio, "I'm ready to move on your mark."

"We copy. You move, and we'll breach when we hear the gunfire."

"Roger that. We're moving." Sam smashed the radio into an empty magazine pouch. Gave Jones a nudge with his foot. "Come on, Jonesy. Let's get this shit done."

***

"I don't understand," Lee said, hollowed out on the inside and trying to tie the disassembling pieces of his brain back together.

Marlin and Worley, standing there in front of him, staring at him. Worley was backed off a pace—he didn't really know Lee. But Marlin knew him. Marlin had made a decision in Butler to back Lee. To try to help them in their fight against Briggs. Now he couldn't even meet Lee's gaze.

That didn't stop his mouth from moving, though. Hateful words coming out as soft as the brush of moth wings, but stinging something deep inside Lee. "You let it get out of hand."

"I *let* it get out of hand?" Lee breathed. "I *let* it? It's a fucking warzone! It's always out of hand!"

Marlin only shook his head, his face pained to the point of sickness. "Things are changing faster than I can even keep up with them, Lee." His eyes sharpened and he finally managed to fix them on Lee. "But you need to listen to me." He leaned in. "We've been living in this bubble, you and I, for the last three years. The private little bubble of a universe where there's no one watching, and it's always up to us." He stabbed a finger towards the ground. "But this? This assault on Greeley? People are watching. People are paying attention. And the things that happen here are going to have repercussions like you haven't seen since everything went to shit. Do you understand what I'm saying?"

"It was a mistake," Lee husked out. "I take responsibility. I told Brinly to get to the weapons depot and not let anything stop him. He was only following my orders."

Marlin's face looked pale. Skin washed out. "Lee, he massacred an entire neighborhood block."

"They were caught in the crossfire," Lee trembled. "These things happen in war."

"You can't just keep saying that."

"Hasn't that always been the case?"

"It's been the case for a long time." Marlin shook his head. "But it's not anymore."

"What about the team with Sam?" Lee felt hope and terrible certainty pulling in opposite directions, tearing at his chest. God, but his pulse nearly hurt it was slamming so hard. A thought he'd never had before in his life—*am I having a fucking heart attack?*

"They've been ordered back. I'm sorry, Lee. This is out of my hands. If it were up to me…" he trailed off, then made an angry face, swore under his breath, and looked away.

Lee found himself breathing heavily. Sweating in a way that didn't feel natural. Tried to control his respiration, but just trying to slow it made his insides feel like they were dying. It was a completely new sensation. Nightmarish. "You're fucking killing me," Lee hissed. "You're killing the whole fucking thing."

Worley stepped forward, frowning. "We're not killing shit. Your boys are killing civilians—and not just a few bits of collateral that can be explained away. Marlin's trying to be gentle, but I'll tell you the truth, Major Harden. War crimes. Crimes against humanity. Have you even taken a moment to think about that? To consider what's going to be written in the history books when you've finished your brawl with Briggs?"

Lee fixed him with his good eye. Old feelings of rage swelled in him so that his fingers clenched and he wanted to grab the man and plunge his thumbs through his eyes. But those old feelings were stale now. They felt musty and rotten. They crinkled and wilted, like paper tigers in a downpour.

"I'm just trying to survive the next twenty-four hours," Lee said, his voice surprising him in its earnestness. "I can't think about anything beyond that right now."

Worley looked saddened. Disgusted, even. "Well, you should start considering it. This isn't like everything else, major. You're not operating in the dark anymore. There may not be much of a world, but what's left of it is watching you right now. This won't go away. This won't get swept under the rug. You need to stop thinking like the world has ended, and you need to realize that it's coming back. When the smoke clears, people will have things to say about what happened here."

"And what about Butler?" Lee asked, looking to Marlin. "You saw what they did. You saw the massacre they caused when they invaded. Is anyone going to tell the world about that shit?"

"I don't know, Lee," Marlin admitted. "But I can tell you that eye-for-an-eye isn't a defense anyone's going to appreciate."

Defense. The way he said it, Lee suddenly saw himself standing in front of a tribunal. A courtroom. Having to explain himself. Having to go through every dirty deed, having every hard, life-altering decision that he'd made in the darkness of utter abandonment brought to light and parsed through and picked at. Judgements rendered in the ivory-white light of re-established order, which always seems to forget the chaos in which the accused were forced to operate.

Would it really come to that? It'd been so long since Lee had considered any power higher than himself and his own sense of justice, that it didn't seem like it could be real. This all seemed so sudden that it felt like a blow to the back of his skull. A sudden, crashing, destructive alteration of how he saw any of this panning out.

And yet, he sensed the truth in it. Did he really think that he was operating in a vacuum? He'd known that wasn't the case the second he'd learned about the envoys from the UK and Canada. Why hadn't he seen this coming then? Other governments hadn't fallen as hard, and now they'd taken an interest in what was happening here. In Lee's white-hot desire to crush the man that had tried to destroy everything he'd built, he'd only seen them as resources that he might use to accomplish his mission.

But they weren't just resources, and he should have known that from the start. Dammit, but politics had always been beyond him. How many times had he tried to tell Angela that? And how many times had Angela tried to rein him in?

These outside governments weren't resources. They were eyes. They were judgements, waiting to be handed down. They were oversight. They were the promise of a cold accountability that would be leveled on him as mercilessly as he'd dealt with his enemies.

Why had he been so blind to that?

Maybe because he'd never really believed that the world could go back to the way that it'd been. The destruction of it had seemed so absolute, for so long, how could there be such a thing as governments, and politicians, and bureaucrats, ever again? How could there ever again be a governing body, with all their uneducated opinions? How could they judge him for the things he had to do to bring them back to life?

But they could. And they would.

Apparently, they already were.

Somehow, they'd pulled themselves out of the shit heap of the world. Slogged themselves out of the grave. And wasted no time looking imperiously down at those with blood still on their hands and dirt under their fingernails.

Was this really happening?

"Lee," Marlin said, his voice plaintive as it broke into the tumult of Lee's thoughts.

Lee realized he'd been staring off into the dusty distance. Dragged his eye back to Marlin.

"Do you understand what we're trying to tell you?"

Did he understand?

Lee found his head moving up and down. "I understand." His voice was a gravel grinder in his ears. "I understand…" He filled his lungs with air again. Pinned his shoulders back. Narrowed his gaze at Marlin, and then at Worley. "That nothing has changed. Nothing ever does. You have your masters, but mine are dead and gone. Your masters are calling you back, with their noses in the air about how I've done my business, but before you get too self-righteous about it all…" And here, he fixed Worley with every ounce of disdain he had in him. "Just remember that your masters could have ended this if they wanted to. But they didn't. They had every fucking chance in the world to help. But they *didn't*. They left us to haggle it out amongst ourselves. Eyes of the fucking world, you tell me? Fuck you, and fuck the eyes of the world. If they cared so much, where was the help? Where were the troops when we were fighting for our lives? Where was the food when we were starving? Where was the medicine when our sick were dying and we had to bury them in mass graves? Where were your holy, righteous masters then?" He found himself taking a step towards Worley, his hand coming up, pointing a finger at his chest. "They weren't here. But I was. I've been here the whole time. Fighting, and burying. Fighting, and burying. Over and over. Never with a fucking hint of help from them. So, if you want to stand there and try to level charges on me, then level away, you piece of shit. It doesn't matter one fucking bit. Because you weren't here. Your masters weren't here. They left it up to me. And I'm going to finish it, because that's what I set out to do. And if the time comes that I have to answer for what I've done?" And he leaned in even closer, his voice deadly and low, staring right into Worley's eyes from a distance so close he could smell the man's sweat and breath. "Then you can come and get me yourself. I'll be waiting."

Worley chuffed, despite the fact that he'd shrunken back. Bravado to cover his fear. "You'll be dead by then."

Lee smiled at him, a haggard, grief-ridden smile. "So many people have tried, Worley. So many people have failed. Who's going to be the one to put a bullet in my head? Is it going to be you?" He shuffled even closer. "If I'm such a monster, if I disgust you so much, maybe you should. Is that what your conscience is telling you to do? Rid the world of me?"

Lee was surprised to find his eye stinging. It felt red and raw. His vision swam. And he realized that he wouldn't mind. Wouldn't mind at all if Worley put one through his head.

Marlin stepped forward and took his comrade by the arm. "Worley."

"How strong are your convictions, Worley?" Lee whispered at him. "Only strong enough for words? Or are they strong enough to actually do something about it?"

Marlin put a hand on Lee's chest, and pushed him back at the same time that he pulled Worley away. Not harsh. Not a shove. Just a steady separation. "Worley, check yourself. Lee..." Marlin met his gaze. So sad and tired. Like all the life had just been wrung out of him. "Don't give them the rope to hang you with."

Lee's death's-head grin widened, even as he felt his throat constrict. "I carry miles of it wherever I go."

The two Canadians backed away from Lee. Two steps. Three. And then they turned their backs on him. Strode towards the little sedan they'd arrived in, and would leave in. Leave for where? Away. Distance. As much as they could make between themselves and the train wreck that was Lee. A train wreck in slow motion. It'd been wrecking itself for three damn years.

As he watched them leave, his eyes strayed to the southern horizon, and there, amid the boiling mirage and clouds of dust, the sun twinkled across dozens of windshields, all in a line, all rushing towards him.

"Hurst," Lee said, not taking his eyes from the horizon. Not looking away from his coming doom. Facing it head on, as he always, stubbornly, rashly, *insanely* insisted on doing.

"Sir?" the specialist said from where he stood, a discrete distance away. Lee could just make out the shape of him out of the corner of his eye. Could only imagine the expression on the man's face. Maybe that's why he didn't want to look.

"Send the assault. Now. And tell our defenders we've got company."

SEVENTEEN

TOUGH LOVE

A NEEDLE IN A HAYSTACK. That's what Abby was.

If the needle was moving, and the haystack was trying to kill you.

They were in the thick of it now, Angela and Nia. The press of gunfire against her ears, surrounding her, battering her senses. Everything was movement, and shifting shapes, and buzzing, unseen things that whisked through the air, keening to take a life. Smoke and fire and destruction. How had it turned into this? How could so few people cause so much damage in so little time?

Angela hit cover, Nia right behind her. Another building. Another wall. Another brief respite of relative safety. Always relative, because nothing was truly safe. A round could find you anywhere. All it would take would be a ricochet, or some asshat behind them that didn't ID their target properly, or maybe some threat that you didn't see because of your tunnel vision in all the swirling chaos.

The wall was pocked with bullet holes. A splash of blood. A body lay facedown, half on the curb, half in the gutter. Angela didn't know if it was one of theirs or one of Greeley's.

Her mouth was pasty, throat scratchy and dry. She felt the layer of dried scum on her lips and swiped at it with the back of her wrist. It didn't remove the scum, but it did wipe a bunch of sweat across her mouth. She licked at it because it was the only moisture to be had.

Angela whispered a series of curses as she put her back to the wall and tried to catch her breath. Whispering was about all she could do. Her throat was so dry it hurt to use her voice.

Footfalls to her right. She yanked around, reactions on a hair-trigger.

Four people in civilian clothes, all with rifles, trundling up to the corner of the building with her. She thought about demanding who they were with, but they didn't seem aggressive towards her or Nia—just looked like they were trying to find a spot where the bullets couldn't get them—so Angela kept her rifle ported.

The man in the lead of the little group stopped, shoulder to shoulder with Angela, craning his neck around her to try to catch a glimpse of the street beyond. "Fuckers," he mumbled. "We gotta break through this block. Any idea where the fire's coming from?"

A bullet struck the sidewalk to Angela's left. She didn't even flinch. She'd already started to get a feel for the nuance of when she was actually in danger and when she could just tuck her toes in a little tighter.

"No idea," Angela rasped out. "We just got here."

Another bullet strike. This one into the dead body on the curb. Just a dull, bloodless *thud*.

The man leaned back, shaking his head. Glanced at Angela. Did a double take. "Hey…"

Angela nodded. "Yeah."

"Are you…?"

"Yeah."

He actually smiled. A big, gormless grin. "Well, shit!"

Angela frowned at him. "Have you seen my daughter?"

The grin faltered. Fell into a frown. "Your daughter?"

"Abby. Ten years old. Curly blonde hair. Have you seen her?"

"The fuck's a kid doing out here?"

Angela shifted her weight, a little barb of anger spiking through her chest. "Have you seen her or not?"

"No," he shook his head. "No kids. Well…" he trailed off, looking guilty.

Christ. Angela felt the anger turn to sickness.

The man shuffled around. "Are you…?" He gestured around the corner.

Angela just waved him off. "After you."

He shrugged, looked back to his little fire team. "Y'all ready?"

A few desultory murmurs.

"On me. I'll post, you move."

Someone swore at him, but it lacked the heat of conviction, and they all bustled around Angela and Nia, stacking up on the corner. The man went low and peered around the corner. The back of his head sprouted a ribbon of blood and brain matter and he simply slumped in place.

One of the others yelped, then thrust their rifle around the corner, chattering away. The others just moved around and sprinted off across the street. The one on the corner held his suppressive fire for a moment until he heard the others start shooting and then he took off as well, spitting curses the whole way.

Angela stood there, staring at the dead man. His shoulder was leaning against the corner of the building. Muscles slowly relaxing into death. He slumped lower. Lower. Then toppled, face-first, with his legs folded under him, so he looked like a kneeling faithful in the midst of a prayer.

"Hey," Nia nudged Angela's shoulder. "Grab his mags."

"Right." Angela bent, hazarded a hand out around the corner, just long enough to snag the man's rifle sling, then hauled backwards. He was a heavy bastard. Dense. Whoever had been sniping at them must've been distracted with the other fire team, because a round never came for Angela.

She got him back around the corner and then she and Nia crouched over his body like vultures, divesting it of anything useful. A half-empty magazine from his rifle—Angela didn't overlook the one in the chamber; every round counted. He had a little chest rig, not armored, but with two magazines in it. Richer than most. Angela divvied this up between them. Found a crumpled, half-empty water bottle in one of the mag pouches and felt like she'd found gold.

"Thank God," Angela breathed. Offered it to Nia first, who gulped down half of what was left and gave the rest back. Angela sucked it down greedily. Enough for a decent mouthful. Enough to wet her vocal cords back into some semblance of sounding human.

And it was right there, crouched over a body, drinking a dead man's water after looting his corpse, that she heard the voice of her daughter.

There is a unique thing that every parent has, and mothers even moreso. It borders on a sixth sense. It's the simple ability to hear your child's voice amidst others. Even amidst gunfire and screams. Even when you're not sure if you actually heard something with your conscious brain, your subconscious took that piece of data and rang a bell deep inside, confident beyond all knowing that you've heard the sound of your own flesh and blood.

Angela sat very still, trying to figure out what exactly she'd just heard, mixed in with all the rest of what her ears could perceive.

Nia noticed her stillness. "What? What happened?"

Angela stood up, the empty water bottle falling from her hand. She turned to the left. Then to the right. "I heard her."

"You heard her?" Nia cinched closer. "Where?"

Angela couldn't answer. Couldn't even really say that she'd *heard* something, because she didn't know what she'd heard—couldn't make any sense of the language of it. Only that she somehow knew it had been Abby's voice.

One little lilt of it. Not even enough to determine if it was a cry, or a yell, or just a word spoken loudly to be heard over the gunfire.

"Where did it come from?" Nia pressed.

"I don't…" Shaking hands, grabbing her rifle up. Neck stretching, as though gaining another inch of height would somehow get her ears above the jetstream of all those other noises. "I don't know."

Her heart sounded just like the bullet that had struck that dead body on the curb: *Thud-thud-thud.*

She did the only thing she could think of: She screamed Abby's name, her voice scratching and breaking painfully. Hands letting go of her rifle so that they could cup around her mouth, and then she shouted it again, taking a heedless step forward.

"Easy now!" Nia hissed, grabbing her and yanking her back towards the wall.

"She's gotta be close!" Angela strained out.

"Are you sure it was her?" As though Nia was the embodied voice of Angela's very logical doubts. Really? Did you *really* hear your daughter's voice, in all of this? Beyond your own thudding heart? Beyond the ringing in your perforated eardrums? Beyond the screams of everyone else?

Or did you just WANT to hear it?

A momentary, auditory hallucination, born from her desperation?

But then she heard it again. She could've *sworn* she heard it. Elusive. A distant sound carried on a breeze. There one moment, and then gone. And what was it that she'd heard this time? A word? A single syllable. A short, sharp, bark.

"Abby!" she screamed again, her feet moving all on their own, like a dog that's caught the scent of something no one else can perceive. She barged around Nia, shaking her grip off and first marching, then running down the sidewalk along the back of that building. "Abby!"

She stopped at the opposite corner. Between her and the next building over was a dumpster that someone had pushed out into the road in a moment of inspiration. Only to discover that dumpsters won't stop the large caliber rounds aimed at them. Three bodies, all slumped against each other and the dumpster, looking like they'd all just decided to take a nap.

She listened again. So much noise. So much superfluous data coming at her. Only one data point mattered.

Peripherally, the sound of Nia—her footsteps, her breathing, just behind Angela.

"Don't run out there," Nia warned.

"Ssh!" Angela hissed.

It came again, so much clearer this time that she knew she must've drawn closer.

"Move!" the little voice cried out. Sounded like a child playing at war. Imitating the things they'd seen from others. And it lanced right into Angela's chest, seized her lungs up—an instant wave of grief, tumbling over relief, tumbling over abject terror.

Move? Why was Abby yelling "move"?

"Abby!" Angela screamed again, but this time with a very different tone. Not the tone of a mother trying to find their child, but the tone of a mother screaming their child's name because they're about to do something incredibly stupid. "Abby, *don't move!*"

"Did you hear her?" Nia demanded. "Where is she?"

Angela sidled closer to the corner. Abby had to be somewhere in this block of buildings. This was where the front lines were pushing. She couldn't be any further away. Unless she'd pushed too far forward. Unless she'd got herself pinned down.

The image of it became a hot iron that seared all reason and logic from Angela. She snatched up her rifle again. Slammed against the corner, and then around it. A chatter of gunfire from down the street, but no buzzing—no rounds coming her way. She ran without thinking—thinking was gone, out of the picture, her logical brain now dead to the world, finally given up the ghost.

Then somebody *was* shooting at her. She fired back, a string of angry, barely-aimed shots at a series of muzzle flashes coming from the rubble of a smoking, half-crumbled façade. Just beyond it, a glimpse of what was hanging up the entire advance: A checkpoint—concrete barriers, sandbags, and guntrucks with their M2s chugging at targets far closer.

Angela cut across the street, angling for a passenger van that had been crunched into the side of a building, its doors still hanging open, fire flickering from under the crumpled hood.

She heard the rounds chasing her. Someone had a bead on her and they were trying to catch up, lead her just the right amount to put jacketed lead through her body—it was simultaneously petrifying and infuriating. They zipped closer and closer as she ran, right on her heels, the sounds of them getting sharper, louder as they split the air, the sonic crack of them piercing her ears more and more—

She leapt at the last minute. Knew it was going to hurt when she hit the concrete, but knew that bullets would hurt more. She hit the curb, trying to break her fall with her rifle still in her hands. The skin ripped right off her knuckles. Her knees hit immediately after, scraping the fabric from her jeans and the flesh right under that.

She clambered for the cover of the engine block. A bullet struck the rear tire with a hollow *thump* and a protracted hiss. The pain was going to come—she felt it hurtling into her. A round skipped off the pavement, scattering chunks of concrete into her face, making her wince and cry out.

She got to the engine block. The panic washed over her, and immediately the pain followed. Shaking, she snapped a glance at the back of her hands. Flaps of white skin, avulsed from the bone. Blood welling and dripping freely. A smattering of spots on the concrete, and big blotches where her torn up knees had blotted themselves as she'd crawled, and...

"Nia!" Angela shrieked when her eyes found the woman.

Still alive, in the middle of the street. Crawling desperately for the van, but sluggish. Her back half not seeming to work—legs just flopping around uselessly while her arms and hands clawed at the concrete, her face all contorted, lips bloodless, teeth bared, eyes wide.

Angela grabbed the sideview mirror of the van and hauled herself upright, sprinkling blood across the dusty side panel. She had to help Nia—couldn't just leave her there in the middle of the street...

"Ryan!" that little, piercing yelp.

Abby!

Angela's head jerked around, looking through the cracked windows of the van to a point about a block away, and catching a glimpse of the thing she'd most wanted to see: A little head of blonde curls.

Angela froze. Every instinct in her body wanted to run to her daughter. Her feet actually stamped at the pavement like they thought the rest of her was already heading that way.

Oh, how she'd wanted to catch sight of Abby. But oh, how it'd come at the worst possible moment.

She snapped back to Nia.

At any second, a round could find Nia and cut her out of this universe as she crawled for safety.

At any second, in all this chaos, a round could find Abby. Kill her when her mother was only a few breathless seconds of sprinting away.

Angela's body and soul knew what she was doing before her mind did. She ran for the back of the van, staring right into Nia's eyes the whole time, praying that the rounds slapping the pavement around her would keep missing…

And then she hung a left. A gut-wrenching turn. Around the back of the van. Heading for Abby, even as a weak cry behind her uttered her name with a mix of shock and grievous knowing. What kind of a person was she? How could she have done that?

But it would have taken more seconds than Angela was willing to give. Every one was precious, attached to a ticking clock with a machine gun nest behind it, and each round that slashed through the air was that much less time for her daughter.

"Angela!" The scream was piercing, melting. Turned her guts to water so that it felt she might piss herself even as she ran. It turned her head to fire so that her ears rang and her face burned and her eyes watered with the horror of it.

But she never stopped.

Blinking and gasping and choking. Thrashing through hellfire and ballistics. The world murky and watery and gray. Shimmering blackness in her vision, carving out the edges of the universe so that all that remained was what lay dead ahead of her: Abby, with a rifle in her hands, firing at the checkpoint, and then screaming someone's name and turning her head, her curls whipping at her face, to look at a man behind the trunk of a bullet-riddled car, sitting in a pool of his own blood.

She wanted to scream for her daughter but feared a nightmare even more—an image of Abby looking back at her, losing focus, not paying attention, and one of those big .50 caliber rounds that were filling the air just crushing her tiny skull to nothing.

So Angela didn't scream at her. She prayed as she ran. Not a prayer of words, but a desperate yearning for Abby to be smart, calculating, and cold-hearted, for just a few seconds more.

Abby scrambled to her feet when Angela was only a handful of strides off, fired a smattering of rounds down the street, and did the unthinkable: She sprinted out of cover, out into the storm of lead, every footfall like a hammer in Angela's gut.

Angela could do nothing but change course. Still would not scream her daughter's name for fear that Abby would falter. Fear, fear, fear, everything was fear—driving, biting, grasping fear.

Abby half-slid, half-tumbled into the cover, squirming through the puddle of the man's blood. And only then did she stiffen, her head coming up, hearing Angela's footsteps as she charged the last few strides. She turned and faced her mother, a look of shock blanking out her face.

Angela launched herself at Abby, more like a linebacker than a loving mother, and flattened her daughter down with no thought for tenderness—this was a different type of love. This was the love that would commit any act, no matter how harsh, to preserve the object of it.

Abby let out a squeal of surprise as Angela mashed her body to the ground, heedless of her daughter's face squelching through blood, as Angela pulled and shoved and pushed and yanked her daughter's body until it was curled up in a ball, and Angela was around her, her own body between her daughter and the incoming rounds.

She was squeezing her daughter and shaking her at the same time, weeping and growling, cursing and demanding reasons even as her own blood-covered hands grappled and stroked and petted Abby's blood-covered face, all of it mixing together into a terrible, slurried mask.

Abby gaped at her. The left side of her face painted red, the right side bright and pale and flushed. "Mom?"

Angela didn't know what she said. Something harsh. Something loving. Something vindictive. Something tender. It all came out at once and made no sense at all, and then she shut herself up by mushing Abby's face into her chest, into her torso, like she could meld the girl back into her where she would be safest.

Abby fought against her. Pushed and pried and yowled like a cat in a bag until she'd got her head free. Anger and panic flashed in her eyes—eyes that ripped back and forth from Angela to the wounded man. She was saying that name again, dull through Angela's befuddled senses.

"Ryan!" Abby was reaching for the man, wrestling her hands free of her mother's grip. "Mom, stop it! I have to help him!"

Angela raised her head and found herself staring right into the face of a man with not much time left. They were close enough that they could have kissed. His mouth was hanging open, his teeth stained red. His eyes were half-empty. Angela tore her gaze from his long enough to take in no less than half a dozen wounds, all across the man's torso. Everything from his chest to his waist was soaked black with blood.

Angela looked him right in the eyes and said, "He's not gonna make it."

Abby's protests turned to nonsensical wails, high-pitched, keening like bullets.

The man's mouth quirked at the corners, his red teeth flashing in something like a smile. "You bitch," he husked, just a breath on the wind.

"Abby!" Angela fought to regain control of her daughter's body as it writhed away from her. Small, but God, she had a wiry strength to her that Angela had never felt before. "Abby! Would you fucking look at me?"

She didn't. She was caught up in her own world of whirling emotions. But wiry strength or no, Angela was a grown woman, and she was only a ten-year-old girl. So, Angela snatched up a big bunch of sweaty, bloody shirt, feeling the threads snap as she yanked Abby's face around. Abby came up with a hand of her own, her thin fingers clawing mindlessly at her mother's face—reminded Angela, just for a flash, of when Abby had been a baby and her little hands would grab at her mother's nose and cheeks, those tiny, wicked-sharp infant fingernails leaving marks—

Angela hauled off and slapped Abby clear across the face. And she didn't give her a chance to recover after that. Grabbed her head in both bloody hands and squeezed it so she couldn't get away, and pulled it close, and fixed her with a stare of death that even the most emotion-addled pre-teen would falter at. "Abigail Houston! You're going to get out of here on your own feet, or I'm going to knock you the fuck out and carry you, do you understand?"

At that, all Abby could manage was a dazed, wide-mouthed nod.

Angela swallowed her up into a hug, burying her face into her hair, smelling it, just barely, just beneath the stink of sweat and gunsmoke. Kissed it. "I love you."

"I know, Mommy."

Pushed her back. Flattening her emotions with a bulldozer of willpower. Eyes sharpening as she blinked the tears out of them. Flashing left, then right. Nudging Abby off of her so she could get a grip on the rifle again. Abby fumbled about and brought up her own rifle that she'd dropped when she'd scrambled in behind the car. Angela stared at it for a half-second, but gave it no more of her time. This was their world.

"Okay," Angela breathed, working to get her feet under her again. All the movement behind the car hadn't gone unnoticed—someone was taking shots at them, the bullets striking the front of the car with harsh, metallic reports, but they didn't seem to have a good angle on them. "We're going to run, back to where you were hiding, okay?"

"Okay."

"We're going to run together. You're going to stay on my left side—do you understand? My *left* side!"

"Okay."

"Stay close to me. And don't stop until we get to cover."

"Okay."

Angela had negotiated herself into a deep squat. Her legs burned and cramped. She didn't know if she had the strength to run fast. But as long as she kept her body between Abby and the bullets…

"Alright. We're gonna do this. You ready?"

"Yes." Her voice was so small.

"Hey," a voice wheezed behind them.

Angela cranked her neck over to look at the dying man. A magazine wavered in the air, wilting out of weak, red fingers.

Ryan gave the barest nod. "Y'all gonna need it."

Angela snatched the magazine from his grip, and his hand flopped to the ground, like holding the magazine was all the strength he had left in him.

Abby let out a whimper and a groan that might've been the man's name.

"Come on," Angela urged. "On three."

She counted it down, and those seconds flashed by too quick for comfort, and then they were hauling up—so slow on her unwieldy legs, pain lancing through the muscles, aching in the abraded knees as they bent and contracted. It'd seemed such a short distance when she'd looked at it from cover, so why was it taking so long to get there?

They crashed into cover, a jumble of limbs, Angela's skinless knuckles spiking with pain as they struck the brick wall of the alcove. Rounds smashed the corner of the brick to shards that peppered the back of Angela's neck and stung against her ears as she huddled protectively over Abby.

"Are you okay?" she gasped.

"Yes—what are you doing here?" Abby said, squirming away from Angela and putting her back against the wall of the alcove.

Love and fury, like a hurricane in her brain. "What am *I* doing here?" she howled. "What are *you* doing here?! You ran away! For what? Why did you do this? People died! Nia…" she choked herself off from saying that Nia had died. Wrenched her gaze around to look back down the street towards the van, not wanting to see, but needing to.

There wasn't much to see. The van sat there, bullet holes like a madman's version of a connect-the-dots. Peering beyond the undercarriage, Angela could only see part of a body and an arm. Brown skin and blood. Not moving.

"Ah!" Angela gagged on the reality of it. Tried to tell herself that she'd done what she had to do to save her daughter, but it wasn't enough to quell the horrible roiling inside of her, the certainty that she'd just crossed over a plane of being that she could never return from. She'd made a choice she could never unmake. She'd traded that woman's life for Abby's, and she'd done it without thinking.

She sobbed and stuttered, tears pouring as she looked back at her daughter with a deep, unwilling resentment. "Why did you do this?" She had the urge to slap her daughter again, or hold her tight, she couldn't decide which. "Why the fuck did you do this?" she screamed in Abby's face.

Abby stared up at her, the corners of her eyes leaking wet, streaking down through the blood all over her face, but her expression was so level and neutral now that she seemed an entirely different child from only moments before when she'd been scrambling to get to Ryan.

And then all at once, Abby's face contorted so hard that Angela jerked forward to grab her, fearing that she'd somehow been shot.

"I'm sorry!" Abby sobbed. "Nothing happened like I thought! It's not what I wanted! This isn't what I wanted!"

Sympathy tried to rise in her, but the image of Nia's dead body and those eyes she'd stricken Angela with when she'd chosen to abandon the woman were too fresh, too hurtful for her to feel sympathy for Abby.

"What did you want?" Angela screamed again. "What did you think was going to happen?"

Abby moved before Angela could react. Darted away from Angela. Oh, God, she was just running, straight down the street towards the van, heedless of the bullets, just trying to get away, trying to be free of the crushing judgement Angela had just leveled on her.

Angela tore after her, yelling her name but getting no response, only cognizant of the need to get her body in the path of the bullets—

Abby was almost to the van when she jerked. Angela watched the little puff of flesh and blood and dust from Abby's filthy shirt. Right there—right at the center of her lower back. Abby's body did a strange thing: her little chest bucked out, arms flying wide as though she were about to take a leap, but her legs just crumpled under her.

And then there was nothing. Everything went white and gray for Angela. Her brain couldn't manage it all. Completely overwhelmed, and the only thing still operating was the animal. She was vaguely aware of her own voice in her throat. No words, just insane noises. Hands touched her daughter's flesh. Danger all around. The weight of Abby's body. Guttering, whimpering sounds. Pain like a distant memory in limbs knocked insensate by the overload in her brain.

Flashes of clarity came only with the cognition of threats. Bullets striking, bullets whining. Everything chasing her, and her just running with her daughter's body clutched to her chest. Running and running, and not feeling any of it, like she was simply floating along the streets like a disembodied spirit.

The danger drove her on, endless, implacable, all-consuming.

The next time her mind came back to her, she was on all fours, tears and snot streaming off her face as she looked down at her daughter's body, horrified by the blood pouring out of it. Couldn't even make sense of the wound. Found herself just staring at all that red burbling out of Abby's lower abdomen.

"Mommy!" Abby squeaked out, shattering the gray that had swallowed Angela's brain.

Angela brought both of her hands together, pressing them down against the wound. Abby moaned but couldn't move away. Angela felt the pulse of her blood in her palms. Felt suddenly paralyzed, as though she couldn't possibly move from that position, she was now locked in, unwilling to release the pressure for fear that it would all drain out of Abby and leave her a bloodless husk. She wanted to move, wanted to carry her daughter out of there, but couldn't move her and keep pressure at the same time.

She found herself screaming for help. But no one came.

Abby was staring at her as though confused. "What's happening?"

What's happening?

Angela didn't even know where they were. The buildings all around them seemed made of the same thing, and it seemed she'd never seen them before in her life. How had she even got to where she was? How long had she been running?

Jace. The van. The extract.

How to get there? She was locked in a maze. No concept of which direction to even go in.

I have to move her. She knew it. Just couldn't figure out how to do it. And even if she could, where would she go? How would she get out of this nightmare? How would she get out of the hell she'd put herself into?

She needed to think, she knew that. But the smallest bits of thought seemed ephemeral and hard to grasp. Simple things became monumental. Every problem a mysterious riddle with an answer that floated out there in the darkness of her mind but wouldn't come closer for her to grasp.

No! You need to THINK! Your daughter's life depends on you THINKING!

Help. They needed to find help. Where? Anywhere. Anyone that could help, be it a passing squad of Marines, or if she had to carry Abby all the way back to the airfield. But she had to get help.

Couldn't leave Abby. Had to figure out a way to move her.

Then where would they go?

Angela managed to rip her eyes from her daughter—even doing that felt like a betrayal, as though her focus could keep death at bay. She needed to figure out where she was, or at least what direction to go in.

South. South was safety.

So she found the sun. Blaring down at her from the middle of the sky. Shadows short, but stretching in one direction—north. Which meant she needed to head into the sun. The sun was south.

Back to Abby.

How to move her and keep pressure at the same time?

"Okay, okay, okay," Angela whimpered to herself. Then, gathering the reserves of herself, every bit of herself that was left, she spoke to her daughter in the calmest voice she could manage. "I have to move you. I have to pick you up." An idea occurred to her, and she had no way to know if it was a good idea or not. Only that she had it, and having it was better than not having it. "I'm going to put you over my shoulder. It's going to hurt you, but it'll keep pressure on the wound."

It would, wouldn't it?

Abby was mewling out her breaths, quick and shallow.

"Up we go," Angela lilted, as though this was some day in the park and Abby was about to ride on her mother's shoulders for the fun of it. She grabbed Abby's arm and pulled her into a sitting position. Smashed her shoulder tight against Abby's wound as she hauled her up onto her shoulders. Abby was so small, and yet Angela's core and her back and her legs trembled with the effort, sapped of strength by panic and lactic acid.

Abby never cried out from pain, but just groaned. Kept on groaning.

Angela faced the sun, and began moving, as fast as her legs would carry her.

EIGHTEEN

THE ROAD TO NOWHERE

The last little redoubt of Cornerstone inside FOB Hampton were holed up behind the stone-veneered welcome desk in the lobby. There were three of them, trying to surrender now.

By the time it got to that point, Sam's little detachment had been radioed to cease fire so that Abe's team could storm the ground floor from the stairwells at both ends of the hotel. Sam moved his people up to either side of the lobby doors. Heard the yelling from inside, the pleas for mercy, and the commands to get down.

Sam keyed his comms, just on the other side of the shattered glass that now glittered across the pavement. "We're coming in through the main entrance! Check fire!"

There wasn't much fire at that point in time. The gunshots had become sporadic—muted by the walls of the place as Menendez and his team cleared the conference rooms that served as command and control for Greeley's operations.

Over the radio, someone gave a curt "You're clear," in a voice Sam didn't recognize, and he moved through the shattered entrance, boots crunching and slipping on the glass.

Bodies were everywhere. Shocking not in their gore, but in their mundanity. The way Abe's men picked their way carelessly between arms and legs and broken parts, boots squeaking across the blood-wet tiles.

Sam had no attention to spare to dead flesh anymore. His eyes went to the living, because they were the ones that killed. The last three holdouts were being dragged by their collars and thrown or booted down in the center of all their dead friends. Sam was more disturbed by their mewling than by their imminent destruction. Hard operatives rendered into hapless, grunting, whimpering golems. It seemed wrong on a level beyond morality.

"Don't kill them!" A familiar voice barked. Abe, storming through the wreckage, his rifle unslung and held in one hand as he marched through the wreckage like a storm, his eyes like thunderbolts stabbing at the three men.

Over the comms, Sam heard the reports trickling in as the distant gunfire from the conference rooms tapered out to nothing. Every report was an added weight, pressing down on Sam's guts. No sign of Outlaw. Briggs was nowhere in the building.

Sam had no orders for his people, and it seemed neither did Abe. He thought, perhaps, he should be securing the outside perimeter in case of a counter-attack. But he found himself morbidly transfixed by the three living Cornerstone operatives, fascinated in a gross way by how thin a thread their lives were hanging by, and knowing that it was about to be slit by the razor of Abe's wrath. And he couldn't look away.

Abe stood over them, his rifle still hanging in his right hand. He scanned the three of them as his men backed off, keeping their rifles trained, in case the prisoners got froggy. But by the looks of them, Sam reckoned any desire to jump had fled them. Kind of a shame, if you think about it.

Because he had to believe they knew what was next. They were only lying to themselves.

Tiny voices in Sam's head cried out for clemency. Urged him to say something, to be a good man and stand up for what he knew was right. But what did that even mean anymore? Sam was just so tired. Right and wrong? Those were concepts for other times, too slippery to hold onto when the gunblasts were still echoing in your head, and the trail of dead friends you've left in your wake was still fresh enough to smell their stress-sweat and the copper tang of their blood.

Abe fixated on the first one. The one furthest from Sam in the line of three. "Where's Briggs?" His voice was vacant. Inhuman. Unfeeling. It leveled the question like a hammer dropping on an anvil, pounding malleable steel flat.

"I don't know!" the man grated back. So odd to see a Cornerstone operative like this. That black polo, that thick plate carrier, the helmeted head. All geared up for war, but sitting on his knees, beaten. Defeated.

Abe only raised one eyebrow. "Care to reconsider?"

"I don't fucking know!" the man spat, trying, in his last moments, for a shred of dignity by way of defiance.

Maybe he got it. Maybe he felt righteously defiant just before Abe leveled his rifle into the man's face and sent a bullet through it.

Sam didn't much care either way. But he did flinch at the report. And again at the meaty thud of the body as it fell.

Abe took a single step sideways. Facing the next man in line. "Where's Briggs?"

This one apparently didn't care to try for dignity. He wept openly, great ropes of snot hanging from his nose, so that when he opened his mouth they stretched and made him look like some horrid swamp monster.

"Please," the syllable puffed out the strand of snot and broke it so it flapped against his chin.

"Please, what?" Abe said, frowning as though the word made no sense to him.

"Please, don't kill me."

Abe made a face like the man had said something disgusting. "Just tell me where he is."

The man sobbed. And it became clear to Sam that he was sobbing because he knew he didn't have an answer that would save his life.

"I don't know," the man whispered, and then, desperate for life, he dragged his fellow man down with him. "He might know! He's the captain!"

"You fuck!" the last man in line hissed.

Abe shot the second man. Moved to the third and final one. "So, you know where Briggs went? That's hopeful. Tell me."

"Not telling you shit."

"But I might kill you if you don't. Like I did to your buddies."

"Fuck you."

Abe speared the muzzle of his rifle into the man's face. A sharp crack of metal breaking bone. The man made a sound almost like he was offended by it. Recoiled in pain, then hunched over himself, blood already pouring out of his broken nose.

"Where is Briggs?" Abe said again, only now with some humanity, but not the right kind. Not the kind that anyone wants to hear. The bad side of humanity. The raging, dangerous side.

The last man gathered a big mouthful of blood, and Abe stepped back, knowing what was coming. The man hocked the wad of blood and phlegm, but it didn't go far enough to reach Abe. Then he stared up at Abe with baleful eyes, their hatred for each other crackling in the air like electricity.

"Not. Telling you. *Shit*. You can just kill me and get it over with."

"Christ," Jones breathed from beside Sam.

Sam blinked, surprised that there were other people watching, surprised that he was not a ghost hovering in the air, alone. He looked to his left and saw they were all strung out in a line, like they'd followed Sam in, but had no desire to go further. Jones, then Marie, then the ones they'd saved from the helicopter. Sam saw empty faces, watching with no more concern than one might for a gory movie that had absolutely nothing to do with them. Watching, it seemed, because they could, and because there was nothing else to watch. Only one of them had a look on their face like they were anything but blank and bored by it. And that was Jones.

Sam was surprised again. Had to do a double take at Marie, who had always been the voice of reason and maturity. But she was just standing there with thin, pursed lips. Eyes narrowed at the last Cornerstone man. And she almost looked hungry. Like she might holler at Abe to ice him and be done with it.

Abe didn't though. He eyed the gob of blood that'd fallen about a foot short of his boots. Then raised his gaze to the man. "He knows. Keep him." He flashed a smile that had nothing to do with happiness. "We'll talk later."

Abe turned away as his men swooped in and clubbed the man hard across the back of his head, just under his helmet, pitching him forward, and then set to work on him like a pack of dogs, ripping his hands behind his back and securing him. As Abe turned, the smile turned into a snarl, and Sam thought that he'd never known him. They were strangers.

His eyes fell on Sam.

"Perimeter," Sam coughed out, spinning away and grabbing Jones as he did. "Set up a perimeter outside. Let's put these leftover machine guns to use."

***

The pin strikes the primer. The primer flashes into the propellant. The propellant ignites. Pressure builds, pushing the bullet out of the casing. The bullet presses its way into the bore. Lands and grooves gouging against the jacket, spinning it. Fire and smoke chasing it. And it departs the barrel, screaming towards wherever you send it.

So much happening in an instant.

Over and over, the process repeated itself inside the bucking body of the M2, and Lee clutched the handles, both thumbs mashed to the butterfly trigger, and he watched those blazing orange streaks, every five rounds, whipping out at the incoming enemy vehicles.

The wind whipped at his back. The vehicle beneath him hit a pothole and, briefly, the muzzle of the gun wavered. Then back to chugging away. Firing on the attackers, while all the rest of his hodgepodge army fled. And he fled too.

There was nothing to be done for it. They'd slammed Lee's hasty defenses with overlapping fire, in amongst the screams of mortars coming from a position Lee had no reckoning on, turning his defenders to so much wasted flesh. He hadn't even known they'd had mortars. How could he? They hadn't used them in the attack on the Butler Safe Zone.

Everything had gone to shit, and Lee sat inside the swirling storm of it and fired the big machine gun like an automaton—without any real thought or emotion behind what he was doing. Just doing it because that's what needed to be done. Because the soldier that had been in the turret before him had caught a round through the neck that had nearly decapitated him, right at the outset of the engagement. So, Lee had heaved his body out of the turret and taken his place.

He watched the final links rattle their way out of the ammo can as the beast hungrily chewed through them.

"Ammo!" he shouted below.

"We're out!" a voice came back.

Looking down between his legs, he could just make out the soldier's dead face looking back up at him with a faint expression of surprise, as though he found it somewhat mystical that his head was hanging from his neck by a thread of gristle.

"Huh," Lee grunted, and fired the last of the rounds as the MATV whipped onto the highway heading into Greeley. The last in line to retreat. Really, he should have left first. That was the *strategic* thing to do, to place his life—and therefore the mission—above all else.

Behind them, in the wake of dust rising steadily higher from their accelerating vehicle, Lee saw Griffin's army swarming across the airfield, but none pursued them. They held up at the perimeter.

Lee shoved his right hand down below and snapped his fingers. "Rifle!"

The familiar shape and heft of it met his questing fingers. He pulled it up with all the willingness of a man meeting a tiresome friend. It'd felt good to have it in his arms only a short time ago. Now it just felt like dumb metal. It's barking arguments worn out and annoying.

He settled the foregrip on the shielding around the turret and started to lower his eye to the optic, but stopped himself. The MATV was moving too much, and the enemy was over five hundred yards away now, the distance increasing with every second of thrumming tires and roaring engine.

The enemy vehicles sent a scattering of rounds at him. Most went high, arcing to his left, but he ducked anyways, and was glad he did as a few zipped the air overhead and one smacked angrily against the shielding, a vibration he felt in his bones.

He tilted his head to the right, peering through the slot in the shielding in which the M2 sat, still streaming smoke. Heat rippled the air around it so that everything that Lee saw was only a watery kaleidoscope.

He sat huddled there for another few moments, counting them off, wondering when they would be out of range, and when Griffin's army would choose to pursue them. Probably not long. Griffin just didn't want to overextend himself. Wanted to clear the airfield, just like Lee had, before he sent them in to finish the job.

How had it fallen apart so quickly?

But then, hadn't he known it was a long shot? Hadn't he awakened that day, knowing full well that their chances were slim, and that the overwhelming likelihood of how it would end was with him struck down and his people scattered to the wind?

It's not over until it's over, he tried to tell himself. But it all just sounded brash and ignorant. More shaking fists at storms. More trite bullshit about never giving up, never surrendering, die in a pile of brass, defy the universe, fight to the last round, die with your boots on, die standing instead of kneeling. Die, die, die. Such heroism! But it always ended in one way: You, dead.

Oh, but now there was a new possibility for an ending to this debacle.

Lee Harden, warmonger, war criminal—*crimes against humanity*—chained up and stripped down and trotted out as an example for the "eyes of the world" to feast on. Who were these "eyes of the world" and why had they waited until now to give a shit?

He could rail against the injustice of it. But no amount of railing ever saved a man from the hangman's noose. Or the firing squad. Or whatever else they might do with him if they got their hands on him.

He realized he was thinking of it as a probability now. Sharing a space in his mind with an image of his body shot full of holes. Both equally likely, at this point.

Where had he gone wrong? Was it his rage that had set him off course? His intemperance? Was it hubris that had animated him to throw hundreds of people into the meatgrinder for the ideal of a dead country? Was he simply a priest, pouring blood onto the cold, marble altar of a false idol of freedom that had never been and never would be?

Or maybe it had started much further back than that. Maybe the seeds of this thing had been planted in his young brain, far before he'd ever considered his own mortality, and would never have dreamed of finding himself in the position he now occupied. The stupid thought that had bloomed in that young man's mind—that the world was somehow broken; and even stupider than that—that he could somehow fix it.

Maybe he'd been hurtling towards this endpoint all his life, and never known it. Maybe he'd ignored or somehow missed every off-ramp on that lonely, nightmare road, and just kept on going, believing that at the end would be some metaphorical pot of gold. Glimmering justice. Freedom for all.

What an idealistic fuckhead.

Now there were no more off-ramps. The end of this road had finally come into view, but there was no way to turn around.

The only way out is through!

God, but he was tired of motivational epithets. They were white-washed gravestones, shining heroically, but underneath was still just worms, and bones, and rot.

He caught sight of a building streaking by. The change in the sound of the engines, now no longer dissipating off of wide-open plains, but reverberating off of the walls of the city. He stuck his head up again, and found it all eerily quiet. Old habits being what they were, he had his gun up and his cheek pressed against that polymer buttstock, and he scanned for threats and felt stale and rote as he did it.

The ball bearings of the turret rumbled mutely as he twisted it around and faced forward.

They were in Greeley now. Ahead of the MATV, leading them by a good distance, the front of the column had slowed, fearing an ambush, but it hadn't met one, and kept trundling forward.

All around them, Greeley seemed dead. Abandoned like so many other cities, though Lee knew that if he could hear beyond the engines, his ears would pick out the sounds of killing out there, somewhere. It just wasn't *here*, apparently.

"Sir?"

Lee snapped his head down, irritated. Hurst peered up at him from below. "What?"

"They've been trying to raise you on the radio."

Lee reached a hand down, about to demand the radio, but thought better of it. The wind would muddle his transmissions. He wrangled himself out of the turret, taking care to avoid stepping on the dead man at his feet. His boots slipped a bit in the blood. He had to grind them through the muck to get traction.

Deuce was standing off to the side, swaying with the motion of the vehicle, and seeming entranced by the dead body. It was odd. Deuce always seemed a tad confused when he encountered the dead. Like he understood that they weren't there anymore, but couldn't quite figure out why. Dogs didn't know how guns and bullets worked, so Lee imagined that, to Deuce, it was probably unfathomable how someone could be just fine one moment, and then thrashing and bleeding and dying the next, without anyone ever having touched them.

Hurst looked pale and sweaty and very determined not to look at the dead man. As though he'd never seen a casualty before. But he had. He'd lived through Butler, hadn't he? Why so squeamish now? Perhaps the taste of defeat had turned his stomach.

Lee frowned at him and grabbed the radio from his hands. Almost transmitted his name, and paused there with the radio to his mouth, PTT already pressed, the line open. Seemed silly to use the codenames at this point. But he did it anyways. "Marshal Actual on the line. Go ahead, last sender."

It was Abe's voice that answered back, calmer and steadier than before. Less teeming anger. "We've secured the objective." A pause, two of Abe's breaths huffing into the radio. Lee knew what the report would be just from the sound of Abe's breathing. "Outlaw is not here. We've torn this place to shreds. He's gone."

Lee swayed in the back of the MATV, sitting there in the quiet of it for a moment, waiting to feel a compounding sensation—defeats stacking up and pressing down. Maybe he did, a little bit. But his last line of thinking when he'd been up in the turret had brought him pretty low. He wasn't sure he could get much lower.

"Any idea where he's gone?" Lee transmitted, as though asking about a dog that's slipped out of the house.

"Not as of right now. I may have a lead. I'll have to…ask some questions."

It was hardly even subtext. Why even bother with it at this point? Why try to sound like anything but what they were? Savages, tearing at each other. So, Abe had a man, and meant to take him down to pieces until he squealed. What difference did it make? The mantle of "war criminal" had already been bestowed. What was one more life to add to the tally? What was one more gristly deed?

"Roger that," Lee said. "Do what you gotta do."

If only they'd snagged Briggs, there might have been a different ending. And he realized that, up until that very moment, he'd still been searching for the off-ramp from this disastrous road. Because if he'd had Briggs, he would have had a bargaining chip. He would have had a way...

Lee pressed the antenna of the radio to his lips. It vibrated slightly with Abe's voice.

"What's your location now?"

Lee stared at the sidewall of the MATV, seeing something else. Seeing a possibility. Because, you don't really need off-ramps. Off-ramps were just for people that didn't have four-wheel drive.

Lee keyed up one last time. "We're falling back from the airfield. Heading your way."

If you got the right vehicle, you can make your own roads.

"Hold what you got," Lee said, speaking slightly quicker. "Marshal out."

He shoved the radio into Hurst's hands, then spun around in the back of the MATV, his boots nearly sliding out from under him in the blood. Found what he was looking for on the floor, a thin rivulet of blood having meandered its way across the steel floor to touch it.

He bent unsteadily and grabbed the satphone, wiping the blood off on his pants and bringing it up. So many satphones floating around, he had to make sure it was the right one before he turned it on and dialed—recalling the last number.

He waited there in the hot, musty, copper-stinking command module as the line buzzed. Buzzed. Buzzed.

"Re-thinking my offer?" Griffin snapped, a tad smugly. "It might not be on the table anymore."

A small tremor went through Lee's guts. The same feeling one might have if they were to make the gamble of a lifetime. All-in, on a slim chance. But Lee was the king of slim chances at this point. He'd grown so used to them, they almost seemed normal—even if they still did quake his stomach.

"We have Briggs," Lee bluffed, with all the confidence he possessed. "So the new offer is this: Stand down and make no more hostile actions towards us, or I'll personally put a bullet through your president's head."

PART 2

I see the bad moon rising
I see trouble on the way
I see earthquakes and lightning
I see bad times today.

Don't go around tonight
Well it's bound to take your life
There's a bad moon on the rise.

—Creedence Clearwater Revival

NINETEEN

TEN DAYS IN GREELEY

"You," Sam said, nudging the bound and blindfolded man with a boot to his kneeling thigh. "Name."

The kneeling man turned his sightless face, trying to hone in on Sam's voice, though he seemed to be facing just a tad to the left. His mouth hung open, lips parched and cracked and bloody. They worked for a moment. A pasty, pale tongue darted out and touched those quivering lips for a moment, hardly wetting them at all.

"Javier," he husked, dryly.

Sam consulted the sweat-limp piece of paper in his hands. Folded and unfolded countless times over the course of the last ten days. The handwritten ink on it had bled a little bit, turning the list of names faded and fuzzy. He scanned down the list, skipping over the ones that had been crossed out—confirmed dead, or already captured.

Mostly dead.

"Javier Cordova?" Sam asked, raising his eyebrows as he felt a dim spark of excitement. Like finding the right puzzle piece for an annoyingly difficult puzzle you didn't even want to be doing. He raised his eyes to the man. "Chief Operating Officer of Cornerstone?"

The man swallowed with some effort. "Can I have some water?"

They'd found Javier—along with five others—holed up in an abandoned house in one of the neighborhoods on the west side of Greeley. The neighborhood had been the site of some intense fighting for the first few days of their occupation, and then it'd gone quiet. It'd been a tip from an anonymous civilian that had led them back into that neighborhood in the wee hours of the morning. The operative on watch had managed to engage them just before they assaulted the house on foot. He'd got about three shots off before Greenman—one of Menendez's snipers—had splashed his brains. Another tried to engage when they breached the back door of the little house. Jones, who'd been on point, had handled him. The rest had gone down in a flurry of gunfire as Sam and his team took over the house.

Javier, on the other hand, had been hiding behind a couch. Not very brave, but then again, he was the only one left alive, so maybe cowardice worked out for him.

Well. Not that it would work out for him much longer.

"I'll give you water when you confirm who you are," Sam said.

Javier's blindfolded head dipped into a bow, his mouth making all kinds of gristly expressions, cracking his lips even worse so that they bled. But, ultimately, it didn't take him long.

"Yes. That's me."

"Super," Sam said, moderately satisfied as he reached around to his cargo pocket and drew out the bottle of water he had there. He uncapped it, and put it to Javier's lips. The man's mouth puckered thirstily at the bottle and sucked it down greedily as Sam tilted it up. He let the man have half the bottle, then pulled back. Javier gasped, smacked his lips.

"More?" Sam asked, charitably.

"Yes."

He gave him more.

"Yo, Sarge!" Jones came through the kitchen and into the living room where Javier had been detained, jacking a thumb over his shoulder. "Ruby's Rebs have been spotted. Looks like they're heading our way. Must've heard the ruckus."

"Christ," Sam sighed, pulling the bottle back, empty now. "Those idiots?"

Jones smirked. "The very same."

No one knew who Ruby was, or whether it was even a man or a woman, but Ruby's Rebels—as they identified themselves through copious amounts of graffiti at the site of their little "terrorist attacks"—had been raising hell for the last week. No one was quite sure whether they were allied with Briggs and Cornerstone, or if they were just opposed to Lee and his occupation.

They'd found a few Cornerstone operatives strung up from a tree, with crude, cardboard signs around their necks, that read TRAITOR. Credit for that little show of savagery had gone unattested. Could've been Ruby's Rebels, or any number of other factions that were sprouting up like mushrooms in a wet yard. Or it might've been some of Brinly's boys who'd just had a bad night. Or it might've been some pissed off civilians—maybe theirs, maybe Greeley's. No one knew what the hell was happening in Greeley anymore. Only that it was a disaster area.

Sam pocketed the empty bottle. "Alright then. Let's load this gentleman up and get gone before shit gets spicy."

They were here for a snatch and grab—not for a damn slugfest with some militia.

As Jones hauled Javier Cordova, COO of Cornerstone, to his feet, Sam transmitted over the squad comms: "Exfilling with one live body. Fall back to your vehicles and meet up at the rendezvous."

Five minutes later, they were hauling east towards FOB Hampton. One cargo van, in which Sam and Jones sat in the back with Javier hogtied between them, Marie in the driver's seat, and one of Menendez's soldiers in the passenger seat with his rifle out the window. Two guntruck Humvees, one in front, one in back, filled with Menendez's men.

They didn't stop for anything. Not for gaggles of kids, throwing rocks and tossing up middle fingers. Not for civilians crossing the road, going about their attempts at trying to pretend that life was normal. Luckily, the denizens of Greeley had learned real quick to get out of the way when they saw a convoy coming, so no one had been run over. Not in the last five days, anyways.

So, when Sam felt the deceleration, he immediately whirled around. "What's wrong?"

Marie was leaning forward, face almost against the steering wheel. "Pack, you see that guy?"

Pack, the soldier in the passenger seat, shouldered his rifle. "Yeah, I see him."

Marie pressed the brakes harder, causing Sam to stumble as he climbed up between the two front seats. "Shit. Divert."

Sam peered through the windshield at the same time that he keyed his comms: "Lead, divert. Go left right here."

He spotted the man easy enough. They were on 20th Street, passing between a series of old commercial buildings. There were a few other civilians about, but they were just doing civilian shit—heads down, shuffling along at a pace that spoke of how much no one wanted to be on the streets any longer than necessary. This guy, on the other hand was just standing there, looming over the curb, with *that look* about him, and one hand hanging tight against his side. Wearing a jacket that was far too hot for this weather.

"Take him out," Sam ordered, his fingertips tingling with foreknowledge.

The Humvee ahead of them hung a sharp left turn on a side street, not twenty yards from the guy. Pack sighted, but Marie took the left turn right at that point, and the man saw that they were diverting. In the slim seconds as the van turned, Sam watched the guy's face turn from sullen watchfulness to rage. His mouth stretched open in a howl that they couldn't hear, and he ripped out an object from his jacket, ramming it down hard on the pavement and then coming upright again as he sprinted into the street, hauling back to throw the thing like a quarterback in a collapsing pocket.

"Mortar!" Sam yelled.

Pack fired fast. Terrible backdrop—civilians screaming now and diving for cover—but all Sam had eyes for was the man, now halfway into the street, the mortar shell in his hand pulled back as far as it could go. Pack's rounds hit him square in the chest and he toppled, halfway into his throw.

"Ah, fuck!" Pack ducked, and Sam cringed, watching the mortar shell spin into the air, half-thrown. Tail up. Nose descending.

The blast hit the side of the van, rocking it and pelting the sheet metal with debris. Jones made an alarmed whoop and the prisoner started screaming for his life.

Sam spun, looking out the tinted back windows to see the gout of dust and smoke wash over the trailing Humvee. The van accelerated with a roar, the Humvee following. Sam transmitted to them. "You guys alright back there?"

"Yeah, we're good," the response came back, a little tense, and slightly bitter. "Fucking asshole."

Jones craned his neck to see out the back window where the explosive cloud was settling, revealing a big crater in the middle of the street. "Great! Another fucking pothole!" Then he turned irritably to Javier, who was still screaming, and poked at his back with the muzzle of his rifle. "Hey! Hey! Cut that shit out! You ain't dying!"

The COO of Cornerstone settled himself with a few whimpers.

The convoy rolled on, everyone ratcheted up to ten, now downgrading, breathing, clutching rifles and steering wheels, and shaking their heads at the ridiculousness of it all. And Sam found himself wondering for the thousandth time in the last ten days, *What the fuck are we doing here?*

***

Angela dreamed of the past.

She was in the yard. The sun was shining down, golden and warm. It was their house in the countryside of North Carolina. The last time anything had been normal. And in the dream, Angela knew that it wasn't real, knew that it would be swallowed up by chaos. But Abby was there. She looked like she did now, except that she was playing like the little girl she'd been. Running and giggling. Barefoot. Blonde hair tossing about.

Angela knew that wasn't real either. Abby would never again run around. And she died inside when she saw how beautiful it was. Had been. Could never be again.

"I want to stay here." It was Abby that had said it, now standing there in front of Angela. Except that the sky had gone dark and mottled.

"I want to stay here, too," Angela said, feeling the tears streaming down her face. "But it's not real."

Abby looked down at her midsection. A tiny spot on her white shirt. Red. Growing.

"No," Angela lurched forward and put her hand on Abby's stomach, trying to apply pressure to the wound. She couldn't let that blood out. She wouldn't. But she couldn't seem to press hard enough. It just kept pouring out of Abby.

"Angela!" The voice shocked her. She hadn't heard it in so long. She looked up and saw her husband standing there in the lawn, his face aghast. "What did you do?"

Abby had somehow wound up on the ground. She didn't look as she had moments before. Her hair was stringy with sweat and unwashed grease. Her skin pale and deathly. Her eyes were closed. Angela kept pressing her hand into the bloody midsection.

"I didn't do it!" she cried. "I didn't do anything!"

Her husband's face turned to rage. "You killed our daughter!"

"No! It wasn't me!"

Gunfire. Her husband's face exploded. His body fell.

Lee stood behind him. His empty eye socket was bleeding. He seemed huge, and gnarled as he stood over her dead husband and regarded her with a blanched sort of sadness in his face. He held out a hand to her, his arm impossibly long, reaching all the way to hover right in front of Angela's face. It was his left hand. Flaps of skin hung open at the wrist. Severed tendons squirmed. The fingers curled in odd ways. Blood dripped from the fingertips.

"The dead can bury their own dead," he said.

***

Angela opened her eyes, knowing full well where she was, even though all she could see was a landscape of blue blanket that had seen better days. A dark stain stared back at her. She'd known where she was even while she'd been dreaming. Her mind might have gone back to the past, but the rest of her had stayed right here, as it had every day for the last ten days.

"Hello?" a voice called from another room. It must've been the door opening that had waked her. "Ms. Houston?"

Angela stayed there for a moment, with her head on the blanket, staring at the stain. "Yeah," she pressed out, her breath foul as it wafted back to her. That, more than anything else, made her pick her head up.

A big square of sunlight glowed on the blanket. It had to be mid-morning by now. She didn't bother to turn and look out the window. She could judge the time by the passage of that square of light.

Now, it lay on Abby's knees. Which meant it was about ten o'clock.

The sounds of footsteps. Padding through the main area of the penthouse. Then stopping at the door to the bedroom.

"How's she doing this morning?" the voice asked.

Angela looked wearily along the shape of the body under the blanket. Finally rested her gaze on Abby's face. It was just as it had appeared in the dream. Eyes closed. Skin washed out. Hair lank. Mouth open and crusted with dry gunk. Angela reached forward and used her thumb to scrape the worst of it off, wiping it on the blanket.

"No change," Angela said, her voice rough.

"Well." The voice drew closer. "No news is good news. You know?"

Angela shifted her eyes to the opposite side of the bed as the speaker came around. He was Pakistani, with dark skin, and darker eyes. A disheveled mess of black curls. Thick five o'clock shadow. Wire-rimmed glasses. A kind smile with which he faced every moment, no matter how awful, like he'd never quite learned how to be angry or sullen like the rest of them.

He set to checking Abby's vitals. Angela watched him work, dully. The constant, aching worry was like a sickness in her bones. A cancer that just kept on growing. She kept thinking, *can I really feel worse than I do right now?* But it seemed she could. And she did. Every day.

Angela picked herself up off the hard stool she'd fallen asleep on and backed up a single pace until she could collapse back onto the king-size bed. She sank into it, slumped, with her hands clasped tensely between her legs. Watching the man with the kind smile.

She sometimes wondered if he were an angel. Corny, perhaps, but there it is. It certainly explained his almost saintly longsuffering in the face of the epic disaster the city had become. And the circumstances of his arrival in Angela's life were…serendipitous, to say the least.

Marines had found her as she'd carried Abby through the hellscape of that first day. One of them had medical training, and had done what he could as they'd hauled an exhausted Angela and a half-dead Abby back across a few blocks to their MATV. Then they'd taken her to FOB Hampton, which had only recently been secured. The bodies had still littered the lobby.

No sooner had Angela arrived, wondering what the hell they were supposed to do next to save Abby, when this Pakistani man came through the shattered doors with his hands up and two soldiers from the perimeter escorting him.

"I'm a doctor," he'd announced, his ever-present smile faltering just slightly and a look of pain coming into his eyes as he saw the human wreckage all around him. "I figured one might be needed."

They hadn't treated him badly, though Abe had emerged from the bowels of FOB Hampton with someone else's blood flecking his face, and had proceeded to perform a rather rapid and harsh interrogation of the man. And after that, they'd worked him to the bone. But through all of it, the man had kept his calm, compassionate demeanor.

He introduced himself as John. He was a surgeon. He had skills, and when the shooting started, he assumed those skills would be sorely needed. Unfortunately, the hospital that he'd kept running through the end of the world was in one of the worst sections of Greeley, and he couldn't go back to it. So, he did what he could here, at FOB Hampton.

They'd set up a makeshift hospital in one of the conference rooms of the hotel that had served as Briggs's command and control. A sizeable detachment of soldiers had been sent to the hospital to secure what equipment they could before fighting and looting could destroy it all. What they'd returned with was a far cry from any civilized hospital, but it was better than what they had, which was basically nothing.

And so John had set to work, and he hadn't stopped in ten days. Angela knew he had to have slept somewhere in there, but she'd never seen him anything but bustling and smiling. Made her feel guilty at her own exhaustion.

She kept watching him as he checked the drip on Abby's IV—which wasn't a standard bag, but a retrofitted mason jar. Abby was on a hospital stretcher so that they could move her about easier, snugged in next to the big bed of the penthouse.

"Why are you doing this?" Angela asked.

John seemed surprised by the question. His thick eyebrows went up over his glasses. Then he smiled again. "Well, what else would I be doing? Sitting on my hands and letting the world burn?" He chuckled. "Of course not. I care for human beings. And human beings are hurting right now. So, I care for them. Doesn't matter who they are."

Angela's gaze narrowed. His answer should have been good enough. She should have just let him be. But she was so tangled up in her own quagmire of emotions that she just couldn't help herself.

"So, you don't care that we're destroying your city?"

John considered it for a beat, then shrugged. "Of course I do." He put his hands on his lower back and stretched, looking past Angela, out the window. "I don't care for many things that I have no control over. I didn't care for the world ending, I can tell you that. I didn't care for Briggs coming in and making this his little fiefdom. I didn't care for your people coming in and making it worse. But I've found that me not caring for something has very little effect on whether it continues to happen." Another shrug. "There's a job to be done, and I have the skills to do it. And so I will."

Angela chuffed, somehow feeling rankled by what he said. In the sickness of her own dilapidated mind, the inner peace of another person smacked of folly and denial. "How the hell did you last this long?"

John laughed at it, rather than become offended by it. "What do you mean?"

Angela shook her head. "Nevermind." She was being a bit of a bitch.

"No, please." John motioned to her. "You need to trust me if I'm going to operate on your daughter."

"You've operated on my daughter three times already. I trust you."

John just stood there, watching her.

Angela rolled her eyes. "You're too nice, John. You should've died a long time ago. So either you have some dark skeletons hiding in your closets, or you're the luckiest sonofabitch I've ever met."

John laughed again. Looked at Abby. "Ms. Houston, I am neither lucky, nor do I have dark skeletons. What I am is *useful*. And I—very selfishly—use my utility to keep myself alive." He grimaced slightly through his smile. Gave her a look over the rim of his glasses. "Does knowing that I'm a utilitarian asshole make you feel better or worse about me?"

Angela regarded him with a suspicious glare. "Well. They do say that a high percentage of surgeons are psychopaths."

He laughed yet again, and suddenly Angela felt like laughing too. She let it out, just a tired chuckle, but it still felt good.

"Ah." He bent slightly and erected the siderail of Abby's bed to keep her from jostling out when he moved the stretcher. "A psychopath I am not." A flash of sadness came over his eyes. "Sometimes I almost wish I were. Life would be so much easier if we didn't empathize. Don't you think?"

Angela shook her head, the laughter dead in her chest. "No, John. People without empathy lead miserable, bloody lives. Trust me. I know a few."

"Hm." He nodded, thoughtfully. "Well, I suppose I'll be thankful for my bleeding heart then, huh?"

Angela didn't feel any humor anymore, but she managed to give him a small smile that felt like there were weights attached to the corners of her mouth.

"Now." He laid his hands on the siderail and grew serious. "Just as with every other time, I have to tell you that this surgery has risks. Even in the best-case scenario, it would have risks. In our current circumstances…well…even moreso."

Angela didn't move. Her fingers clenching into bloodless knots.

His dark eyes narrowed just a bit. "I need you to understand that I cannot fix Abby. If all goes well, I can keep her from getting any worse. My hope for today is to get her to a point where she can begin to heal on her own. But I want you to have realistic expectations. Her spinal cord was severed—I cannot make her walk again. I'm not saying that she won't, only that it's beyond my abilities. Also…I cannot wake her up. I can, and I will, put her body back together to the best of my abilities, so that the vital functions inside of her can do what they're supposed to do. But that is as far as my skills reach. Whether or not she wakes up, and how she heals after that, will be up to her. But she's young and she's strong. If anybody can make it, Abby can."

It wasn't new information to Angela. And yet it still stabbed her in the gut.

She managed a single, shaky nod.

"I expect the surgery to last anywhere between four and six hours. That's assuming all goes according to plan. And you know what they say about plans." He sighed, giving Angela a soft, apologetic look. "In the meantime, I think you should sleep."

"I just slept."

He shook his head. "No, I mean *real* sleep." He moved to the head of Abby's stretcher and pushed her away from the wall. "And look—you're almost there already. You're in a king-size bed in a penthouse. What better place?"

Angela nodded, mostly because she didn't want to argue with him.

She wouldn't sleep. She'd spend the next four-to-six hours staring at the ceiling, and wondering what was happening in that goddamned travesty of an operating room down there, and whether or not John would come through that door with a sad look, or a happy look. And how that would feel if he came in with a sad look. And even if he came in with a happy look, whether or not she'd ever see her daughter open her eyes again, or laugh, or even just speak a single word.

TWENTY

THE POD

SAM CROUCHED OVER JAVIER CORDOVA as the van negotiated its way around the barricades surrounding FOB Hampton. "Javier, I need you to listen to me. Are you listening?"

"Uh-huh," Javier nodded as best he could in his hogtied position.

Sam nodded to Jones, who whipped out a pair of wire cutters. "We're going to cut the restraints from your feet. When I tell you to move, I want you to move quickly. This is for your safety."

"My safety?" Javier whimpered.

Jones snipped the cord connecting his feet to his hands. "Lot of people out there would like to see you dead."

"Me?" Javier seemed shocked by the revelation. "Why me?"

Sam patted him on the back as Jones cut the zip ties around his ankles. "Maybe because they think you have information. Maybe because they think you're a traitor. Maybe because they just want to kill Cornerstone."

"So...it's your own people that you're worried about?"

Sam sighed as the van pulled around to the front of FOB Hampton and rocked to a stop. "I'm worried about everybody, Javier. Now come on. It's time to move."

The two guntrucks sidled up next to the van, blocking most of it. Menendez's soldiers poured out, rifles up, creating a perimeter around the front entrance and scanning the rooftops and streets all around them for anyone that might have *that look.*

Jones yanked the sliding door open on the passenger side as Sam hefted Javier upright.

"Scoot forward on your ass," Sam directed, helping his torso along while Jones grabbed his feet and pulled him to the edge. "Put your feet down. Good. Stand up. Okay. Now *move.*"

Marie and Pack covered their backs while Sam and Jones hustled the blindfolded figure through the front doors. There was only a narrow gap to get through, the rest of the shattered windows having been blockaded by stacks of sandbags pilfered from other defensive positions.

The soldiers on guard inside had already been notified that they were coming in with one. Their attention remained outward, giving Sam and Jones a cursory glance to confirm who they were, and then waving them through, closing up the gap behind Marie and Pack like water filling in open space.

The lobby looked very different from ten days ago. The bodies were gone—immolated in a big, hasty pile with diesel as accelerant. The blood had been wiped up, though a few streaks and spots remained if you took the time to look. Now the tile floors were covered in a mix of bedding, crates and cans of ammunition, and various foodstuffs that they'd plundered from points unknown. Weapons—both from the depot and from enemy bodies—crowded the area behind the bullet-riddled welcome desk, and had become so numerous that Sam could spot the tops of entire mountains of them that had started out as neatly stacked teepees, and now were just tossed on with all the others. Good problem to have, though.

A few soldiers not on duty were lazing in their "racks," which is what they called it, but it was really just flattened cardboard boxes and blankets. Like they were a bunch of hobos. They watched the blindfolded man pass by with minimal interest and went back to doing whatever they were doing—one man flipping laconically through a titty mag, another two playing a card game on the bit of floor between their bedding.

A pathway was religiously maintained through all the junk, leading straight through the center of the lobby and back to the conference rooms. Sam hung a left down the hall, relaxing now that he was inside the building.

He passed by the conference room that had been turned to a makeshift hospital. Soldiers and civilians—literally anyone that had any sort of medical training, and even a few that didn't, but could follow simple instructions—bustled about what looked more like a homeless shelter than a hospital. Just a big, open space, crammed full of the dead and dying. Stinking like piss and shit and disinfectant. In the back, the plywood walls that had been constructed to give offices to the higher-ranking had been repurposed to make one large, rather rickety-looking structure that served as the operating room.

Sam wondered about Abby and whether she was under the knife right at that moment. He knew she had another surgery planned for today. Had the urge to run in and check on her. But he had other duties to fulfill.

He continued on past the hospital. The next conference room was largely as it had been found, but not much of the technology inside could be used, as their little demolition on the substation was still beyond their abilities to repair.

At the last conference room, Sam stopped. Two Marines stood guard at the doors.

"Checking one in," Sam said. "HVT. Javier Cordova."

One of the Marines raised his eyebrows. "No shit?"

"No shit."

"Aight." The Marine took a radio from his chest rig and keyed up. "Sergeant Ryder here with one HVT, Javier Cordova."

A brief pause, followed by Abe's voice: "Send him in."

The Marine reached over and opened the door for them. Silently, a series of expressions: The Marine eyed Javier, then made a face at Sam as though to say, *poor bastard*, and Sam just shrugged and gave him a look that said, *What're you gonna do?*

Sam and his squad led Javier through the doors and into…what to call it? A name hadn't been officially declared. Unofficially, however, all the soldiers and Marines whispered names that were half-joking and half-disturbed. Names like The Chamber, or The Pit of Despair, or Darabie's House of Horrors.

If Sam were being honest with himself, being in here gave him the willies. It shouldn't have. They were all friendlies here. Sam himself was in no danger. But the knowledge of what Abe was doing, and, if you wanted to get metaphysical, the *spirit* of the place, hung like a rancid fog over everything, so that even the lights—the same ones that illuminated every other conference room—seemed dimmer, the shadows deeper, the air danker, and when you were there, everyone's expressions seemed just a bit more grim and hard.

Personally, Sam thought that The Pit of Despair was the more apt name. It even made a nice acronym: The POD. So that's what he'd come to think of it as, and that's what his team had taken to calling it.

Into the POD they marched. Here, the plywood offices had been kept. No longer offices, but cells. Places to store people that needed to be questioned. The doors and walls weren't all that secure, so the people trapped inside were kept loosely hogtied. They could still roll around and sit up if they wanted to, but they couldn't walk or run or kick the walls. Couldn't piss or shit, either. Unless they just did it in their pants. Which they did. And it smelled like it. Worse than the hospital because at least the hospital smelled of disinfectant.

Somewhere in there, one of the prisoners was crying. Deep, gasping whimpers and sobs. Sam couldn't figure out if it was the sound of pain, or the sound of despair. Was there that much of a difference? It made his spine tingle and his skin pucker and his hairs stand up.

Javier heard and smelled the environment and it turned his more or less willing gait into a slow, plodding, passive resistance so that Sam had to tug him along a few times, like a dog that doesn't want to go on a walk.

Sam found Abe, sitting on the desk of one of the little cubicles in the center of the room, Lee standing and leaning against the divider wall.

Pack held up, as though he sensed bad juju. "You need me anymore?"

Sam glanced over his shoulder at the man. Gave him a wry smirk that he didn't feel because he didn't feel any better than Pack did about it, but he had a job to do. Pack's job was done, though. "Go ahead, man. We're good."

Pack tossed a parting salute in the direction of Abe and Lee, neither of whom returned it, and then hustled back out at a somewhat overeager pace.

Sam stopped just outside the cubicle. Abe and Lee looked over the prisoner with some combination of distaste and feral hunger. Deuce was there, sitting between them and when he saw the prisoner he stood, took a step forward and let out a grumbling growl. Lee put his foot out and used it to push Deuce back a few inches with a corrective, "Leave it."

"Where you want him?" Sam asked.

Abe inhaled a great breath then craned his neck to see over the top of the cubicles. He scanned the plywood offices, on which big black numbers had been sprayed painted on the doors. "Put him in Number Four."

Sam turned and nodded to Jones and Marie. Marie moved in to take Javier's arm as Sam released it, and they guided the man off towards Number Four, speaking in surprisingly gentle tones to the man. As though everything would be okay. As though he had nothing at all to fear from them.

"Debrief?" Lee asked, scratching under his ruined eye as he watched the prisoner depart with the others.

Sam unslung his rifle and set it against the cubicle wall. Abe kicked a rolling chair towards him and nodded at it. Sam was all too happy to take a load off. Wearing armor all the time was starting to make his back and shoulders hurt. Wasn't he too young for that shit? He didn't feel young anymore. Woke up with aches and pains he'd never had before. Felt like time counted differently in Greeley. Days wore the weight of years.

"Tip was right on," Sam said as he lowered his ass to the chair and leaned back. "Six Cornerstone operatives. Five dead. Mr. Cordova was hiding. No casualties on our part." Sam unbuckled his helmet and doffed it, running a hand through the sweaty mess of his hair. "Had Ruby's Rebs move in on us while we were exfilling, but no contact." Deuce sauntered over to give Sam's crotch a solid sniffing. Sam squeezed his thighs together to get the nose out of his junk and then scratched the dog behind the ears. "Some asshat tossed a mortar at us on the way back."

Lee took some interest in that. "Where?"

"Twentieth and Thirty-Fifth," Sam answered. "We diverted. No damage. Pack took him out as he was winding up. Fucker pretty much just blew himself up. But there's a nice crater in the middle of the intersection now."

"Bastard." Lee shook his head. "Gonna have to take that route off the rotation."

Abe let out a disgruntled noise. "At this rate, we're gonna run out of streets. Gonna turn into a maze out there. Take you twenty minutes to move a mile."

It was hyperbole, but only just. Somewhere along the line, someone that didn't like them had come into a stash of mortar rounds. Now every idiot with a bone to pick was flinging them in all directions. Blowing up more civilians than anything. And there were some launch tubes out in circulation, too. The thump-whistle-boom of mortars had become a common background noise, and the attacks were inching closer and closer to FOB Hampton every day. The snipers and marksmen were being worked like rented mules, trying to keep the attackers at bay. Poor old Greenman hadn't had any downtime in a damn week—18 hours behind the gun, and six hours of sleep. If he was lucky.

Problem was, the snipers and marksmen would kill the would-be mortar-men, but by the time ground forces made it to the location, some other collection of idiots had crept in and stolen the equipment away. It was getting to be a thing.

Sam shrugged against the weight of his armor. "Other than that, everything went off as well as can be expected."

Abe grunted. "Javier Cordova, huh?"

"That's what he says."

Abe and Lee exchanged a loaded look. Lee's turned rapidly to caution and he held out a hand towards Abe. "Let's not get our hopes up."

Abe laughed. "Abandon hope, Lee. Don't worry. But still. COO is the best we're gonna get. If he doesn't know where Briggs is, I'm not sure we're gonna find out."

"We *need* to find out," Lee said, darkly. "We can't stall Griffin forever. He's been demanding proof of life since day one, and my stalling tactics have pretty much turned into not answering the phone."

Abe made a face. "That's gonna rankle him."

"He's been rankled. Scouts reported a detachment moving towards the north end of the city. Probing some of the areas we haven't been able to get to. But so far, the truce remains. He still thinks we got him by the short and curlies and he's afraid of a misstep that might get his president dead. But that won't last forever."

"Frankly, I'm surprised he hasn't sent in some sort of black ops."

Lee shook his head. "Maybe he has. Point being, I'm surprised the bluff has held this long. And if it breaks, we're fucked. We can't hold out against Griffin's forces if he starts moving in on us. We need to find that bastard."

Sam nodded in the general direction of Number Four. "Mr. Cordova doesn't seem like much of a hardcase. If he knows where Briggs is, I think he'll spill."

"Maybe," Abe said, thoughtfully. Perhaps imagining what he was about to do to the man. Sam was glad to see that Abe didn't smile. Instead, he turned a wary gaze on Lee. "But then what?"

Lee seemed to slump into the divider even more. Like just the mention of "then what?" was a weight his body could hardly carry. He seemed relieved when Marie and Jones reappeared.

"He's secured in Number Four," Marie said. Despite her gentle words to the man, she had a cold look about her when she looked at Abe. "What's it gonna be today, Abe? He seems a bit bookish. Might be able to get it out with a few hard slaps. He's awful prone to crying."

"Desk jockey, as I understand," Abe said. "Used to be head accountant for Cornerstone back in the day. Not sure why Briggs shoved him up to COO. But he ain't a warfighter by any means." He nodded to Sam. "Probably why Ryder found him hiding."

"Well." Marie shrugged. "At least break a few ribs for me."

Abe flexed his knuckles—they were swollen and red, the skin missing in several places. "Don't know how much more my hands can take."

Jones let out an unguarded snort. Glanced around as the others looked at him. Took on a defensive posture. "Because...you know..." He gave up rather quickly. "Ah, fuck it. Nevermind."

But Sam knew what he'd laughed at: Abe, complaining about his knuckles, when there was a trail of dead bodies, broken by those very same hands.

Sam slapped his thighs, signaling that he didn't want any more of this conversation, and stood. "Is there anything else you need from us?" He looked between Abe and Lee.

"Case of beer?" Lee suggested.

"A good-looking hooker?" Abe countered.

"Cocaine?"

"Some weed? Even just a little bit?"

Sam smiled and shook his head. "Really? You think I'd give that shit to you if I found it?"

Abe gestured between him and Lee. "Commanding officers, half-boot."

Sam rocked to attention and saluted crisply. "I shall search for aforementioned beer, whores, and narcotics. No stone shall remain unturned."

Abe and Lee both waved his salute off, Abe with a protracted raspberry. Strange how things had shaped up. Military etiquette had mostly gone by the wayside a long time ago—even before they got to Greeley. But there were still some moors that were upheld—ranking structure, in particular. And yet Sam, Jones, and Marie had somehow become exempt from that. There was, obviously, still an understanding that Lee and Abe's orders were to be followed, quickly and without question. But outside of direct orders, the relationship had started to sound more like Sam's old squad. Back before Billings, and Chris, and Johnson, and Frenchie, and Pickell had bit it.

Frenchie.

Sam recoiled from the memory of it. It sapped the humor out of him as fast as an icy wind cuts through a thin shirt. He dropped his salute and averted his eyes so that Abe and Lee wouldn't see the sudden change in them. Avoided looking at Jones and Marie too.

Lee seemed to sense something was up and spoke more seriously. "Y'all get some rest and chow. But stay ready for deployment." Lee pointed skyward. "It's a hot one, and we got a full moon on the rise."

Sam nodded to him. "Always ready." Then with a half-hearted smirk. "*Major*, sir."

***

Lee watched them leave, thinking about that full moon, while the old song rattled through the back of his head: *I see a bad moon rising. I see trouble on the way.*

What else is new?

He dragged his eyes back to Abe. Continued the conversation they'd been having before Sam arrived. "Brinly says there's some faction or another pushing on Zone Five."

"The Ruby idiots?"

Lee shook his head. "Not them. Someone else. As of yet unidentified."

Abe let out a low whistle. "Popping up like weeds. Everyone wants a piece."

Loyalties were out the window at this point. If there were factions of insurgents in Greeley still loyal to Briggs, it was hard to tell them from the dozen others that just wanted to feed on the destruction and set up their own little kingdoms in the power vacuum.

The power vacuum that you created.

So far there were socialists, communists, fascists, anti-fascists, religious extremists, and a whole set of groups that didn't know what the hell they were and didn't have any clearly defined ideas of what they were doing, but were still all too happy to shoot and lob mortars at them, and sometimes at each other. Greeley had turned into something of a gangland, with sections of the city carved out into "territories" and a parade of shifting alliances and new leaders with better ideas that had probably killed the old leaders with shittier ideas and took their place. Everyone saw an opportunity for their own utopian ideals to take hold, and they were making a hell of it.

And it was all because of Lee.

"Hey." Abe leaned forward, peering at Lee. "You got the sad-puppy look again. Don't go to your dark place."

"We're losing control of this." Lee scoffed at himself. "If we even had it to begin with. Our civilian troops are trickling away, falling off the radar, bit by bit. I don't know whether they're getting the fuck out of Dodge, or if they're falling in with some of the factions. Shit, they might be creating their own for all I know. How long can we keep this up?"

"Not long," Abe admitted, quietly.

"And then…" Lee crossed his arms over his chest, hunkering down, troubled to the core. "There's the ever-present question: What's next? What do we do when we find Briggs—*if* we even find him?"

"We kill him, for starters," Abe said.

"Or do we hold him as hostage so we can get out of here?"

Abe frowned. "What? Like we're bank robbers? We gonna give Griffin a list of demands? A helicopter and some pizzas? And what about everyone else? We still got hundreds of people under our command. We gonna get all of them out too?" He shook his head. "Something tells me there's not a way that pans out for us. How are you going to keep Griffin at bay? How are you going to keep him from just coming after us, wherever we go?"

Lee looked down at his boots. "Maybe not bank robbers. But we are criminals."

"Oh, this shit again?" Abe rolled his eyes. "The fucking war criminal thing?"

Lee looked at him sharply. "The label's been applied, Abe. And once it's on you, there's no way to get it off."

Abe squinted at him. "You really believe all that horseshit about the 'eyes of the world' and all?"

Did he?

Lee nodded slowly. "It's become real to me. *The world* might be an exaggeration. Right now it's Canada and the UK. But they're watching us, and that's a certainty. And they don't like what they see. That much was made clear when Marlin lit out. Who knows what kind of backing is behind *them*? What other parts of Europe are with them? What other countries have survived, or have some sort of working government? Are they allied with the Brits?" He shrugged. "We don't know, but it seems likely."

Abe went quiet and pensive for a moment. "We don't know what the future holds for us."

"No, we don't."

"So, we focus on the next step. One foot in front of the other. Cross bridges when we get to them, and all that shit. Right now?" Abe met Lee's eye. "We find Briggs. Once we have him…well, then we can start worrying about what to do afterwards."

Lee took in a heavy breath. His chest shuddered slightly, as though he had to fight to get air past a massive weight sitting on his sternum. "Well, then…get me a location for Briggs."

Abe stood up. "Yup. That's what I'm trying to do." He reached across the desk and hefted a battered Louisville Slugger.

Lee stared at it, remembering a dark night in a basement with a man strung up from the exposed rafters. Remembering Julia. The look on her face when she took up the bat. Swinging for the fences. The dull thud of impacts on flesh. And strangely, he didn't feel disturbed by the memory. He felt…nostalgic. He felt love for the Julia that had been, and still lived in his memories. He pictured the savagery in her eyes as she broke that man to pieces, and he didn't care about the morality of it, he just wanted her back, mean streak and all.

When had they turned into this?

Where had Lee gone wrong?

He pushed himself off the divider. His hip, which he'd been keeping the weight off of, complained with its usual spike of pain. "Come on, Deuce," he said, patting his thigh. Then to Abe: "I'll let you get to it, then."

***

Abe stepped into Number Four, alone.

Javier Cordova lay on his side in the middle of the plywood room. Hands bound behind his back, ankles lashed together, and the wrists and ankles connected by a bit of cordage long enough that Javier could stretch his body to its full length, but not much more. The blindfold was still tied to his face, but he'd managed to finagle it so that one eye peered up at Abe, filled with tears and fears.

Abe closed the door behind him. Even with the door closed, he could still hear the other prisoner moaning and groaning wordlessly. Wordlessly, probably, because he had no teeth left in his face and his jaw was broken. A less-than-cooperative company commander of Cornerstone. He was the highest-ranking Cornerstone they'd recovered so far. But now that Javier was here, Abe figured he didn't have much use for the other man anymore.

He stepped closer to Javier, dragging the bat along the floor and then leaning on it like a cane. "Javier," he said, amiably. "Do you remember me?"

A shaky expression wriggled across Javier's features. Like he couldn't decide if it was good or bad that he recognized the man standing over him with the baseball bat. "Abe Darabie."

Abe nodded. "It's been a long time, Javier. And look at you! Chief Operating Officer of Cornerstone! My, my! Moving up in the world, huh?"

"Look. I didn't want it. I never did. But you don't understand! Briggs was insane! Paranoid! I couldn't say no—he would have killed me if I said no! He was completely off the reservation!"

Abe knelt, rested his chin on the base of the bat. "I know," he said, sympathetically. "Briggs has always been a madman. Why do you think I left in the first place? All those civilians he killed, just because they spoke out against him?" In the back of Abe's minds, lurking behind those words, was the knowledge that *they* had massacred civilians too. But it hadn't been *him* that'd done it. So was he truly a hypocrite? "All those people he starved because they wouldn't toe the line."

Javier didn't say anything. Like he suspected every word was a trap, and any response would get him beaten with the bat.

"But you have a chance to make it right," Abe said, still keeping that friendly tone. "All I want is Briggs. That's the only reason I'm here, Javier. So let's just start this out on the right foot, huh? We're on the same side. We both know that Briggs was an asshole. We both know that he deserves what's coming to him. Now, all you have to do is tell me where he is. If you tell me where he is, then there's no reason for me to hurt you. I don't *want* to hurt you, do you understand that?"

Javier remained silent, though he managed a very dubious nod.

"Tell me where he's holed up, and then we can be done."

"Are you going to kill me after I tell you?"

Abe felt his heart do a little stir in his chest. That was the closest he'd come so far to an admission of knowledge of Briggs's whereabouts. Everyone else had simply claimed they didn't know. And maybe they didn't. Abe had sure caused them a lot of pain. Enough that he'd begun to suspect maybe they really *didn't* know.

Back to the matter at hand: Was he going to kill Javier?

Abe shook his head. "I don't think you're a bad guy, Javier. I think you're an accountant that got sucked into a bunch of bullshit. I see no reason why you need to die. As long as you're cooperative."

Javier swallowed. Seemed to struggle with it, maybe because his mouth was dry.

Abe raised his eyebrows. "You do know where he is, don't you?"

Javier's mouth worked. "Look. He didn't tell me everything. Like I said, he was paranoid!"

Abe's heart fell. He almost felt bad for the man. He stood up.

"I can't tell you what I don't know!" Javier cried. "Please, you gotta believe me!"

Boy, had Abe heard *that* one before. He shook his head sadly and hefted the baseball bat. "We'll see, Javier. We'll see."

TWENTY-ONE

CALLING BLUFFS

"How much longer are we going to let this charade go on?"

It was Worley that had asked the question. Seemed to Griffin like he was the more outspoken of the four envoys. And it irritated the shit out of Griffin, but when you have envoys from two world powers that are on the cusp of lending you serious assistance, you figure out how to grin and bear.

"As long as I need to," Griffin answered, levelly. "To make sure I get the best outcome."

Guidry and Worley exchanged a glance between them. Marlin and Wibberley had kept silent so far. Marlin in particular. He seemed a man of few words, and Griffin couldn't tell if that was simply his nature, or if he regretted leaving Lee behind.

They were in a quiet corner of the main hangar of the Greeley-Weld Airport. After securing it ten days ago, Griffin had immediately erected a FOB inside the main hangar as soon as it became clear that he wasn't going to chase Lee into Greeley. Now it was filled with soldiers and Cornerstone operatives, and two of the fuel tankers they'd managed to capture before Lee evacuated the area. At the moment, they were the most valuable things Griffin had, so he liked to keep them secure, where he could see them.

There were six of them in all—the four envoys, and Griffin and Paige—sitting in a rough circle of some folding chairs they'd appropriated from one of the other buildings. With only Paige to back him, Griffin felt a little outnumbered, and had to remind himself that these people were here to help. Even if their constant demands for updates and action tended to cramp Griffin's rather patient approach to this whole debacle.

"You know he's lying, right?" Guidry finally piped up.

"Do I?" Griffin asked, arching an eyebrow. "Do you?"

Guidry huffed and rolled his eyes. "If he had Briggs he would've given us proof of life at the very least. Now he won't even answer the phone. We haven't heard from him in four days. Everyone in this circle knows that Lee Harden is full of shit. He doesn't have Briggs, he's just stalling for time. And God knows what he's using that time for. The longer we wait, the longer he has to set up something tricky. We need to stop playing his games on his terms and change the paradigm."

Griffin leaned forward and rested on his elbows. "And what if he's *not* lying?" He held up a hand to settle their rumpled annoyance at that. "I understand what you're saying. And I've had the same thoughts. Yes, you're right. Chances are, Lee's full of shit and he doesn't have Briggs in hand. But we don't *know* that. There is a chance, however small, that he's telling the truth *and* stalling for time. As long as it's a possibility that he has Briggs, I cannot take the risk of pissing him off. We're talking about the president of the United States here. I'm not rolling the dice with his life."

Paige pitched in, ever-faithful. "If he is lying, he's got the whole city bamboozled. Our last incursion made contact with some of the folks we've been feeding ordnance to. They're under the impression that he has Briggs locked up in FOB Hampton somewhere. Of course, I acknowledge the fact that this belief is based on hearsay, and Lee might've spread those rumors himself to bolster his deception. Point being, like Griffin said, we don't *know*. And until we know, we have to operate like Briggs really does have a gun to his head."

Guidry flapped his lips. "How many teams do you have inside?"

"Three," Griffin answered. "They've been embedded for the last week, causing chaos, listening to chatter, and trying to coordinate some sort of alliance. But the going's been slow because they have to be cautious—if they're identified as mine, and Lee catches word of it, then we run the risk of killing the president."

Wibberley rubbed his chin thoughtfully. "Is there no way they can work their way in with Lee's forces?"

Griffin shook his head. "Lee's got everything buttoned up tight. From what we can tell, he doesn't even allow his civvy-soldiers inside FOB Hampton. It's strictly for his military guys, and, from all accounts, they're loyal to him. Getting a man inside FOB Hampton is not in the cards."

Guidry sighed theatrically. "Alright, then. What happens if we learn that Lee *doesn't* have Briggs?"

Griffin shrugged. "Then we end this."

"If Briggs isn't in FOB Hampton," Worley said. "Then where is he?"

"Hiding?" Griffin suggested.

"Or dead," Marlin finally broke his silence.

Griffin looked at him. "That is another possibility."

"Lee might've killed him during the assault on FOB Hampton," Marlin continued, his voice somewhat deadpan, like he'd rather not be saying these things, but was simply being a slave to duty. "Maybe they did it intentionally. Maybe he got killed in the crossfire. Maybe that's why we can't get proof of life."

"It's a possibility we should prepare for," Wibberley agreed.

"Regardless of Briggs," Worley said, dismissively. Like they were talking about a random street bum and not the fucking POTUS. "Time is of the essence. We've been in contact with our command, and they want to see definitive actions taken. They're not blind to the fact that there is a humanitarian crisis happening inside Greeley, and they want it stopped."

Griffin couldn't help himself. A sharp guffaw came out of him before he could tamp it down. "Humanitarian crisis?"

Guidry and Worley frowned at him, as though he'd just kicked a starving war-orphan.

"The whole fucking country is a humanitarian crisis," Griffin snapped, the humor fading as rapidly as it had appeared. "Their concerns are noted, but don't you think they're a little fucking late?"

Worley straightened, looking almost primly offended. "I'm simply relating their feelings on it. Don't kill the messenger."

Easy, Griff. These are not the people to piss off.

He fixed his eyes on Worley. "Alright. You want business handled. Let's talk turkey. What assistance can your people give me? Or are they just going to lay down their demands from afar? Sure would make me feel a whole lot better if they were willing to dip their toes in the water with us."

Guidry harrumphed, defensively. "That is still being discussed."

"And we're not at liberty to tell," Worley added.

Be cool.

"I understand that they're eager to have things settled. So am I. But if they want decisive action, some assistance would be helpful."

"I've already passed on your requests," Guidry replied.

"So then why don't I have satellite imagery and air support?" God, he was doing a shit job of being political, but he just didn't like these two. He was neutral on Marlin and Wibberley. But something about Guidry and Worley just rubbed him the wrong way. Made him feel like he was being *handled*. Like they thought themselves some masterful puppeteers.

Worley sighed and rubbed his thighs. "I don't know, Captain Griffin. Again, all I can do is repeat what I'm told to repeat. I'm as frustrated at the lack of response as you are. But I can tell you this: Pieces are being moved into place. They are taking this very seriously." A weird glimmer in his eyes. "They are taking *you* very seriously."

Griffin's brows furrowed. What the hell was that supposed to mean?

And, at that point, he'd had about enough. He'd hoped for some good news, but the powers-that-be were still dragging their feet, or making their backroom deals, or whatever else they were doing. For all he knew, they were busy divvying up the states into new territories for European powers.

"Well, gentlemen," Griffin patted his lap, as though signaling that court was adjourned. "I look forward to hearing from you at our meeting tomorrow. Hopefully you'll have some better news for me."

Guidry rose from his seat. "If we get good news, we won't wait for the meeting."

Griffin pasted on a brittle smile. "Please don't."

Guidry and Worley departed, Griffin watching them as they left. Marlin and Wibberley stood and, for just a second, Marlin seemed about to say something. Of all the men in the circle, he was actually the one Griffin wanted to hear from most. But he must've decided against saying whatever had rolled through his head, because he just zipped his mouth up tight and gave Griffin a curt nod. He and Wibberley followed their other two countrymen away into the hangar.

Paige waited until they were out of earshot before letting out a low whistle. "Man, you really don't like those guys, huh?"

"What's to like about 'em?" Griffin grunted. "Their meddling is the reason we're in this shit to begin with."

"How's that?"

"Those two fucks—" Griffin wagged a finger at the retreating figures of Guidry and Worley. "—were with Briggs. They encouraged his invasion of the east coast. And now look where it got us." He chuffed darkly. "Besides that, I don't care for the switching sides. They're on Briggs's side, and then they defect to Lee, and now they're back with us. Don't trust 'em as far as I can spit. At least Marlin and Wibberley have only turned once." He rolled his eyes. "Christ. Listen to me. Only turned once? As though being a one-time traitor is any better."

Paige shrugged. "Enemy of my enemy is my friend."

"Yeah, well, fuck you, Sun Tzu. Because the enemy of my enemy is *not* my friend. It's a dubious ally, at best. Someone you have to keep an eye on because they'll stab you in the back the second your interests diverge."

Paige was frowning. "Don't think that was Sun Tzu."

"Whatever." Griffin grumbled and pushed himself backwards in his seat until his spine let out a couple of pleasant pops. "How many more refugees did we take in overnight?"

Paige snapped a finger. "Ah, that reminds me. We took in seventy-eight, but fourteen others peaced out, so the total is now…" he looked skyward, doing the math. "Three hundred and twenty-three? I think?"

"Got almost as many refugees as I've got troops." Griffin shook his head irritably. "Can't feed all these people. Humanitarian crisis," he scoffed. "Have they taken a look at all the sad bastards crammed into Hangar Two? So fucking worried about their *humanitarian crisis*. Where's the water and food then, if they care so much?"

"Easy, Old Man. Don't work yourself up. Not good for your ticker. God, you get saltier by the day."

Griffin waved him off. "Was that it? You said you were reminded of something."

"Right. Yeah. Took in seventy-eight last night. Fifty-eight of which were from Greeley. The other twenty were from down south."

Griffin closed his eyes and pressed his fingers to his temple. "Jee-zus. Please don't tell me they're from one of the settlements that prick Smith burned to the ground."

A slight moment of silence that made Griffin open his eyes and look at Paige. A wordless communication passed between them, cooling Griffin's ire. Canada and the UK were bemoaning the civilian casualties, but did they have any idea of what Briggs had done in Greeley? What Mr. Smith had done on their way up here? All the people that'd been massacred. All the people that Griffin had *helped* massacre.

Everyone's hands were dirty. Not just Lee's.

"No, actually," Paige finally said, looking away. "They were from a different settlement. Down Oklahoma way."

"The hell are they doing all the way up here?"

"They were seeking asylum in Greeley. Didn't realize it was under siege, I guess. But they were fleeing. From a horde of infected."

Griffin let his hands drop from his temple. Sat there a moment. "We don't have hordes in the interior. That's an east coast problem. We have packs."

Paige just shrugged again. "That's what they said."

"They said 'horde'?"

"Well, I don't know. I didn't talk to them directly. Just heard about it from one of my guys."

Griffin stood up, feeling a small pressure inside of him. A tightening. "Are they in Hangar Two?"

"Yeah." Paige stood up with him.

"Then let's take a walk."

***

"It wasn't no pack," the man said. "I know what a pack look like. This was a horde of 'em."

The man's name was Heel, or at least that's what he introduced himself by. He reminded Griffin of a lodge-pole pine tree—as tall as he was rail-thin. He had that taut skin that told Griffin he'd always looked malnourished, and it wasn't just an effect of the current circumstances, though Griffin doubted that helped. Heel had squinty, shifty eyes that never stayed on one thing too long, and seemed to prefer to ramble over the distance instead of making eye contact. When he did make it, it was brief and needle-sharp.

Griffin nodded slowly. "How many are you calling a 'horde'?"

His thin, almost hairless brows squinched together as though it was a stupid question. "Didn't count 'em. Just ran. Me and the others."

"Right, but can you give me a ballpark? Was there more than ten?"

"Mhm. More than ten."

Griffin waited for further, more accurate numbers, but Heel just stood there with his hands stuffed into his pockets, swaying slightly back and forth on the balls of his feet.

"More than a hundred?" Griffin prompted, irritated at having to play twenty questions.

Heel considered this. "Not sure what a hunnert teepios even look like."

"Teepios?" Paige asked.

Heel flashed a glance at Paige. "Crazies. Infected. But not the old ones—the new ones. Teepios is what we call 'em down our way."

"Teepios," Paige said again, with a questioning glance at Griffin, who simply returned it with a shrug.

"So," Griffin drew a circle in the air with his finger, like he was trying to slowly reel the skinny man into a more robust explanation. "Maybe not more than a hundred?"

"Didn't say that." Heel shook his head. Seemed to grow exasperated. "How many teepios runnin' makes the ground shake? How many teepios hollerin' their heads off sound like a tornado coming?" He shrugged. "I dunno."

Griffin and Paige exchanged a glance. The way the guy was talking, it sounded almost Biblical. Or the guy had been so scared shitless that his perceptions were warped. Fear could distort memories in all kinds of ways.

"That sounds like an awful lot of infected," Paige said.

"Mhm," Heel confirmed.

Against his will, Griffin was seeing swirling hordes, like they'd seen take over Fort Bragg. But they didn't have that out here in the plains. The only reason there were hordes in the first place was that the population centers along the east coast had created them. Out here where there were more towns than cities, and even those were massive distances apart, hordes were just…not possible.

So how did a horde get into Oklahoma? Migration? And what were they actually dealing with? Because, if Griffin were being honest with himself, the concept of dealing with hordes like the ones on the east coast was…disconcerting. He didn't *want* to believe it.

"How did they act?" Griffin pressed.

That look again, like Griffin was being a dullard. "How'd they act? They acted like fuckin' teepios. Runnin', jumpin' off of things. Howlin'. Tearin' folk to pieces. How else you ever seen 'em act?"

"Organized," Griffin said, deadpan.

Heel met his gaze, and for once, held it. For a good, long, uncomfortable moment. Then away again. "Sanctuary..."

"Beg pardon?"

"I wasn't finished," Heel snapped. His hands ruffled about in his pockets, his swaying heating up for a moment with irritation. "Sanctuary. That's the name of our settlement. Or it was. We had two hunnert folk in there. Now we got twenty. Including me." Heel took a breath, and Griffin resisted the urge to prompt the man for more.

After a moment's stare-down with something over Griffin's shoulder, Heel went on. "Didn't have no fences, but we had deer stands, right? For sentry posts. Two guards per post, all day every day. We've had packs try to come fuck with us, but once the sentries get to shootin' they'd always back off. Smart fuckers." Another long, excruciating pause. "Didn't happen this time. No shots at all. First inkling we get of it is when we're damn near surrounded. Wake up to screamin'. Folk dyin', runnin' around. Then there was some shootin'. But it was too late."

Heel unearthed one of his hands—long, skeletal things, except for the pads of his palms and the ends of his digits, which looked thick and heavy with calluses. He rubbed his stubbled chin with it. "Eight sentry posts. Eight deer stands. That's how many we got. *Had*," he corrected, finding an errantly-long chin hair to pluck at, right under his mouth. "Sixteen sentries. None of 'em fired a shot. They were all dead and torn up by the time I even opened my eyes." He looked at Griffin, as though he needed to explain why his eyes were closed. "Happened about two in the mornin', so I'zasleep."

"Got it," Griffin murmured.

"Now, you tell me, sir…" Heel squinted his sharp little eyes at Griffin. "Takin' out eight sentry posts with nary a shot fired and havin' the better part of Sanctuary overrun by the time we knew what was happenin'? That sound organized to you?"

Griffin nodded again. "It does."

"Yeah." Heel nodded along with him and looked away. "I thought so, too."

Griffin let out a long breath through his nose, trading glances with Paige again, who now looked about as disconcerted as Griffin felt. "So, you and nineteen others get away. How?"

"Bus."

"You had a bus?"

"That was the plan. Evacuation. Just in case. Kept a bus—short bus, you know? For the retards?—fueled up and ready all the time. Never used it in ten years. 'Cept for that night."

"And how many days ago was that?" Paige asked.

Heel squinted one eye almost shut, and looked skyward with the other. "Five days," he decided.

"Why'd it take you so long?"

"Popped into another settlement, 'cuz we didn't know where we was goin'. They's kind enough to take us in for a few nights, but they didn't have much extra, and we didn't want to impose. We warned 'em about the horde. They told us to go up Greeley way. And now we're here." A sardonic look at Griffin. "Though it seems y'all got problems of your own."

"Don't I know it," Griffin sighed. "You ever catch sight of that horde again?"

"No." Hesitation. "But..."

Griffin waited. Watched the man's mouth work like he had something stuck to his tongue. "Yes?"

"That other settlement? Ranger Ridge is what they called 'emselves. They had a HAM radio. And I got one in the bus, too. We were supposed to check in with 'em ever'night." He finally got that chin hair plucked. Winced as he did it. Then sneered at it like it was a bloated tick and flicked it off his finger. "They didn't answer up last night. Right before we got here. Tried 'em again this mornin'." His face seemed dark for a moment, but then he shrugged. "Maybe we're outta range now."

"Where is Ranger Ridge?" Griffin asked. "I'm not familiar."

"Not far," Heel answered. "We left there yesterday mornin'. Got here in the evenin'." Another shrug of his bony shoulders. "Not far."

"So about eight hours' drive?" Paige tried.

"No. Less." Heel twirled his hand in the air. "Had trouble with the bus. Had to go hunt for parts. Took me damn near half the day. No, I'd say Ranger Ridge is...what? Four hours due south?"

"How fast your bus go?" Griffin's guts were getting tighter and tighter.

"Hell, it don't haul ass, that's for sure. Tops out around fifty. Think it's got a gov'ner on it. Man, I tried to find the damn thing and take it off so I could go faster, but...never worked."

Griffin turned to Paige. "What is that? Two-hundred miles?"

Paige nodded, looking equally worried.

Griffin looked to Heel one last time. "Thank you, Mr. Heel. You've been very helpful."

"Just Heel," the man corrected.

"Right. Heel. Thank you."

Heel stood there for another few beats. He looked a tad worried himself. "You thinkin' them things gonna come up this way too?"

Griffin tried to be comforting by being dismissive. "If they do, I'm sure we can defend ourselves."

Heel just stared at him blankly. Then his mouth quirked in a weird, flat smile. "Sure you can." He took a big breath. "Well, I think we might just head on, anyways. Seein' as how Greeley don't seem like no place for fam'lies at the present."

And without waiting for a response, he spun in an almost perfect about-face and strode off through Hangar Two, towards where a little white short bus was parked on the far side.

Griffin and Paige watched him go, neither having the gumption to say anything humorous about the oddity of the exchange.

"Paige, I want you to send a scout team south. See if they can't find this Ranger Ridge, but even if they can't, have them drive a few hundred miles south and make a nice big loop through the countryside. See what there is to see."

"Christ. If it's a real horde—like the one we saw at Fort Bragg—"

Griffin cut him off with a series of negative noises. Held up a finger. "Just…see what there is to see."

TWENTY-TWO

PAST AND PRESENT

SAM HAD GONE UP TO THE PENTHOUSE to see if Abby was awake, but all he found was Angela, sitting alone at the big dining table in the first room.

He stood in the doorway, somewhat frozen for a moment. Angela looked terrible. She had a bottle of water clutched in her hand, the sides of it so scuffed and worn from use that it made the water inside look cloudy. She was staring at it intently and didn't even seem to notice him, though it had been her voice that answered when he'd knocked.

He glanced behind him at one of the two soldiers on guard, but the guy just gave him a weary shrug, as though to say, *You were the one that wanted to be let in.*

Now Sam wasn't so sure. He'd come because...well, he loved Abby. For a while, he'd chafed against the strange—and in his mind, false—familial bond they'd forged. But that was because he hadn't known who he was.

He was getting a better handle on that now. Things had changed. He had changed. The things that mattered to him when he'd been a half-boot in Fort Bragg seemed far away and childish, even though it hadn't been that long ago. Now he just felt bad. Wanted to hold Abby's hand and talk to her. Something in him was afraid he wouldn't ever get the chance again, and it made him regret all the times he'd run away from her, so that he could go feel tough and strong about himself, toting a rifle on sentry duty, and bro-ing it up with the other half-boots.

But being in the presence of a mother's grief was not what he'd come up here for. It was too big. Too heavy. Too monolithic for him to face right now.

Too late.

He couldn't very well turn around. So, he closed the door behind him, with a big—but quiet—steadying breath.

"Sam," Angela said, still not looking at him. "How have you been?"

Her voice sounded far away. Her thoughts on other things. She didn't really care about how he'd been. Or if she did, it just didn't hold a candle to the worries over her own daughter. But she'd treated him like a son once, just like Abby had treated him like a brother.

Another wave of shame and guilt. He'd pissed that away too, and for the same reasons. Why is it that we have to be broken down to see what's important? Why can't we see it before it hurts to look at?

He stepped into the room. "Oh, you know," he said. "The yoozh."

A tiny glimmer of a smile tweaked the corners of Angela's mouth. She finally wrenched her eyes from the bottle and looked at him. Really...*looked* at him. He stood still for a moment, not sure what to do while her eyes ranged over him from top to bottom. What was she seeing? Was it him? Was it what he used to be?

Was there a difference?

Sam was starting to think there wasn't. He was still Sameer Balawi. Harder, more sure of himself, better trained, more accustomed to violence, less scared, but not because he was any braver—simply because that's what happens when you're in danger, day in and day out. You figure out how to work with it. You learn coping mechanisms.

"Do you want to sit?" Angela asked, making a small, almost absent-minded gesture at the chair across from her.

He didn't. But she looked so lonesome sitting there, one person at a table meant for eight. Seven empty chairs, and not an ass to fill one of them. Did she not have any friends? Did she not have anybody besides Abby?

He crossed to the table and sat in the chair. His clothing still smelled stale from being under the armor. Hadn't completely dried from his sweat either. He leaned forward on the table and interlaced his fingers in front of him.

"Is she still in surgery?" he asked, glancing towards the bedroom.

Angela nodded. "Hour four." Her face gave a miniscule spasm. "John said four to six. I hope it's going okay."

"Me too."

Silence descended. If it was uncomfortable for Angela, she didn't seem to notice. Sam inwardly writhed against it for a moment, but then just sort of submitted himself to it. He knew at the door this wasn't going to be comfortable. Some things just need to be done, even if they make you squirm.

Angela blinked. Looked around, like she'd forgotten something. "I'd offer you something to drink, but this is it." She held up the water bottle and raised an eyebrow. "Thirsty?"

He managed a smile. "I'm fine, thanks." He looked over at the wet bar. Crystal tumblers glimmered in the sunlight coming through the bank of windows. No bottles, though. "Bastard took the booze with him, too, huh?" Sam shook his head wryly. "Rude."

"Extremely," Angela concurred. "God, but I could use it."

She looked like she could, but Sam figured that wasn't helpful to point out. Noting the heavy luggage piled up under her eyes, Sam decided to be a little more tactful. "Have you been able to sleep?"

"Some," she said, in a way that Sam understood as *Barely*.

"Has…" He hesitated, wondering if he should steer clear of asking.

Angela looked at him, exhausted. "Go ahead Sam. We're practically family."

Practically family.

Not long ago, he would have recoiled from that. What a petulant little prick he'd been. *You're not my mommy! I'm a big, strong man!*

The thought made him laugh before he could restrain it.

Angela frowned at him. "What?"

Sam waved it away quickly. "I wasn't laughing about the family thing. Well…I guess…in a way."

Angela watched him with mild curiosity. Maybe a little defensiveness. And didn't she have the right? Hadn't she earned the right to call him family? She'd taken him in. Cared for him. Treated him like he was her own.

Sam sighed and leaned back in his seat, one hand still perched on the table. "I was just laughing about how I…" God, but it's hard to admit what a shit you've been. He grimaced at his own struggle with the truth. "Look, I was an asshole. To you. And to Abby. I should have appreciated what you did. I should have *wanted* you to be my family. I'm sorry that I fought against it. I wish I hadn't."

Angela's face softened. "Oh, Sam. We're all fucked up in the head." She chuckled at her own ungilded words, and Sam found himself smiling with her. She shook her head and looked out the window, one hand rising to her cheek. It looked so thin. Was she even eating? And what were all those heavy scabs all over her knuckles? He hadn't noticed them before. He wondered when she'd gotten them. "What did any of us expect?"

"I don't know," Sam admitted.

"After everything we've been through, after everything we've seen, everything we've lost, everything we've ripped away from others?" Her face sagged into her palm, eyes going cold again. "How can we possibly expect each other to act like humans?"

He didn't think she meant it as a jab at him, but it still stung.

She spoke again, almost whispering. "How can we expect *ourselves* to act like humans?" She let out a hollow breath. Sounded like wind in a cave. "Whole generations were lost, and those of us that survived are *still* lost. Even if we were able to remake the world like it was..." She looked at him with sunken, haunted eyes. "The scars, Sam. The scars we'll take with us. They won't go away. We'll pass them down to our children, and they'll pass them to their children. And whole generations afterwards would be just as fucked up as we've become."

That's heavy, Sam thought, but just nodded in silence. He hadn't given much thought to the next generations that might come after them. Hard to think about your progeny when you don't even know if you're going to survive. Maybe you had to be a parent to see the truth of it, but he sensed it, even if only academically.

He wished he were back down with Jones. Jones, who'd never really let the darkness take him. He danced around it instead. Poked fun at it. Turned the horrible into a joke, and slyly robbed it of its power. Sam wished he could be like that.

He returned to his original question with a soft clearing of the throat. "Has Abby woken up at all?"

"John says she might not."

"She will," Sam said, as though he knew it for sure.

Angela looked at him, doubt in her eyes.

She needed encouragement, so Sam decided to double down on his rather limp conviction. "She's got fight, Angela. I know I haven't been around the block as many times as you, but from what I've seen, the ones that have fight in them are the ones that survive. She'll survive this."

Angela sniffed, and it sounded wet, though her eyes were dry. "You are right about that, Sam. I'm just..." Her eyes seemed to be seeing something disturbing, hovering in the air between them. "I'm not sure how much she wants to live."

Sam opened his mouth to deny it, but Angela suddenly stood up, doing an odd little shake, like a dog just coming out of water. "Ugh. Doesn't do any good to think like that. We need to stay positive." She didn't sound like she believed her own advice. "How are things down below? What's happening?"

Sam raised his brow, not quite sure what he was free to talk about.

Angela sensed his reticence and drew herself up a bit, hands on her hips. "I am still technically the president." A frown. "Even if I don't know what exactly I'm the president of, at this point."

"Hasn't Lee been up to see you?" Sam tried to deflect, still unsure about opsec.

Angela's face was very still. A façade, hiding the emotions inside. "A few days ago. He's been...very busy."

"Well. You know. Wrangling civilians. Dealing with Briggs. Dealing with Griffin."

Angela gave him a sardonic stare. "Sam. I know we don't have Briggs."

Sam felt a flush on the back of his neck. "Right."

"Any progress on that front?"

Sam shifted in his seat. "Some. Not a lot."

Angela rested her hands on the back of her chair. "What about Abe?"

Sam met her gaze for a long moment. "He's working on it," he replied, guardedly.

"Torture," Angela said, flatly.

Sam looked away. Couldn't help glancing at the door, wishing he could escape.

"Huh," Angela grunted. "Maybe I'm *not* the president of anything anymore."

"I'm sorry, Angela. It's just that...Lee's been on us about opsec. Keeping our mouths shut about things. If word gets out that we don't actually have Briggs..."

"I know," Angela said softly. "But who am I going to tell? I'm just a used up old woman in the penthouse."

Sam winced, sighed out some of his discomfort.

"I know what Abe's doing down there. And you know what?" A grim, haggard smirk touched her lips. "I don't care anymore. There was a time when I would've railed against it. I would have a shouting match with Lee and Abe about it. I'd tell them, 'This isn't the way,' and 'We have to be better than our enemies,' and all that other horseshit." She shook her head, snorting softly through her nose. "But I can't stop them. I never could. They'll do what they do, as always."

She slumped against the back of the chair, mouth hanging open for a moment. "I'm tired of picking up their pieces. I'm tired of running around trying to stop the bleeding. Trying to keep the chaos from swallowing us up. I'm just *tired*, Sam. Too tired to care about it anymore."

"They're just trying to do the right thing," Sam said, sounding lame even to his own ears.

"The right thing," Angela echoed, with bitter blankness. "What's the right thing, Sam?"

Sam felt his chest heat up, anger rising as Angela impugned everything he'd fought for. Devalued the sacrifice of his dead friends, and so many others. He found himself struggling to keep the glare out of his eyes. "Keeping your word. Doing what you said you were going to do. Even when it hurts. Even when you feel like quitting."

Angela's expression didn't falter. She didn't believe a word of it. She gave him that look again—up and down, appraising—and it wasn't kind. Like she was seeing something entirely different now. "Oh my. So you're one of them now."

Sam stood up. "I don't know what that means."

Angela smiled, mirthlessly. Wielded it like a razor, slicing through him. "Look at you. You're just like Lee now."

It was only the strength of his sudden rage that stopped him. It flared up so hot and irrational that he immediately drew back from it. He looked away from her, fixed his eyes on the door, and didn't try to hide it this time. He couldn't stare into those mocking, judging eyes. They would only infuriate him further.

"I'd like to see Abby," he said, a little thickly. "When she wakes up."

Angela didn't respond.

Sam just kept staring at the door. "Will you let me know when she wakes up?"

"If she wakes up," Angela said. And Sam wasn't sure if she'd just agreed to let him know or not, but he wasn't going to ask again.

"She'll wake up," Sam said to the door. Then, bitingly: "We just have to stay positive."

He waited for Angela to say something else, even though he couldn't imagine she would have anything to say that he wanted to hear. When she didn't speak, he nodded to himself with a sort of cold finality, and stalked to the door.

As he opened it, she finally spoke.

"Sam."

He stopped, teeth clenched. Looked over his shoulder, but never quite looked *at* her.

"Stay safe out there," she said, softer now. Maybe even apologetic.

"I will," he said, then stepped through the door and closed it behind him.

***

This was a dry land.

The Alpha knew to keep its mouth shut against the dry air. Sweat slicked its body, and as it kept pace with the others, the wind of movement cooled it. But it would need water soon. It did not worry itself, though. It smelled the water in the distance—dank and marshy, but water nonetheless. Its nostrils flared wide to take in air, and to follow the scent.

It could see the scent, as well as smell it. Like the Glow the females gave off when they were ready to mate, but different. This glow was not as bright, but it hung there, like gossamer strands of spider's webbing, teasing at its nose.

The Alpha needn't have followed its nose to water. It was, in fact, no longer the Alpha, but had become simply one of the Many. And the Many were all heading to water. It could have simply followed.

For many days it had traveled hard and fast with the Many, all of them following the strands of scent left by the Prey that had escaped them in the place they had come from—a place with much more water, the Alpha remembered, but dwindling Prey. And where the Prey goes, the predator must follow.

The Alpha had not understood at first, but now it did: The Omegas were growing heavy with their offspring. They would need to feed, in order to give them birth. They would need much Prey to feed them all. More Prey than could be found in the place they had come from.

The Strange Ones were wise to have brought them here.

But now the Many had to leave the scent of the Prey behind, and follow the scent of water. Water brings life first, so that the hunt could continue, and the Prey could be had, and the Many could feed, and the Omegas could have their births that would make the Many even stronger.

They traveled into the sun for a time, until it baked their faces and shoulders, and their sweat slowly dried from lack of replenishment, and their need for water became fierce. The Many became a body of one, churning the ground beneath them in their haste to reach the source of water, the dust from their treading feet coating its nostrils and throat. The scent of water grew stronger now, filling the air so that when the Alpha picked up its head to smell, the sky seemed heavy with all the strands of water-scent in it.

They found it in a mostly-dried-out river bed, with just a skim of greenish water flowing sluggishly along muddy banks. They plunged down the sides of the banks, grunting and gasping and snapping, their desperation causing a few scuffles to break out in the panic to drink.

The Alpha's hands and feet plunged into mud that smelled heavily of rot and stagnation. It surged for the water, growling at a smaller male that tried to cut in front, then gnashing its great teeth at it when it failed to yield. The smaller male bared its teeth and tucked its backend up to protect its testicles, jostling sideways into others as the Alpha shouldered past it.

The Alpha sank its jaws below the layer of scum. Tepid water struck its tongue and it lapped and sucked at it greedily. It tasted as it had smelled—strongly of dirt, and rot. The many others sloshing through it only stirred up the silt more, but the Alpha did not care. It had secured its place, and it drank and drank until its belly felt swollen. It paused to look up, muddy water streaming from its jowls. The sunlight dazzled across the frothing water. It's stomach spasmed with the weight of water and tightened, sending a jet of it back up. It hunched and vomited a small splash of water back into the mud. It had taken its fill, and more. As had all of the Many, and now the mostly-dried-out river had been drained down to the mud.

It climbed the bank of the river, slower than it had gone down. At the top, it scented the air again, sitting on its haunches, and looked around.

Several Strange Ones stood, only a few strides away. Their lithe bodies dripping with water and caked with mud. They looked in the direction of the Prey—away from the sun, now.

The Alpha watched them for a time, its jaw working as instincts writhed within it. Fear of the Strange Ones. But also love. And a slithering feeling of want that confused the Alpha, because it knew it could not have them, and it could not decipher if it wanted to feed on them, or rut.

The Omegas, now filled with water themselves, converged on the Strange Ones. They went low onto all fours, while the Strange Ones stood on their legs, tall and erect, like the Prey stood. The Omegas circled the Strange Ones, all of them moving in a river of flesh around them, letting out plaintive whimpers and hoots.

One of the Strange Ones turned around and looked at the Alpha, and the confusion of feelings grew stronger, so that the Alpha averted its eyes, knowing that it was not good to think of rutting or feeding on the Strange Ones. For the Strange Ones were wise, and they would lead them to the Prey, and they would make the Many stronger than they'd ever been.

The Strange Ones sank down from their tall standing, and disappeared into the swirling circle of Omegas, and made the noises with their mouths that the Many could not make. And the Omegas understood them, and then raised their voices in a chorus of howls that the Alpha and the Many *did* understand.

They had drunk, and the water had given them life. Now the hunt would continue.

The Alpha smelled the air, but could not see the strands of Prey-scent.

But it did not worry itself, for the Strange Ones knew the place where they had left the scent, and would lead them back.

The Omegas, with the Strange Ones embedded within their tight circle, took off at a run, and the Many followed.

TWENTY-THREE

CORPORAL RIZZO AND THE BUFFALO STAMPEDE

"So, then I was like, 'Motherfucker, if you had that much of a problem with it, why didn't you say anything? Why didn't you *do* anything?'" Corporal Rizzo swirled his urine stream in a circle, then side to side as he spoke. "And then this dude's like,"—he lowered his voice and pursed his lips to sound big and dumb—"'He had a gun.' Can you fucking believe that shit? 'He had a gun,' this guy says. And so I was like, 'Yeah, so do you, you dumb fuck. If you were feeling froggy, you coulda jumped, but you didn't, 'cause you're a fucking pussy, and you need to shut the fuck up.'"

Corporal Rizzo couldn't see his sergeant's face, but if he had, he would have seen an eye roll. "You didn't say that."

"Yeah, I did."

"You didn't."

"What are you talking about?" Rizzo's voice pitched high in indignation. "You weren't even there!"

"I was standing two feet away. And that's not what you said."

"I didn't hear *you* say nothin'," Rizzo shot over his shoulder.

"That's 'cause I'm not always trying to pick a fight with the assholes. We gotta work with these people, you know."

"Man, fuck Cornerstone," Rizzo snapped.

"Bet you wouldn't say that in front of them."

"Pffff—I already did! Said it right to his face."

"No, you didn't."

"Rizzo, you're so full of shit," the gunner piped up from the turret. "Hey, don't freak out, but there's a big ass spider crawling towards you."

"Shit!" Rizzo flailed, his urine stream splattering and cutting off, tucking his goods in like he thought the spider might jump up and bite his pecker off. "You serious?!"

"Oh my God, it's running for you! Run, Rizzo, Run!"

Rizzo did a little spin, both hands covering his junk. Then realized there was no spider, to the cackling of the others sitting in the MATV. He jabbed a middle finger up at the gunner. "Fuck you, man." Then turned back around to resume his business.

"Christ, you got *more*?" the gunner moaned. "What are you, a fucking camel?"

"I stay hydrated, bro," Rizzo snapped, irritated.

"So, here's what happened," the sergeant narrated, for the benefit of the others. "Right after Griffin popped that Mr. Smith's noggin, this one Cornerstone guy—big bastard, big old operator beard, tribal tattoos, you know the type—"

"Wiley X's?" the gunner suggested.

"Right, Wiley X's, of course. Anyways, this Big Bastard is bitching about it, talking about how he should've stopped it. Then Rizzo over here says,"—the sergeant put on a nasally, wheedling voice—"'Uh, excuse me, Mr. Operator Man, but you can't talk about my Daddy that way.'"

"Oh, come on!"

"You shut the fuck up, Rizzo! I'm telling the story now! Anyways...Big Bastard looks right at Rizzo and says, 'What, do you suck his cock?' And—swear to God—Rizzo goes sheet fucking white—"

"I didn't!"

"—His knees are all a-shakin'—"

"That's bullshit!"

"—His lips are all a-quiverin'—"

"Come on, man!"

"—and, I'm not positive about this, it might've been the lighting, but I thought I saw some tears in his eyes."

"Fucking lies!"

"So, Rizzo's staring up at this Big Bastard with his pale face and maybe just, you know, a single tear, glimmering, right there on the edge of his eyelid, ready to fall, just looking like he was about ready to shit himself, and Big Bastard just kinda gives him a look, you know? Like he's a little confused. He thought this was an army of hardcore killers, and here's this little wop kid, trembling and crying at the injustice."

"That's racist!" Rizzo shook himself off.

"So then Big Bastard says, 'Something wrong with you, boy? You tryna get *stomped* today?!' and Rizzo—man, he's barely holding it together at this point—adrenaline's pumping, I mean, he's looking death right in the face. What's he going to do? What are his *tactical options* here? What *strategery* will he employ to save himself from the curb-stomping that's about to befall him?"

A long, dramatic pause, as Rizzo buttoned himself back up, shaking his head.

"Well, our brave little guido, he's only got one option at that point. He knows what he's got to do. So he does it. He moves quick! Lightning quick! Dives into his pocket aaand…"

Another breathless pause.

Rizzo turned and glared at his sergeant, who smirked back at him, eyes twinkling.

"…And that's when I heard the rape whistle."

"Dumb," Rizzo grumbled, turning his back on the laughter of his squad. "Y'all are dumb. Wasn't even funny."

"Look, look!" the sergeant cried, pointing. "I just saw another tear!"

"He's gonna fucking pout now," the gunner poked. "Come on, Rizzo, stop pouting."

Rizzo remained facing away from them, staring into the distance.

"Give him some time," the sergeant sighed. "He's got to get a handle on his emotions—you know how emotional those Italians are."

Rizzo raised a hand and pointed south. "What's that?"

"What?" the gunner said, still laughing. "Your dignity? That shit's gone, bro, you'll never catch it."

"Seriously," Rizzo barked. "What's *that*?"

Sergeant, gunner, and one other troop in the back all peered south at the same time. And saw it: A pale, tan smudge on the horizon.

"That a dust storm?" the gunner asked.

"It ain't even windy," Rizzo answered.

"Well, it could be the wind coming in, you know. Weather changes, dickwad."

"You a fucking meteorologist now?"

"It's a fucking, uh…" the troop in the back snapped his fingers, searching for the right word— he didn't use words much and his fellow soldiers suspected it was because he was significantly below nominal intelligence. "Buffalo stampede."

The sergeant looked into the back with a pained expression. "A buffalo stampede?"

"Yeah."

"This ain't the Wild West, Slows." They called him Slows for obvious reasons. He didn't care for it.

The gunner nudged at Slows with his knee. "Fucking Daniel Boone over here."

"Don't call me Slows," Slows said, sullenly.

The gunner kept on nudging him. "Why don't you get out and put your ear to the ground, Slows? Tell us how many buffalo are coming."

"Stop," Slows shoved at the gunner's leg.

The gunner kept nudging. Almost kicking him now. "Go on, use all those skills you learned when you lived with the Indians that one time, Dances With Wolves."

Slows reared back and punched the side of the gunner's leg, hard.

"Ow!" the legs retracted halfway into the turret, the gunner's hand coming down and rubbing his thigh. "You dick!"

"You're the dick," Slows grumbled.

"Oh, good one, *Slowsville*."

"No, no," Rizzo announced, still standing outside the passenger side of the MATV, but now with his arms held out at his sides, palms facing the ground, as though divining something from the earth. "I think he's right. Can you guys feel that?"

For once, and perhaps only because they knew what they'd come to scout for, no one lambasted him. It was a rare occasion for Rizzo to be taken seriously.

"What?" the sergeant asked, keen enough to see when Rizzo wasn't screwing around anymore.

Rizzo vibrated his hands in the air. "The ground's shaking."

"See?" Slows elbowed the gunner's leg again. "Buffalo."

"Stop!" the gunner snapped at him, pulling his legs away again. "I'm gonna kick the shit out of you."

"Alright, alright, alright," the sergeant grouched at them, using the tone they all knew meant that play time was over. "Rizzo, get in the truck."

Rizzo seemed fascinated by his ability to sense the vibrations. He was bending lower now, hands still hovering. "I can fucking *feel* them."

The sergeant gazed laconically forward and took his foot off the brake, letting the MATV roll forward.

"Hey!" Rizzo squawked, dashing to catch up. "Wait!"

The sergeant jammed on the brake so Rizzo slammed into the door. "Told you to get in the truck. That's what you get for being insubordinate."

Rizzo grumbled under his breath as he clattered back into his seat and shut the door.

The sergeant began accelerating towards the dust cloud in the distance. Slows and the gunner were still sniping at each other, albeit more quietly now. The sergeant took up the radio handset. "Hey, could you two chill out for two fucking seconds? Tryna transmit here."

They froze into silence.

The sergeant keyed up. "Recon Two to Recon One, we spotted a large dust cloud south of us, maybe four or five klicks out. We're gonna get a little closer, try to figure out what's stirring it up."

"Recon Two, we copy. Ain't got shit on our end. Let us know."

"Roger. Out." The sergeant set the radio back in its cradle.

The gunner, meanwhile, had squirmed his way down and now had his head in the vehicle with them. "Man, oh, man. There's gonna be a fucking wampa."

The sergeant made a face. "What?"

Slows looked concerned. "What's a wampa?"

The gunner looked intensely earnest. "This is just like that scene in Star Wars, where Luke sees the probe droid land, and he tells Han he's gonna go check it out. So he creeps in closer and uses his little binocs to scope it, right? But then when he turns around?" the gunner made claw motions with his hands. "Fucking wampa."

Slows stared at those hands. "What's a wampa?"

"Fuckin' *ice beast*, son!" the gunner practically yelled it, pawing at Slows, who did not look amused.

Rizzo started laughing in that derisive way of his. "Fucking nerd."

The gunner was incredulous. "It's the greatest movie series Of-All-Time!"

"Nerrrrrrd," Rizzo sang to the ceiling.

"Everybody loves Star Wars!"

"Nerrrrrd," Rizzo sang in a baritone.

"What, you don't like Star Wars?"

Rizzo flapped a raspberry out. "Sorry, my childhood was filled with, you know, normal-people shit. Like sports and girls."

The sergeant shook his head, exasperated. "Oh, Rizzo."

"What?"

"You do this to yourself, you know."

"What'd I do?"

"You're just so full of shit. This is why we make fun of you."

"I'm not full of shit!"

"If you're ever crying yourself to sleep at night, wondering why we're so mean to you, it's because of this shit right here."

"I played sports!"

"Oh, we know," the sergeant waved his hand in the air, inviting the gunner to join in, which he did, and they harmonized, word-for-word, the oft-quoted triumph of Rizzo's yesteryears: "You scored forty-six points in a highly-competitive basketball game."

Rizzo was flummoxed by their disbelief. "I did. Hand to God, I did."

The gunner shook his head, almost apologetic. "No proof."

"Whatever, man," Rizzo huffed. "Least I had a girlfriend while you were jackin' off to Princess Leia." That got a snicker from the sergeant, so Rizzo went with it, pumping his fist over his crotch and turning his voice to a childlike falsetto. "Oh, Leia! Let me shoot my torpedoes into your exhaust tube!"

Rizzo and the sergeant fell out laughing, the sergeant rocking in his seat, Rizzo animatedly slapping at his shoulders, breathless and red-faced.

"See?" the gunner said, pointing at Rizzo. "You *have* seen Star Wars!"

Rizzo ignored him, heaping it on. "Here, it comes, Leia! I'm flying into your trench! Oh, help me, Obi Wan Kenobi!"

They were cresting a slight rise in the land, and the sergeant's eyes were clouded with tears from laughing so hard, and when they hit the top of the rise, he blinked, saw what lay ahead, and stomped on the brake.

Rizzo slammed into the dash, his jokes cut off with a yelp and a few curses.

"Shit," the sergeant breathed, the humor rapidly draining out of his chest.

Rizzo righted himself and looked ahead. The sergeant snapped his fingers and demanded the binoculars, but Rizzo was already fumbling for them, found them, and shoved them into his sergeant's hand.

The sergeant raised it to his eyes, adjusting the dials. "Get back in the turret," he said to the gunner.

The gunner went up top. The turret swiveled around. A quiet exclamation from above: "Oh, fuck."

The dust cloud swam in the sergeant's vision, coming into focus, drifting down from the tops of the billowing clouds, down to the ground. Shapes in the dust. Hundreds...no...more than that. He fiddled with the focus again until they stood out sharply.

His heart pounded in his chest as he lowered the binoculars. With the naked eye, the dust cloud spanned a massive swath of the countryside, and at the front of it, tiny shapes churned inexorably towards them. A stampede, yes. But there were no buffalo in there.

Rizzo had retracted his usual bravado and spoke in a dead-serious whisper. "There's gotta be fucking thousands of them."

"That's not..." the sergeant breathed, clinging to the faint hope of a notion: That maybe this was some holdover horde of the original infected—the smaller, weaker ones, the ones that had been so numerous at the outset, but had died off. The ones that could be killed with a few well-placed rounds, rather than the new ones that had taken over—the ones that took half a fucking magazine to bring down.

Hoping against hope, the sergeant looked through the binocs again. Tried to steady his hands and focus in on one. It was hard—not just because of the tremor taking his arms, but because they skipped and bounded and churned all around each other. But he saw enough. He saw their size. He saw glimpses of their savagely-muscled frames. Snippets of mouths too wide to be human.

And the way they *moved*.

Maybe three klicks out, and eating up the distance with worrying speed.

The sergeant tossed the binocs into Rizzo's lap and grabbed the wheel, yanking it to the left as far as it would go and spinning the tires with sudden acceleration. "We need to get the fuck out of here," he said, unnerved at the pitch of his own voice. "Those are the bad ones."

TWENTY-FOUR

PROGNOSIS

IN THE WANING AFTERNOON LIGHT, Angela and John sat at the dining table of the penthouse, Angela in the same seat she'd been in before when Sam had come to see her, and John sitting caddy-corner to her at the end seat.

John had just returned Abby to the bedroom after a five hour and thirty-seven minute surgery—Angela had counted every minute. After getting Abby set up, they'd retreated, Angela knowing that John had something on his mind, as his demeanor was not quite as chipper as it usually was. Not depressed, but simply…flattened out a bit.

He laid both of his hands flat on the table, and Angela thought he looked like a man about to take a lie-detector test. So still and erect. His eyes were naturally dark and deep-set, but they seemed to have retreated further into his skull, as though something in him was shrinking and creating a vacuum.

"We need to talk about the options," John said, breaking the silence with his quiet, gentle voice.

Angela nodded, feeling nauseas from a combination of anxiety and a gnawing hunger that had no appetite to back it.

He took his glasses off and rubbed the bridge of his nose where two little red spots clung to his dusky skin where the glasses rested. He looked spent. Exhausted. Like some inner well had been sucked bone dry.

He inspected his glasses, blew an offending eyelash off of one of the lenses, then seated them back on his face with a sigh. "First off, the surgery was a success in my book—I accomplished what I told you I wanted to accomplish. So that's a good thing. That means that Abby's body is, for the most part, doing what it should be doing. Her internal organs should be operating normally, and getting better." A long pause told Angela that was the end of the good news. She clasped her hands together, steeling herself for the rest.

"If I had all the resources I *should* have, we would have installed a port for a colostomy bag. Unfortunately, I don't have those resources. So it's a bit of a roll of the dice. Now, I did a very thorough job piecing the intestines back together, but there is still a chance for leakage until the tissues heal completely. If that does happen, it will almost certainly lead to sepsis. And that is the first big part of the bad news: We are almost completely out of antibiotics. I've kept Abby on a strong round of it until today, but...I only have one more bag of intravenous antibiotics. Now, there might be a temptation for us to save the bag in case she experiences sepsis, however, my very strong recommendation is to use it now, as soon as the one she's on runs dry. If we keep her on antibiotics, it'll have a better chance of preventing infection, and hopefully give her intestines time to seal themselves up. If we wait for the infection to happen, my concern is that a single bag won't be enough to kill it off." He looked at her. "Does that make sense?"

Angela blinked. "What happens if we use the bag and she develops sepsis anyways?"

John looked pained and averted his eyes, choosing instead to stare at his hands. "If that happens, there isn't anything we can do, Angela. At that point, all we can do is hope and pray that her body is strong enough to fight the infection on its own, but I should caution you..." he grimaced. "Hope is a wonderful thing. But only if we are realistic. I don't want you to be unrealistic, do you understand?"

Angela was very still for a moment. Her voice quaked when she spoke again. "So if sepsis happens, her chances are..."

John simply shook his head.

Angela wrestled with it, feeling the thickness growing in her throat, her eyes beginning to burn. "Isn't there, like, chances? Like odds or something? A percent chance that she'll survive it on her own? Do you know?"

"I don't. Everyone is different, so it's not realistic for me to give you a hard number on her odds. I can only be plainspoken about it, and tell you that most patients that experience sepsis require antibiotic intervention."

"So her chances are...what? *Nothing*?"

John raised a single hand. "Not *nothing*. But...low."

"Christ." Angela leaned into the table, her hands raking up through her hair. She felt like pulling it out.

"Right now, your biggest battle is just going to be staying positive, loving her, talking to her, even if it doesn't seem like she can hear you. There's plenty of evidence to support that people in comas do better when they have a loved one caring for them and talking to them. That's really all you can do at this point."

Angela tried to nod, but couldn't quite make it happen. Didn't want to acknowledge her utter powerlessness. It made her feel like she had on the streets of Greeley, lost, scared to death for her daughter, and unable to do anything to help her. All she wanted was a solution. Would have given anything—*anything*—for a solution.

John reached over and touched her elbow gently. "It's okay to experience bad emotions about all this. You're allowed. We just have to remember to pick ourselves up and try our best to stay positive."

"Okay," Angela murmured, thinking that sounded impossible at this point.

"Should I go on, or do you need a break?"

Angela's fingers tightened around her hair. There was more bad news. He was offering to save it for later, but what would she do? Sit around and just imagine what the other shitty news was? Better to simply have it all out at one time.

With painful effort, she extracted her fingers from her hair, smoothed it out so she didn't feel like she looked like a crazy person, and nodded, trying to be as stalwart as she could manage. "No, I'm fine," she lied. "Go ahead."

John patted her arm and retracted his hand. "Our other obstacle right now is nutrients. Abby's body needs nutrients to work and heal properly. Right now, we have her on an oral solution. I have some left, but I want you to be aware so that it doesn't take you by surprise: I only have enough for another week, on her current feeding schedule."

"Should we ration it?"

"No," he said. "Best to give her body everything it needs. But we need to be aware that we're running out of the oral solution that you've been putting into her feeding tube. If she hasn't woken up in a week, we're going to need to figure out another option."

"Can't we just blend food? Make our own solution?"

"Actually, yes," John said, for once showing a silver lining to the bad news. "And we can talk about the right way to go about that, but it is possible—might be a bit of a challenge, but I'm also sure that we can come up with a reasonable solution. But for right now, let's forget about that. If we get to the last day or two and she hasn't woken up, then we'll talk about how we might make our own. I just wanted you to be aware."

Angela felt marginally better that the last bit of bad news actually had a solution to it. Better than the antibiotic problem. She even managed a careworn smile. "Okay. Cross bridges when we get to them."

"Exactly."

He left after that, with his usual good wishes and admonishments to sleep and to eat something. But Angela didn't rise from her chair after he'd closed the door behind him. Part of her wanted to go see her daughter. Part of her just felt like floating there, pretending that none of this was actually happening to her.

She was supposed to be positive. Loving. Go in and talk to her daughter. And she would. She just needed a moment. She knew she needed a moment, and yet she didn't spend it thinking about anything that might have revitalized her. She couldn't. There were too many other things to think about, and she was alone, so no one else was going to think about these things for her.

The food was a lesser issue.

But the antibiotics were the ticking clock, and she felt the swinging of that pendulum in her bones. Whether or not Abby woke up wasn't the issue. It was whether or not something in her body did something that Angela had no control over.

No control. Powerless.

In her mind, it wasn't a question of *if* Abby's sutured insides were going to leak into her abdominal cavity and create sepsis. In her mind, it was happening right at that moment. And she was Abby's mother, and Abby could not help herself, and so it was up to Angela to figure out how exactly she was going to keep her daughter alive.

She would give anything—do anything—to keep her daughter alive.

And now, she began to consider just what *anything* might be.

***

"What's on the menu tonight, Rough Ryders?" Lee asked as he stepped into the little plywood office that had become the crash pad for Sam and his team. Deuce padded along beside him and wagged his tail at the familiar faces and smells.

Sam looked up from where he was reclining on an office chair, his hands cradling the back of his head. "You heard about that, huh?"

"I hear everything," Lee said, leaning over Marie, who had a pot of something sitting on a hot plate that they'd wired to a car battery. He found it darkly amusing that they'd all become so accustomed to shit being so janky that he barely even noticed the haphazard wiring. It was just how things were done when you were scraping by. Repetition turned it into normalcy.

"Well," Marie said, stirring something in the pot. "We're going to start with an aperitif of wheat berries, just to whet your appetite for the main course of wheat berries, and then we'll finish it off with an amuse-bouche of wheat berries." Deuce pressed himself in next to Marie, nose questing closer and closer to the cooking food until she gently elbowed him away. "But if y'all don't mind, I'll just put them all in the same bowl."

Jones, who was lying down against the wall with his forearm draped over his eyes, raised his other arm and made a limp little jazz hand in the air. "Yay. I love wheat berries. Can't get enough of them."

Sarcasm notwithstanding, Lee knew they'd been lucky to find the grain stores unharmed. A handful of big silos on the northwest end, just outside the city, that apparently none of the militia groups had thought to sabotage or rob. They'd taken what they could from the silos a few days ago, and found them smoking ruins the next morning.

Lee stared down into the steaming pot of wheat berries as they slowly absorbed the water. Lee had enough wheat to keep his people fed for the next week or so. After that, they'd have to start getting creative, or hope they came across another store of food.

Lee shook his head, tiredly. He'd come to Sam's little crash pad, hoping to boost his mood a bit, but there were just too many reminders of all the ticking clocks that Lee had to manage. Never before had time become so consequential. Everything measured in hours and days. How long could they last? How long could they keep this up? What happened if they started to starve before a resolution could be found?

Marie rapped her stirring spoon on the side of the pot and looked up at Lee. "You staying for dinner? I got enough for you and Abe."

Lee smiled, remembering back to Camp Ryder, and how Marie would run their kitchen there, sweating in the hot little room where they'd constructed the wood stoves, making huge pots of whatever they had to make to keep everyone fed.

Being in Camp Ryder at the time, Lee didn't think he'd ever look back at it with nostalgia. Things had seemed so bad, so dire. And they were, in a way. And yet they were simpler. Easier.

When had things become so complicated?

"If you don't mind," Lee said.

Sam pulled his feet from the office chair he was using as a footstool and shoved it towards Lee. "Have a seat, then. Make yourself comfortable. Deuce need some?"

"Don't let him fool you—I already fed him." Lee spun the seat around and sat in it with a huff and a grumble that sounded too geriatric. Hips and knees hurting. Bad arm aching. Eye-socket burning and itching. If he kept losing bits of himself, there wasn't going to be much left after a while. Yet another ticking clock, but this one, at least, was the least demanding. Provided Lee didn't have any more unfortunate encounters with projectiles. Which was never a guarantee.

There was a knock on the plywood door.

"Password!" Jones demanded, still with his arm over his eyes.

Abe pulled the door open far enough to stick his bearded face in. "File Transfer Protocol."

Jones raised a thumbs-up. "There you go. Welcome to our humble abode."

Funny how little things take on a life of their own, Lee thought. They used humor to disarm the terror. It had begun as a mantra, only a few days into the occupation of Greeley: "Fuck This Place" was murmured by everyone from the lowest boot all the way up to Lee himself. Then it had been shortened to FTP. And, when asked by someone who wasn't a part of the joke, what exactly FTP meant, they were told it meant "File Transfer Protocol."

Bad news just kept coming, and rather than be buried under it, the soldiers and Marines housed up in FOB Hampton would simply shrug it off and say, "File Transfer Protocol." He'd even heard some of their civilian troops begin to pick up on it. One might say it was a failure of morale—morale being a laughable concept at this point—but Lee didn't see it that way. It was a way to guard your mind against the terror of your circumstances. To turn the disastrous undercurrent of fear into a joke.

It was a way to stay sane.

Abe pushed the door closed behind him, sniffing the air. "Smells like wheat berries!"

There were five of them now, crammed into the small, ten-by-ten box. Gear and weapons piled in corners. Lee and Abe both kept their own offices with their own gear and bedrolls, and they'd go there to sleep, but Sam's little room had become the meeting spot for five like-minded survivors to gather, and to talk, and to pretend, for a time, that this camaraderie was the extent of their existence, and that they wouldn't eventually have to exit that room back into a dark world where you were never sure what was going to come at you next. Here was their little microcosm of banality in a world gone wild, and they all clung to it, addicted in a way, to the brief sense of well-being it gave them—a bright spot in otherwise dark days. There'd been no decision, no plan to make it happen, no talk about what it meant to any of them. Talking about it would only break the delicate suspension of disbelief that it provided. By unspoken agreement, they just kept gathering here, and here, they were not ranked, they were not who they were on the other side of the plywood, they were just…friends.

Sam made to stand and offer his chair to Abe, but Abe waved him down and chose instead to lean against the wall. The plywood panels creaked and shifted, but the structure was sturdy.

Marie leaned back from the pot of wheat and crossed her legs under her, looking up at Abe. "Get anything useful out of Javier?"

Abe grimaced. "Unfortunately, no. Not anything I didn't already know, anyways." Abe shoved his hands in his pockets and spread his feet a bit, leaning harder against the wall. "I think he's being forthcoming. Trying to be cooperative, at least. So I can say with relative certainty that Briggs *is* in Greeley somewhere. Javier says he had a place to go to ground—like a panic room or something. And it's somewhere in the city, or in close proximity to it at least."

"Well, that's good," Lee observed. "At least we know we're not searching for somebody that ain't even here."

Abe nodded. "Problem is, Javier says he has no clue where this safe room is. He says Briggs was paranoid about it. He's the only one that knew its location, and wouldn't let anyone else in on the secret. And I believe him. He doesn't know where the safe room is. But he thinks Briggs is still there. Said he went to ground the morning we hit. Went without an escort, just up and skedaddled and didn't tell anyone where he was going."

"Been ten days," Lee said. "How long can you survive in a safe room?"

Abe shrugged. "Guess that depends on the safe room. We talking about a steel closet somewhere with a few jugs of water and some MREs? Or are we talking about a big ass bunker? I don't know. He might be running out of food and water as we speak. Or he could be set up for life in there. Who knows?"

"And Javier can't offer any insight on that?" Sam spoke up. "He was the head of accounting before he was COO, right? Is there anything he might've seen or noticed, like maybe Briggs stockpiling food and water somewhere?"

"I asked," Abe said with a sigh. "But he says he doesn't know. Said that if Briggs did that stuff, he didn't leave a paper trail."

"Hm." Lee's eye wandered back to the pot, watching the steam rise. Between the steam and the five bodies and their breath, the room was warm and muggy. But he didn't mind. He flicked his eye up to Abe. "Javier still with us?"

A single nod from Abe. "He is. I didn't bang him up *that* bad." A small smile, directed at Marie. "You were right—he caved quick. Lucky for him. And I believe he's told me everything he knows."

Lee started at a vibration in his right leg. Slapped a hand to the pocket, realizing it was the satphone going off. Griffin's satphone.

"Ah," Lee sneered, removing his hand from the phone. "Just Griffin nagging me again." He acted cavalier about it, but it belied the painful drop in his stomach, the mushroom cloud of anxiety bursting right there in his sternum.

"Eventually, you're going to have to answer," Abe said.

Lee nodded. "You're right. But not today. I got nothing to say to him that I haven't already said. He'll demand proof of life and make threats. But if he actually intended on making a move, he wouldn't be calling to tell me about it. What do you plan to do with Javier?"

Abe drew his hands out of his pockets and raised his arms, stretching languidly. "I was gonna ask you the same question. I mean, the guy's not a warfighter. We don't have to worry about him doing shit. He's a bookworm that got shoved into COO. Not a threat. Then again, I'm not sure that guarantees him mercy. He's still Cornerstone."

"Did you guarantee him mercy?" Sam asked, quietly.

Lee watched Abe's face as he felt the satphone finally stop vibrating.

"I did," Abe acknowledged. "That doesn't mean I have to honor it."

Sam popped his eyebrows up in a facial shrug. "Guess that's up to you and what you can live with."

Abe gave him a sardonic look. "Ooh-hoo. Look at who's all morally superior."

Sam rolled his eyes and raised his hands in surrender. "Didn't mean it like that. I just meant exactly what I said. Don't read into it. Do what feels right."

Abe frowned at Sam, but it lacked malice. "Thank you, Oracle of the Half-Boots. Glad I have your permission."

"Just kill him," Marie said, as dismissively as if they were talking about a troublesome rat, pilfering their grain.

The satphone started buzzing again.

It was a muted noise inside Lee's pocket, and yet everyone heard it and looked over.

Lee frowned at the lump beneath the fabric of his pants.

"Boy," Jones said, sitting up finally. "He's insistent today."

Lee grumbled under his breath and drew out the satphone, looking at the little readout, thinking, for some reason, that maybe it wasn't Griffin that was calling after all. But it was. Lee wasn't sure who else he expected. He set the satphone on his leg without answering.

He refocused on Marie. "That's some cold-hearted talk, there, young lady."

Buzz, buzz, buzz went the satphone.

Marie shook her head. "Just being practical, Lee. Can he do anything around here that would make it worth the food to keep him alive? I doubt it. We don't need an accountant. So we let him walk away? Someone will learn about it and wonder why we let a Cornerstone guy go. Keeping him costs food. Letting him walk costs respect. Killing him costs nothing but a bullet. And frankly, would probably be a mercy. Let the poor bastard loose, you're just feeding him to the wolves."

The satphone stopped buzzing again.

Lee relaxed a little when it did. "Jones? Sam? What's your take on it? Just for, you know, conversation's sake."

Jones made a noncommittal noise. "I don't really care either way. I mean, I get what Sam's saying. If you promise him life, maybe just let him go. Marie's right, he'll die anyways, but at least you kept your promise. Then again, Marie's also right in saying it might just be better for everyone if you cap him."

Sam listened, then shrugged. "Guess I don't have much to add. If I was Abe, I would let him go. But that's just me. And..." Sam looked at Abe earnestly. "I really don't care, Abe. I already know you're a mad bastard."

Abe snorted. "Hey. I have feelings."

Sam nodded quickly, feigning guilelessness. "No, yeah, of course you do."

The satphone started buzzing again.

"What the fuck?" Lee barked at it, sitting up.

They all stared at it again. Then at Lee.

Abe pushed himself off the wall. "Maybe you should see what he wants."

"Motherfucker," Lee mumbled, snatching the device up and jamming his finger on the answer button. "What is it?" he practically barked into the phone.

Griffin's cool voice immediately came back: "We need to meet. In person."

"I'm not—"

"Let me talk for ten fucking seconds," Griffin suddenly snarled, the air of calm collectedness shattering in a way that surprised even Lee.

"Okay," Lee ground out after a moment's pause. "Talk."

"We've got a situation that affects both of us. It is urgent, and it is serious. I will meet you at any neutral location of your choosing."

Lee sat forward in his seat, the others craning closer to hear the dim sound of the other line and try to suss out what was being said. "You're serious about this."

"I already said that I was," Griffin snapped back. "You pick the spot. You wanna bring some guys, go right ahead. I'll bring some of mine, but I'm operating under truce, do you understand? This is for talking only."

Lee frowned, staring into the middle distance, his heart keeping a steady, hard rhythm. "And when are you talking about meeting?"

"Now," Griffin said, immediately. "Right now."

TWENTY-FIVE

THE MEETING

OF ALL THE PEOPLE under Lee's command, Brinly had held his shit together the best. It almost seemed to Lee, that while the rest of them were wearing down with each day, Brinly was somehow energized by it all. There were times, looking at him, during some of the shittiest situations that they'd had so far, where he appeared darkly radiant.

None of that wrathful radiance was evident now, though. He glowered, arms folded across his broad chest. Eyes dangerous little slits of suspicion. Mouth a hard line of distaste.

"I don't like it," he declared.

"You know," Lee said, cocking the eyebrow over his good eye. "Several years ago I had this same conversation with some other folks about meeting *you*."

Brinly glanced up from the map laid out on the table. "Maybe you should have listened. We almost killed you. A few times."

"Why in person?" Abe wondered. "Why not over the phone?"

"Get a better read on me, I assume," Lee said.

"If he wants to see if you're lying about Briggs," Marie put in. "Why give him that advantage?"

Lee shook his head. "This isn't about Briggs. Not saying it won't come up—I'm sure it will. And yes, maybe he'll try to read my bluff. But he's talking about primals—infected. Something's got his dander up about it."

Brinly managed to somehow frown even deeper. "You think they're giving him problems out there?"

"What? A few packs of primals against his entire army?" Lee didn't buy that. "It's gotta be something else." He chopped a hand through the air. "In any case, that's all beside the point. I already agreed. We need to just figure out where and how."

Brinly huffed through his nose. "Just trying to make sense of why you agreed."

Because we need to break this stalemate? Lee thought. *Because I'm running out of ideas? Because something in his voice worried me?* All thoughts best kept to himself. But that last one made him wonder: Was the fear he heard in Griffin's voice just his own bluff? Was he feigning weakness to draw Lee into a trap?

Lee didn't discount anything. But that didn't change the fact that he knew he had to go to this meeting, whether he could be honest with the others about his reasons or not. Something had to give. Something had to break, or bend. Because Lee was stuck. And yes, there was a possibility that he would be the one being broken or bent. But it also felt like he didn't have a choice. For a week he'd been trying to figure a way out of this, and he'd come up with nothing. Now, there was a chance, however slim, that this meeting might illuminate a way. And Lee's brain was so sore and sick from hashing over the same failed thought patterns that he found himself desperate for that chance.

"Right, well..." Brinly leaned over the map on the table and stabbed his finger down on it. "Based on my experiences, I'd say the bridge on the south end. The same one I came over during the first assault. I noted on my way in, the lack of places to put snipers for overwatch on the south side of that bridge. Tree line will be sparse on his side, and thicker on ours. So, we'll mitigate his ability to have effective overwatch, and maximize our own."

Lee nodded, looking down at the map. "Also forces him into a bottle-neck, if he's planning some stupid shit like trying to push through. At the very least, he won't be able to flank us on a bridge. Though I don't think an assault is what he wants—if it were, there's no reason for him to let us pick the spot, or give us any warning. If he wanted an assault, he could pick a thousand different entry points and be deep into Greeley by the time we even knew it."

"Agreed," Abe noted. "Assault doesn't make sense. Even so. Shouldn't rule it out."

Lee was staring at the hand-drawn lines that denoted the bridge. Picturing it in his mind, putting himself there in the center, facing Griffin. "I like the bridge. The bridge makes sense to me. And it's as good a spot as we're likely to find. Anyone have any counter-points we haven't thought of?"

No one spoke up. It was just the six of them—Sam and his three team members, and Lee, Abe, and Brinly, all crammed into the little office that Lee had chosen as his personal room. The map laid out on the desk, and the six of them all standing around it.

"Alright," Lee straightened. "I want our guys there before I even tell Griffin where we're meeting. Brinly, I want four machine gun nests, two on either side of the bridge, but back in the woods, with overlapping fields of fire. Then I want two more guntrucks on the road, just north of the bridge, but with a clear line of sight to engage if shit goes wonky. Put Greenman in with them. I want him on the roof of a MATV, ready to splash Griffin's brains if I give him the signal."

Brinly nodded along. "Which is?"

"I'll go in with an open line on the satphone. I want you there with Greenman so you can hear everything at the same time he does. Keep it on speaker. Audible signal will be 'helluva ride.' Visual signal, I'll raise my hands in a surrender position." Lee looked to the others, sweeping his eye across all of them. "Y'all are going in with me. But you'll stop at the edge of the bridge. Only me and Griffin on the bridge. Anyone else steps foot on it, then it's go-time." He rubbed the back of his neck. "We gotta assume Griffin will have similar plans. In which case…" he met each of their gazes in turn. "If I go down, you leave my ass there. Do not get sucked into a trap with me as bait, you guys got that?"

They all nodded, the seriousness of their undertaking seeming to settle on the room like a heavy fog.

"If the shooting starts, I'm not running all the way back across the bridge. I'm gonna pitch myself over the side and into the river. Brinly, just tell your boys not to rake me with fifty-cal if they see a shape coming up out of the water."

"Understood."

"If I go down, Abe has control. If shit hits the fan and I toss my ass in the river, Abe has control until I can get back with you guys. If Abe goes down, Brinly, you'll have control." Something in Lee's gut did a slight twist at that, and he found himself glancing at Brinly as he said it, though the Marine was still staring at the map.

It wasn't lost on Lee that Brinly had been the cause of Lee's new label as a war criminal. Yes, Lee was responsible for telling the man to do whatever he needed to do—when someone got creative with their orders, that was the fault of the man who had issued the orders. Lee had left it up to Brinly's interpretation, and for that, Lee was at fault.

But Brinly was the one that had chosen to interpret it in the way that he had. And that was on him.

He didn't want Brinly to have control of what happened in Greeley if he and Abe were to go down. But who else was there? Sam, Marie, and Jones had all turned out to be valuable operators, but none of them had command experience like Brinly did. They were good in a firefight—but that didn't mean they knew how to organize troops. Besides that, they would be with Abe, and if he went down, there was a good chance they were going down with him. So they were not an option.

Angela was out of the picture. Hell, he hadn't even seen or heard from her in several days. If she had any intention of acting as their civilian leadership, Lee hadn't witnessed it. Even if she was there with them at that moment, Lee thought he would have still chosen Brinly.

There simply wasn't another option.

Lee was finding that to be the case with a great many things, lately.

"Alright," Lee breathed. "Brinly, get your Marines into position. Have the rest on a hair-trigger standby, just in case. Abe, disseminate that same readiness to the rest of the troops around here. I want everyone ready to fight for their lives if Griffin tries to pull an invasion on us." He put on a confident smile for the benefit of the others, even though it felt like cracked and weathered wood on his face. "Let's hope for the best and prepare for the worst."

***

It was ninety minutes later, under a red-painted dusk, that Lee found himself standing on the bridge over the South Platte River. Looking across it to the opposite side, he saw the glimmer of headlights approaching. He'd only given Griffin thirty minutes to respond and get here, which had hopefully taken away his ability to plan much and station troops ahead of time.

Still, Lee stared at those approaching lights, wondering if there wasn't a massive convoy of assault vehicles behind the set that he could see. Were they going to just plow straight through and begin their assault? Was this the moment that Griffin called Lee's bluff?

Lee shifted his weight, and worked his shoulders underneath the armor. He'd considered not even wearing it—if he had to ditch over the side of the bridge, the armor certainly wasn't going to help him swim. But he figured he'd be more likely to catch a round on his way over the side, so he chose to wear the armor. He was rather tired of catching rounds at this point in time in his life.

Still, he'd left the armor loosely strapped so he could get it off quickly, and he'd opted to go in with only the pistol on his hip, so he wouldn't have to mess with the strap of the rifle if he found himself drowning.

The headlights blazed brighter as they drew closer. Lee stiffened, waiting for the moment when they wouldn't stop, just keep coming over the bridge, right at him. It's difficult to track the movement of a light that's staring you right in the face, but after a moment of squinting at it, he realized that it had stopped, as instructed, just short of the bridge.

In the waning twilight, Lee could just make out the shadows of doors popping open. The sound of them slamming reached him. The movement of figures caused the headlights to appear to flicker. Soldiers, taking up positions. Lee had expected no less. Griffin likely wasn't keen to be drawn into a trap either.

After another few tense moments of peering at those lights, Lee caught sight of a lone figure striding out onto the bridge.

"I guess that's him," Lee said over his shoulder, taking one last glance at Abe, Sam, Marie, and Jones, who were standing there in full kit. "Wish me luck, and be ready for anything."

They all nodded in response, eyes staring past Lee to the other side of the bridge.

Lee turned back around and began walking out. The bridge was roughly three hundred yards long. They were going to meet in the center. Just the two of them. Lee and Griffin, face to face for the first time in many, many years. Even before the pandemic had struck, they hadn't seen each other in a few years. That last time Lee had seen Griffin in the flesh, it'd been on one of the Coordinators' occasional get-togethers. They'd met at a bar in Cincinnati. The last memory Lee had of Griffin was his lean face, clean shaven, under an old ballcap, smiling and draining a longneck under dim, reddish lighting.

Again, that odd sense of nostalgia washed over him as he kept count of his steps. He'd been fighting for so long for survival in the present, he'd barely ever had a chance to look back at much. Now, perhaps, because he was locked in a stalemate, not knowing what was in front of him, he found his memories searching backwards more often.

Lee had counted a hundred and twenty-nine steps when Griffin stopped, just a short distance from him, apparently deciding that he had reached the halfway point. Maybe he'd been counting his strides too.

Lee continued forward for another handful, each step coming a bit slower as he got closer and closer to the man. More of Griffin's face came into focus through the backlighting of the headlights behind him. Not too different from what he remembered, though he had a short beard now. No ballcap. No longneck beers to share. And any semblance of amiability had been stricken from him, so that his face was made up of unkind lines and harsh angles as he watched Lee come to a stop, separated now by only a few feet.

Griffin sized him up clinically, but Lee just watched the other man's eyes. Maybe searching for some scant breath of friendliness that had survived the war they'd waged on each other. If it was there, he couldn't see it.

"Well," Griffin remarked. "You look like shit."

Lee gave a small shrug. "My body's seen better days."

Griffin's eyes went back to Lee's face and coursed between his good eye and his ruined socket. "When'd you lose your eye?"

Lee smirked without humor. "When you assaulted the Butler Safe Zone. When'd you lose your sense of honor?"

Lee wasn't jabbing randomly. He'd intended to see how much of a rise he could get out of Griffin, and he wasn't disappointed. Griffin's eyes flared like something had detonated deep inside of him.

"Really?" Griffin seethed, his anger well-controlled, but evident nonetheless. "That's your opening sally? This, coming from a man who just massacred the civilians he claimed to be liberating?"

Griffin had always been a cool customer. Frankly, Lee was surprised he was even able to get an emotional response out of him. He'd assumed he'd have to press much harder to get it. Now, seeing it clearly, and so quickly, he noted it to himself and allowed Griffin's words to wash over him. *Be cooler than he is. That's one advantage. Maybe your only advantage.*

Lee sniffed, displaying calm imperturbability. "No, massacring civilians isn't really my forte. I was introduced to the concept fairly recently, when you vaporized a bunch of them with your Predator drones, again, in Butler."

"That wasn't my decision," Griffin bit back.

"Well, neither was what happened in Greeley."

Griffin shifted his weight. "Honor," he spat. "What about treason, Lee? What about the oaths you took?"

"I live them every day," Lee replied, coolly.

Griffin shook his head, his teeth catching the light, flashing in a grimace. "Oh, that's rich. You forgot the part about obeying your Commander-in-Chief."

"I didn't forget," Lee said. "I don't have one."

"You do. His name's Erwin Briggs."

"I don't consider self-appointed despots to be eligible for the position."

"And what do you consider yourself?"

"Someone who's doing their fucking job," Lee snapped, letting himself loose, but just a little bit. "*Subvenire Refectus*. Rescue and rebuild? That ring any bells for you?"

"We had something built," Griffin hissed, jabbing a finger over Lee's shoulder. "Until you came along and fucked it up."

Lee smiled. "I wouldn't be here at all if you hadn't fucked up what *I* built."

Griffin shook his head. "You were operating illegally. You were a nonviable asset. Does *that* ring any bells? It started the day you left your bunker against your orders. Everything after that, no matter how well-intentioned, was tainted by the fact that you did it illegally. You made yourself into a criminal, Lee. Don't blame me for bringing the law down on you."

"Because you were just following orders, right?" Lee asked, raising his eyebrows.

Griffin gave him a nasty look and leaned forward, his voice dropping to a dangerous, low tone. "I'm not the one that's gonna be on trial, Lee. That's you. A war criminal."

"Ah. Sounds like you've been talking to the Canadians and Brits." He watched Griffin carefully after leveling that statement, but Griffin wisely kept a poker face. He said nothing to confirm or deny that he had their backing now.

"I'll tell you what, Lee," Griffin said, straightening his shoulders and seeming to smooth the anger out of him into a glossy calm. "You send President Briggs out right now, alive and unharmed, and give yourself up as a war criminal and a traitor to your country, and I will allow all of your people to surrender peacefully."

Lee didn't move. "I think we both know that's not going to happen." He put on a pained face. "Were we just going to rehash the same bullshit? Or did you have something else to talk about? Infected giving you some problems?"

It was like all the tiny muscles that animated Griffin's face suddenly went slack. In the absence of any expression, it was only his eyes that bore into Lee, and in them Lee saw the fear that he had heard on the phone, and it transmitted to him like a sudden illness.

"They're going to be a problem for both of us," Griffin said quietly.

Griffin's face may have gone slack, but Lee's face had hardened, tightened. Everything—lips, eyes, brow—tense. "Explain."

"This morning," Griffin said, his voice quietly intense, every word a deliberate action. "I received reports of a horde of infected coming from the south."

Lee quirked his head slightly. "For clarity, what type of infected are we talking about?"

"The original kind are all dead. These are the ones that took their place."

Primals. "And did you investigate these reports?"

The ghost of a ghastly smile touched Griffin's mouth. "Investigated, yes. And confirmed. I sent two recon teams south towards the last known location of the alleged horde. They came into contact with them roughly sixty miles south of us."

Lee's brain was already doing the math. Already forming the timelines. He knew how fast those things could eat up distance. Not only were they fast, they didn't seem to tire like a normal human would. Sixty miles was nothing for them to cross in a day. *Less* than a day, even.

"I've already done the math, Lee," Griffin said, apparently seeing the machinations in Lee's face. "Why do you think I demanded the meeting so quickly? I'd love to say that we don't have much time, but the fact is, we don't have any time at all."

There was one piece of arithmetic Lee was missing, though. "How many?"

Griffin shook his head once. "They couldn't give an accurate count, as the horde was raising a massive dust cloud. The recon team that put eyes on gave me a rough estimate of anywhere between two and five thousand."

Lee would have choked if his throat hadn't gone suddenly dry. He could actually feel the blood draining out of his face. "And they're heading this way?"

"They're heading north," Griffin replied, his voice a little odd, almost distracted, as though he were picturing what would come upon them soon. "The predators go where the prey is. And right now, all the prey within hundreds of square miles is right here in Greeley." His eyes became serious. "Including my men."

Lee squinted at him. Even as his pulse pounded and his palms moistened with the prospect of it—images from the fall of the Moody Safe Zone racing through his brain; the people being carried off and torn to pieces; the primal latching onto his wrist, making it ache now with the memory of its teeth ripping at his tendons—all of that was happening at the same time that another thought occurred to him.

Was this a ruse? A bluff? Was Griffin trying to get Lee to willingly open the doors to him? Trying to unite them against a fictitious enemy so that he could break Lee apart from the inside?

"What are you trying to do right now?" Lee husked.

The anger came back to Griffin's face—genuine, or an act? "What am I doing? Pull your head out of your ass, Lee! A few hundred of those fucking things were enough to lay waste to your Safe Zones, and you're asking me what I'm doing when I tell you about several *thousand*?"

Lee stood there, trying like hell to soak Griffin in, to see every twitch in his face, every micromovement of his features, searching for some evidence of falsehood, and coming up empty-handed.

"I'm talking about complete fucking annihilation," Griffin snarled, droplets of spit catching the light of the headlamps. "Not just for our armies, but for every human being in Greeley. And I don't know if you know this, Lee, but a lot of those civilians have fled your warzone and are now hunkered down in a hangar in that airport. We all have our asses hanging in the wind right now."

"Well, what the fuck do you want me to do about it?" Lee growled.

"I don't know yet," Griffin answered, honestly. "That's why I needed to talk to you, face to face."

"You think I have some magic dog whistle to call them off?" Lee was flabbergasted, set on his heels by the revelation of thousands of primals bearing down on them, and only worsened by the odd powerlessness in Griffin's face. And, if Lee were being honest, he likely had something similar scribbled on his own features.

Two men with armies at their backs, and yet nowhere to run, no ideas of how to survive something as unstoppable as a force of nature. And it *was* a force of nature, wasn't it? It was evolution gone awry. The product of out-of-control mutations, and a mass of them too numerous to fight off was right around the corner.

"Give me Briggs," Griffin suddenly said, clenching a fist like he thought Briggs was something he could just reach out and grab. "This is beyond what we're fighting for Lee. This is beyond politics. This is survival."

But Lee was already shaking his head. Not just because he didn't have Briggs to hand over in the first place—hell, if he did, he might've actually considered it—but because now it felt to him that Griffin was simply using a terrible circumstance to try to gain the upper hand. And that was something Lee would not allow.

"Lee!" Griffin barked in his face. "Give me the president! If you give me Briggs, we'll leave—you can leave too! We can all get the hell out of here, head north, and maybe the Brits and Canadians can give us enough air support to take the horde down to a manageable size."

It took a moment, in all of the rippling sensations of deep-seeded fear and misgivings, for Lee to realize that the satphone was buzzing in his pocket. He twitched when he felt it, still holding Griffin's gaze, while his hand touched his pocket. It was supposed to be an open line so that Brinly could listen into what was happening. Had it been accidentally disconnected?

A worse possibility dawned on Lee: Maybe Brinly had *intentionally* disconnected so that he could call him. Because something bad had happened.

Were they here? Had the horde arrived already?

Lee dove into his pocket and shucked out the satphone. Griffin frowned at him, but didn't object, though he did draw back a half step and blade his body, as though he thought Lee was going to come out with something dangerous.

Not sure what exactly to feel in that moment—fear of the possibilities, anger at the interruption—Lee stabbed the call button and put it to his ear. "What?"

Brinly's voice was quiet. "I'm keeping my voice down so he doesn't hear. Lee, Briggs has just started transmitting on a broad radio frequency. He's saying that he is not in our pocket, and he's calling for the people to fight for him. And, Lee…if we've picked it up, you can bet your ass that Griffin's folks have."

The only thing Lee could think of to do in that moment was turn away, so that Griffin couldn't see the crashing panic all over his face. He didn't know what to say. Anything he did say might give him away.

Brinly must've been thinking the same thing. "Lee, if you've heard and understood my message, just say yes."

"Yes," Lee said, the word rotten and swollen like a dead thing tumbling out of his mouth.

"You need to disengage—immediately. If Griffin doesn't already know, he's gonna know any second, and this truce is gonna go up in gunfire."

Should he tell Brinly about the primals? Should he act like everything was okay, not show any weakness, then simply tell Griffin that their talks were done and get the hell out of there before Griffin got word—

"Go ahead." Two words. Griffin's voice. A quiet murmur.

Lee turned, frowning, and saw Griffin wasn't even looking at him. He had his head tilted to one side, as though listening to something. The headlamps behind him illuminating the coiled acoustic tube of his radio earpiece.

There was no way to know what was being said on that other line. And yet…Lee knew. He saw it in the way Griffin was so very still—unnaturally still, like he didn't want to give anything away. Just like Lee hadn't. The slight furrowing of his brow, as though he were trying to come up with a strategy for what to do next.

Disengage. Get out of there now, before he can come up with something.

Lee left the phone on, but lowered it. He looked right at Griffin, and Griffin raised his eyes, looking right at him, and they both knew in that moment exactly what the other person knew. Their fragile truce teeter-tottered on the moment.

"We're done here," Lee rasped, and turned to walk away.

He was stopped cold by a sound on the wind. It touched his ears, and lit off a reaction that skittered unpleasantly up from the center of him, crawled up his spine, and down his arms and legs, tingling darkly in his fingers and toes.

A howl. Long, and clear. And not too far away.

Someone less experienced with that sound might've wondered if it was a coyote, or maybe even just the wind. But Lee knew it from so many times before, and his mind painted the image even as his eardrums still hummed with the noise of it.

He turned halfway back, his eye wide as he stared at Griffin.

Griffin was looking right back at him, his lips squashed to a thin, shadowy slash. But his head was turned slightly, like a cat that's heard something behind it.

Lee's arms hung at his sides, his right hand very close to his holstered pistol, twitching slightly with each slamming pulse of his heart.

In the wake of the howl, the silence seemed to roar.

Could he get off this bridge before the shooting started? Was Griffin going to initiate it? He knew, dammit, he knew! But the howl had come from the south—behind Griffin's men. Would he risk all of them to take Lee down, or would he do the more cautious thing and retreat while they still had their skins?

And what are all those primals going to do to Greeley?

All Lee had to do was raise his hands, or utter the words, "helluva ride."

But he was surprised to realize that he didn't want Griffin dead.

Did Griffin have any such reservations about him?

"What happens now?" Lee asked, his voice plain.

Griffin's hand moved closer to his own holstered weapon. "You put your hands up and surrender."

"You don't want me to do that."

Griffin's gaze flicked over Lee's shoulder, knowing in an instant what Lee meant by it. His thumb touched the backstrap of his pistol as he refocused on Lee. "You tricky sonofabitch," he sneered. "I'll admit: You've always been hard to pin down."

Time's up.

Lee lurched for the side of the bridge.

Griffin let out a yelp. The scrape of a pistol being drawn, and suddenly the night was crashing and booming, Lee hobbling as fast as his bum leg could go for the concrete wall of the bridge, muzzle flashes dancing in his peripheral, the air suddenly filled with humming and screeching and whining, a cavalcade of noise that exploded into existence like the devil himself had just ruptured through the crust of the earth.

Lee hit the concrete wall as a round smacked the pavement just behind him. He glanced to his right, trying to see if it was Griffin shooting at him, but Griffin had turned his back and was hauling ass south, framed by blooms of rifle fire from his men.

Lee shoved his torso up and over the wall and was a hair's breadth from pitching himself over, when he caught sight of dark shapes rippling through the water below him. For a tiny second, he hoped they were just whorls in the water, but then he saw the dim, red light from the western sky, glinting off of wet skin.

Then he realized his momentum was still carrying him over the edge. He tried to pin himself back with his left leg, but the shattered hip ground and screamed through his body, weakening his muscles. He was going over. Fighting for a handhold. The satphone fell from his grip, spiraling down into the darkness. His weak left hand slipped, concrete scraping his calluses off. His right hand shot up and seized a narrow gap in the concrete, wedging itself there, despite the pain it caused.

His legs swung down over empty air. Shoulders and wrists straining against the sudden weight. Dammit, but if he hadn't worn the armor…

Boots scrabbling for purchase as he gasped, staring down past his thrashing feet, and seeing one of them looking up at him. Red twilight glimmered across its wide, bared teeth, illuminated feral eyes. But then it looked away, disappearing into darkness again as it slashed its way for the northern shore.

He had no comms, no phone. No way to warn the machine gun nests of the threat coming up below them. No way but his own dim voice, screaming into the thundering darkness: "Primals! Primals in the river!"

TWENTY-SIX

THE BAD ONES

GRIFFIN HAD BEEN SHOT THREE TIMES before he crashed into the brushguard of the MATV. Two of the shots had hit him square in the back—stopped by his armor. One of them had damn near knocked him off his feet, and definitely knocked the wind out of him. He was still wheezing as he clawed his way around to the passenger side, looking down at the third shot, which hadn't been caught by his armor.

His left pant leg was dark, just above the knee on the outside. Strangely, the pain hadn't hit him yet—just the knowing that it was bad. The certainty that something was irreparably broken. His left leg had no stability to it anymore, wobbling every time he put weight on it.

A round splashed against the MATV's armor, spall ripping across his shoulder and slicing at his face. He cried out, one eye squinted closed as he ripped the passenger door open. "Get us out of here!" he screamed at the driver, who looked all too eager to comply.

A flash of movement to Griffin's left as he tried to haul his wobbly leg into the vehicle. He had his pistol in hand already. Jammed it out as something nightmarish came looming out of the darkness at him, painted red by the MATV's taillights. He dumped his magazine, every round striking the target, too close to miss, but not seeming to have any effect. It just kept coming, thrashing towards him, jaws gnashing. Blinding panic shrunk his entire world down to his own muzzle flashes illuminating a gaping maw of bared teeth.

He barely heard the heavy impacts, but he felt them against the door that his hand was still on. A smattering of big rounds—machine gun fire—and then they traced up and took the top of the creature's head off and all that feral madness in its glinting eyes went out like a light.

The thing collapsed into him, twitching and writhing, knocking him into the crook between the door and the body of the vehicle. God, it was heavy! He realized he was still mashing at a dead trigger, then started hitting the thing in its mushed face with his locked-back pistol. Rammed the weapon into its throat and pressed with everything he had until he felt the weight of it roll off of him.

"Get in!" the driver was screaming. "Get in! Get in!"

Someone fired on full-auto, the ear-piercing staccato crack of 5.56mm cartridges.

Griffin grabbed the back of the passenger seat and pulled himself in, twisted, grabbed the door and slammed it—or tried to. The door rebounded off of flesh, and he caught sight of a long-fingered hand groping for him.

"Gah!" he yelped, slamming the door again, and again, until the bones broke and the creature roared outside the window, straining against his door. "Go! Go! Go!"

The engine revved. They were in reverse. The force of the acceleration threw Griffin forward and ripped the door open, but the infected on the other side couldn't get out of the way fast enough, and the bottom of the door clothes-lined it right across the chest, spinning it under the front tires.

The vehicle lurched as it rammed over the creature. The driver spun the wheel, all the rearward momentum suddenly turning to centrifugal force as the big vehicle was whipped in a J-turn maneuver that it had no business doing. Griffin caught himself on the frame of the door before he was thrown out of the vehicle. Headlights flashed across running shapes, leering teeth, predatory eyes—so many of them.

The vehicle rocked to a brief stop, already back in forward gear, tires squealing through dust and scree, the door slamming back into Griffin's face, the cold glass punching him square in the nose.

"Go!" he burbled through a numb mouth, filling up with blood.

But the vehicle was already flying forwards again, ramping back up onto the road and turning hard to the right so Griffin was tossed back into the driver, who elbowed him roughly back into his seat with a yell and a grunt of effort.

Griffin's vision cleared just enough to see a body flying at the front of the vehicle, slamming into the brush guard with a terminal *BANG* and disappearing underneath, the rear of the vehicle jumping as the knobby tires smashed across the infected's body.

"Fuck! Fuck! Fuck!" Griffin screamed his throat raw at the windshield, blood from his mouth and nose speckling it. *Blood.* He remembered his leg wound, and with his remembrance, a tidal wave of pain nearly laid him out.

"You okay?" one of his guys was shouting, he had no idea who—everyone's voices sounded indistinct and muddy.

"Ah!" was all Griffin could get out as his shaking hands—his right still holding the empty pistol—bumbled about his chest rig until he felt his fingers hit the tourniquet strapped there. He ripped clumsily at the straps. Dropped the pistol in his lap. Eyes going down into the darkness of the cab where he could only see a glimmer of wetness by the glow of the headlights.

"Hey!" A warm hand latched onto the side of his sweat-cold face. "You with me?"

He recognized *that* voice. It was Paige, from the backseat, now jammed into the space between the driver's and passenger's chairs.

"Uh-huh," Griffin choked out, ripping the tourniquet open. God, but his fingers were not working properly.

"You need me to do that?" Paige's voice stabbed at Griffin's ears.

"No!"

"Can you listen?"

"Yes!" Griffin looped the tourniquet around his thigh, above the wound. Took a deep breath and readied himself for the pain to get worse.

"I told 'em to evac the airfield and move north, away from Greeley."

Griffin yanked the tourniquet tight. Hot, broken pain shot through his thigh and up into his pelvis. "Motherfffff…!"

"You want me to cancel that?"

"Not you!" Griffin seethed, blood frothing through his teeth. "Fuck!"

"Lemme do it," Paige snapped, his body crashing over Griffin's shoulder, his hands batting Griffin's away as he seized the windlass. "This is gonna suck."

"Stop talking."

Paige stopped talking, and got to cranking. Every spin of the windlass was like a vice being tightened right on the wound. Every revolution an exponential compounding of pain. Griffin could do nothing but grab his hands together and ram his right leg hard against the floorboards.

He was going to be a one-legged gimp now. Just like Lee.

***

Right about the time that Griffin was slamming into his MATV and registering the fact that he had a hole in his leg, Lee was dangling over the side of the bridge, and realizing that his own orders might be the thing that killed him.

He'd managed to get his boots onto a narrow ledge of concrete and pull his body back up. Everything in him shook and strained. He put the side of his face against the top of the concrete barrier—it was the only way to balance himself in his precarious hold.

He ground his chin in, using it to hold him there while he got his right hand out from where it'd been wedged in that gap. The skin was missing from his knuckles. He grabbed the top of the concrete, and finally didn't need his face for balance anymore, so he looked south.

There were bodies coming across the bridge, glimmering in the wild sweeping slashes of Griffin's headlights. Not soldiers—the outlines were all wrong. Primals. Primals were pouring across the bridge.

And he'd told his team *not* to try to come after him.

Lee froze there, clinging to the side of the bridge and staring at the nearest primal as it sprinted along on its muscled legs. He couldn't drop into the water. He couldn't run. His best chance was to stay hidden and hope to God the primals didn't notice him on the side of the bridge—

And right when he thought that, the lead primal snapped its head over and looked right at him.

Lee bared his teeth at it. No escape now. No running. No swimming. No help.

He looped his left arm over the side and snatched his pistol out with his right hand. Leveled it at the charging primal. Tried to estimate the distance, but depth perception was a bitch when you only had one eye. He held high, thinking the primal was fifty yards and closing, but when he fired, he couldn't tell where the round had gone. So he fired again. And as the distance shrank, he fired faster and faster, until finally he saw them slam into the thing's chest, but didn't stop it—they never did.

And Lee was oddly calm about it. Everything in his body was screaming for survival, an earthquake of adrenaline shrinking his peripheral vision, shaking his limbs, putting his heart and lungs into overdrive. But his mind was somehow clear. The clarity of death.

He knew it was going to end this way. He'd always known it.

People like him didn't get to die any way but violently.

His slide locked back, and it was over, ticket all but punched, and he considered if he should just pitch backwards and take his chances with the river, when a massive tan shape came screaming up out of nowhere and slammed into that leading primal, sending its body flying in a boneless arc.

Abe's face, mouth wrenching in a scream, as he clung to the side of the MATV, reaching for Lee, but Lee couldn't hear what he said, because the turret was thundering, raking the incoming primals.

Abe's hand grabbed onto Lee's right wrist. The empty pistol fell out of his grasp and there wasn't time to pick it up. The MATV's headlights illuminated the glut of shapes storming towards them, the wall of lead laid down by the turret creating a small bubble of safety that was rapidly collapsing.

Lee stumbled over the wall, found his feet, registered Sam clinging to the side of the MATV as well—there was no room inside the vehicle. Was Lee going to have to—?

"Hang on!" Abe shouted in his ear, propelling him into the side of the MATV.

Lee scrambled for holds, getting his feet on the running boards and squashing his hands down next to Sam's on the only handhold there was—a small, black bar between the front and rear doors. Abe smashed himself against the sideview mirror, using it as his handhold and slapped the window manically.

Lee knew what was coming but was still shocked by the force of the acceleration as the MATV went squealing into reverse. His hands, slaked in blood from his torn-up knuckles, slipped, his left leg shaking as he was forced to use it to keep from flying off the vehicle. His body leaned hard into Abe, and he tried to pull back, but the forces were too strong to fight.

The concrete whirred by beneath them in a blinding blur. The shapes of the attacking primals began to retreat. The speed grew even greater, but Lee's body managed to overcome the break of inertia and right itself. He jammed his hands harder into the handhold with Sam's. Took a glance at the kid, words of encouragement halfway to his tongue, but what he saw was a man's face, and it was Sam that used his elbow to pin Lee tighter to the vehicle.

"Hang on, Lee!" Sam yelled at him.

Lee didn't know whether to feel proud or humbled. He was a bit too shaken to feel either.

He looked past Sam. Saw the treeline, belching with machine gun fire at the primals on the bridge, giving them precious seconds to get the hell out of there, but who was going to get the machine gunners out?

The treeline whipped past.

"Stopping!" someone screamed, and Lee could do nothing but wrench down tight again as the forces now pulled him into Sam, who didn't have a sideview mirror to hold him in. Lee bore down and sunk his body lower, so the heaviest part of him didn't impact Sam. He felt barely-healed tendons in his left hand popping, his fingers slipping.

But then they were stopped, moving forward again, this time in a tight turn, now facing the dark city of Greeley, and already accelerating again before Lee could think to give a command that might help the machine gunners.

But what command could he give? What could save them at this point?

He wanted to tell Abe to make the MATV stop. He wanted to run down into the woods and tell the machine gunners to fall back before the primals in the river could climb the banks to them. But he knew in an instant that it would only kill them all. He couldn't stop the vehicle. And he couldn't run fast enough to save them.

Powerless. He was powerless to stop the coming destruction.

TERMINUS

***

They came upon the city like a killing wind. Silent, but for breath and the pounding of their thousands of feet. They slipped through darkness and stuck to shadows. The swept through alleys and found the places where their prey was hiding. And their prey did not know that they had come until it was too late.

No one knew until knowing could do them no good.

The sound of a door shattering in on its hinges. A father thrashed awake in the darkness, hearing the footsteps and thinking of soldiers from one side or the other come to kill them, and he tried to surrender, but the things that loomed up in the gloom of the little house where he and his wife and children slept had no mercy. He screamed when he saw them and tried to cover his family with his body. But it was too late.

A mother on the street with her twelve-year-old son heard the footfalls and turned to see the mass of them churning towards her, and she was struck dumb by the sight of it. Could do nothing but pull her son into a hug as they crashed into her. Her son was ripped, screaming, from her grip and thrown into the air like a doll, only to be snatched out of his pinwheeling freefall by another and his head dashed to the pavement. She watched it happen and screamed, until she was mounted, and a great, clamping pressure sank into her throat and turned her last moments into muted, choking terror.

A daughter went to a window, already shaken by the rising chorus of screams from outside. Her parents yelled at her to get back, but it was too late for her too. The glass shattered, and she was torn from the house by a multitude of iron-strong arms, then born up like a prize so that she could see her parents reaching for her, and they could see her as she seemed to float away on the darkness, before being sucked down into it and disappearing forever.

The family yelled their daughter's name as though they could pull her back to them by sheer volume, but all that came back through the window was a tangle of muscled limbs, seeming a single organism it was so tightly packed with leering faces and stringy, dreadlocked hair. Claws and teeth, and a strength beyond any man, and they fell under the tide of it.

They swept through the south side of Greeley, creeping ever northward. Through neighborhoods already shattered by war, people that had counted themselves lucky to have survived the endless nights and days of gunfire were torn to the ground and ripped open. Others were mounted and their arms and legs were pulled out of socket.

As the tide of panic began to outpace the tide of death, people tried to run. People tried to hide. People tried to stand their ground and fight. Those that ran were outpaced. Those that hid were found. Those that fought were overwhelmed. Many were fed upon. Many more were simply slaughtered. None were taken away, for the horde had found its breeding grounds, and there was no need to carry them away—they had everything they needed right there.

There was no escape. Hell had come to Greeley, and you cannot escape hell.

TWENTY-SEVEN

LAST DITCH

Angela pushed the stretcher through the mess of chaos that FOB Hampton had turned into. Any semblance of military order had been disrupted—it seemed every squad of soldiers was doing something different, and none of them knew what they *should* be doing, except get as many weapons loaded and deployed as they could.

"It's okay, Abby," Angela murmured through the din of shouted orders, clanking ammo cans, and running boots. "We're gonna get through this. I'm gonna get you someplace safe."

A Marine in a dead sprint nearly toppled the stretcher, skidding to a stop and jostling Abby's inert form. He juked around the stretcher with a mumbled "Sorry, ma'am," and kept running towards the main entrance.

She pressed the stretcher through the mess as fast as she could, angling around men and women and bedrolls and crates and a tripod-mounted M2 that someone had decided to plop right in the center of the lobby, the barrel pointing towards the doors.

She felt like a running back, spotting a narrow lane and charging the stretcher through it, towards the conference room turned hospital. Shouts rose behind her—the pitch different, less controlled, more irate. She managed a glimpse over her shoulder and spotted a gaggle of civilians badgering their way inside. No one seemed to know whether they were supposed to batten down and defend the hotel, or evacuate.

In another time, playing another woman, Angela might have tried to assert some order back into the chaos. But not now. She had other problems to deal with. She had her daughter to think about.

She skimmed through the open doors of the hospital, narrowly missing a woman with a stethoscope still stuck in her ears. Angela didn't wait to spot the man she was looking for, she just added her voice to the cacophony of others: "John! John! I need your help!"

She stopped in the middle of the room, breathing hard and fast, eyes roving across the patients that littered the floor, many of them trying to rise, some of them hobbling off, favoring their wounds. Many of them were too weak to rise, their hands in the air, grasping at anyone that passed by, their frail voices just an undertone of panic to all the rest.

Someone grabbed her arm, and Angela spun, thinking it was one of the patients trying to get her to help them.

"Angela!" John stared at her wide-eyed. "What are you doing down here? How'd you even get Abby down the stairs?"

The soldiers guarding her doors had helped her, right after they'd delivered the news that they were under attack by a massive horde of primals—no other details given—but Angela didn't bother to explain that to John. She seized him by his upper arms, fingers squeezing into his thin flesh.

"John, you have to help me get Abby out of here!"

John goggled at her. "I've got hundreds of patients!"

Angela wasn't having it. Her face twisted into a snarl that brokered no argument. "Just help me get her the fuck out of here!"

John glanced rapidly about, but relented with a quick nod. "Okay. Okay, where are we taking her?"

Angela didn't give him the whole truth, because she didn't have time for him to argue with her. "Out the front! Help me get her in a vehicle!"

John gave no response to that, save to seize the foot of the stretcher and begin pulling it while Angela pushed.

"Make a hole!" John shouted. Soldiers, Marines, and civilians pressing their way inside jostled about and pushed themselves to the sides, creating a narrow alley that John plowed through with his hand up as though he might face-palm anyone that stood in his way.

He wouldn't. But Angela would. She'd already decided that she wouldn't be stopped. Not by anything. Not by anyone.

The stretcher rattled as it passed over the entryway, Abby's head flopping about, dead to the world. The sky was fully dark, a skin of black clouds blocking the stars, but the outside was lit in yellows and whites and reds by hundreds of headlights and taillights.

So many vehicles. A gridlock of them. How the hell was she going to get out of here?

She'd ram her way out, if she had to.

"Which vehicle?" John demanded, turning to face Angela as he pulled the stretcher backwards, elbowing through a crowd of civilian troops.

Angela craned her neck to see over the shoulders of the others, but she wasn't tall enough. Some of them recognized her as she passed, and the fear in their faces turned to shock at seeing her single-mindedly fleeing.

"Are we evacuating?" a man shrilled, jutting his face so close to Angela's that she recoiled and shoved him violently backwards. She didn't bother answering, even as he screamed the question twice more at her back.

They emerged from the crowd and Angela spotted a white utility van sitting unmanned towards the edge of the jam of vehicles. She pointed at it, whirling the head of the stretcher around to head that way. "That one! The white van!"

They pulled up to the rear of the van.

"Are you putting her in the back?" John asked, even as he ripped the back doors open.

"Lemme make sure it has keys," Angela said, running around to the driver side. The keys were supposed to be left in the vehicles, but sometimes people forgot. It'd been an issue that she'd thought inconsequential. Now she wished the rule had been enforced more strictly.

She tore through the driver side of the vehicle until she spotted them in a cupholder in the center console. "Got 'em!" She jammed them into the ignition and cranked. The van started up. Her eyes glanced over the dash, noting that it had a half a tank of fuel. More than enough.

She thrust herself back out and ran to the stretcher. John was already crouched in the back, his hand on the foot of the stretcher, ready to lift. Angela grabbed the bar just below Abby's head. "Ready?"

"Lift!" John said, grunting as he pulled the stretcher up into the back.

Angela strained at the weight of it, but got the wheels onboard. It wasn't a collapsible stretcher, and Abby's face was close to the ceiling of the van, but it would have to do. John pressed himself to the sidewall as Angela shoved the stretcher all the way in and then jammed the heel of her palm down on the wheel brakes.

John started to squeeze towards the back, but Angela closed one of the doors on his face.

"Hey! What're you doing?"

"Sit tight!" Angela snapped. "Just trust me!"

She was going to betray that trust, but she didn't care. She'd already decided that she'd do anything, and this was one of the many anythings she was willing to do.

She slammed the other door on John's incredulous huff of indignation. Ran around to the driver side. The van wasn't pinned in by the clog of vehicles. She had a clear shot, right out of the parking lot. She jumped into the driver's seat, slammed her door, and yanked the shifter into gear while John wheedled from the back: "Angela, I've got patients in there! This is an emergency situation! Where are you taking me?"

She was about to press on the gas, when a MATV with bodies clinging to the sides of it came hurtling up and blocked her in. For a terrified moment, she thought they were primals, trying to get at the people inside the truck. Then one of them hopped down and turned. It was Marie.

"The fuck?" Angela hissed, raising her palms from the steering wheel in a classic traffic-jam gesture. As though the MATV were an inconsiderate motorist.

Marie squinted against the headlights of the van, then recognition crashed over her face, and her lips moved to Angela's name.

"Goddammit." Angela thrust her door open, but didn't get out. She leaned to clear her head from the van and shouted. "Marie! Move that vehicle! I need to get out!"

Marie glanced back and forth between the MATV and Angela, like she couldn't figure out what the hell was going on. The doors flew open and Marines began getting out—the driver, too, Angela saw. Other figures were pouring around the side of the vehicle, and Angela was suddenly staring right into Lee's face.

He looked banged up. Again. But Angela could find no pity for him. She could only think about Abby.

"Angela?" Lee said, stalking around to her side, limping a bit more than usual. "The hell's going on?"

"Lee," Angela grated through clenched teeth. "I need you to move that vehicle. I need to get out."

He was shaking his head in bewilderment. "Where are you going?"

Where am I going?

She dodged the question. "I need to get Abby to safety! Move the truck!"

Lee grabbed onto the door, his knuckles skinned and ruddy with dried blood. "Angela! This situation is not controlled! We need to figure out what we're doing and—"

"I know what I'm doing!"

"The safest place for Abby is here in the hotel!"

"That's bullshit and you know it!" Angela screamed, leaning into his face so hard that he actually leaned back, surprised. "This place is going down and I'm not gonna let my daughter get stuck here!"

Lee's eye jagged to the left—to the crowds of people. Some of them watching. His face flashed savage and he hissed, "Keep your fucking voice down."

She tried to wrestle the door out of his grip, but he held on and jerked it back. "I'm getting Abby out of here! Move the truck!"

"You're panicking," he snapped. "Take a fucking breath!"

And she did take a breath. Just so that she could blast him with it. "I'm taking her to Griffin!"

A pall of ringing silence suddenly slammed into them. Angela's breath raking her throat dry. Lee staring at her, disbelief all across his face. And Marie. And Sam. And Brinly. And a cluster of Marines. All standing there. All watching her.

"Griffin?" Lee asked, dumbly.

"I'm not going down this road with you anymore," Angela said, her voice suddenly quieter, but no less hard. No less determined. "In another time, I might've. But not today. Not now. Not with Abby like this. I need medical supplies, and *we don't have them.*"

"And you think Griffin does?" Lee growled, anger starting to overcome his shock.

"He might! And I know that we don't!"

"Angela—"

"Move the truck, or I start ramming."

Lee blinked several times, like something was caught in his eye. His jaw muscles pulsed rapidly. From behind the van, a woman shouted, "Angela! Take us with you!" and Lee must've seen how this was going to go, how there was no way to deter her except to use an amount of force that he wasn't willing to dish out to her. His teeth flashed, and he whirled away from the door, shoving it hard against her so that it latched and struck her elbow painfully.

He waved at the MATV. "Move the truck."

The Marine that had driven it in hustled back around and got in. Angela waited, hands wringing at the worn-out vinyl steering wheel. She watched the driver eagerly, but then her eyes drifted, and bounced across Marie's—full of betrayal—and then to Sam's—full of accusation.

"Angela, you can't take me with you!" John said from the back.

Angela didn't respond. The MATV backed up.

"Angela!" John pressed. "I need to stay and help!"

Angela waited until there was a gap just wide enough, and then stepped on the gas. She heard John grunt and tumble in the back.

"Help my daughter," she said as she swung the van around, heading north out of the parking lot.

***

Lee stared, dumbfounded, at the back of the van as it retreated into the night. Something inside of him bumped at the deeper parts of his chest, something bucking to be recognized, to be dealt with. A soul-sick pain that surprised him.

But there wasn't time. He gulped a breath. Smashed it down where it couldn't be felt anymore, and then whirled, finding Brinly's face glowering in the darkness. "Brinly, I need all of your Marines on a perimeter, *now*. Push south as far as you can. I need to know how fast this horde is progressing through the city."

Marie stepped forward. "Lee, we should evacuate."

Before Lee could answer her, Abe elbowed his way to the front. "Fuck that. We can hold."

Marie's eyes widened. "Hold? For what?"

A distant thump cut through any more words. Then several more. All of their heads snapped to the west, where the sound had come from.

"Are you kidding me?" Lee spat, just as one of the Marines shouted at the top of his lungs: "Incoming!"

There was a scramble of movement and a cry of fear that went up from hundreds of voices. Some people dashed for the hotel entrance. Others dropped in place, hands over their heads, faces to the pavement. Lee jolted for the nearest vehicle and dove, hitting the ground and sliding just underneath the grill of it.

That whistling noise.

Lee gritted his teeth and tucked his legs in tight, trying to get as much of his body behind his back plate and under the truck's engine block, not knowing where the mortar was going to strike—you never knew, you could only just clench up and hope it wasn't close.

The first blast fell short—a bright flash of light from far behind Lee—but he felt the tremor in the concrete. With his hands still covering his head, he peered towards the hotel entrance. A few people tried to make a break for it. Lee didn't move—there'd been multiple mortars fired, and as a peppering of falling debris struck the hood of the truck and the concrete around him, he heard a chorus of whistles, all different tones, different distances, creating a strange, warbling effect.

Two explosions—closer than the first, close enough that Lee felt the shockwave hit his back, felt a flash of heat on his neck. Then a sedan that had been parked just behind the van Angela had taken flew into pieces in a dusty, fiery crash, scattering jagged chunks of sheet metal that whined over Lee's head and embedded in the bumper of the truck.

He felt that one in his lungs—the way it pulled the air out of him.

The next two hit the pavement, directly outside of the entrance, and Lee watched in mute, breathless horror as bodies simply disappeared, and others flew to pieces. A wet smack of something hit the bumper of the truck just over Lee's head, then slid down and slapped against his face. He recoiled and swatted it off, leaving a hot, wet smear across his cheek.

How many had been fired? How many had fallen?

His ears were ringing so he could barely hear anything. Soldiers and Marines and civilians were all straggling to their feet, some of them running and dodging around others, some of them dragging wounded friends and family members, some of them ambling about in a daze.

A man tried to pull a woman up from the ground by her arm, but it simply detached and he fell backward staring numbly at the limb in his grip. The woman on the ground didn't react, didn't move.

Lee realized he was rolling out of cover. His body moving on autopilot. His concussion-addled brain trying to scoop up the pieces of his fractured cognition and figure out what to do. He scrambled to his hands and knees, everything as numb as blocks of wood. Then up to his feet. The world tilted and he staggered to right himself. Rebounded off the hood of a vehicle, trying to make his way towards the entrance to the hotel. Got another two steps before he remembered the others and turned, swaying drunkenly.

Jones and Sam, arms slung around each other, faces ghastly. Lee couldn't tell who was supporting who. They stamped past him, Sam shouting something at him, but everything sounded like Lee had his head underwater. He tried to reach out and shove them on, but only succeeded in ruining his delicate sense of balance and having to shuffle about to get it back.

Brinly, Abe, and Marie. They were alive. As were the rest of the Marines. One big huddle of bodies surging towards Lee.

Abe shouted and waved at him to go, so Lee turned again, fighting a sudden rush of nausea as everything in his body and everything in his vision disagreed as to what direction he was facing and whether or not he actually was leaning hard to one side or the other.

Help, was the first conscious thought that Lee had. *Find a way to help.*

He stumbled over something. Looked down and saw that it was a leg with no body attached. Kept going, searching the ground for someone that needed help. But everyone he came across was obviously dead. Blank, dust-encrusted eyes. Gaping mouths. Stilled chests. Disemboweled. Dismembered. There must have been a dozen dead, all cluttered there around the two gaping craters at the front of the hotel.

He was caught up in a tide of bodies, and realized that it was Brinly and Abe and Marie pushing him along. Small flames guttered from struck vehicles. Lights bloomed, uncomfortably bright in his vision, creating bright halos. He blinked against them and they focused just enough that he realized he was looking at the lanterns and flashlights that lit up the lobby of the hotel.

Dimly, he perceived the word *incoming*, shouted again.

He thought about dropping, but he was so close to the hotel. Just a few more strides. He could make it.

A blast nearly knocked him off his feet. He stumbled and recovered, coughing and wheezing for air that his shocked lungs couldn't figure out how to get, and he turned, fearing the worst. Two Marines had soaked up the brunt of the blast and fallen short in a tangle of limbs. One was dead on the spot. The other rolled, hands shaking in the air, grasping at nothing.

Lee reached out towards him but was pulled back by Abe and Marie, who were now on either side of him. A third Marine skittered out of the crush of bodies and stooped, grabbing the wounded man by both arms and pulling him backwards towards the building.

Three more detonations. One was a direct hit on the top of the very MATV that they'd just ridden in on. The other two slammed into empty space, out in the parking lot.

Why now? Why had they started mortaring them *now*? Didn't they know what was going on out there?

Then they were inside the hotel. The air was hot and stinking. Too much noise created a river-rush in his ears. He spun around, surrounded by bodies, searching for the faces of his friends.

"EE!" the sound rattled in his eardrums. "EE!"

He frowned, turning again, and found them all right there. Abe was right in his face, a hand grabbing the back of Lee's neck. "Lee!" he was shouting to be heard over the noise. "Lee, you with me?"

Lee blinked and shook his head to clear it. "Yeah, I'm with you!"

Pieces of strategic concerns started to batter their way back into his brain. Primals. Mortars. They needed some fucking breathing room.

"Hey!" Lee bellowed. "Hey!"

It had no effect. The noise of panic didn't diminish a single decibel. He needed to get control of this shit and quick, because they didn't have time for mass panic. Some of the soldiers and Marines heard him and started adding their voices to his, cupping their hands around their mouths and roaring in true leather lung fashion.

"Everyone shut the fuck up!"

"Quiet! Everyone be quiet!"

Lee was already thrashing his way through the crowd, spotting the top of the reception desk. He needed a damn bullhorn, but his cracked voice would have to do. He elbowed his way up to the reception desk, Abe and Marie and a few soldiers creating an alley for him to get through. He hoisted his body up onto the desk and clumsily swayed to his feet as the continued commands for quiet started to take some effect.

Being three feet off the ground wasn't a fantastic idea with his balance as busted as it was, but Lee planted his feet wide to steady himself. "SHUT—UP!" his voice ripped out of his throat.

The noise finally dropped to a level that Lee could work with. A good portion of the soldiers and Marines were already looking at him, and the civilians started to follow their example, their faces masks of animal fear.

"Everyone put a lid on it so we can coordinate!" Lee shouted at them. "Wounded into the hospital! If you're not helping a wounded person, I need you to get a weapon if you don't already have one and standby right here for orders!"

Another series of explosions from outside rocked the lobby to a ripple of frightened gasps. Only three impacts this time. They were slowing down, or running out of ammunition. But Lee couldn't count on that, and he couldn't do shit until he could move his troops out of the hotel.

"Menendez!" Lee demanded, scouring the crowd with his eye. "Where's Menendez! Sergeant Menendez!"

"Here, sir!" A hand shot up, and Menendez squirmed his way around a cluster of civilians and locked eyes with Lee.

"Two squads! Clear out whoever the fuck is lobbing those mortars at us!"

Menendez raised his hands to his mouth and hollered, "Squads One and Two, get to the reception desk!"

A dozen bodies immediately started snaking their way through the crowd towards the desk.

Lee found Brinly's face and pointed at him. "Brinly! Get on the horn with any assets you have in the field! I need that perimeter, and I need to know where those fucking primals are and how far they're pushing!"

He needed to organize the civilian troops, but without Angela there, he had no idea who was in charge. "Who's leading the civilian troops? Sound off!"

A tall man right at Lee's feet shot up. "That's me!"

Lee looked down at him. "Name?"

"Name's Pope."

Lee tried to lock that down to remember it. "Pope, I need all your people holding this hotel. I need an outer perimeter at three hundred yards, an inner perimeter at fifty, and a reserve holding the lobby. Got it?"

Pope nodded with his mouth hanging open. He didn't look like much. Lee hoped he was up to the task, but there was no time for an interview process. He'd have to do.

"Are we not evacuating?" someone shouted. Lee couldn't tell where the voice had come from.

"That's undecided," Lee barked back at the crowd. "We need to stabilize this situation first, and then we'll decide what the best course of action is. Get with your squads and your teams, get loaded up, and be ready for anything."

With that, Lee slid stiffly from the counter as the crowd began moving again and the noise ratcheted up once more.

Marie was right there when he put his feet on the ground. "Lee," she hissed, just loud enough to be heard. "We cannot hold against that amount of primals!"

And, again, before Lee could answer, Abe was there, fury and pleading in his eyes. "Lee, we gotta hold. You gotta give me some time."

"Time for what?" Marie demanded. "We have no time!"

Lee pointed a finger at her. "We don't know how much time we have, and I'm not gonna make a knee-jerk reaction until I know. It's a big-ass horde and I understand the threat that they pose. But this is also a whole city, with a lot of people in it…" he cut himself off, realizing what he was saying as Marie's eyes widened at him. Then he clenched his fists and shook his head at her. "Fuck it. You know what we don't have time for? Sparing feelings. So yes, I said it! There's thousands of civilians that are going to soak up the brunt of that horde and keep them occupied."

Marie's mouth worked, but then something cold fell over her face, and Lee knew that she was seeing it from his perspective. He didn't relish the death—wished he could do something to stop it. But he couldn't. And facts were facts.

He shot his eye to Abe. "Now, what are you talking about needing time?"

Abe's eyes were feverish with rampant hunger. "Briggs. He's out there. He's transmitting on a radio, Lee! This might be our one chance at finding him. I gotta take it. You gotta give me enough time to find him."

Lee just shook his head. "I can't give you time that I don't have, Abe. If we gotta evac, we gotta evac."

Abe nodded rapidly. "I understand that. I'm just asking for as much of a chance as you can give me."

Brinly shouldered up to them, clutching a radio in one smoke-blackened hand, Sam and Jones riding in his wake. "Got sitreps from a half-dozen posts." He took a breath and let it out steady. "We might have some time. But I need the map."

Ninety seconds later, the six of them were smashed in around the map again, in the dim confines of Lee's plywood office, with Deuce furiously sniffing at their pants legs, as though he smelled the explosives and the blood from the mortar attack and found it concerning. Rifles leaning against walls with their lights splashing across the ceiling, giving just enough light to see the map.

Brinly had the radio turned down so they could talk over it, but the transmissions were coming in a near-constant stream. Brinly used the radio antenna to point to a wide swath of territory on the south side of Greeley, and then extending west in a lop-sided semi-circle.

"Outposts all through here have visuals, but no real contact at this time," Brinly said. "I have no idea why, but it seems like the horde hit the south side and then just peeled to the west."

"Neighborhoods," Sam said, glowering down at the map with his arms crossed over his chest. "They're sticking to the neighborhoods. For now."

Lee looked at Sam until he glanced up from the map and seemed surprised that everyone was watching him now. He cleared his throat. Pulled one arm out and wagged a finger at the section of Greeley that Brinly had already indicated. "Those are all neighborhoods through there. Further north, it turns into commercial area. Less people. They know what they're doing. They're following the easiest path to more prey."

"But what happens when they run out?" Marie said, glancing at Lee. "Better question: *when* are they going to run out?"

Lee shook his head. "No way to know."

Brinly rested his fists on the desk and leaned on them. "My outposts—checkpoints, really—can provide some overwatch and early warning. I've got the rest of my Marines deploying to those positions in a staggered perimeter. When they start pressing in towards us from the neighborhoods, we'll have some warning."

"*Some* warning," Lee emphasized, pointing to the distance between FOB Hampton and the sketchy line of Marine checkpoints. "We've only got…what? Maybe a mile between us and those checkpoints?"

Abe nodded. "That's about right."

"That ain't much warning."

"No, it's not," Brinly conceded. "But my boys know how to do a fighting retreat. They can stall."

"I know they can," Lee said, hesitantly. "But we still have no idea if we're talking about thirty minutes, or an hour, or a fucking day."

Jones didn't usually speak up—while young, he was an old-school soldier that believed in letting the higher ranks do the thinking while he did the obeying. But things change. He shouldered his way up between Sam and Marie. "We can evac this place in less than thirty minutes. We've got plenty of fuel and vehicles. It'll be a mad rush, but we can get it done."

If this were any other day, Lee might've been more encouraging to the guy that rarely spoke up with anything but jokes, but it wasn't any other day. It was this day, and there was no room for gentle words. "What's your point?" he demanded.

Jones was unfazed. "My point is, be ready to evac, but we have an unknown amount of time until the checkpoints start getting pushed. When they get pushed, we call the evac. Until then, we can try to find Briggs." He glanced around. "That is pretty much the only reason we're still here, right?"

Lee stared at the man and realized with a certain cramping rush of realization, that Jones was right. He had no reason to still be here, to still risk everyone's lives. He should be calling the evac—hell, should have called it already. Except that Briggs was out there.

Was he really going to do this? Was he really going to keep risking everything to find Briggs? Because it hadn't gone well so far, and all the missteps and risks that hadn't paid off were starting to compound. The price for Briggs's head was skyrocketing into levels that Lee wasn't sure he was willing to pay.

And yet, they'd paid so much already. He knew that was a logical fallacy—the fallacy of sunk costs. But what was he supposed to do? Throw up his hands and say, "Guess all that death and destruction was for nothing, let's go"? The possibility of it felt like a hand clamped around his throat. You could say all you wanted that it was the logical decision to cut their losses, but Lee didn't think he could live with it.

Then again, he didn't know if he could live with losing everybody either.

"Shit," Lee murmured, wiping a hand across his face. The salt from his sweaty hand stung the multitude of scrapes across his cheekbones and chin. He looked to Abe. "Do you even have a plan to try to find Briggs?"

"I haven't exactly had a lot of time to think," Abe shot back.

Lee snapped his fingers a few times. "Well, now's the time, Abe! Think!"

Abe raked fingers back through his thick, black hair, pulling his scalp tight and giving his eyes a wide, wild look to them. "He transmitted over the radio." Abe was thinking out loud, staring at nothing. "We don't have the equipment to triangulate. Do we?"

Most of them looked like he'd just asked them for a lesson on quantum physics, but Brinly and Lee both shook their heads.

"Can't triangulate," Lee said. "What else?"

"Ah…shit…" Abe was manically tugging at his beard now. "He had to have power to transmit. There's no power in the Greeley grid. He was getting his power from someplace else." He shot a look to Sam. "Solar panels? Sam, your team seen any solar panels out there? Brinly, have your Marines?"

Sam blinked. "We weren't exactly looking for them."

Brinly remained silent, his lips pursed.

"So, you don't recall seeing any?" Abe pressed.

Sam shook his head. "Not that I recall."

"What about radio towers?"

"Yeah," Sam said, eagerly, but then frowned. "I mean, I know they're out there, but I can't recall exact locations. And with it being night, how the hell are we gonna find 'em?"

"He didn't transmit from a radio tower," Marie asserted. "Any radio towers in Greeley are from the old world, which means they would be tied into the grid. Which means they don't have power."

"He could have spliced some power in," Abe tried to reason, desperate now. "Maybe with solar panels or a genny?"

"Come on, Abe," Marie huffed, exasperated. "And no one would have noticed that shit? Someone would have seen and talked. Someone would have heard a genny. And he transmitted after dark, which means he couldn't have been using solar panels to power it unless he had battery backups."

"It's not impossible," Abe said.

Lee reluctantly had to side with Marie. "Not impossible, but extremely unlikely."

"He didn't use existing radio towers to transmit," Marie said with finality. "He got that message out some other way."

A thunderous banging on the plywood door of the office sent Lee's already stressed heart into his throat. Deuce let out a little bark of surprise, and for a second, Lee thought it was more explosions from mortars rattling the walls, until he heard the voice immediately following, just outside.

"Lee! Lee, it's Pope!"

"Christ!" Lee exhaled. "Come on!"

The door ripped open and Pope came tumbling in, shying away from Deuce, who was posted up at the entrance and growling at the newcomer. Pope slid around the dog with a worried glance, then pointed emphatically towards the front of the building. "We got a guy just showed up on a dirt bike! He says he's with one of the militia groups, but wouldn't say who. He says he has information for you."

"What kind of information?" Lee stalked around the desk.

"He wouldn't say," Pope gasped. "Said he'd only talk to you. Do you want me to bring him in here?"

"Hell no," Lee snapped, already heading for the door and motioning Deuce to stay. "I'll come to him."

TWENTY-EIGHT

ASYLUM

Griffin saw the lights in the northern sky before he heard the rotors. A single helicopter, coming in fast and low. It was the type of day where you just assume the worst, so his first reaction was that it was some sort of attack, and he grabbed Paige by the shoulder and jammed a finger at the incoming lights.

"Who the fuck is that?" He demanded, realizing as he said it that there was no way Paige knew the answer. "Put some guns on that thing! I don't want it—"

"Captain Griffin!"

Griffin spun, searching for the source of the call. Everything was in a tumult. They'd already evacuated the airfield and moved rapidly northward into a little abandoned burg called Eaton on the maps, about eight miles north of Greeley. Griffin himself had only just arrived a few minutes prior and had just been trying to find where they'd relocated their damn field hospital, only to realize that nothing had been set up yet—vehicles were still flying back and forth, soldiers still running around trying to set up some sort of perimeter. And they sure as hell weren't ready for visitors.

He caught sight of two men running towards him through the darkness, their bodies flashing through splashes of headlights so that it took a moment for Griffin to recognize Guidry and Worley. Worley was waving at him manically.

Griffin waited until Worley was within a few yards before he pointed at the sky again. "What is this? Is this one of yours?"

Worley nodded rapidly as he and Guidry stamped to a halt in front of him. "Yes! Don't fire on it!"

Griffin looked over his shoulder at Paige. "Cancel that last order."

Paige held up his hands. "Hadn't even had a chance to give it."

Back to Worley. "The hell's going on? Why is there a helo inbound?"

"It's friendly," Worley said. "Colonel Donahue is on board."

"Colonel who?" Griffin demanded, having the urge to grab Worley up by the shirt and shake more clarity out of him. The pain in his leg was horrendous, clouding his judgement, making it hard to focus, and setting patience far beyond Griffin's grasp. "I've never heard of Colonel Donahue."

"You asked for help," Guidry said, a little hotly. "And now it's here."

Griffin scowled at the two operatives, his breathing unnaturally fast. His scalp was prickling a bit. Vision getting a bit muddled at the edges. How much blood had he lost? He turned to Paige. "Get me a medic." Then to Worley and Guidry. "Whoever the fuck Colonel Donahue is, he can come see me right here. I need to sit."

Luckily, Griffin hadn't even had the chance to walk away from the MATV once they'd come skidding to a stop, so he simply limped backwards and slumped his ass onto the running boards. Taking the weight off his leg seemed to help the pain. He looked down at the hole in his flesh. He'd gotten it stuffed with hemostatic gauze and wrapped in an

Israeli bandage. He pulled the bandage back with one finger, grit his teeth, and gently touched the wound. It felt like needles, and he had to focus past the pain in his leg to even register the sensation from his probing finger.

It wasn't oozing anymore. The tourniquet and hemostatic gauze had done its job. That was good. At least he wasn't going to pass out from blood loss.

God, what he wouldn't do for a delicious fentanyl lollipop, but that was a luxury he couldn't afford right now. He needed to keep a clear head.

The roar of helicopter rotors became all consuming, Worley and Guidry standing apart from Griffin and Paige, Guidry with his satphone in hand and held to his ear, waving emphatically at the Blackhawk. The pilots must have spotted him—likely wearing NVGs—because the bird angled towards them and then came into a hover and began to lower to the ground, about fifty yards from Griffin's MATV. Soldiers scrambled to get out of the rotor wash and clear the landing zone.

"Medic incoming," Paige yelled over the rotors.

Griffin squinted against the dust and wind and spotted one of their medics skirting around the outside of the landing zone with his shoulders hunched and his head ducked, giant medical pack strapped to his back.

As the Blackhawk reached about ten feet off the ground, Worley and Guidry both jogged into the rotor wash, arms up over their faces to block the flying dust and debris.

The medic came sliding in, already shucking the pack off. "Where you injured, sir?"

Griffin responded by angling his left leg towards the medic and pointing at it.

"That it?" the medic asked, going down on one knee and rapidly checking over what had been done already.

"That's it," Griffin answered, then batted the medic's hands away. "It's fine—bleeding's controlled. Just stick me with an IV."

"Lemme take your blood pressure first," the medic said, trying to reach for Griffin's wrist.

Griffin jerked his hand back. "My fucking BP's fine! Just give me the fucking IV!"

The medic lifted an eyebrow. That was the thing about medics—they were soldiers, but they were also doctors, in a way, and had to ride a line between listening to their superiors and doing what was best for the patient. Hard to do when the patient was the superior, and being surly to boot.

"Alright," the medic conceded with a shrug. "IV it is."

As the medic set to unpacking an IV kit, Griffin brought his eyes up and watched as Worley and Guidry greeted a tall, older man in a combat uniform as he climbed out of the Blackhawk, along with a half-dozen well-equipped soldiers that struck Griffin as special ops of some kind.

The whole conglomeration of them came trotting out from under the rotors, straightening as they did, and winding up all clustered around the MATV. The soldiers—Canadians, Griffin was pretty sure, based on their rifles and camouflage—spread out into a tight circle. A few glanced in Griffin's direction, and, was he mistaken? Or did they have a distinct look about them like they didn't want to be there?

Griffin's attention was drawn back to the older man with unfamiliar officer's insignia on his collar, as he jutted a hand out at Griffin.

"Colonel Donahue," the man said. "You must be Captain Griffin."

Griffin grabbed the hand, peering up at the colonel. "That's me. Sorry for my manners. I got a hole in my leg."

The colonel gave his leg a grim smirk. "I can see that. You gonna make it?"

"Yeah. Why are you here?"

The colonel gave him a neutral look and brought his other hand up from his side. He was holding a chunky data-pad that Griffin hadn't taken note of before. The colonel dashed a finger across the screen and turned it to face Griffin. "Assistance," he said. "So we can end this travesty."

Griffin peered at the screen, taking a moment to realize what exactly he was looking at. The whole thing squirmed with white blobs moving around black and charcoal geometric shapes. For a second, Griffin thought it was a screen saver.

"Satellite imagery would've been useless," the colonel declared. "We have a plane orbiting Greeley. Much better imagery, and it's real-time."

Griffin leaned closer to the screen. The shapes were bodies—white-hot on thermal imaging, moving around the charcoal rectangles of cold houses. Now that he was paying attention, he could see the difference between the normal people and the infected. The infected were bigger, and their shapes moved rapidly, hunkered low to the ground. Griffin watched in a sort of muted, detached horror as one of the big shapes tackled one of the small shapes. A spray of white on black, which quickly began to turn gray. And that same thing was playing out all across the screen.

Griffin swallowed. Glanced up. "May I?"

The colonel nodded.

Griffin took the data-pad. It was a touchscreen, and within seconds, Griffin saw that the controls were similar to what one might expect. Pinching two fingers on the screen zoomed the image out. Then he dragged it around, noting the compass direction on the upper right corner. And breathed a tense sigh of relief.

He'd been afraid that the infected would have chased them north, through the airfield, and might even now be encroaching on their new position. But between what looked like a galaxy cluster—that would be them—and the Milky Way of violence that was Greeley, there was only empty, black countryside.

The colonel had repositioned himself to look over Griffin's shoulder at the screen. "We've already noted a few things. First, what you just saw: It looks like we have a bit of a reprieve. Those things aren't coming for us—yet. The second thing…" And here he leaned in and swiped the screen to move the image south to center on Greeley. "…Is this right here." He pointed to a globular mass of white, right in the middle of the south side of Greeley, which was one, big, band of white shapes milling in all directions.

Griffin's throat clenched up. He zoomed the image in to that mass, and saw the movement within all those shapes. A black nucleus—a large building of some sort—around which massive numbers of infected swirled in a constant circular motion, like glowing water moving down a drain.

He'd seen that behavior before. "They're not just here to attack," Griffin breathed. "They're making a new home."

He looked up and found the colonel frowning at him, doubtful of his conclusion.

"I've seen this before," Griffin explained. "When they overran Fort Bragg."

"Is that so?" the colonel said, softly.

"Yes. Any chance that plane you've got orbiting has artillery in it?" He was speaking of the AC-130 Gunship, and crossing his fingers.

"Unfortunately, no," the colonel said.

"Dammit." Griffin clenched his fingers around the data-pad. "Not complaining about the intel—it's useful. But please tell me you've got some firepower to back you up."

Griffin didn't know how to interpret the colonel's face after that. Everything in it went stony and solemn. For a heartbeat, Griffin thought that maybe the colonel hadn't been authorized to offer any real firepower to help them. But that wasn't right, because the colonel nodded to Griffin's question.

He had firepower. But for some reason, he didn't want to use it.

The colonel took a deep, heavy breath. "Let me explain our options."

***

Lee limped out of the front entrance of the hotel and immediately spotted the man who'd come to meet him. He was framed by two civilian troops, and he didn't look much different from them, except he didn't have a gun on him that Lee could see. He was a young kid, no older than Sam, with a mess of dirty blond hair that hung in his face, making him look like he'd be much happier stoned and on a surf board.

Wouldn't they all?

"You search him?" Lee growled at his side where Pope was keeping pace.

"He had a rifle, pistol, and two knives," Pope answered. And then, as though it needed to be said: "We removed them."

Lee was now within a few paces of Surfer-Dude, and saw the kid's mouth open up to say something, his eyes glinting in an almost sarcastic way as he took in Lee—and probably his limp and his busted face. Lee never gave him the chance to say whatever smart shit was curling his lips. He grabbed the kid by the front of his collar and drove him backwards until he rammed the kid into the side of a Humvee, then spun him around and pulled him close.

"Hey, whoa!" the kid yelped. "What the fuck?"

He tried to pull back but Lee gave him a harsh yank that let him know he might be busted up, but was still immensely stronger than Surfer-Dude. "Just in case," Lee grunted.

"In case what?" Dude said, glancing about.

"In case you got a sniper that wants to put a bullet in me." Lee smiled savagely. "Now he'll have to shoot through you first. So, we'll both get to die in each other's arms. It'll be great."

Dude blinked a few times, any smartness now yanked up by the roots like a troublesome weed. He felt the kid go slack in his grip as he stared at Lee's eye and his own—big and clear-blue—started to sparkle with fear.

"Okay, okay," Dude said, his voice a breathy tremble.

"Well?" Lee snapped.

Dude looked confused. "Well, what?"

Lee widened his eyes. "You had a message for me or not?"

"Oh." A few stammered, unfinished syllables. "So, you're Lee Harden?"

"You see any other one-eyed gimps around here? Yes, motherfucker." He shook him again. "Speak."

Dude swallowed. "Right. Uh. Ruby sent me."

Lee twisted his grip on the guy's jacket. A few threads popped. "Ruby, like Ruby's Rebs?"

A faint whiff of defiance in Dude's face. "That's right."

"Well, it's a dumb fucking name. What'd Ruby want to say?"

The kid was silent for long enough that Lee started to wonder if he'd forgotten what he'd come to say and might need it shaken out of him.

Then, in a low voice: "We can give you Briggs."

Lee's eye narrowed. He searched the kid's face for any sign of guile. But that was just old habits. Lee'd been lied to so many times and believed it that he couldn't even count on his impressions of honesty anymore. Still, there was nothing obviously false lurking behind Dude's eyes.

Lee pulled the kid closer to him so their noses were just inches apart. "Were you the motherfuckers that just mortared us?"

"No. Swear to God, that wasn't us."

"Why would Ruby want to help us?"

"She doesn't." So, it was a woman. Didn't mean much to Lee, but at least one mystery had been solved. "But we need this shit to end."

"End?" A mad laugh burst out of Lee's mouth. He bit it off with bared teeth. "You have any idea what the fuck's going on right now?"

"Uh…"

"Does Ruby know that there are several thousand infected that just breached the south side of Greeley?"

Dude blinked a few times like he couldn't fathom what Lee had just said. A mix of suspicion and terror came rising up to the surface. "Wait. You're serious?"

God, they really didn't know, did they? Guess Ruby's Rebs weren't holed up in the south side. Must be safely hiding in the north, and word hadn't reached them yet.

What Ruby knew and didn't know was immaterial, and might actually change the dynamic, so Lee shrugged, covering his tracks with a nasty smile. "Is anyone serious, Dude-man? Or are we all just players in a sick comedy with no punchline? How's Ruby going to give me Briggs? Explain."

Dude's eyes dashed about, trying to make sense of Lee's rapid-fire subject changes.

"Hey!" Lee was tempted to slap him out of thinking too much, but decided to just shake him again. "How's she have Briggs?"

"Well…" Dude squirmed. "We don't *have him* have him. But we can tell you where he is."

"How do you know where he is?"

"Because he's in our territory. We spotted him once, right after the invasion, sneaking into this big burned-out McMansion. He paid us in weapons and ammo to keep it quiet."

Lee's head was reeling with the new information and he had to fight to keep his face from showing surprise. He didn't want the kid to feel that he had the upper hand at any point. He wasn't even sure he believed it. Could just be bullshit that Ruby came up with to lure them into an ambush. She apparently didn't know that they were being overrun by primals, and being ignorant of that, she might have decided to proceed with whatever cockamamie plan she'd come up with.

So, Lee kept trying to poke holes in the story. "Where'd he get the weapons and ammo?"

"I don't know," Dude's voice had taken on a whining quality and he'd started to look over his shoulder like he wanted nothing more in the world than to be free of Lee's grasp. "From somewhere in the mansion, I guess. Look, do you want to make a deal or not?"

"Deal? I didn't realize we were making a deal. See, I thought you came to give us Briggs so we wouldn't massacre your whole militia."

Dude swallowed. "Well. Right. That's the deal. We give you Briggs, and you leave Greeley."

Lee had felt Abe hovering behind him the whole time, but it wasn't until now that he came around Lee's shoulder and spoke to the kid.

"Why's Ruby think giving us Briggs will make us leave?" Abe said, stone serious.

Dude looked confused again. Or maybe that was just his face. "Well...because...why else are you here?"

Lee and Abe exchanged a glance, entering into that silent communication that they had. Abe wanted it. He wanted to go for it. And why shouldn't they? It was indeed the only reason they were still here. And while it might be a trap, it was also the only lead they had on Briggs. The only tangible lead they'd ever gotten.

Lee looked back at Dude. "Tell me where he is."

***

It was only by happenstance that Angela actually knew where she was going.

As the two soldiers that guarded her door in the penthouse had helped her negotiate Abby's stretcher down the stairwells, they'd mentioned to each other that their scouts had reported Griffin's army pulling out of the airfield. At the time, her stomach had dropped and she'd feared she wouldn't be able to find them. But by the time they reached the ground level, another report had come in.

Griffin's army had been spotted once more, by one of their checkpoints on the northern end of Greeley—a massive snake of taillights hauling ass north on Highway 85.

And that had been enough for Angela.

So, she'd put the van on Highway 85, and headed north, with nothing but a hope that she would run into them eventually.

And she did.

After driving for about five minutes on that lonesome highway, listening to John trying to reason with her from the back of the van, he was silenced by blooming headlights and spotlights that turned the road ahead of them into a starburst of white.

"Who is that?" John wheezed out, terrified. "Is that them? Are you sure they're not going to fire on us?"

TERMINUS

Angela had not slowed down when she'd seen the lights, and John's question was answered when three tracers went arcing just over the roof of the van. There's something incredibly convincing about watching those glowing streaks rip right over your head, and even in her panic to get Abby to somebody that could help, Angela stomped on the brakes.

John yelped as he toppled in the back, and Angela felt the stretcher hit the back of her seat, the locked wheels squealing against their brakes. She twisted to look in the back, her eyes jumping right over John as he tried to wrangle himself up off the floor, and going straight to her daughter. Abby still lay, unconscious, her head and body slightly twisted now with the jostling of the sudden stop.

"Okay, baby," Angela whispered to Abby. "It's gonna be okay."

"Angela—" John started again, but she was already on her way out the door.

She had not expected a warm reception, so she wasn't surprised at the takedown. She put her head down and pressed through it with nothing but that small hope of salvation for her daughter to quell the fear and uncertainty.

She knelt on the blacktop, as instructed by a voice over a loudspeaker, her hands clasped on the top of her head. John emerged from the van, causing another uproar of shouted commands. He eventually found himself about an arm's length from Angela, and in the same position.

She glanced over at him, but it seemed he refused to look at her. She couldn't tell if it was because he was afraid to move with so many guns trained on them, or if he was so furious with her. And only then did Angela feel a modicum of remorse for how she had so callously violated his trust.

"I'm sorry," she whispered to him, as the sounds of boots on pavement drew closer behind them.

John didn't move his head, but his eyes turned as far as they could towards her, not quite far enough to make eye contact, but far enough that Angela felt at least that he was *trying* to look at her. His lips quivered, and he gave the barest shake of his head.

"I hope you know what you're doing," he whispered back.

That only made Angela feel worse. Because she had no idea what she was doing. She was simply running on a prayer.

"Nobody fucking move!" a voice bellowed at her back.

More boots, stamping up to them. Hard hands grabbing her up. Twisting her around. Pulling her arms behind her back.

"My daughter," she started to say.

"Shut the fuck up!" Someone grabbed her by the hair and shoved her head down so she could do nothing but stare at her feet and the blacktop.

"My daughter's in the van!" she strained out, not fighting the grip, but trying to straighten her neck enough that she could raise some volume from her throat.

"I said—"

"She's injured and she needs medical attention!" Angela belted out.

Her body was roughly whirled around. A soldier with his rifle trained on her chest, glared at her, his face just angry shadows, backlit by the spotlights. "Why the fuck do you think I care?" he demanded.

And whoever had their hand in her hair tried to push her face down again, but this time she *did* fight against it, thrashing her body and straining against the pain in her scalp as she wrenched her head up again, looking that soldier right in the eyes once more.

"I'm Angela Houston!" she shouted at him, trying to get all the words out before they manhandled her into submission again. "I'm the former President of the United Eastern States, and I'm turning myself into Captain Griffin!"

Everything ground to a halt.

The soldier with his rifle pointed at her chest straightened a bit, his eyebrows arching in shock. "You're Angela Houston?"

She did her best to nod against the fingers still gripping her hair. "I'm Angela Houston," she confirmed, not knowing whether that was a death sentence or a reprieve. "And I'm seeking asylum for myself and my daughter."

TWENTY-NINE

A RECKONING

For once, no one argued with him. Lee almost didn't know what to do with himself. Once again, they were crowded into his office—all but Brinly. They hung over the map with drawn faces, and every single one of them knew two facts.

First: It could be a trap.

Second: They were going in anyways.

On any other day, they'd have manpower and time. They'd run their own intelligence operation to confirm the validity of the tip. And if they found it worthwhile, they'd go in hard with plenty of guns.

But none of that was possible now. They didn't have time to confirm it. Nor did they have the resources. It was just Abe, Marie, Sam, and Jones. Lee drew the line there—he wasn't going to pull resources he might need to hold the line and give them time to evacuate.

Abe was the first to give voice to the thing that was *really* gnawing at Lee. "You're really not gonna roll with us?"

God, but it felt like a jab in his gut. That little note of disbelief in Abe's voice. But Lee had already swallowed his pride and stepped back from this operation. Maybe that's why they hadn't argued with him so much.

Lee shook his head, grimacing at the very real, physical pain he felt in his stomach. There was still something inside of him that kept telling him

You should get in there, this is your mission, you need to be leading it, you can FIX THIS!

But he couldn't. And there were too many factors against him.

"I'm not leaving Brinly in charge of this evac," Lee said, glancing over his shoulder as though he expected the big man to be standing in the doorway of the office. "He's gone some place I don't like, and I..." He winced as the words came to his tongue, then spat them out like bile. "I don't trust his judgement anymore. I'm worried he'll stay too long, fight too hard, and get people killed for no reason."

No one came to Brinly's defense. It wasn't that anybody disliked him. Only that they knew exactly what Lee was saying. Lee could see in their faces that they were thinking of all those dead civilians Brinly had left in his wake.

"If we leave it up to Brinly," Marie said, softly. "He's going to turn FOB Hampton into the Alamo. You can see it in his eyes."

Lee nodded. "Besides that, as of right now, the people in this room are the only ones with this intel on Briggs. Someone needs to stay behind, and I'm the logical choice."

There was no judgement in their eyes. They knew that it wasn't because of his bum leg, or his one eye—though they were certainly factors. They all knew that Lee would go in with them if there was any other way to do this.

Lee straightened and gestured to Abe. "You're team lead on this. Take it away."

Abe hesitated for a moment, staring at the location on the map that they'd identified. It wasn't precise, due to the constraints of a hand-drawn map, but they knew the main roads they'd take to get there, and they had the rest of the information from the messenger.

"Jones," Abe started, dropping swiftly into gear, putting the hesitation behind him. "Secure a vehicle. You're driving. See if you can't nab a MATV. If not, one of the technicals will do, but I want a turret in case shit goes sideways. And a full tank. Sam, you'll be in the turret on approach and egress. For now, Sam, gather up as many spare rifle mags as you can. Make sure everyone's loaded to bear. Marie, I want you to track down whatever med supplies you can swipe from the hospital—you're gonna be medic if one of us goes down." Abe took a breath. "No clue what we're going to deal with inside this mansion, so I'm going to try to rustle up some breaching equipment."

Jones spoke up in a sort of dreamy voice, eyes still fixed on the map. "Menendez had a box of C4 and detonators. If he hasn't made off with it."

"Roger that," Abe nodded. "Last thing: Everyone take a pack with some water and food. Don't weigh yourself down, but take as much as you can handle and still be light on your feet. There's a chance the evac gets called and we get left behind. Might need to go to ground for a few days."

"Guys," Lee said. "It's the last thing in the world I want to do. But I'm gonna call the evac the second our perimeter starts getting pushed, whether you're back or not."

They all nodded. They knew it was the reality they were facing.

"Last-last thing," Abe said, looking at the other three in turn as he spoke, slowly and deliberately. "This is primarily a kill mission. *If* we can take him alive *and* extract him without creating undue risk to ourselves, then we will attempt to do that. Otherwise? If he gives us any problems, or if time and mobility have become an issue? Just put him down."

And all at once, it all came down.

Lee felt his pulse stretching his carotid arteries. Felt a cold sweat ringing his hairline. The white-hot glow of a weaponlight that was glaring into Lee's eye made him squint and shy away from it. Ears not ringing this time, but instead drowning the others out with a strange, watery, rushing noise.

Sam and Marie and Jones were shuffling towards the exit, saying something to him. Jones reached up and slapped the top of the doorframe like a championship ball player taking the field. Sam and Marie turned their faces away from him and he was certain he wasn't going to see them again.

Abe leaned over the desk, looking at Lee with a note of concern. "You alright, man?"

Lee barely heard it. Took a moment to comprehend it. Then hastily nodded. "Yeah, I'm fine. Just need some water. Keep 'em safe. And keep yourself safe."

Abe reached out and slapped Lee on the shoulder, then let his hand linger there for a moment. Lee realized his core was trembling like it couldn't hold up the weight on his shoulders anymore. He wondered if Abe could feel it.

Abe gave him one last squeeze, then took his hand away and departed, his face also vanishing into what seemed like an endless void.

They're gonna die. Everyone around you dies.

Lee realized with a distant sort of dismay that his shoulders were hunched, his body bent, like he was walking into an icy wind. Dismay, because he knew he needed to be strong right now. But the dismay couldn't outpace the rampant sensation of inevitable doom that was coursing through him, robbing him of anything but a desire to somehow be anywhere else, doing anything else, in a place where he didn't matter, and his choices didn't always fall with the weight and sharpness of a guillotine.

He wanted to close the office door. He feared being seen like this. But in that instant, he didn't think he could make it to the door. He leaned forward onto the desk, hoping that taking some weight off would help to center himself. But his knees just started quaking even harder, his quadriceps bouncing erratically.

He barely got his ass into the office chair behind the desk. Collapsed into it so hard it almost tipped backwards. Rolled a foot away from the desk. He brought shaking, clammy hands to his face. His palms were cold. His face was hot. Skin tingling. He tried to rub some normalcy back into himself, but his flesh just felt like feverish pins and needles.

"God," he murmured, his diaphragm pulsing, making the single syllable tremble in his throat.

Deuce crept around the corner of the desk and eyed Lee with what looked like canine concern. He couldn't know the ins and outs of what was boiling through Lee's brain, but it seemed the dog could tell that something was very wrong.

The rushing sound in Lee's ears seemed to carry with it an unstoppable tide of images. He saw himself as a younger man, with so much life still in him, so confident in every decision he would make, as though the hand of the universe was guiding his every action, as though he was infallible. Where had that young man gone? What had killed him?

He saw Angela's face by the light of a dim lantern as they lay side by side. He saw her eyes looking at him with love, and yet he could never love her back the way she needed him to, and he wondered in that moment what had been broken inside of him? Why hadn't he ever been able to love her?

He saw Abby's unconscious form, shot through the back and covered in blood.

He saw Abby, alive and vibrant, laughing as she sat shoulder to shoulder with a younger version of Sam, who toted that little .22 rifle around with him, his eyes still lit with some inner sense of peace that he'd lost somewhere along the line. Then he saw Sam as he was, only moments before, with dirt in the creases of his face, and a hard set to his mouth and a darkness in his eyes that was ages beyond the years that he'd lived. And Lee wondered, what harsh metamorphosis had occurred to produce that new version of Sam?

He saw the dead, and the dying, in a drowning wave of images both experienced and imagined. He saw the women being carried away by the primals. He saw the dead ones in the warehouse where they'd been held. He saw the piles of bodies with their arms and legs broken so that they couldn't get away, stored there like a wasp stores its paralyzed prey for its new brood. He saw pieces flying off of people, human beings turned inside out by violent hands and demolitions, children and mothers and fathers in every state of death, in every position that they'd fallen, an endless trail of them that seemed to mark Lee's path through life.

Everyone around you dies.

Why hadn't *he* died yet? Why hadn't he suffered the same fate as all those others that he'd commanded to put their lives on the line? And for what? Because he thought he could fix an unfixable world?

God forgive him, but they'd all believed in him. They still did. They were still doing it. *He* was still doing it. Had just done it to the last four friends he had.

And yet, he didn't even believe in himself anymore. He knew that he couldn't fix the things that had been broken. He *knew* this. And yet it was like he was animated by some other creature that lived in him and refused to die, refused to listen to the things that Lee had learned through loss and grief, a creature that would only ever scrape and claw and devour life in an infinite, mindless, obsessive loop.

He saw himself emerging from his bunker, so many years ago, a man on a mission, full of belief and conviction. And what had that mission been? *Subvenire Refectus.* Rescue and Rebuild. But what had he rescued? What had he rebuilt? For every person whose life he'd saved, there were dozens—maybe even hundreds—that had died because of him. For every stone he'd stacked on another, entire cities had crumbled to dust. He had not rescued or rebuilt. He had murdered and destroyed.

"God!" he seethed, doubled over now, pulling at his hair, while his gaping mouth sweat as though he might vomit, and he watched a silver strand of it dip to the floor between his boots. Boots with blood and dirt caked on them. A patchwork history of violence and gore.

Now I am become Death, the Destroyer of Worlds.

A man had uttered those words once, as he had watched the first fireball of a nuclear detonation.

He'd known, just as Lee knew in that moment, that he had been the cause of something unholy, that he stood at the edge of a drop, beyond which nothing could ever be the same.

In a dizzying jerk, Lee's mind seemed to lurch out of his body. He saw himself, bowled over in the dim office, with his dog staring at him, worrying. He saw the hotel sitting in a blackened city, surrounded by death. He saw that dark city in the plains, and those plains were framed by mountains to the west, and to the east, and beyond all of that was only more death. And he saw the world beyond those borders, and didn't know it anymore—it was drenched in total darkness—and the darkness leered at him and leveled the sword of judgement on him, and he felt it hack him to pieces.

Death. The Destroyer. *War criminal.*

He was not a man anymore. He had become a force of chaos, of nothingness, and everywhere he went, death followed, and fire burned. Structures crumbled, and rivers ran red. He was an apocalypse unto himself, a plague worse than FURY could ever be, because he had set himself on this course and ignored what should not have been ignored, and saw it now only at the point that he knew he could never go back, never redeem what had been abandoned. He had made the irrevocable choices. He had rendered so many lives into dust. He had sacrificed everyone he had ever cared about in his dogged pursuit of Briggs.

Could he sacrifice the last four people that he loved? All to kill a single a man?

Was that justice? Or was it simply rage? Hatred? Mindless lashing out?

What the fuck was he doing here?

If he called the evacuation, he could save the lives of so many of his people. But then the city would be overrun, and the four people that he truly cared about would be abandoned, trapped in a sea of primals.

If he didn't call the evacuation, he could give those four people a chance to complete their mission and find Briggs and get back to safety. But so many of the Marines and soldiers and civilians would die while holding that perimeter.

Could he sacrifice all those people outside his office? All of Brinly's Marines, all of Menendez's soldiers, all of the civilians that had taken up arms because he'd sold them a bill of goods about the righteousness of their mission?

Could he sacrifice his friends?

Everything had been spiraling to this point of compression where all things hung on a single choice. Would he commit to the path of vengeance at all costs? Or would he level his pride, his convictions, his *obsession*, but in doing so become a stranger to himself? A husk of directionless humanity that had sucked the life out of the very country he claimed to love, and then given up at the penultimate moment?

Which was worse? To remain stalwart and defiant, *bloody but unbowed*, but thereby consign his soul to destruction? Or to bend and break, to shatter his identity, to hollow out the convictions that had made him who he was for so long that he could barely remember being anything else, but thereby save the lives of so many?

Something was about to die. He held the knife. He had the choice. It would be him that committed one of those things to destruction.

Which one could he stand to sacrifice?

Which part of himself was he willing to murder, and how many would wind up dead with it?

THIRTY

THE MANSION

THERE WAS A STILLNESS to them now, Griffin perceived. Him and Paige, and all four of the envoys from Canada and the UK, and Colonel Donahue. The gravity of it had frozen their bodies, but not their minds. Griffin's own thoughts were a nightmarish whirling dervish.

He had never thought it would come to this. The option on the table so onerous that he wanted to flat out deny it and scrub it from his reality. But instead, he found his weary eyes tracking up to Colonel Donahue, who looked down at him with some form of pity and dread.

Rather than strike it from the table, Griffin sought to know more, and hated himself for it, even as he rationalized it away: *A good commander needs to know the ins and outs of each option on the table. Only then can I make a sound decision.*

"Tell me about the payload," Griffin heard himself say.

Colonel Donahue's nostrils flared, and he tucked his chin like a fighter wading into a brawl. "The submarine is equipped with Trident D5 missiles, with yields ranging from five to one hundred kilotons."

Just hearing the word *kilotons* made the hairs on the back of Griffin's neck stand up and his stomach sink. Why was he even considering this?

But he was. Because a good commander considers all his options.

"Been a while," Griffin said, quietly, frowning. "Can you remind me what type of blast radius we're talking about?"

"Depends on the yield. Each missile can carry up to twelve warheads. A five-kiloton warhead will produce a blast radius of roughly three to four square kilometers. A hundred kiloton warhead would be between forty and fifty square kilometers."

"Christ," Paige murmured. "That's the whole fucking city."

Griffin shook his head. "That's too much." But he was still thinking about the smaller yields. How twelve of them could be packed into a single delivery system. "What's the flight time?"

"The submarine is positioned in the Mississippi River, just north of Kansas City. Estimated flight time would be roughly ten minutes from the time you ordered the strike. *If*...you order the strike."

Griffin was still shaking his head, slowly, side to side, even as he kept on thinking about it. "Well, obviously it's not an option while President Briggs is still in the city."

Worley cleared his throat and took a single step forward. "Captain Griffin. Let's put our cards on the table. At this point, if we're considering this—and we *should* consider this—we need to speak plainly with each other." He fixed Griffin with a grave, evaluating look. "Neither Canada nor the United Kingdom has any desire to get into bed with Lee Harden *or* Briggs."

Griffin looked at him sharply, heat rising up the back of his neck. "The hell is that supposed to mean?"

Worley was unperturbed. "They're mad dogs tearing at each other, Griffin, and they have been for years. Lee is a psychopathic warlord, and Briggs is a delusional tyrant. I speak for the command of both Canada and the United Kingdom when I say this: We do not want either of them."

Griffin still couldn't quite believe what he was hearing. Or could he? There was a small measure of him that knew exactly what Worley was saying, and it echoed some of Griffin's own thoughts. Griffin had abided by the oaths he'd taken, and under those oaths, he obeyed Briggs as the commander-in-chief. But there was no skirting around the issue: the man was paranoid to the point of self-destruction. If it hadn't been for Briggs's rashness and paranoia, the invasion of the United Eastern States would never have happened, and they would not be in the situation they now found themselves in.

As for Lee…

Yes, he was a mad dog. Griffin had said as much himself. Yes, he was a warlord. Yes, he was a war criminal.

Was it odd, then, that deep within Griffin, he recognized a stronger emotional reaction to the prospect of consigning Lee to a nuclear fireball than his own president?

All of these thoughts, as Griffin continued to stare at Worley. Then he squinted at the man. "Well, if we're just going to burn the whole thing down, then what the fuck are we even doing here? I came here to rescue Greeley, and to save Briggs." *Did you?* "If both of them are dead, then who the hell is Canada and the UK trying to back?"

An eerily out-of-place smirk came to Worley's mouth. "Who are we backing?" He pointed a finger at Griffin's chest. "We're backing *you*."

Griffin wanted to lurch to his feet, but his busted leg wouldn't allow it. "Out of the question. I'm just a soldier. I have no qualifications for what you're implying. And on top of that, the people need a representative government—they need democratic, *civilian* leadership." He glared at Worley. "That's kind of what this country is founded on."

"All due respect," Worley returned, calmly. "It's not *out of the question*. And the people don't need civilian leadership right now. They need stability. You can't have a democratic government without stability. Once stability can be restored to the United States, *then* the democratic process can continue to take place. But until that day comes, someone is going to have to be in charge." Worley looked around, a bit theatrically. "And the rest of us aren't even Americans. Granted, the pool is small, but you're the most qualified American for the job."

"I'm a captain," Griffin snapped back. "How the hell is that *qualified* to stabilize a country this size?"

"Rank is immaterial at this point," Worley dismissed, blithely resolute in his argument, as though it had all been decided and the only thing left to do was smooth Griffin's hackles and get him to accept it. "You successfully invaded the United Eastern States, chased Lee's rebels, and now have them cornered. I see no other individual American more qualified than you. I'm not saying that it will be easy for you—obviously there will be a steep learning curve. But you will have the full support and backing of both the Canadian and the British governments, as well as other European powers that have a vested interest in seeing the United States restabilized so that it can take its rightful place amongst the world powers."

Griffin looked to Paige, hoping for support, hoping that his second-in-command would confirm that this was a ridiculous idea and shouldn't even be considered. But Paige was looking at the ground, thoughtfully nodding. When he realized Griffin was looking at him, he glanced up and shrugged. "They have a point."

"Goddammit, Ron!" Griffin barked.

Paige held up his hands in surrender. "I know you don't want to hear it, but they're right. You're the most qualified. They're offering their backing and support. And that's something we need right now, Griff. If we ever want to see this country brought back to life, we're going to need outside help. And we have it now. And all they're asking for is that you accept it."

"No." Griffin pointed a finger in the direction of Greeley. "They're asking me to nuke an American city."

Worley sighed. "We're asking you to put the final nail in the coffin of a bullshit conflict that should never have even started in the first place. But it did start. And now we're here, and you're here, and the options for resolution are *extremely* limited." He put his hands on his hips and his face became earnest. "I get it, Captain Griffin. No one wants to be called upon to push the button on their own city. But the circumstances are extreme, and the solution needs to be equally extreme."

"What about all the civilians still left in Greeley?" Griffin demanded.

It was Colonel Donahue that responded, this time laying a hand on Griffin's shoulder and looking down at him sadly. "Captain. The numbers don't lie. The images don't lie. We've already done the math, and you have too. Those people are dead—they just don't know it yet. There is no practical way to rescue them. There is no practical way to deal with a horde of this magnitude, embedded in a city. If we wait, the death that those civilians experience will be nightmarish beyond what you can imagine. The longer we wait, the more of them will die that way. I'm not and have never been a proponent of the nuclear option. But from a purely human perspective...it would be a mercy.

"The situation on the ground is this: We currently have all our enemies contained in one place—Lee, Briggs, and the infected horde. Yes, there are civilians mixed in. But they're going to die anyways, Griffin. It sucks, but it's true, and you know it. If we don't strike now, we run the risk of a continued, protracted, bloody conflict. And that's a best-case scenario. Worst case scenario? This horde of infected wipes out the civilians anyways, continues to procreate, continues to grow, continues to spread, and continues to threaten not only your country, but mine. The size and scope of it is unprecedented. And it calls for unprecedented action."

Colonel Donahue looked suddenly exhausted and sick. Grieved by the reality descending on them. "I did not want to be the one to offer this up. My hands will have blood on them as well. It will haunt me for the rest of my life." He looked at Worley. "But he's right. There's no way around the facts. We've tried. You've tried. You've done your best. Your men have done their best. But you're painted into a corner now. And there's only one way out."

***

They approached the mansion in darkness so thick that Sam could only make out the shape of the structure, ink-black against a charcoal sky of thin clouds. "Mansion" was, perhaps, a generous term for the house, but it was large. Hard to tell just from the shape and sprawl of the dark shadow, but Sam guessed it was several thousand square feet.

The property itself was not large, but it was overgrown, and the massive trees only threw them into even greater darkness. And anyone could have been hiding in that darkness. Sam had the nearly-overwhelming urge to splash his weaponlight into the blackness engulfing them, but Abe had strictly forbidden light until they made entry, and Sam knew he was right.

They didn't overcomplicate the entry. They knew virtually nothing about who or what might be waiting behind the doors, or what entry points might or might not be barricaded or guarded, and so the simplest plan was straight through the front entrance.

They moved quietly up a cobblestone drive, their treads made even quieter by the layer of dirt and rotted leaves that covered it. No verbal commands yet—they all knew what they were supposed to be doing as they approached the front of the structure. Sam on point, followed by Abe, then Jones, then Marie.

Sam could make out a wide front porch. Dark columns of brick or stone—he couldn't quite tell. As he drew closer to the front steps, he glanced up at the roofline and saw that sections of it had fallen in, likely during the fire that had gutted the structure. As he climbed the three stairs to the front porch, he was close enough now to make out windows without glass—just yawning, charred openings in a hull of fire-blackened brick.

And the doorway. Not a door at all, in fact, but a warped piece of plywood, just leaning there, covering the opening.

Sam took his position, standing just to the right of the doorway. He stayed locked on that opening, the only light the dull glow of his red dot optic dialed down to its lowest setting. Abe moved around him, taking a position to the left of the doorframe, then waiting until Jones and Marie stacked up behind Sam.

Jones put his hand on Sam's shoulder, snugged in tight, the muzzle of his rifle poking out over Sam's right shoulder.

Abe reached out and placed an open palm against the plywood. He seemed to give it a slight press to test whether it was backed by anything sturdier, but Sam saw it move even with that slight pressure. It really was just sitting there.

Of course, there might be a couch or a bookshelf just behind it, but they wouldn't know that until they gave it a hard push. Which was pretty much their only option at that point. That, or blow the thing up with a breaching charge, which seemed excessive.

Abe turned his face to Sam. In all the darkness, and with his dark hair and beard, all Sam could make out was the slight, wet glimmer of his eyes, fixed on Sam.

Sam nodded.

Abe turned, put both hands to the plywood, and shoved.

Sam's feet were already moving. He watched the plywood panel wobble and tilt back, and then fall to the ground with a muted *whump*. Sam had been expecting a noisy crash, and was unnerved by the sepulchral silence as he moved through the doorway, feet tramping lightly over the plywood, feeling it crack and squish beneath him, nearly entirely rotted out.

He thumbed his light as he moved. Blaring white brought the environment into stark, monochromatic relief. Their stealth blown now, Sam's heart ramped up as he moved through a massive entryway with the skeletal remains of a spiral staircase to the right, and an enormous chandelier right in the center of the entryway floor where it had fallen who-knew how long ago, it's twisted, spindly arms making it look like a spider that had curled up and died on its back.

He stopped there in the entryway, moving to the right a bit so the others could file in behind him. He played his light across the scene. An old, rank scent of charcoal and woodsmoke filled his every breath. Everything was black. The walls had crumbled in many places, the sheetrock lying in piles like sloughed off skin, and the studs within poking up like burned bones.

Jones passed Sam and pulled to the left so that he stood next to the smashed chandelier. Marie came in next, going even further left and taking position on another, wide opening that appeared to lead to some sort of sitting room, but it was difficult to tell as the furniture had been burned to tattered remnants. Abe came in swiftly on Marie's heels and held up, right next to Sam.

Abe spoke the first words they'd said since exiting the MATV they'd driven in. "Two story structure," he noted, eyeing the staircase to the right, then bringing his eyes to the floor and playing his light over a stampede of various footprints in the soot. It was clear that *someone* had been coming and going, but that didn't necessarily mean it was Briggs. If the place had sat, burned out and abandoned for years, it could've been local kids.

Sam eyed the staircase and shook his head. "No one's going up that thing." The treads were completely burned out. The banister gone until about halfway up, and the upper half hanging off at an angle. The framework of the staircase was still there, but blackened and looking like nothing Sam cared to test his weight on.

"Marie. Jones." Abe pointed to the ground. "Hold this entryway. Sam and I are going to clear the ground floor, try to find another stairwell up."

Marie and Jones nodded their understanding, and Sam and Abe set off, moving through the remains of the house at a deliberate and controlled pace. Little more than a walk. They cleared fire-gutted rooms that held no sign of life save for vestiges of graffiti that made no sense to Sam. One side of the house had caved in completely, and Sam made the observation to Abe that it looked like that would be where the additional stairwell to the second floor would be—they hadn't found it anywhere else.

The only other stairwell they found was a concrete one, leading down into a basement off of the kitchen. Abe stood in the frame of it, staring down into that blackness for a moment. Then he spoke in a low whisper, without taking his eyes or his weapon off of it.

"Go get Jones and Marie. I'll hold this."

Sixty seconds later, they were descending the stairs into the basement, with Abe at point.

The wall to the right of the stairwell fell away as they went down, and Abe panned his light across a wide expanse of concrete. Sam, one stair tread behind him, glanced into the basement and was surprised to see it virtually untouched by the fire, but then he figured that made sense, since it was mostly concrete.

At the bottom they paused, because there was nowhere else to go. There was no exit door to the basement, apparently. It was large, but had no rooms. A pool table stood near the center of it. A few leather couches faced a wide-screen TV with a skin of pale dust on it. Neon Budweiser, Miller, and Pabst Blue Ribbon signs hung dark on the walls.

"Briggs has a man-cave?" Jones murmured as he began angling to one side of the basement.

They spread out, checking nooks and crannies with a sinking sense of having been duped. Sam checked the area behind a wet bar—nothing, no one—and came up thinking the same thing that probably all of them were: "Basement's a good place to ambush us." His eyes strayed to the stairwell up, half-expecting a grenade to come tumbling down the stairs at them.

Jones was eyeing the stairs too. "Be like shooting fish in a barrel. Maybe we should get out of here."

Abe was silent on the matter. Appeared to not be concerned with it. Or was, perhaps, too obsessed with the possibility of finding Briggs and just couldn't let go.

"Abe," Marie said. "It's a bust. Unless Briggs has a ladder and has been living on the second level." She seemed to consider that possibility. "I mean…he *might* be."

Abe stopped at the leather couches, staring down at them for a long moment, his rifle held loose in his hands. He brought it up and played his light over the largest couch, the one directly across from the TV.

"Abe," Marie said again, more insistent.

"Hold up," Abe said. He seemed inordinately interested in the armrest. Kept angling his light around it. Then reached over to the back cushion and ran a finger along it. Held the finger up to the light. Sam could see the dust on it from where he was standing.

Jones had drifted closer to look over Abe's shoulder. Sam found his dread turning to curiosity and pulled himself out of the wet bar and approached with Marie.

"Dust on the TV," Abe said, quietly. "Dust on the rest of the couch. No dust on the armrest." He pointed to it. "Just this armrest."

Sam connected the dots, but Abe beat him to it, kneeling down quickly and shining his light on the underside of the couch. Sam went down anyways, and saw what Abe had illuminated.

"My, my," Abe huffed. "Bingo."

Sam jolted to his feet, already slinging his rifle to the side and seizing the armrest. "Help me move this thing."

As Abe clambered to his feet again, Marie and Jones grabbed the hefty couch and helped Sam drag it backwards several feet. Then they all stood up, and all of their lights crept to the same point in the floor that had been covered up by the couch.

Jones tilted his head. "That's a mighty big floor-safe."

It was a giant metal slab, maybe three-by-three, set into the floor so that it was flush with the concrete. What looked like a numeric keypad sat squarely in the center of the metal panel.

Abe knelt at the edge of it. "That's 'cause it's not a floor-safe. It's a hatch." He rapped his knuckles on the top. It gave up a dull noise that sounded a helluva lot like very thick steel.

"Shit," Jones muttered. "That asshat give us a code to go with the tip?"

Abe shuffled on his knees closer to the keypad. He jabbed a finger down on one of the buttons and the screen lit up. "Keypad's live. It's getting power from somewhere."

Sam stalked over and peered down at the keypad. "You got any idea what the code might be?"

Abe shook his head. "I wouldn't even know where to start. And we don't have time to go through a thousand possibilities." He reared back. Seemed to take a moment. Glanced up at the others. Then started shucking his backpack off.

"How many breaching charges you got in that thing?" Sam said, tapping the toe of his boot on the metal panel, and then on the concrete, as though he hoped it would make a hollow sound. It didn't. "Because that's some thick-ass concrete and thick-ass metal."

"Four," Abe said, ripping his pack open. The first thing he took out wasn't a breaching charge, but a length of steel. "And a crowbar."

"You think that'll be enough to get through that thing?" Marie sounded doubtful.

"I don't know," Abe said, a little irritable. "But would you rather not try at all?"

She didn't respond.

The crowbar clanked to the concrete floor as Abe set it off to the side and pulled out his pre-set breaching charges. Began unspooling the wiring from around them.

Jones made an uncertain noise. "Bad a shape as this house is in, four charges might bring it down on us."

Abe snapped his head up. "Well, I guess we shouldn't be down here when they go off then." He fixed each of them with a furious gaze. "This is what we're doing. You want out, then piss off."

"Whoa, easy," Marie said. "We're just making points."

"I don't give a fuck about your points," Abe said, his movements growing sharper as he got angrier with them. His whole mood had changed the second that they'd left FOB Hampton. A darkness had come over the man. He was so close to the thing he so badly wanted, and he wasn't going to let anyone or anything hold him back.

Marie raised her eyebrows and glanced at Sam, as though she thought he should say something. But Sam only shook his head. Hell, they'd come this far. Why not blow the breaching charges and see what happened? If the house came down, then at least they'd bury Briggs underneath it. If, in fact, he was somewhere beneath that hatch.

Abe worked furiously, sweat beginning to bead on his nose. The rest of them were silent as Abe spliced wiring together, seated blasting caps, and fused the four charges to go off at once.

Sam backed up from his work, not worried about Abe setting it off prematurely, but becoming more and more unnerved by how long they'd been in this concrete death-trap. He moved over to the stairs again and took a position so he could see up to the top. Kept his light off so that if anyone was coming, they wouldn't know he was watching. The stairwell was doused into gloomy blackness.

After another minute, Abe grunted, standing up, snatching his backpack onto his shoulders and feeding fuse as he backed his way towards the stairs. He stopped at the first tread and swore, staring down at his hands.

"I don't have enough fuse to get up the stairs," he said with a hollow voice.

Sam, Jones, and Marie all exchanged a glance, as though not sure what the next move was. Oh well, we don't have enough fuse, let's call it a day? That didn't feel right. Nor did just blowing the damn thing while they were still down here.

Abe dropped the fusing to the floor and marched towards the couch. "Y'all help me with this thing."

"Abe, what're you doing?" Sam pressed, but followed after him.

Abe grabbed one side of the couch and waved Sam to the other, Marie and Jones standing at the back of it. "I'm gonna move this couch over to the stairs and hide behind it."

"You fucking kidding me?" Jones rasped.

"No, I'm not fucking kidding you!" Abe shot back. "Now help me move the fucking couch!"

As the four of them slid the couch along the concrete—no longer trying to be quiet—Marie kept trying to speak reason, and Abe kept not wanting to hear it. He was like a freight train at max speed. You couldn't reason with it. All you could do was get the hell out of the way, because it wasn't stopping for anything.

"Couch ain't gonna protect you if the house caves in," Marie said as they shoved it up against the stairs.

"Then oh-fucking-well," Abe growled. "I'm not leaving this house until I've exhausted all the possibilities. You see a better way to get in that hatch? Huh? No? Anybody?" He only paused long enough to take a breath. "Alright then. Go upstairs. I'll count it off. Don't come down after me unless I tell you to, you hear?"

They heard, but no one made a verbal acknowledgement. Sam looked at him as he trudged up the first stairs, but Abe was focused on his work, wiring the fuse and detonator, hunched over it like a madman, squashed in tight behind the leather couch. At least the couch was heavy and solid. Sam didn't know how much that counted when you were about to blow off four charges.

At the top of the stairs, Sam panned his light around again, just to make sure no unwanted visitors had arrived. Part of him hoped that he'd find Briggs standing there in the kitchen, just as pretty as you please. At least that would keep Abe from blowing himself up.

"You all upstairs?" Abe called from down below, his voice husky and tense.

"We're all up here," Sam answered.

"Alright." There was a long pause. Long enough that Sam thought maybe Abe was getting cold feet. But then Abe's voice came again: "Three!"

"Shit, he's actually doing it," Jones squeaked, backing away from the basement door and raising his fingers to plug his ears.

"Two!"

Sam plugged his ears too, cringing and leaning away from the doorway as though that would do any good. With his ears plugged, he barely heard the one count, but he heard Abe's call of "Fire in the hole!"

And then the whole house shook.

The shockwave seemed to punch Sam's entire body at once. A massive gout of gray dust came swirling up from the basement door, rushing into the kitchen, catching the glare of their weaponlights and turning the whole room into a gray-out.

Coughing and waving his hand futilely in front of his face, Sam charged back towards the doorway, sparing a glance to the walls and ceiling around him for any obvious signs that the house was coming down, but he couldn't see shit with all the dust in the air.

"Abe!" he choked out between coughs. "You okay?"

Sam was hearing Marie and Jones cough, but then realized one set of coughs was coming from down below. Which meant that Abe was alive, at least. Hopefully still in one piece.

Sam put one foot down on the first tread, but stopped himself. "Abe, you with us? We clear to come down?"

More coughing. Then, haggard and trembling and a little nasally: "It's clear! Come on down!"

The three of them came banging down the stairs. Abe was upright, with all limbs attached, though his entire body and face were covered in dust, making his black beard look gray. Bright red blood seeped down one side of his face, coming out of his left ear. His eyes were wild and a little dazed.

He was blinking a lot and Sam couldn't tell if it was because of the dust or if Abe was maybe seeing six of them instead of three.

He put a hand to Abe's chest, fingers curling around the collar of his plate carrier. He felt a slight sway in Abe's movement, and his eyes seemed to be struggling to focus.

"You okay?" Sam asked again. "You get your bell rung?"

Abe nodded. "I'm fine." He turned away a bit jerkily and started climbing over the couch. Sam followed, moving through the haze of dust, squinting against it, his nostrils and throat filled with it. He tried to hold an elbow over his face to mitigate the dust he was breathing, but it didn't seem to help much.

Abe stopped where the charges had gone off, waved his arms at the air, trying to get it clear enough to see some detail in the chalky gloom. Sam went down on one knee, getting closer to the hatch in order to see. It took Abe a minute to lower himself, grunting like something was hurting him—probably everything.

The hatch was intact and unmarred, save for minor scorch marks at the corners where Abe had pressed the explosives. But the concrete was shattered. Peering closer still, Sam saw that they'd blasted just enough concrete away to see the solid steel frame of the hatch.

Abe began frantically searching around on the ground. "Where's the crowbar?"

"You looking for this?" Jones offered up, plucking the crowbar from where it had embedded itself in one of the front cushions of the couch. "Jesus, man. Good thing it didn't go right through and spear you."

Sam felt his face blanch a bit as he realized Abe had left the crowbar on the ground and the blast had hurled it into the couch. A few inches higher and it might've gone through the back of the couch and into Abe.

Abe seemed to not care one whit. He snatched the crowbar up as Jones approached with it, then spun and started jamming away at the narrow gap between the concrete and the frame of the hatch. Abe got the flat bill of the crowbar into the gap and started prying, the muscles in his forearms standing out as he groaned with the effort.

"Help me with this!" Abe snapped, and Sam added his weight to Abe's. At first it seemed like they were just prying fruitlessly at concrete, but then Sam felt a little give to it and glanced down long enough to see the entire hatch assembly lift out of place by about an inch.

Spurred by the hope of progress, Sam and Abe redoubled their efforts, gasping and grunting as they pressed and pulled. Jones and Marie hustled over and tried to add their weight behind it, four people all yanking at the same crowbar.

Coughing and spluttering and cursing, the four of them made slow progress, all the way around the hatch, grinding away at the concrete, chipping the edges with furious blow, and then prying again and again, each time the hatch and frame getting a little looser, the concrete losing its grip.

After about five minutes, they were all soaked with sweat. The air in the basement was cool, but heavy and humid, and the dust and sweat combined to make a thin paste across their skin so that in the washed-out glow of their lights, they looked like they'd rubbed spackling on themselves.

Arms burning from the effort, lungs rasping and rattling, grown phlegmy with the cruddy air, Sam stood back to mark their progress. "I think we might be able to lift the whole hatch out."

"Fucker must weigh four hundred pounds," Abe gasped, then hocked and spat off to the side. "Sam, help me lift the edge. Jones, Marie, see if you can't get in there and lift it."

"Oh, God," Jones groaned, readying himself into a crouch at the edge of the hatch with Marie while Abe got the crowbar seated. "Don't drop it on my fingers. Please. I'm asking nicely."

"Ready?" Abe said, as Sam got his hands on the crowbar too.

"Go ahead," Marie said, focused and intense now that their efforts had paid off.

"Lift!" Abe strained out, and he and Sam pulled with everything they had left in them.

The hatch and the frame lifted out. Two inches of space between the metal edge and the concrete. Jones let out a little mewl of terror and then he and Marie jammed their fingers into the gap and heaved. The hatch lifted even more. Abe kept pressure on the crowbar, working it deeper with a few jerks. The gap grew to six inches. Jones and Marie were huffing and seething.

"Help them lift!" Abe commanded.

Sam moved as quickly as he could between the crowbar and the hatch. It dipped an inch as his strength left the crowbar and Jones let out a squeal but didn't let go. Sam smushed himself in beside Jones and grabbed the hatch, lifting with his legs, pulling, pulling, slow progress, a few more inches, gasping and swearing, a few more.

Then the massive hatch assembly was cradled on their forearms and Abe dropped the crowbar and lurched into position, should-to-shoulder with Sam, all four of them lifting it now and suddenly it wasn't so hard as the hatch reached a tipping point about forty-five degrees off the ground. Low, red light emanated from the space below.

"One more push!" Abe strained out, and then with all of them working together they lifted the hatch assembly nearly straight up and then thrust it over.

It smashed to the ground with an ear-pummeling crash of metal and concrete.

Sam was already grappling with his rifle, his over-stressed hands unwieldy as he brought the weapon to his shoulder and stepped up to the opening, shining his light down.

There was a ladder—steel rungs embedded into the side of a square concrete tunnel. The tunnel descended for maybe ten feet and then there was concrete floor. Sam's bright light washed out the red glow, but he could tell that the passage under their feet was lit by red lights.

Abe peered down into the hole. "Well, I'll be fucked," he murmured breathlessly. "That look familiar to anyone else?"

Sam had been thinking the same thing—an inkling of recognition pulling his mind back across the years, searching for a matching image that he knew lurked in his memory. And then he found it and realization rammed into him, even though he wasn't sure what exactly it all meant.

"It's just like Lee's bunker," Sam breathed. "Like the one underneath his house."

THIRTY-ONE

THE BUNKER

ABE WENT FIRST.

Sam, Jones and Marie stood topside, leaning over the hole, watching him descend the ladder. When he was about five feet off the ground, he dropped, boots hit the ground, and he spun, rifle coming up. A few seconds passed in silence.

"There's a passageway down here," Abe's voice lilted up to them. "Long-ass tunnel. It's clear."

Sam immediately slung his rifle to the side, sat on the edge of the opening and then dipped down, getting his feet and then his hands on the rungs. He trundled down rapidly, curiosity and eagerness and fear all mixing together into an electric charge that sparked through his brain.

At the bottom, he whirled, bringing his rifle up, registering the sounds of Jones and Marie descending after him.

He was staring down a long passageway, maybe eight feet wide and eight feet high. Grated lights fixed to the concrete ceiling cast the entire tunnel in dull red. The bunker had electricity, then. And more than that, the passage was practically an exact match to his memory of Lee's bunker beneath his house in North Carolina. The size and shape of it. The red lighting. The way the ground sloped gradually downward.

"Is this a Project Hometown bunker?" Sam whispered.

Abe took a moment to respond. "There was no Coordinator stationed in Greeley. It *shouldn't* be a Project Hometown bunker. But hell if it doesn't look nearly identical. Shit's giving me deja-vu."

Jones and Marie joined them.

Jones let out a low, whispery whistle. "I guess…we're now going to go into the Red Tunnel of Death, huh?"

"Single file," Abe said in response. "Stack up behind me. We take any fire, just haul ass back here—we got no cover."

And with that, Abe set off, and Sam and the others followed.

The passage was even colder than the basement had been. They kept their lights off since the red light was plenty to see by, but in the glow of it, Sam had to admit, there was something to what Jones had said: It felt like they were slowly descending into hell.

Abe kept his pace slow and steady. The gentle downward slope of the passage caused the ceiling to act as the horizon, so as Sam went along, he kept his eyes on what he could see just beyond the ceiling. Little bit by little bit they progressed down the tunnel, more and more of it coming into view as they did, until finally, after nearly five minutes, the passage ended in a massive, vault-like door.

Just like the one in Lee's bunker.

Abe pulled to a stop as the vault door came into view. "Hang on a second."

They all stopped behind him, peering over his shoulders at the door.

"No way we're getting through that," Jones said. "We'd need a helluva lot more explosives."

Abe stared at the door, his jaw working. "This's *gotta* be a Project Hometown bunker. Same vault door. Same passageway. Even the length of the passage is the same." He shifted his weight. "Who the hell put a Project Hometown bunker in the middle of a neighborhood in Greeley?"

"And how the hell did Briggs get access to it?" Sam muttered.

"And why is this the first I'm learning about it?"

"Maybe he had it all along and kept it a secret?"

Abe shook his head. "Briggs didn't even know about Project Hometown until he took on the presidency. And he didn't have access to the bunkers until he ordered all the Coordinators to hand over their access codes."

Sam considered it for a moment. "You know, I've always wondered why he picked Greeley to set up his base. Do you think he chose Greeley because of this bunker?"

"What are we doing, guys?" Marie urged from behind. "Either we keep going and see what can be done about that door, or we pull out while we still have time. We don't know when Lee's going to call that evac."

Sam frowned, something tickling his consciousness. "Abe, you heard any radio chatter in the last few minutes?"

Abe cocked his head to one side. "As a matter of fact, I haven't."

Abe was the only one with the radio—they didn't have enough to go around. He reached up and put his finger on the PTT but didn't press it for a moment, seemed to be listening. Then he transmitted: "Stranger Actual to Marshal Actual, you copy?"

A long stretch of silence pulled at Sam's nerves. The walls around them seemed to get a little tighter. The ceiling felt heavier. Like there was an entire mountain over their heads.

"Stranger Actual to any station, you copy?"

Abe's words gave a faint echo down the passageway, sounding lonely and abandoned.

"Anyone picking up this transmission?" he said one more time, his tone a bit clipped, like he already knew the answer. After another moment of silence, he shook his head, and pointed to the ceiling. "I'm not receiving anything, and I don't think anyone can hear me. The concrete's too thick. Signal's not getting out."

"Shit," Marie hissed. "He might've already called the evac and we don't even know it."

"We don't know that," Abe grunted. He took a cautious step forward, and then another, and then he was striding towards the big vault door.

"Abe!" Marie shot at his back, unmoving. "You should go topside and see if you can get a transmission out!"

Abe just shook his head, still moving forward. "Wouldn't change anything."

Marie started after him, and Sam and Jones followed.

"What are you gonna do?" she demanded.

"Knock and see who answers," Abe tossed over his shoulder.

***

Lee stared at the radio with wide eyes, his hands clasped in front of his mouth. He wished he could stop thinking. Stop thinking, and start doing. He wished he was on the front lines, facing down the encroaching horde. He wished his world was just gunfire and targets and moving and weapon manipulation—all the simple things that he could do so well.

Anything but this. Anything but sitting there with all of those lives teetering on his rickety decisions. How had he ever been okay with making these types of calls? He could remember making them and pushing the baggage underneath, never dealing with it. But there was, apparently, only so much room in that place where he'd pressed everything down inside of him, and now he couldn't fit this in there too. It was too big, and the depths of him were too filled up with all the things that he'd done.

He berated himself. Chastised his cowardice. Belittled his emotions. Commanded himself to push through, nut up and shut up, do what needs to be done. All the things that he had always used to keep himself going, to keep himself sane.

But was he? He didn't feel like it now. He felt unmoored. None of the tools that he'd used to keep himself upright were working. The rigging was broken, and all the ropes were swinging loose in the storm and he couldn't seem to grab a single one of them, and he felt the ship of his mind listing, sinking.

"We're taking heavy contact at Thirty-Fifth Avenue!" an unnamed Marine transmitted, his voice sounding tiny amid the arhythmic battering of the guns. "I got a large pack, maybe twenty-strong, moving south, trying to get around our position!"

Brinly's voice, cold and calm: "Hold what you can. I'm sending reserves to plug that gap."

Was this it? Was this the pressure on Brinly's lines that Lee had promised to call the evac on? It felt too soon. But the line was straining, if not yet breaking. Hadn't he planned to call the evac *before* they broke? How long was he going to leave those Marines out there holding the line? If he waited too long, they'd get overrun and surrounded.

Lee unclasped his hands. Started to reach for the radio. Then stopped. Laid his palms flat on the table. He'd said he wouldn't wait for Abe. He'd said he'd call the evac. That's what he'd *said*. Why was he hesitating?

You have four friends left in this world. Do you really want to abandon them?

But he also had hundreds of people that trusted him to make the right call before things were too far gone.

He reached his right hand out and grasped the radio. Pulled it a little closer. But didn't hit the PTT. He glanced past the radio to the map, where 35th Avenue was labeled. How far was that from FOB Hampton? Maybe a mile? Slightly less?

"Five-Seven to Actual," another, calmer Marine spoke up. No gunfire in the background of his transmission. "Be advised, just spotted a sizeable chunk of primals crossing Twenty-Third Avenue, heading northwest, maybe a half mile from our line."

Brinly: "Actual copies."

Confusion and irritation in the voice of another: "Two-Six, Actual. I got about fifty civilians at our checkpoint, trying to get out of the neighborhoods and go to FOB Hampton. What do you want me to do with 'em?"

"Two-Six, tell 'em to get lost," Brinly said. "We can't have militia coming in and wrecking our shit at the worst possible moment."

"Actual, I copy, but…I don't think they're militia. There's families in here with kids."

"We don't have time to search every backpack and toddler for mortars and grenades. Tell them to get lost, and if they give you any problems, you're cleared to engage."

Lee brought the radio up to his mouth, almost ready to belay that order and tell Brinly to let them through. But still, he didn't press the PTT. Brinly was right. Wasn't he? So why did it turn Lee's stomach? He'd always said the right thing wasn't necessarily the correct thing. Was Brinly only correct, but not right? Should Lee be right? Was he ever right?

Slowly, he lowered the radio. Acid boiled up his throat.

Who the hell was he? And who was he going to be when this night was over?

Was he going to be an ousted war criminal, running away with his tail between his legs, having wrecked a city only to leave it in shambles, empty handed, because he didn't have the balls to stick it out?

Was he going to fight it out to the bitter end for a chance to get Briggs, because that's what he'd promised to do, and he always did what he promised, no matter the cost?

Why couldn't he see which way was the *right* way?

Was there even a right way?

A vibration drew his attention to the left. The satphone had lit up. It was buzzing softly against the desktop, squirming slightly as it did. For a moment, he wondered who might be calling him on his satphone, but then he realized it wasn't his satphone. That one had been dropped into the river. This was the satphone Griffin had given him.

He clutched the radio in his right hand, and grabbed the satphone with his left. Brought it up and stared at the face plate. It was definitely Griffin calling. But what did he have to say? Was he going to try to bury the hatchet and loan Lee some troops? The thought was laughable, though Lee didn't think he could laugh. More likely, Griffin was going to tell him that his time was up, his bluff had been found out, and now Griffin was coming into Greeley to solve this once and for all.

The thought gave him a minor stir of anger, and he tried desperately to seize upon it and wrap it around himself to bolster him out of this insanity. But then it was gone like smoke in the wind.

He answered the call and put the satphone to his ear.

"What do you want?" Lee growled.

"I want you to close your mouth and listen to me, Lee," Griffin said, every word honed and pointed and thrust right into Lee's chest. "Don't say shit until I'm done talking."

So, Lee closed his mouth, and let Griffin talk.

***

The vault door was nearly as big as the tunnel itself, save for the space of about a foot on either side. And in that space, on the right side of the door, was a control panel. Alphanumeric keypad. And a little, silver button. And a speaker.

Abe stared at that panel for a long time, and Sam's eyes went back and forth between the impassable door, and Abe, and the control panel. What the hell were they going to say if Briggs was in there? There was no way they could get him out. Did Abe think that he could simply talk him out?

"That look like an intercom to you, Ryder?" Abe asked, his voice quiet and seeming lost in thought.

Sam shrugged. He supposed it did, though he had no experience with such things. Even before the fall of society, he hadn't lived in an area where intercoms were used, like in an apartment building. And after the fall, there wasn't much use for them.

Abe tilted his head to one side. "They didn't have intercoms on our bunkers." His eyes ranged over the massive door. "Figures that Briggs would have a nicer bunker than we did."

No one had mentioned evacuation since Abe had shut them down a few moments before. Maybe they were all thinking about it, though. Sam knew that he certainly was. He felt time slipping out of his grasp like an oil-slicked rope. But Abe didn't seem bothered by it. He had one reason for living, and he didn't care if the evac happened without him.

Did Sam? Did it even matter at this point? For all they knew, the evac had been called already and everyone was miles north, and the mansion over their heads was overrun with primals.

Maybe the best thing to do would be to simply commit. Go to whatever dark place Abe had gone. Kill your fears and your desires for a life that extended any further than this moment. Sink into it, and let vengeance be the only thing that mattered.

Abe grunted as though reaching a final decision. Then he shrugged, leaned forward, and pressed the silver button. "President Briggs," he barked, his voice sharp, then echoing softly back.

Nothing happened for a long time. Sam glanced over his shoulder and saw Marie and Jones, their attention wrapped up in the intercom. Waiting to hear the voice of the man that had taken everything from them.

Was he even in there? Or were they just talking to an empty bunker at this point?

Sam's heart was beginning to sink—everything that they'd done, everything that they'd sacrificed, all the hell that they'd been through, only to wind up here and now, facing an obstacle they had no way to get past, standing around with their thumbs up their asses and no big fish to fry in all their fire and fury.

And then the intercom crackled, and Sam's heart skipped, then hit the ground running hard.

"This is President Briggs," the voice came through. It was a loud, cocksure voice, as though it didn't belong to a man who'd had his regime toppled in the matter of hours and was now living in a bunker. Sam immediately felt ferocity buzzing in his chest, wanting to get through that door and get to this man.

"Who'm I speaking to?" the voice demanded after a pause.

Abe stood there, very still for a moment. Then he looked up and around, and Sam realized he was looking for a camera, but there didn't seem to be one. Briggs didn't know who it was lurking outside of his door. Was Abe going to try to bluff his way in?

Abe's fingers wiggled in the air, as though conjuring words, then he pressed the button. "This is Lieutenant James. Javier Cordova sent me. We found out where you've been hiding. The threat has been dealt with. We have Lee Harden in custody. It's safe to come out."

Sam didn't breathe. Couldn't. Everything was locked up, as though Briggs might hear through the slab of steel, and be frightened off by the sound of a single huff of air.

"Lieutenant James," Briggs came back after a long moment—too long. "That's excellent news. I'm sure Javier provided you with the all-clear?"

Abe snapped his head towards Sam, his eyebrows going up.

Sam raised his hands desperately, shaking his head and mouthing, "Password?"

Abe seemed to mirror Sam's desperation, throwing up his hands and shaking his head, his eyes wide. He had no idea what the password might be. After a moment of exchanging glances and similar body language with Jones and Marie, Abe turned back to the intercom. Raised his hand, one index finger protruding, visibly shaking. He stabbed the button.

"President Briggs, I'm sorry to say, I was not given an all-clear password, if that's what you're asking for."

"Goddammit. Well, get on the horn with Javier and have him provide it."

Abe swore under his breath, hands clawing at his beard, muttering, "Javier never said shit about a password." Then he pressed the intercom again. "Uh, Mr. President, unfortunately that's not possible at this time."

"Why?" Briggs demanded flatly.

Abe bobbled his head, cringing. "Because, sir…the concrete in here is too thick. I can't get a transmission out."

"Jesus Christ," Briggs snapped. "Am I the only one with a brain around here? If the concrete's too thick, then go *outside* and get Javier on the radio! In fact, better yet, how about you just have Javier come down here and handle this shit himself!"

Abe's hand had balled into a fist. His body had inched closer to the intercom so that he hunched menacingly over it.

"Abe," Sam whispered, but Abe was done.

He jammed his thumb on the button this time, practically pressing his face against the speaker. "Alright, jig's up, motherfucker. You wanna know who this is? It's Abe Fucking Darabie, you piece of shit, and your chickens have come home to roost. Here's your password: Your city is in shambles, your Cornerstone goons are dead or fled, and you're out of options. We own Greeley, and we're not going anywhere. Now, you can come out now and be treated like a prisoner of war, or I can collapse this fucking tunnel and you can while away your time in there, clawing at the walls while you die of starvation. How's that sound, Mr. Fucking President?"

THIRTY-TWO

SURRENDER

LEE WAS ALREADY SCRAMBLING out of his office before he even terminated the call, Deuce at his heels, tail low and still, sensing that something was off. Satphone in one hand, radio in the other, Lee jerked to a brief halt, glancing back over his shoulder at his rifle. But he didn't go back for it. He had a pistol. That was all he would need.

Out of the empty conference room and into the pell-mell of civilian troops rushing about, trying to make their final preparations to defend against the horde. But they wouldn't be. They were going to evacuate. But Lee needed to get out first. Not to save his skin, but to save theirs. He needed a vehicle, and if he called the evac, panic would inevitably take hold, and he might not be able to find one.

A calm had come over his mind now. Not because the situation had improved—no, it had only gotten worse. But at least now Lee knew what he had to do. At least he was not stuck in that hellish dilemma. All the options had been taken away, leaving Lee with only one course of action—the *right* course of action—and it was blessed relief, even as it came with a cold, grievous certainty that it was all over.

Lee came to a stop in the lobby, craning his neck and looking over the heads of a multitude of civilians huddled near the front entrance, peering out into the dark night where the crackle of gunfire could be heard in some indeterminate distance.

He caught one of Menendez's soldiers, hauling four ammo cans—two in each hand, two clamped under each arm. "Where's Brinly?"

The soldier barely broke stride, jerking his head in the direction he was heading. "He's out in the parking lot."

Lee put his head down and pushed into the crowd of civilians. As they saw who it was hobbling through their midst, hands touched him and grabbed at him, though none of them dared to actually pull him to a stop. Their questions wheedled at his back, desperate and panicky.

"What's going on?"

"Lee! What're you gonna do?"

"What's the plan?"

"Are we evacuating?"

"The primals are right over there! We need to evacuate!"

Lee ignored them all. Limped through the front entrance with Deuce's flank pressed against the side of his legs, and spotted Brinly standing at the hood of a MATV, one of his Marines attending him, juggling radios, and scribbling notes directly onto the hood of the MATV—squad positions and reports, Lee assumed.

Brinly spotted him coming and gave him a curt nod, then went back to relaying some command over the radio that Lee didn't hear—he'd turned his own radio down while speaking on the satphone with Griffin. Or rather, *listening* to Griffin in shell-shocked silence.

"Brinly," Lee said, coming to a stop at the man's side.

Brinly finished his transmission, shaking his head. "Primals are circling around to the east and west. Not really pushing our lines just yet, but it seems like they're trying to find a hole to squirt through and flank us." He grimaced, or maybe it was a rueful grin, Lee couldn't tell. "Fuckers get smarter every goddamn time."

"Brinly," Lee said again, quieter, waiting for the Marine to look at him, and when he did, Lee held his gaze for a moment, communicating in that tiny slice of time that everything had changed, and the words that would come next would be somber and serious.

Brinly raised his eyebrows in question at Lee's stare. Then frowned, sensing the weight of the moment.

"Griffin is going to launch nukes," Lee said. No point in beating around the bush about it. As always, they were short on time. The one thing you couldn't get back.

Brinly didn't react for a moment. Then: "Did he tell you this?"

Lee nodded. "I just got off the phone with him. And he's serious. It's going to happen. The Brits gave him access to a nuclear submarine in the Mississippi River. He means to end it right now."

Brinly blinked a few times, then looked up at the dark skies and sighed. "Well. Ain't that a bitch?"

"Listen to me," Lee said, stepping closer and putting his hand on the grill of the MATV. "I'm going to call the evacuation. You need to gather up your men and the civilian troops and head north. Griffin will accept your surrender."

Brinly cocked his head and frowned again. "What about you?"

"Don't worry about me. Griffin's got his own plans for me. Right now, we need to save the troops that we have. Get them out of here before the primals rush us. Griffin's army is stationed eight miles north in a town called Eaton..." Lee trailed off as he watched Brinly shaking his head slowly from side to side. "What?"

Brinly looked at him like he'd just said the dumbest thing in the world. "I'm not surrendering to that fuck. And neither are my boys. Not a chance in hell I'm gonna have my Marines kneeling in the dirt and tried as war criminals. He can go right on and fuck himself."

"Brinly, did you not fucking hear me?" Lee pressed himself even closer. "He's going to drop nukes. He's going to wipe this city off the face of the earth. We're out of options."

"I'm not," Brinly declared with a resolute sniff.

"What the hell do you think you're going to do?" Lee asked, truly wondering what Brinly was thinking. "You can't stay in the city, Brinly. You can't go south through the primals. And if you go north, you're only going to run into Griffin's army—and your boys might be great fighters, but you're outgunned and outmanned."

Brinly curled his nose in disgust. "We'll see."

Lee stood there a moment, just watching him. The background of radio chatter and distant gunfire. Brinly listened to another transmission and pointed to the hood, looking at his assistant, who took up a pen and scrawled another note across the tan paint.

"And what if I order you to withdraw and surrender?" Lee asked evenly.

Brinly's only response to that was a chuff and another small shake of his head.

"Huh." Lee leaned back a bit. "Marie was right about you, Brinly. You're gonna turn this into the Alamo and kill everyone under your command."

"You go ahead and call your evacuation," Brinly said, leaning over the hood to consult the notes. "Sounds like you got places to be. Is that what Griffin wanted? You to turn yourself in to him?"

That was true. So Lee nodded, though Brinly wasn't looking at him. "Those were his terms. It's the only way to guarantee our people can surrender and be treated as prisoners of war, instead of terrorists and war criminals."

"Hm." Brinly grunted. Looked to the south, towards their perimeter where a few muzzle flashes twinkled in the night like fireflies. "Well. You do what you gotta do, Lee. I'll do what I gotta do."

"Is this really better?" Lee said. "Holding out for no reason? Committing all of your Marines to death and not getting anything out of it? Is that the *right thing*?"

But Brinly didn't even respond. Didn't even turn to look at him. He wanted his Alamo. He wanted the "honor" of it. Would rather die than surrender. Simply doing what Lee himself had considered doing only moments ago. But it was an empty honor. Their deaths weren't saving anyone, weren't keeping the threat at bay, weren't even making a point. It was just hoorah bullshit, being enacted more out of stubborn habit than any true necessity.

But Brinly was as resolute in his decision as Lee was in his. He could not be turned away from it, and neither could Lee.

"If I can," Lee said, his voice quiet and sad. "I'll try to radio you when the nukes are inbound. If you can go to ground you might be able to save your men."

Brinly was lost to him, like a gulf had been fixed between them and neither could cross it. He chattered into his radio and bent over his hood, while his assistant glanced rapidly back and forth between Brinly and Lee, his eyes showing his own personal struggle with what he'd heard.

Lee just gave the man a sympathetic nod, and then turned away from Brinly, leaving him to his self-administered doom.

His legs felt stiff as he stepped away from Brinly, but his pace quickened anyways, the urgency retaking its hold on him. The animal in him that always wanted to continue the struggle kept hounding his heels, telling him that this wasn't the way, this was cowardice, this was defeat. But Lee had already decided. He had decided not to listen to that animal. He had decided that this was the right course of action. For the people that had put their trust in him, at least, if not for himself.

He found a small pickup truck. Not one of their technicals, just an old, rust-red beater with an extended cab. He picked it out of all the others because it would not be missed in the evacuation. He let Deuce jump in, then found the keys already in the ignition. He cranked it and it sputtered to life. A quarter-tank of gas, but it would be enough.

As he drove out of the parking lot, crossing through a checkpoint of confused soldiers at the outer perimeter, heading north, Lee raised the radio to his lips and pressed the PTT. "This is Lee Harden to all units, Lee Harden to all units. I am calling the evacuation. You've all done a helluva job. Thank you. I'm sorry that it came to this. Evacuate. Evacuate. Evacuate."

And then he let it go, set it in the passenger side of the old, tattered bench seat next to Deuce, and let the darkness of night swallow his little truck as he drove north towards Eaton and Griffin's army.

***

"You're lying," Briggs's voice trembled over the intercom.

"I'm not," Abe responded, his voice level, barely disguising the malice and hatred that Sam saw written all over his face. "Cornerstone broke after a matter of hours, Briggs. They didn't have enough trained fighters. You drained them when you threw them all into North Carolina to try to kill us. There were more civilians than operatives by the time we got here. We've owned Greeley for the last ten days."

"It's a lie," Briggs hissed into the microphone. "It's a trick! You're just trying to get me to surrender because I made that announcement, calling for the people to rise up against you!"

Abe laughed, pressed the button so that Briggs could hear his mocking chuckle. "How do you think we found your bunker? Those people that you wanted to rise up and fight for you? They were the ones that turned you over to us. They were the ones that told us where to find you. They don't want you, Briggs. You've never been their president, just their dictator. A tyrant. Hated by all, no friends in the world, and now hiding in a bunker." Abe frowned around at the big door. "Which, by the way…is this a Project Hometown bunker? Sure looks like it."

"This is bullshit!" Briggs practically shrieked. "I'm not coming out! You're a madman, just like Lee Harden! If I open this door, you're just going to kill me!"

"I told you that you would be treated as a prisoner of war. But only if you come out willingly. Otherwise, I collapse the tunnel. How much food and water you got stocked away in there, huh? Same amount as the usual Project Hometown bunker? Or did you pilfer some of it to up your food supplies when you set up your little dictatorship?"

Silence. Briggs didn't respond.

Abe bared his teeth for a flash. Shifted his weight. Pressed the button again. "So maybe you can hold out here for a while, even if I do collapse the tunnel. Maybe you think you can claw your way to the surface eventually—find a way out. But you know, there's something else that I haven't told you yet. You ready? Primals—infected, but we call them primals, the big nasty ones that took over and ate all the original ones, you know what I'm talking about? Anyways. Primals. They're pushing into Greeley right now. A huge horde of them. Thousands, as I hear it. So even if you do stay in your bunker, and even if you do manage to dig your way out after I collapse your tunnel, you're just going to emerge into a den of primals. You'll be hunted for your meat. I don't think you'll last long. You know what they've started doing, these primals? Smart fuckers. Getting smarter all the time. They've started immobilizing their prey. You know how they do it? They break the arms and legs so you can't run away. Then they save you for later. Let their spawn feed off of you. Imagine that, Briggs. You, laying on the ground, half-starved, legs and arms pulled out of their sockets, unable to get away, while a brood of little primal juveniles just starts nip-nip-nipping at you. Then taking bigger chunks. I imagine you'd go into shock at some point in time, but until that happened…Whew. Terrible way to go."

"More bullshit," Briggs declared, but he didn't sound so certain this time. He sounded shaken by the image that Abe had just painted. If Sam were being honest, the thought made him a little ill. "There are no hordes out here. Just small packs. You're…you're telling me monster stories! Trying to scare me!"

"Well, see, that's the irony of it, Briggs," Abe said, leaning his shoulder into the wall and taking a conversational tone. "You didn't have hordes out here. But we had hordes on the east coast. The best I can figure, this particular horde followed us up here. So, in a way, you brought this horde upon yourself. How's that for irony?"

A long pause in the talking. Abe leaned there, his finger making little caressing circles around the intercom button. Waiting, as though they had all the time in the world.

"It wasn't…" Briggs finally said. He sounded choked up now. "It wasn't supposed to be like this."

Abe snorted. "I know, right? But you know what they say—you reap what you sow."

"No," Briggs growled into the intercom. "The infected! The plague! It wasn't…It wasn't supposed to be like this! You have to believe me!"

Abe stiffened at those words.

Sam felt something in him tighten up. The skin around his neck and scalp suddenly felt taut and itchy, like there were tiny bugs crawling in his hair. He looked at Abe, then at Jones and Marie. Everyone wore the same expression of ghastly confusion: brows furrowed over wide eyes.

Abe waited for a moment, but when Briggs didn't seem inclined to say anything more, he pressed the button and spoke in a surprisingly gentle voice. "Are you saying that you knew about the plague before it happened?"

Another long silence, but this time Abe let it hang. Waited Briggs out.

After almost thirty, long seconds, Briggs came over the intercom again, his voice childish and haunted. "I didn't know *everything*. You have to believe me. It was The Corporation. It was their...their...*plan*. I don't know if they knew what it would do, or if they just didn't care. But I didn't know! No matter what happens, you have to believe me, and—and—be witness to it! I. Didn't. Know!"

"Holy shit," Jones breathed out. "Is he confessing?"

Abe cut him off with a hiss and a wave of the hand. Then eased his finger onto the button again. "Who's The Corporation, Briggs?"

"I don't even know who they are," Briggs mewled. "Just...people. Powerful people. People with enough resources and money that it might as well be infinite. They had different names for different operations in different sectors, but they were all just pieces of one massive conglomerate. I only ever knew them as The Corporation."

Abe made his voice an accusation: "What did you do, Briggs?"

"I didn't do *anything*! If they take me as a prisoner, you have to tell them that I didn't do it! I...I only did what was asked of me. I had no part in the plague. That wasn't part of what they asked me to do. I didn't know when it was going to happen, or even how bad it was going to be. If I'd known..." he trailed off and the intercom clicked.

TERMINUS

Sam's heart was stuck in his throat, beating against the bottom of his brain. Why was Briggs saying all of this? Why was he suddenly spilling all these secrets? Was it because he thought that someone already knew them? Or had the last ten days of him sitting alone and staring at the walls simply undone him? They say people stuck in solitary confinement get strange after a while. Lee had told him that was one of the reasons why Project Hometown recommended pets in the bunker with the Coordinators—to stave off the worst of the madness that solitary could wreak on a mind.

By all accounts, Briggs had been paranoid, and getting worse. Maybe he believed that Lee had uncovered something about his past when he'd taken Greeley. Maybe that gnawing worry had, over the course of seemingly endless days and nights in solitude, convinced him that his darkest secrets had been brought to the light. And now he was trying to justify himself, his blubbering mouth spurred on by the simple need to speak and be heard that had metastasized in all that loneliness.

Ten days didn't seem like *that* long to Sam, but then again, maybe Briggs hadn't been exactly right in the head when he'd gone into it.

Abe's demeanor had shifted. The anger was still there in his eyes, but when he spoke, if Sam were to close his eyes, he would not hear a wrathful man, but a practiced interrogator, drawing his suspect out. "Help me understand, Briggs. What *was* your part in all of this?"

"To take control of Project Hometown," Briggs said, almost immediately, as though it were obvious, as though it were a commonly-known fact. "Why do you think they gave me a bunker of my own? Hell, it was The Corporation that designed and built Project Hometown in the first place!"

THIRTY-THREE

ABSOLUTION

A BLINDING SPOTLIGHT hit Lee in the face and he squinted his eye and raised both his hands. He'd already taken the pistol from his holster. He'd only needed it to get from FOB Hampton to this lonely stretch of Colorado road. In case someone tried to stop him. Or in case he decided to stop himself. Now it lay on the bench seat next to the radio, Deuce standing over the two objects, not sure what the hell was going on.

An amplified voice blared at him from the checkpoint ahead—nothing in his vision except for a collection of white lights, like a UFO had landed and he was about to be pulled into the mothership. The voice competed with the squawking of the radio next to him—the evacuation had turned into bedlam, as he'd known it would. Brinly's Marines were trying to keep the primals back, but their perimeter was crumpling in key areas.

Lee focused past the hit-and-run transmissions, radio discipline mostly disintegrating, and complied with the voice on the loudspeaker as his heart and his mind went in two separate directions and seemed to be tearing him straight down the middle.

"Place both of your hands outside the window!"

Lee knew the drill. He'd rolled down his window in anticipation of it. He stuck his hands out.

Deuce looked confusedly between the bright lights and Lee and let out a whine.

"It's okay, boy," Lee whispered. "You stay."

"Using the outside door handle," the loudspeaker continued. "Open your door."

He did so, nudging it open with his knee.

"Exit the vehicle."

The animal in him told Lee he still had a chance. He could jump back in the vehicle and throw it in reverse. Chances were, they had a sniper trained on him, but maybe if he juked enough...

Or maybe he could just bolt into the darkness and disappear.

His hip sent a spike of pain through him as he stepped out onto the dusty blacktop, as though to mock him. *Who the hell are you kidding? You're not running anywhere.*

He knew they were going to tell him to spin in a circle, and put his hands on his head, and interlock his fingers, and face away, and go down to his knees, and cross his feet over each other, and sit back on his heels. But he let them give their commands anyways, going through the motions even as he wrestled with his compliance, like a beast, shot through the heart, will still struggle to live, though living is hopeless.

On his knees now, he listened to the sound of boots running up to him, the clatter of gear and weapons. He stared southward, into the darkness beyond which Greeley sat, and he thought what a waste it had all been. Everything he'd done, he'd done in the name of some forlorn hope of freedom, and now he was going to end that journey as a captive.

It was a selfish thought, and he knew it. All tied up in how he viewed himself, in his pride, in the identity that he'd carved for so many years before he'd even heard a whisper of something called Project Hometown. Again, that thought that he'd been traveling down a dead-end road, knowing that it went nowhere, and now he was staring at the end.

Except it wasn't quite like a road. As he'd said before, all you need to get off the road is a decent four-wheel drive. No, this had been a long haul on an express train. No getting off. No other rails to ride. Just one path, heading in one direction, for his whole life, and here he was, looking back at all the miles, and thinking himself the world's biggest fool for having even got on in the first place.

For a time, that train had been packed with friends and allies. It had felt like there was some control to it. At times, Lee could have convinced himself he was the engineer. But now all those people that had populated it were gone, and it was just Lee, chugging to his final stop. The only destination that could ever be. The terminus of his life's work.

"You move, you die," a loud voice sounded behind him. They sounded young. As young as Lee had been once. Did that rifle-toting kid behind him think he was fixing the world too? Probably. Everyone always thought they were fixing the world. Everyone always thought there was some bright, beautiful end to it all that would justify all the dark, ugly things they'd done to get there. That's what they told themselves to rationalize the blood on their hands. Hell, that's what Lee had told himself.

Hard hands grabbed him by the wrists. Wrenched them around to his back. The zip of plastic handcuffs. The pinch of the bands tightening over his skin.

"Stand him up," another voice said. And this one Lee recognized.

They hooked him under the armpits and hauled him to his feet. Turned him around to face Griffin. The spotlights had gone out, but the headlights of several vehicles still glared at him, casting Griffin's face into stark whites and blacks. There was no joy on his expression. No revelry in his victory. He had his man, but everything in his eyes said *Big fuckin' whoop.*

"You look like shit," Lee said with a small smile, echoing Griffin's first words to him when they'd met on the bridge.

Griffin chuffed without much humor. "I've seen better days."

"You look like a man that's about to launch a nuke at an American city."

Griffin's mouth pursed. Worked around, like he was gathering enough spit to speak with. But he didn't say anything.

"You don't have to do it," Lee said, with all the conviction of a man that knows he's speaking to the deaf. "The civilians that were with me are evacuating right now. It's not necessary."

"And what about your Marines? And your soldiers?" Griffin raised an eyebrow.

Lee only shook his head.

"And what about the infected?"

Lee took a heavy breath. "You're going to kill your own president."

"I don't have a president anymore."

"Careful," Lee said. "You're starting to sound like me."

"Briggs is through," Griffin said in a big gust of air, as though he were admitting something to a priest. "Canada and the UK have decided they don't want to be in bed with him anymore than they wanted to be with you."

Lee looked at the ground, breathing hard through his nose. That should've been good news. It should have been a *Well, at least Briggs won't be a problem anymore.* But that's not what he felt. It just felt like more waste. He'd sent Abe and Sam and Jones and Marie after a man that had no hope of living anyways. He'd committed his last friends in the world to a suicide mission that didn't even yield anything of value, because the target was going to go up in smoke anyways.

"Why'd you do all this, Lee?" Griffin suddenly cried out, a wind of released emotion and tension scouring away the affected calm.

Lee looked up at him, squinting. Griffin had his arms spread out wide, his face incredulous.

"Are you happy with what you've done?" Griffin bit out. "Are you pleased with yourself? Are you sitting there thinking, 'Mission accomplished, Old Boy! We've wrecked enough lives, how about we call it a day!'?"

Lee winced. Looked away from Griffin.

"Fucking answer me!" Griffin demanded. "I want you to nut the fuck up and answer me! You've done all this shit, now I want an explanation!" He stepped closer and jammed a finger roughly into the side of Lee's head, pressing it in hard. "I want to understand what the fuck's going on in that brain of yours!"

Lee shook his finger off, his face pained.

Griffin put his hands on his hips, waiting, his eyes wide and furious. Lee heard the man's breath wheezing rapidly in and out through his nose.

"I was gonna..." Lee started, then stopped. Tilted his head back and looked at the vaulting blackness above. "I was gonna recon my AO."

"What?" Griffin breathed, the single word riddled with accusation and disbelief.

Lee lowered his head and looked at his old friend. New enemy. "That first day when I left the bunker. The whole reason why I was declared a nonviable asset."

Griffin's ire softened, but only slightly, overtaken by a sort of morbid curiosity.

"The feeds were dead," Lee continued. "Hadn't heard from anyone in charge in a long time. No internet. No news. I had no idea what was going on topside. And I knew I was going to have to go out into that in just a few days. I was supposed to rescue people and rebuild the United States, but I didn't even have a clue what I was facing out there. That's why I left the bunker. And after I'd left the bunker, everything just...everything just went sideways. Time and time again. One thing leads to another, and before I know it, I'm running a camp of survivors, and Briggs is sending men to assassinate me."

Lee laughed, soft and mystified. "I didn't even know who Briggs was. I didn't know I'd been declared a nonviable asset. I thought I was still doing my mission. I was...blown away, Griff. Couldn't even fathom why some guy in Colorado wanted me dead so bad. And then Abe came along, and he told me about the shit that was going down in Greeley, the people that had been starved for speaking out. And I thought to myself, 'That's not America. That's not the thing I was supposed to be rebuilding. This man's an imposter.'"

Lee shook his head, still chuckling sadly to himself. "And that's where I went wrong, Griff. I thought I could actually accomplish the mission I set out to do. I thought I could fix what had been broken. But all I knew how to do was fight. So, I fought. I fought the infected to keep them from running us over. I fought people that were trying to dismantle the tiny little shred of democracy that I'd established. I fought the cartel. And, yes, I fought Briggs. Because I saw him as a part of the problem. I saw him as the thing that was holding the nation back. But I didn't know how to solve that problem. I didn't know how to fix it. I never did, Griff. So, I just fought. Because if you throw enough men and weapons and ammunition at a problem, that's sure to solve it, right?"

Lee scoffed at himself. "Why did I think I was going to succeed when I'd seen that way of thinking fail so many times before? I don't know. Pride, maybe? Lack of imagination? Hell, I've been trying to pin down where it went wrong for quite a while now, Griff. Been thinking about it long before you and I even knew we were fighting each other. And the best answer I can come up with is that I didn't know how to solve the problem any other way. All I knew was how to fight." He shook his head. "So, I fought. And here we are."

Griffin stared at him in silence for a few beats. "And here we are," he echoed, voice tense and quiet. "Because you fought."

Lee sighed. "I was a good operator, though."

Griffin leaned back. "One of the best," he conceded.

"But you can't rebuild a nation with operators," Lee said, wistfully. "That's something Project Hometown got wrong. Rebuilding nations takes civilians, not fighters. It takes people that know how to build, not just kill and blow shit up."

Griffin's eyes narrowed at him. "You know this doesn't change anything."

Lee nodded. "I know." He peered at Griffin. "You haven't launched the nuke yet?"

"I'm going to," he said. "As soon as I get back there. This is going to end tonight. I've already made up my mind."

Lee steeled himself. Felt the way his heart was bumping faster, as Lee came to a crossroads. "We found out where Briggs was holed up. And I sent four of my friends in after him. I lost contact with them. Couldn't get them on the radio. They don't even know that a nuke's incoming."

Griffin watched him carefully. He was a stone wall, not giving an inch. And yet Lee was going to throw himself upon it. Because it was his last chance to do the right thing.

"Griffin," Lee said, his voice quiet and pleading. "They're the last four friends that I have in the world. I don't have anybody else. I know you don't owe me shit. But let me go after them, Griff. Let me try to save them."

Griffin's face screwed up. "Are you fucking high?"

Lee pushed desperately forward, but was yanked back by the soldiers holding him. "Listen to me. You've got me. You won. I'm here. I turned myself in. Now let me go back there and at least warn them to get out." Griffin's head was shaking, but Lee pressed on, pressed himself into that unforgiving wall, praying that it would give, just a little bit. "My word might not mean much to you, but I don't give it lightly, and I still stand by it. I give you my word, that I'll come back. I'll turn myself back in to you. If I don't die in the blast, that is."

Griffin made a negative noise, but he didn't flat-out deny Lee's request, and that was something. It was just enough to put some hope in.

"You'll still win, Griffin. You didn't even want me in the first place, did you? You were going to let me die in the blast anyways. Isn't that what Canada and the UK wanted? A clean slate?"

Griffin stabbed a finger at the ground. "I wanted you here, because I wanted to look you in the face and hear why you did all this shit in the first place."

"And I've told you. And I know that doesn't fix anything. Nothing is different, and it won't be. I'm not trying to make it be different. I'm just trying to save the last four people that I love. And I'll either die when the nuke hits, or I'll come back here to you, and you can put me on trial, or do whatever you want to do with me. But, please...let me at least *try* to save them. It costs you nothing. And if you still want me as your prisoner, I'll be cooperative. I'll be compliant, even if it means a firing squad or a fucking noose. And if I die, then you still win. Any way you cut it, *you still win*. Just give me a chance..." he swallowed against a knot of desperation forming in his throat. His voice was hoarse and broken when he finished: "Give me a chance to fucking sleep at night, Griff!"

Lee watched the image of Griffin swirl and muddy, and realized he had tears in his eye. He felt nothing about it. No sense of shame tied to his pride. He had none of that left. He'd already given up everything he was to stand there in that moment. All he wanted now was a chance to make things right with Abe, and Sam, and Marie, and Jones.

His ruined eye socket ached as though it wanted to spill something from its scarred tear ducts, but couldn't. It itched fiercely, but he couldn't scratch it with his hands behind his back.

Griffin stared at him for a few beats, then looked away for a few more. Swore quietly under his breath, but Lee couldn't tell if it was the sound of the wall giving in just a tiny bit, or if it was just a man disliking the nasty decision he would have to make.

Finally, he looked back to Lee. "Where's this location that you think Briggs is holed up in?"

A frown crossed Lee's brow. Why did he want to know? But then the answer came to him just as quickly as the question formed in his mind. "So you can drop a nuke right on top of it?"

Griffin didn't answer. Just stared, waiting.

Lee grimaced. Hung his head. "You know the Bittersweet neighborhood?"

Griffin nodded once.

"It's there. At the dead-end of West Eighteenth Street."

Griffin spent a moment inspecting Lee's face, as though searching for any bluff, but Lee's bluffing days were over. Then Griffin snatched a pen from one of the loops in his plate carrier and scrawled the location on the back of his hand. Capped the pen. Set it back where he'd got it. Raised cold, unyielding eyes to Lee.

"I'm going to drop a five-kiloton warhead on that location," Griffin announced, then paused, as though waiting to see what reaction Lee might have to this.

"Fine," Lee said. "Just give me a chance to warn my friends. It's just four people, Griffin. Four people I need to try to save."

"You wouldn't have much time," Griffin said. He glanced at his wristwatch. "I get back there in maybe five minutes, at which point I am *going* launch those nukes and strike targets throughout Greeley. It's a ten minute flight time. Maybe a bit less. So, you'd only have roughly fifteen minutes."

Lee's chest felt like it was going to burst. All of his insides felt like they were squirming up his throat. "Are you telling me that I can go?"

Griffin didn't answer directly. "If I drop that nuke right on that location, you know you can't survive it, right? Even if Briggs is in a basement, or underground, or wherever he's hiding. The blast will collapse everything at ground zero."

"Are you going to let me go?" Lee urged, voice rising.

"You're not going to have enough time to get there and get out. You're going to die."

"I know that," Lee hissed. "But I've got to try. Even if I die with them, at least they'll know that I didn't just…" he choked. Swallowed. Croaked out three more words: "*Throw them away.*"

"You'll be committing suicide."

"Why do you care?" Lee demanded. "I'm dead anyways, aren't I? Whether I hang as a war criminal or die in the blast, it doesn't matter. Dead is dead."

Griffin leered at him. "You trying to die on your terms? Trying to take the easy way out?"

Lee was honestly shocked at the accusation, because it hadn't even crossed his mind. "None of this has been easy. The only easy day was yesterday. Except that yesterday sucked too. I'm not trying to make a statement or escape justice, Griffin. I've already admitted everything I can admit to. I've already admitted that I fucked it all up! I'm not trying to take the easy way out; I'm just trying to do the right thing!"

"Fine," Griffin snapped.

Lee blinked. "Fine?"

Griffin looked at the soldier over Lee's right shoulder. "Cut him loose." Then he brought his wristwatch up and tapped it at Lee. "You got fifteen minutes left to your life, Lee Harden. Go ahead and try to clear your conscience. I hope you die well."

Then he turned and started to walk away with a pronounced limp that Lee hadn't noticed before.

Right then, Lee remembered Deuce, still sitting in the truck. And there was no way he was taking the poor dog into a nuclear blast zone. It seemed an odd thing to worry about at that precise moment, but Deuce deserved better. Lee had made his bed, but Deuce had only ever been loyal.

"Griffin!" Lee hollered, just as he felt the cold steel of a knife slide along his wrist, and the pressure as the soldier behind him jammed it down against the plastic cuffs.

Griffin stopped and looked over his shoulder, perturbed.

Lee felt the plastic snap through on one wrist. "I'm leaving my dog!"

Griffin turned fully. "What?"

"Just feed him!" Lee hollered, as he felt the second cuff break away from his wrist. He was already backpedaling for the truck. "He's skittish, but he's a good boy!"

Lee didn't wait. He had fifteen minutes—maybe less—and he wasn't going to waste a single second of them. Even as his mind swirled with disbelief at being set free, he spun and ran for the pickup, his bum hip forgotten, the pain drowned in urgency.

Deuce wagged his tail as Lee hauled himself into the pickup, and it broke his heart. He held the driver's door open with one foot and pointed out. "Deuce." His voice cracked. "Go."

Deuce tilted his head, like he hadn't understood, but he knew the command.

Urgency fought with a powerful wave of grief. Deuce understood the command, but he wouldn't understand being left with strangers. He wouldn't understand that it was for his own good. "Deuce, go!" Lee commanded, louder.

And Deuce padded over his lap. And Lee resisted the urge to touch him, to give him one last bit of attention, one last scratch behind the ears, fearing that it would cause the dog to stall. So he let Deuce just hop out onto the blacktop, and then he slammed the door.

Deuce turned and looked up at him.

"You're a good boy," Lee husked. "Now stay!"

And then he yanked it into gear and spun tires in a tight U-turn, Deuce watching him the whole way.

As he put the pedal to the floor, the little six-cylinder engine screaming as he accelerated southward towards Greeley, he palmed the radio from the bench seat. He waited for a break in the cavalcade of transmissions, and then cut in with his own.

"Lee Harden to Brinly and all units still in Greeley! There are nuclear warheads inbound to Greeley! If you can get out of the city, then get out! If you can't get out, then get underground! Detonation in *fifteen minutes*!"

THIRTY-FOUR

HISTORY LESSONS

SAM'S REALITY SEEMED TO SHIFT AND CRACK. All of the sudden, he was launched into a new, terrible perspective, as though he were looking down at the reality he'd believed for so long and saw the grim truth that lay behind the façade of misinformation.

Abe's voice was barren when he spoke again. "The very same people that created Project Hometown, and advised on its design, and built our bunkers...they were the same people that unleashed FURY." He was hunched against the intercom still. His breath was audibly shaky. He still had the button depressed. "Why? Why design Project Hometown to preserve the nation, if you're just going to slaughter it with a plague?"

"Because you were never supposed to *preserve the fucking nation*!" Briggs bit out, his breath causing static over the speaker. "All that Rescue and Rebuild bullshit was just what they had to say to convince a bunch of twenty-something, gung-ho, patriotic operators to sign their lives away. Rebuilding the nation under the US Constitution was never the point. That was the *opposite* of the point. The point was to dismantle it! Destroy the Constitution. Destroy the democracy that had rotted us out for hundreds of years of subjugating the people that *should* have the power to all the idiots in the world that don't know their ass from a hole in the ground! They wanted to start from scratch. Not to rebuild the old, but to build something completely new. Get us back to the power systems that worked for thousands of years before we entered into this time of 'freedom' and 'democracy,' which has *ruined us*."

Briggs made a series of nasty scoffing noises, but didn't release the intercom. "The world's too complex to be left in the hands of the *people*. People with everyday worries about everyday bullshit can't possibly know what to do with their vote, so they just vote for all the wrong reasons! They don't understand how the world works, how governments work, how wars are run, how the economy functions—they don't understand anything! How are we supposed to be successful laboring under that type of idiocracy? You can't just turn the reins of government over to the idiot masses! They'll vote for movie stars, because they *like the characters they play on screen*! It's utter madness! It's like letting your children run your household. No. The children need parents, because children don't understand money, and cleanliness, and eating their fucking vegetables. But that's what democracy has done. It's turned our world over to the least capable people. The world needs parents, you see? Oh, they hate the rich and powerful, the *elites*. But they're rich and powerful for a reason—because they know how the world works. Might makes right. That's what they wanted to build. Because a benevolent dictator will *always* be the best form of government. But you can't build a completely new structure while the old one stays standing. So, you have to tear it down to the ground. Bulldoze it. Clear the lot. Then you can build from a clean slate. That's what they wanted. That's why they released FURY on the world. And that's why they designed Project Hometown. Not to re-establish democracy, but to establish dictatorships. Why do you think they chose a bunch of soldiers? Because you lot are so fucking good at government and economics? No! Because you can fight! And all of that fighting was supposed to be turned over to *me*! Project Hometown was supposed to be the core of a new military, under *me*, and not beholden to the masses!"

It almost sounded like he was weeping in rage. "You had the chance to be lords under a king, and you threw it away. You could have been great, but you preferred your familiar prison."

The rambling diatribe came to a sudden end as the intercom clicked off. As Briggs had spoken, Abe had slowly wilted a bit, his forehead now against the concrete wall, staring at nothing in particular.

Watching the former Coordinator, Sam realized that however jarring he felt this shift in perspective was, he wasn't feeling anything close to what Abe was feeling. To have it all rendered down into nothing—your life's work. All the honor and the duty that he must have felt as he strived to complete his mission, now thrown back in his face as the bitter punchline in a madman's tirade.

Sam wanted to deny it, wanted to tell Abe, and maybe tell himself, that it was all bullshit—just Briggs talking out of his ass. But as terrible as the revelation was, it fell into place with such a confident click, that Sam's doubts were snuffed out.

"I thought," Jones ventured hesitantly into the silence. "That Project Hometown was a part of the Army. How could they have let this happen?"

Abe took a deep breath. Sighed it out as he spoke. "The Army contracted nearly everything they have out to third parties. Weapons, munitions, uniforms, bases." He turned his head slightly, but didn't actually look at any of them. "I doubt they knew about any of this. But still...they chose the wrong third party."

The intercom crackled to life again. Briggs's voice was calmer now, almost apologetic. Whining. "But I didn't know what the bacterium would do to people. I don't even think they knew. Or maybe they did, and just didn't care. If I'd have known..." he trailed off into silence. Grunted. Then released the intercom.

Abe immediately took it. "It doesn't matter if you knew what FURY would do to the world. You still decided to let it happen. You still wanted to be the dictator of America. You still destroyed *everything*. Just because you wanted the power."

Sam stepped forward and gently put his hand on Abe's, and when he didn't get a harsh reaction, he eased it down until Abe's finger let go of the button. "Don't get him riled up, Abe. We need him to come out, not have another argument."

Abe pulled himself up from his slouch. Looked at Sam long and hard, and in that moment, Sam didn't know what the hell was going through Abe's brain. His eyes looked somehow both empty, and full of wrath, and grief, and something like bitter, black humor. Sam couldn't tell if Abe was about to listen to him, or go off the rails.

But then he nodded. Pressed the button again, this time standing straight. "President Briggs. We have heard you. You've told your side of the story." He bared his teeth, as though the next words came out with a bit of his soul. "*Thank you*. It's time to come out."

For a long moment they waited for a response. Sam started to wonder if he might hear the massive door unlocking instead of Briggs's voice. But as mad as Briggs clearly was, socked away in his little hovel underground, he was still savvy enough to think about his own skin.

"I have demands," he said. "And I want total immunity."

***

Brinly watched his perimeter crumble like sandcastles against high tide.

Marines were dying out there. Being ripped to shreds. All semblance of order had gone up in smoke. It was like a medieval rout. Command and control were ignored, and men were running now, simply hoping they were faster than the man behind them. Brinly felt a wash of shame for them, but at the same time, that was just human nature in most cases.

The civilians were still pouring out of the hotel. Scrambling around, trying to find a vehicle to get into. A sedan skidded out, so many people piled in that they were laying on each other like stacked wood in the back seat, and someone was clinging to the roof. They weren't going to get far, unfortunately. When they'd reworked the barricades after they'd taken FOB Hampton, they created a solid wall with only one entrance and exit. Great for defense. Really bad for a panicked evacuation.

Now the vehicles were bottlenecking at that one exit point between two jersey barriers. A traffic jam of hundreds of vehicles, the din of screams and car horns and revving engines, but no one was going anywhere. Panicked people had abandoned vehicles, seeing that they weren't going to make it out in time, and left them behind to run north on foot. Left those unmanned vehicles as one more blockage for everyone else to get around.

The radio had devolved into insensible chatter. Marines screaming for support. Screaming to fall back. Sometimes just screaming to be heard in their last moments. Everyone's transmissions stepping all over everyone else's. Brinly hadn't even bothered with the radio since Lee made his last transmission, calling for the evac. No one was listening, and he wouldn't be able to get a word in anyways.

Even if he could, what would he say?

It was all kind of farcical, if you looked at it a certain way. But that's how humans were, Brinly concluded. Take away the fear of death, and it all just became a ridiculous stage play.

Captain Gosling was yelling at him. Brinly turned and raised his eyebrows to the man. He felt that stab of shame again—the man looked like he was ready to run. Hanging on by a bare thread of military discipline.

"What's that?" Brinly said, inclining his ear to try to hear the captain over the waves of noise assaulting him from all directions.

"I said, we need to get the fuck out of here!"

Brinly frowned at Gosling, and then looked south, where he saw more squads dashing on foot, a few hightailing it in vehicles. And beyond them, a dark rippling mass of shapes, surging through their perimeter. Less than a mile away, and closing fast.

"Where the hell you think we're gonna go?" Brinly asked with a sardonic smirk.

"Anywhere but here!"

Brinly sighed and clapped his hand on Gosling's shoulder. "Captain, you're relieved of your duties. You've been great. Go anywhere but here."

Gosling stared at him, and for a moment, Brinly wondered if he'd heard him. Then he wondered if the man was going to do some honorific thing like come to attention and salute him, which would just be more hilarity, as far as Brinly was concerned.

Gosling didn't. His stare became shocked, and then furious. And then fearful. And then he turned and ran.

Brinly shook his head and looked back to his nonexistent perimeter. The civilian troops that had held the two inner perimeters around FOB Hampton had already up and retreated. There was no one now between the wolves and the sheep. The massacre was no longer a hypothetical, but simply a matter of time. Mere minutes, actually.

Brinly moved around the hood of the MATV. Someone had tried to take it a few moments ago, but Brinly had denied them at the muzzle of his pistol. He wondered if, even then, he'd known what he was going to do.

He was smiling airily as he pulled open the back door and climbed in, shutting it behind him. He poked his head up into the turret. It was one of the few that they had with an enclosed turret, but even that wasn't complete protection. There were still gaps in the armor.

He checked the ammo cans. There were three of them, stacked up next to the M2. One already loaded and ready to go. Satisfied, Brinly climbed into the turret and settled himself. Opened the ammo cans. Pulled the first links out, then laid the lid back on them so spent casings wouldn't fly in and gum up the works. Reload time would need to be quick.

When was the last time he'd done a combat reload on a Ma Deuce? Oh well. He'd have to refresh himself on the fly.

He wrapped his fingers around the grips of the gun. Squeezed. Worked his hands. Swiveled the gun around smoothly. Then reached forward and hauled back on the charging handle. That big, clunky *chu-chunk*. Enough to put a smile on any Marine's face.

He rotated the turret until it was facing the closest bulge in the encroaching wave of primals. And he fired. The gun roared and trembled in his grip, spitting raw power. Tracers blazed through the darkness, and he angled them down a bit until he was chewing through ranks and ranks of bodies. Through the muzzle flashes, he could barely make out the damage, but he knew he was doing it. He was wreaking havoc on them, those big rounds cutting down multiple bodies in a row. He couldn't see it, but he could imagine it. Shearing their arms off, exploding their chests, ripping their heads off their necks, limbs spinning off into oblivion.

He swung the turret around, prioritizing the threats by how close they were getting. There was only one sheepdog left amongst the wolves, and while the sheep were fleeing in terror, he was all too happy to do the one job he'd been put on this earth to do: Kill wolves. And in killing them, he gave the sheep a little more time to live. Every primal killed was seconds added to the lives of the evacuees. Hell, maybe some of them would actually survive.

He spotted another mass of shapes, now only a quarter mile out. He fired into them until the last links spat through. Ripped the cover off the top as he chucked the empty ammo can. Seated a fresh one in. Pulled the links into place. Slapped the cover down. Charged the handle. And went right back to shooting.

Now to the right. And then pivoting to the left. His blood was singing in his veins, and the thrum of the weapon in his hands was like a deep basal vibration that resonated with something inside of him.

Less than three hundred yards now.

How many sheep had escaped? He could ponder those things in this moment, because he was working on automatic, his weapon was cyclic, and all was right with the world. Another crowd of primals was razed to the ground, cut down like wheat before a harvester, and Brinly added perhaps another minute to the lives of the fleeing civilians.

Right, and left, panning back and forth in wide, destructive swaths, like painting with death.

Less than a hundred yards now. He was having to move faster, change angles quicker. And now they were coming from the sides more, flanking around him, maybe to get to him, maybe to get to the civilians. So, he soaked them with lead, first to the right, and then chattering all the way across to the left, and letting them have it.

He couldn't hear anymore. Everything had become a dull, peaceful hum. All the panic and the screaming and the gnashing of teeth, silenced under the onslaught of his wrath, so that it was like sinking to the bottom of a deep pool, where sound could not reach, and neither could worries of logistics, and perimeters, and war crimes. All of that was pulled away, burned away in the pall of gunsmoke, and it left Brinly pure and cleansed as it wafted around him and through him and into him.

Another reload, faster this time, but they were too close. Churning over the barricades now. By the time he charged the weapon again, they were on him, on the vehicle, leaping and bounding, harder to hit, but hit them he did, and now he had the pleasure of watching them fall, watching them be dismembered, watching every second he bought.

He was spiraling up, not down. Up, and up, and up, into a place that he thought he'd never taste again. His heart was slamming in his throat with the unbridled, savage joy of it all as he spun, spun, spun, and destroyed flesh, and added time.

Spinning and spinning as the bodies lay in heaps and more came surging towards him, so many that he couldn't even see the hood of the vehicle. Hands reaching, and then blasted off. Jaws gnashing and then shredded. Eyes flashing in the yellow glow of the muzzle blasts, and then gone in puffs of red.

He was a whirlwind. He was a carousel of annihilation. And he was transcendent. He was above it all, even as their hands thrust through the gaps and their claws ripped at his uniform, and then at his flesh, and he only laughed at them and killed their brethren.

In that moment, he was what he was, and he was complete. And it was beautiful.

God, he thought, still roaring with laughter. *This is really something, isn't it?*

THIRTY-FIVE

MINUTES

11 MINUTES LEFT.

Lee drove at ninety-miles-an-hour down the road, straight from Eaton to Greeley. He tried to push it faster, but the backend started to get squirrelly as soon as he touched ninety-five. He swore and hazarded taking one hand from the wheel to roll up the window. He didn't know if the reduced drag would help him keep control of the vehicle, but it was worth a shot. He'd try anything to shave seconds at this point.

The clock on the dash was off by hours. It read 12:38, when Lee knew it couldn't be past 10:00 p.m. He'd got in the vehicle when it read 12:34, and each time the number changed, it felt like a hammer punching one more nail in his coffin.

There might have been a faster way to get to Abe's position, but Lee didn't know the roads, and couldn't afford to get lost. He'd have to stick to the roads he knew, which meant he had to drive straight into Greeley on the same road he'd taken out.

He leaned forward, gripping the wheel in both hands now, feeling that unpleasant floating from the back wheels. Every bump and washed-out section of road threatened to send the pickup into a spin—or worse, a roll. If it spun out, it would cost him seconds. If it rolled, he was fucked, and Abe and Sam and Marie and Jones with him.

"Come on," he whispered to the vehicle, as though words could increase his speed and stability. "C'mon-c'mon-c'mon!"

He crossed into the city. Spotted his turn hurtling towards him and eased on the brake, then clamped it down, nearly locking up the tires in an effort to slow enough to take the turn. Spun the wheel rapidly, hand-over-hand, felt the backend loosen...

Headlights blinded him.

He yelped, having to cut a tighter turn than expected and nearly colliding with an oncoming vehicle. Their sides touched—a squeal of metal-on-metal—and his left sideview mirror went spinning off. He corrected, almost overcorrected, then spun the wheel back and righted himself, hammering down on the gas again. He glanced into the rearview mirror, but then sent his eye forward again just in time to spot another cluster of vehicles—five or six of them—screaming onto the road, skidding tires as they turned off, nearly T-boning him.

His throat tightened with compounding stress. Why were there so few vehicles? Where were the rest of them? Had only a few people heard his call to evacuate? Surely word would've spread...

He realized with a sudden blast of dread that he'd missed his turn. He should've turned on the same road the escaping vehicles were coming out of—it was the path that he was familiar with and he knew those roads weren't blockaded.

He jammed on the brakes, and for a microsecond, considered spinning a U-turn and going back, but then his headlights splashed over a street sign. 35th Avenue. That was one of the streets that bordered the Bittersweet neighborhood—he remembered that from their planning.

He yanked the wheel and cut a hard left turn onto 35th Avenue, heading south again, pedal to the floor, going thirty, fifty, sixty...

A glance at the clock.

12:40.

Dammit! How had two minutes already slipped by?

He was going eighty miles-an-hour when his headlights splashed over naked figures, running straight at him up the street. Instinct made him hit the brakes. They locked up, the pickup starting to drift sideways. His brain sparked with panic and told him to run them over, but he couldn't hit them going this fast—

Too late.

WHAM!

The whole vehicle shook, the wheel thrashing in his grip, the front end jumping. A massive spray of gore washed over the windshield as half of a body went tumbling over the hood and the bottom half went under his tires.

He lost control. Saw a light pole looming up in front of him and stood on the brakes. The pickup skidded, swirled, and then slammed into the light pole on the passenger side. Pebbles of safety glass shot through the cab, stinging his face.

Shrieking noises. He couldn't tell if it was his engine screaming, or the primals just outside of his vehicle. The pickup rocked and he saw a shadowy shape, bathed in red brake lights, clambering into the truck bed.

He seized the shifter, pulled it into reverse and slammed on the gas again. The engine responded, but the acceleration was slow and the noise was wrong. Steam jetted out of his crumpled hood. As the pickup went backwards, the primal in the bed pitched forward, slamming into the back glass.

Lee hit the brakes again, snatching up his pistol as the primal tumbled back into the tailgate. The pickup jolted to a stop. He twisted in the driver's seat, pointing the pistol backwards with one hand and fired three rounds. The blast in the enclosed space was like being punched in the ears. The back glass cracked—one hole, two holes—then shattered.

Something hit the driver's door. Tried to yank it open. Lee immediately pivoted, screaming, grabbed the handle and fought it closed again, then fired from the hip, four rapid rounds that disintegrated the glass and punched through the door, striking the chest, neck, and face of the primal outside and knocking it back.

Pistol still in hand, Lee slapped the shifter into drive and hit the gas. The take-off was even slower than before. The engine was overheating, straining, on the brink of giving out. Shapes swirled around him, leapt at the trudging vehicle, trying to get their arms in the broken windows, but by then, Lee had the pickup surging through the hole crowd of them at thirty miles-an-hour and gaining.

A muffled gargling from behind him.

He twisted again, heart in his throat.

The primal from the bed was slithering through the back glass, half its face hanging off, drooling streams of dark blood and jabbering non-words. Lee had no breath left to scream. The thing reached for him. He tucked his pistol into his body, knowing that he couldn't thrust it into the back or it would be snatched away from him. He jerked the wheel side to side, now going fifty, and the primal thrashed, off-balance, and fell into the passenger-side floorboards, feet kicking at Lee.

Lee gasped, snarled, angled the pistol through the flailing legs and fired until he was empty. Felt the horrible sensation of the slide locking back. No time for a reload, and the primal was still moving, still squirming, rolling, trying to right itself and come for a second attack, but its head and chest were still down on the floorboards.

Lee had no more weapons. He dropped the pistol. Switched his left foot to the accelerator and brought his right foot over and started kicking at the thing's face. Breath came back into his lungs again and was wrenched out of him in a series of rhythmic, guttural barks. He caught the thing in its half-demolished face and put all the strength he had into it, the strength of pure survival—kill or be killed in its truest form.

The thing clawed at his leg, the nails gouging deep into his flesh, trying to pin it, trying to restrain it. He just kept stomping at it, trying desperately to keep his swerving vehicle on the road at the same time. He shouted with each stomp and finally, like a gust of cool air, felt the relief of bone giving way. The primal tensed as Lee rammed his heel into its crumpling skull again, its claws going deeper as it started to shake.

By some miracle of the subconscious, Lee thought *Don't miss your turn!* in the midst of all this, and glanced up just in time to see the big, ornate stone sign that read BITTERSWEET. He pulled his left foot off the gas and hit the brakes again. As the pickup squealed to a halt, he gave one final kick to the primal, this time feeling his heel go nearly all the way through the gristly, bone-sharded muck that he'd made in the floor board.

"Fucker!" he roared at it, then ripped his leg out of its taloned grasp, yanked the wheel to the right, and entered the Bittersweet neighborhood.

Shaking, with goosebumps riddling his skin, Lee could barely keep his eyes on the road—he kept looking down at the primal, expecting it to come swimming back to life. It was still moving. Chest still bucking for air, hands still clenching and unclenching, but its head was demolished. It was dead, even if its lizard brain didn't know it yet.

Where the hell was he? Unfamiliar street signs whipped past. The engine was knocking now, and the accelerator was going to the floor and not providing much speed. He was topping out at forty, and watched in horror as the speedometer started to fall.

He was in the process of unleashing a streak of invectives at the vehicle, when the headlights flashed across the rear end of a MATV.

He angled around it, now just coasting, no power at all left in the gas pedal. Craned his neck to see as he rolled past, but the MATV was so high and the pickup was too low. He was almost certain that it was the MATV that Jones had taken…

And then he saw the street: W 18th Street Lane.

He pulled the pickup truck onto the street, rocking back and forth like a kid trying to make a cart go faster. He saw the burned-out hulk of a massive house, knew that it had to be the one—had to be, or they were all screwed. He rolled the truck right into the driveway, and braked, shuddering to a stop right before the front steps.

He was out of the vehicle by the time it stopped. Didn't even bother putting it in park— simply let it roll forward with a diminutive *crunch* against the brick stars. Both legs stiff and painful—from his old hip wound, and from the fresh claw marks on his right thigh. But he hauled himself up those stairs and into the dark house.

How much time was left? He'd forgotten to check the clock on the dash. Couldn't go back now. Were the missiles in the air yet? They had to be. Streaking up into the stratosphere. Detaching from their main boosters, the re-entry vehicles arcing back down to earth.

He pushed through blackness so thick that he had to move with his hands in front of his face, bouncing off of walls. He should've taken the damn pistol so that he could use the weaponlight. So many things he *should've* done.

"Abe?" he shouted into the darkness, never letting his feet stop. "Sam? Anyone?"

Precious time slipped away as he fumbled through the darkness. With his breath heaving and his heart pounding and everything going topsy-turvy, his perception of time was lost. He only knew that he was losing what he could not afford to lose.

Of all the senses that could have helped, it was his nose that led him into the kitchen. The stink of high explosives hung thick in the air. Ambient light was coming in from a bank of windows in the kitchen, only visible to him because his eyes had been searching the darkness. With that barest of illumination, he was able to see a slightly blacker square in all the blackness around him, and figured it for an open door. He hobbled towards it, and found, as he neared it, that a dull red glow emanated from within.

He stopped at the door, but only for a second. He saw a set of stairs lit by red, as though blood had been spilled on the treads. He thrust himself through the door, bracing his hands on either wall as he stilted down the stairs on awkward legs.

At the bottom, a surreal scene was painted in crimson. Some sort of man-cave. A couch pushed up against the stairs, a thin sheen of smoke still hanging in the air. In the center of the room, the red light was coming from a blasted-out hole in the floor, like a tunnel to the earth's core.

Grunting and swearing, Lee climbed over the couch and stumbled up to the hole in the floor. The details of the scene made little sense to him, but he only spared a single second to peer into the hole and judge the depth. There was only one place to go now, and this was it.

He dropped down, swung onto the ladder, knees nearly buckling. Grip sweaty and shaky. He hadn't realized how much the fight in the vehicle had sapped him. But there was no stopping. Only moving.

How much time?

He hit the bottom, turned, and for a moment, it all just hit him. The tunnel. The red lights. The basement under a house.

This was just like his first bunker.

He never stopped moving, though. Hauling those uncooperative legs as fast as he could, the muscles cramping, pain arcing through him with every step. Did they even have enough time to get out? Maybe. If they hurried. If they ran. If they got to their MATV quick enough and drove away fast enough, they might be able to get out of the main blast radius.

It occurred to him that the others might have to leave him behind. He couldn't run as fast as they could. And the second that he had that thought, he knew that he was okay with it. He hadn't come here to preserve his life. He'd come to try to save theirs. If they got away, that would be enough for him to die with a clear conscious.

That would be enough for him to know that he'd finally done the right thing by the people that he cared about.

The tunnel felt endless. Light after red light passing over his head. Sucking the time away.

And then he heard voices. They were unclear over the rapid shuffle of his legs, the slap of his clumsy footfalls, the huff of his breath, the pounding of his pulse. He couldn't stop and listen, only keep charging forward, but there was something off about the voice. It was a man's voice, but it didn't belong to Abe, or Sam, or Jones. It was a voice that Lee had never heard before...

They came into view—those four people that he had left in the world—and something like relief came over him, shot through with redoubled urgency.

"...Total immunity," the unfamiliar voice was saying, the words becoming clearer as Lee got closer. The sound of his approach finally reached the four figures, and they all turned at once. Rifles came up—an instinctive reaction to the battered visage now shambling towards them. Then they lowered, and Marie took a step forward, her face shocked.

"Lee?" she said.

The stranger's voice continued, tinged with something that could only be described as mania: "I have details about certain individuals that ran The Corporation! I can help bring these people to justice! But I *demand* immunity from any prosecution!"

Realization almost ground Lee to a stop. The voice could only be one person. The person that he'd sent his last four friends to kill.

It was Briggs, speaking to them from behind the massive vault-like door. A door just like the one outside of his original Project Hometown bunker.

Disparate facts rammed into each other in Lee's head, for a moment clouding his reasoning with confusion as part of him tried to connect the pieces together—Briggs, in a Project Hometown bunker, demanding immunity—

The nuke. That's all you care about.

Lee staggered to a stop, grimacing and gasping for breath, stitches clawing at his sides from the efforts of his awkward run down the tunnel. Abe shot forward and grabbed Lee by the arm as he started to double over, trying to catch enough breath to speak with.

"That's the only way I'm coming out!" Briggs shrilled.

Questions battered at his ears:

"What are you doing here?"

"Did you call the evacuation?"

"Christ, Lee, what happened to you?"

"Lee!" Abe hauled him upright and stood face to face with him, eyes searching. "What's wrong?"

Lee gulped air, and spilled it all out at once: "Griffin launched a nuke. It's going to drop right on us. You need to get out."

THIRTY-SIX

THE SHADOW OF DEATH

LEE KNEW THERE WOULD BE CONFUSION, and he saw it all across their faces. They didn't have the groundwork to get from Point A to Point B. They couldn't understand how Griffin even had a nuke to launch, or why he would do such a thing, or how Lee knew about it. But there wasn't time to fill them in on how they'd gotten to this point. They had to just accept the facts as they were.

"Go!" Lee shouted at them. Jones and Marie took a step, as though they were about to run, but hesitated. Lee pulled at Abe, trying to spur him into movement. "You've only got a few minutes left to get out of here! Go! Get to the MATV and drive any direction but south!"

But Abe yanked backwards, freeing himself from Lee's grip.

Sam was shaking his head. "What?"

"No time to explain!" Lee snapped, starting to backpedal, hoping that his movement would draw them in. Again, Jones and Marie seemed ready, but Abe and Sam weren't moving. "What are you doing?" Lee shouted. "You need to be running!"

Abe thrust a hand back at the bunker door. "We found Briggs."

As if on cue, Briggs spoke again: "Are you listening to me?" And Lee realized that he couldn't hear them.

"I don't care about Briggs," Lee said. "I care about you! I came to tell you that the nuke is in the air. I need you—all of you—to get out of here!"

"How long?" Abe asked, his voice oddly quiet amid the seething fear, the reality now settling into all four of them as they eschewed trying to understand how it had come to this, and instead simply accepted that it had.

"I don't know," Lee said, finding himself downshifting to match Abe's tone, despite the urgency driving every particle of his body. "Five minutes? Maybe less?"

Abe's face made a strange twitch. "How big?"

"Five kilotons."

Silence.

Then broken by Briggs: "Are you listening?" he practically shrieked. They all startled at the sudden venom in his voice, looking at the intercom speaker. Then Briggs spoke again, suddenly sounding like a child that's been lost in a dark room. "Are you there? Are you still there?"

Abe snarled wordlessly, then took a step to the control panel and pressed a button. "We're here. We're working things out. Standby." Then he whirled on Lee. His mouth worked for a moment before he dredged the words out. "That doesn't seem like enough time."

Lee waved his arms down the tunnel, exasperated. "It'll be enough if you go *now*! If you get in the MATV and drive! You can get out of the immediate blast radius, and the MATV can protect you from the worst of it!"

"What about Briggs?" Abe growled, that old fury invading his face again, scouring away the fear of his circumstances.

"Fuck Briggs," Lee gasped out. "I don't give a shit about Briggs anymore! He'll be buried under the blast. I just…" He swallowed. Centered himself. Put every ounce of earnestness into his voice that he could muster. Bared himself before these four people, no shame as his voice cracked. "I just need you guys to live. I need that one thing. Please, Abe. Please run."

"Oh, shit, shit, shit," Jones whispered, rubbing his scalp manically, turning in small circles.

But Abe was shaking his head again. "No. I've only got a few minutes left? I want to look this fucker in the face. He'll come out. He's close to coming out."

"And then you're both going to die," Lee snapped.

Abe blinked as though processing the inevitability of his terminus. And then he relaxed. Raised his head. "I'm going to look him in the eyes. That's what *I* need." He waved a hand at the others. "You guys get out. You don't need to stay with me. This is between me and Briggs." He pointed, commandingly. "Go."

But no one moved.

Lee stepped up to Abe, his face crinkled up. "I'm not leaving you down here." He turned to the others. "I can't even run anyways. You guys can make it. But you have to leave *now*."

In the silent seconds that followed that, Lee's gaze went from Sam, to Marie, to Jones, mentally urging them to go over that razor's edge of decision that they all were teetering on. And at the same time, realizing, as he made eye contact with each of them, that they weren't going to.

It seemed to come over them one at a time, and Lee witnessed it with a sort of humbled awe.

First, Sam. He bowed his head. Worked his shoulders. And when he looked up again, he had that same expression that Abe had. A knowing. An epiphany that this was the end. And an acceptance of it. Then Marie. She blinked rapidly, tears coming to her eyes, but her face remained rock-steady. Her thin mouth set. She took a deep breath through her nose and sighed it out, and as it came out, she too, accepted her death.

Jones had to talk it out. "Minutes. Minutes to live. I'm going to be dead in a few minutes. Less than five minutes you said? Okay. Alright. Fuck. Are we doing this? You guys look like you're doing this. *FUCK!* Alright. I'm fine. I'm gonna do it too. God*dammit*!" He stomped his feet a few times as though trying to block out some horrendous pain. Anger flashed across his features, but it wasn't directed at any of them. He thrust a hand at the control panel. "Well, fucking get him out here!"

It was so strange to watch. It seemed to have happened at such a surreal pace. How can you jump from clawing for survival to simply accepting your death in so little time? Perhaps because there wasn't time to get comfortable with it. It was a feat of willpower, Lee thought, to simply suppress your animal instinct, knowing that it was simply a decision—to stay or to go. They had all made their decision, and in so doing, through a monumental power of the mind, they all silenced the animal.

And in it, Lee felt a strange sense of peace wash over him. It washed the animal right out of him, like so much dead flotsam caught in a flood tide. Carried it away from him, so that only he remained. He had listened to that animal for so long. It had guided his life, his decisions, his constant *fighting*. Now there was nothing left. And it felt to him that he had somehow been cleansed of something he hadn't even realized had been consuming him like a cancer.

It's kind of a shame, Lee realized. *That I only figured it out now.*

"Lee," Abe said.

Lee turned. Abe had his hand on the intercom button. He raised his other finger to his lips. "Don't say anything."

Lee nodded, understanding: If Briggs knew that Lee was in the tunnel, that might be the one thing he was unwilling to face. It might be the thing that pushed him back from coming out.

Seconds ticked by. Closer and closer to death. But they were always moving closer to death, of course. All their lives had always been moving towards this moment. And it didn't feel constraining to Lee anymore. There was some quality to it that he couldn't quite put his finger on, but now it didn't feel like he'd been trapped on a hurtling train. No, now it felt that he'd been on a river. And he was now reaching the end of it, where it emptied into the great, big ocean. And it could only have led to this ocean. It was destiny. And in that knowing, Lee relaxed into it. Let himself be carried by the tides, instead of always fighting against them.

The tiny sound of the button being depressed. The cuticles on Abe's single finger going white, he was pressing it so hard. "President Briggs. We understand your demands. They will be honored. If you can help us bring The Corporation to justice, then you will have total immunity from any prosecution."

Lee frowned. What the hell were they talking about? Clearly, he'd missed something. But it was easy enough for him to understand that Abe was speaking to someone who wasn't entirely mentally stable. There was no way that Abe could make those guarantees. But Briggs was a man of such monumental hubris, that he could never actually accept reality as the five people on the other side of the door just had. In his unending sense of self-importance, he could not conceive of a world without him, and so assumed there must be a way to preserve himself, however illogical. He preferred the madness of his fantasy to the crushing weight of the truth. And so he let Abe lie to him, and in the ensuing silence, it seemed Briggs accepted it.

Briggs never responded. They stood in the red tunnel, Lee counting the seconds. Wondering when the earth was going to shake, and the tunnel was going to collapse down on them. Would they be crushed by the mountain of earth and concrete over their heads? Or would it all be incinerated? Would they feel anything?

Lee turned away from those thoughts, fearing that they might unnerve him. He had only moments left to live, and he didn't want to spend them in fear. He wanted them to be spent in this newfound sense of self, this calmness that had taken him in the wake of his acceptance.

A loud *clack* reverberated through the tunnel, and they all jumped, thinking that it was the first sound of their imminent doom detonating over their heads. But the sound was immediately followed by the whir of large, electronic motors, coming from the door. The sound of massive bolts being drawn back. The door was being unlocked.

Briggs was coming out.

Lee and the others moved to the right side of the door. Abe stood closest, right there at the edge, with Marie and Sam to either side of him. Jones and

Lee standing behind. All of them staring at the seam where the steel met the concrete. Waiting for it to open.

A slight groan rumbled through the structure. A shoosh of hydraulics. And the door began to open. Just a crack at first. And then widening. Widening.

White light blazed from inside, seeming brighter than it really was in their red-dimmed eyes. Lee squinted against it, patient and eager at once. None of them spoke. None of them breathed. As though any tiny disruption might spring the trap too soon and scare their quarry away.

As Lee's eye adjusted to the light, the small sliver of the bunker beyond that his angle of view provided, came into focus.

A well-appointed living room. The arm of a plush couch. A Persian rug. The corner of an end table with a half-empty bottle of scotch standing open next to an empty tumbler.

Warm, dry air wafted against his face, and Lee smelled something pleasant, like a fragrant candle burning, mixed with a tinge of unmistakable cigar smoke. It was almost enough to make him laugh. While the world was burning over Briggs's head, he'd been sequestered here, getting drunk on fine liquor, and smoking fine cigars.

And then the man himself emerged.

Erwin Briggs. Former Secretary of State. Former Acting President of the United States. Former self-appointed dictator. Current…nothing at all.

Lee wasn't sure what he had been expecting. But as he peered from between Abe and Sam, and soaked in the view that now confronted him, he almost laughed again.

For so many years, Briggs had been a spectral, powerful figure in Lee's mind. A dark overlord that stood tall and imperious with outstretched hands, maneuvering the forces that were arrayed against Lee like some malevolent puppet-master.

What he saw before him now was just a man. He was neither tall nor short. Neither skinny, nor fat. Neither strong, nor weak. Salt-and-pepper hair stood out at all angles, matted in the back as though he hadn't washed it in some time and had just woken up from a hard sleep. His face was long and angular and deeply lined in all the wrong places—wrinkles that hadn't developed from laughter or smiling, but rather frowning and scowling and shouting and pursing the lips into sneers of cold command, so that it seemed a permanent expression of derision had been fixed upon him. But there was no derision in his eyes. They were a watery blue, and bloodshot, and filled with a brand of madness that only a life of paranoia and narcissism can bring. He was dressed, not in the presidential attire of a dark suit that Lee had somehow always pictured him in, but instead a rumpled pair of brown slacks, and a white t-shirt, sweated through at the armpits. Bare feet scuffed softly on the concrete as he shuffled out, moving sideways to them, as though trying to keep his distance, a pair of smallish hands with the long, thin fingers of a pianist worked nervously at each other.

A strange, almost genial smile came to a thin mouth unaccustomed to such displays. "Why, Abe Darabie," Briggs's voice lilted, as though they were old friends. "It's been a long time since I've seen…"

He trailed off as his eyes fell on Lee. And Lee instantly knew that Abe had been right when he'd told Lee not to speak. Recognition came over

Briggs with all the force of a sudden and unexpected waking nightmare. He knew Lee's face, even though Lee had not known his, and seeing it now, Briggs's mouth shuddered open and his watery eyes widened, and he took a halting step backwards.

"It's *you*," Briggs trembled.

Lee pushed between Abe and Sam. Briggs leaned away from him, but it seemed his sudden terror had rooted his naked feet to the cold floor, his lips working with unmade syllables.

Lee limped up to the man that he'd fought for so long that he'd built him up to a tyrannical demigod in his mind, and now found rendered down to this meek form, so banal and mortal, that it almost seemed he couldn't possibly be who he claimed to be.

He stared at Lee as though he couldn't believe who stood before him. Even though he would have known what Lee looked like, that would have been based on old images from long before, when Lee was a different man altogether. He could not have expected the battered form that now stepped up to him, with its scar-riddled face, and its missing eye, and old-mannish, halting gait.

"Lee Harden?" Briggs breathed, and the words reeked of booze.

"Erwin Briggs?" Lee answered, just as quietly.

"Yes?"

And then Lee cold-cocked him right in the jaw. He hadn't even known he was going to do it until he swung his fist, so hard that he felt his knuckles immediately shatter. So hard that Briggs's jaw audibly cracked with a sound like a dry branch snapping. So hard that Briggs's feet lifted an inch off the ground, and he spilled, his boneless flesh slapping on the concrete.

Lee stared down at the man as he made a weird huffing noise, sightless eyes crossing, his body shaking in the twilight of unconsciousness. Blood was dribbling out of his gaping mouth, his jaw set strangely in his face. Then, laboriously, Lee sighed and stepped to the downed man, gently flexing his broken hand against the growing ache in it. He bent over with a tired grunt, and laid his hand on Briggs's face and patted it a few times, not unkindly.

Briggs was coming back slowly. Eyes moving, but not quite in sync with each other yet. He was a lucky man to have both, though. Even though he'd only have them for the next few moments. Lee wished that he had both eyes to look at his friends with. He doubted that sight would be as good to Briggs.

"There you go," Lee encouraged him. "Come on back. You only got a little bit of time left. Don't waste it thrashing on the ground."

Briggs goggled up at him, an expression of mystification on his face. He didn't know that he could hurt this much. He didn't know he could be this powerless. But Lee watched that reality dawn on him as his eyes cleared and shifted to the others as they stepped up to Lee's side. Four people who had already accepted their deaths, staring down at him and knowing him for what he truly was: Just a man. Just another suit of meat, in which resided a sadly warped soul.

Briggs tried to speak, but his tongue lolled out and spit and blood pooled all over his chin and into the cavity of his neck.

"Ssh," Lee said. "Don't bother trying to talk. We won't understand you. Your jaw's broke." He squatted lower and hooked his arm under Briggs's. "Come on. Stand up. No good to die laying down."

Briggs whimpered, uncomprehending but terrified nonetheless, as Lee pulled him to his feet and steadied him there. He swayed, panicked eyes tracking between all of them. He still had an animal in him trying to live, the poor, dumb bastard. He just didn't know.

Abe held a finger up. "Don't speak. Just listen."

Briggs honed in on him, oddly childlike in that moment. Trying to understand who he was in this moment, how everything he thought he'd been was suddenly stripped away, and simply unable to grasp it. Lee pitied him in that moment. Pitied him for the madness of his mind that would prevent him from ever experiencing the acceptance of destiny that all five others had already achieved.

"There's a nuke in the air," Abe said. Emotionless. Simply explaining, as you would a fact of life to a young boy. "It's going to hit us any second now. I lied. There will be no trial. There will be no immunity. There will, in fact, be nothing. Any moment now, we're all going to be vaporized. But I wanted to look in your face, and I wanted to watch you understand…that you're about to die."

Briggs's breathing was rapid and shallow. He was fixated on Abe's face, as though it was a dark hallucination. Everything in his expression showed incomprehension. Denial, even, that this was his end, right here, right now, in a red-lit tunnel underground, surrounded by people he didn't know, and who had no warmth of feeling towards him. No shred of human compassion for the man that had shown none in his life.

Lee didn't want to look at him anymore. He meant less than nothing to Lee in that moment. So he looked at Abe, and found the other man frowning, as though caught up in a dilemma. Abe realized he was being watched and cocked his head to Lee.

"You know," he said. "I don't really care to die in his company."

Lee nodded, understanding the unsaid. Briggs meant nothing to him, and so it had no effect on Lee whether he died in the man's presence, any more than he would care if they shared their last moments with an erstwhile cockroach. It simply didn't matter.

To him. But clearly it did to Abe.

Lee brought his hands up, mimed wiping them off, and then showed his palms—clean, though they were anything but.

"Huh," Abe grunted. Then he pulled his slung rifle away to his side, unholstered his pistol, and shot Erwin Briggs between the eyes.

Lee didn't even bother to watch the body fall. Why would he? He'd seen it many times before. And he'd seen it happen to better men than Briggs. So, the cockroach had been crushed. It was neither here nor there.

Lee just watched Abe. And then he watched Sam. And then Marie. And then Jones. They all stared down at the body of the man they'd come to kill. Mission accomplished. And yet there was no joy in their faces. There was no pain, either. They were not miserable or regretful. They were looking at a dead man, but they were seeing their lives.

Abe sighed through his nose and holstered his pistol. "Thought that would be more satisfying than it was. But still. I do feel…relieved."

Lee put a hand on his shoulder. Then he pulled him in and hugged him. Abe hugged him back. No wallowing in emotions or imminent mortality. Just an embrace of two brothers, knowing their journey with each other was at an end.

When they separated, Lee looked at the others. "They were good lives. Your lives. You're good people. I'm glad that I get to go this way. I'm glad I get to go in your company. I wouldn't have it any other way."

Abe pulled his rifle off and chucked it to the ground as carelessly as a piece of trash. Then he unclipped his holstered pistol and did the same. Then started unstrapping his armor. "Not gonna go with all this shit on me, that's for damn sure."

Marie seemed to agree and followed suit.

"I dunno," Sam said, sinking down to the ground and sitting cross-legged. Shifted inside of his armor as though testing the heft of it. "It's kind of like a weighted blanket, you know? Kinda comforting."

Lee lowered himself to the ground too, much slower than Sam had. Abe sat down with them, freshly stripped to his sweat-soaked shirt and pants. Marie sat next to Sam. Then Jones scooted in. He wore a brave smile, despite the haunted look in his eyes. Always trying to cheat the gravity of every moment, turn dread into humor.

"Should we hold hands?"

Marie snorted, and it was half a sob. But she reached out and took his hand. "I'll hold your hand, you big baby."

Jones looked at her with those fearful eyes, as though she'd just done the kindest thing anyone could do. He squeezed her hand tight, that false smile still hanging onto his lips. "Thank you." Then he blinked rapidly as though to cover his earnestness and peered into Briggs's bunker. "Hey, there's still some whiskey in there. Do you think we have time to—"

And then the earth shook.

THIRTY-SEVEN

ANNIHILATION

Eight nuclear warheads, each individually guided, had separated from their entry vehicle somewhere in the upper atmosphere, and now they detonated.

Griffin didn't watch. Didn't need his eyes cooked by the blast of light, but he saw the world flash white as though someone had triggered a giant camera flash that threw everything into blazing white or deep black.

Griffin flinched as he felt the impacts and saw the light all around him, but kept his eyes glued to the screen of the datapad, standing shoulder to shoulder with Colonel Donahue and Lieutenant Paige. The image from the circling plane far above the earth went blank for a moment—just a white screen. And then slowly, as the earth began to rumble under Griffin's feet, the white faded to grays, and then coalesced around the eight targeted locations in Greeley. Massive fireballs bulged into mushrooms, and as the image clarified further, Griffin could actually see the firestorms sucking the city into those blooming, all-consuming clouds.

An involuntary shudder worked down Griffin's spine. For a moment, a spike of panic jabbed right through the center of him. God, what had he done? Why is it always the moment when you can't take it back that you realize the fullness of what you've done?

Colonel Donahue spoke into the satphone he had against his ear, as the first shockwaves reached them, shaking the MATV they were huddled behind. "Detonation confirmed. Standby." He pulled the satphone speaker away from his mouth and looked at Griffin. "All targets accounted for?"

Eight warheads. Eight fireballs. Eight targeted locations vaporized, buildings blown to dust in the immediate blast radius, and then spreading like a slow tide of destruction, outwards, as superheated structures crumbled and bodies spontaneously combusted in the unimaginable heat of the blast. It seemed like it would never end, would just go on eating the world until nothing remained.

"All targets down," Griffin murmured, shaken by a mix of shame and awe.

"All targets accounted for," Colonel Donahue said into his phone. "Confirming eight nuclear detonations."

Only now did Griffin raise his eyes to the horizon, and witnessed first-hand what he had done. One man. One decision. One command. And from that had been borne this scene of cataclysm that engulfed the southern sky. Eight roiling, churning, blackening clouds, rising from the earth, connected to it by funnels of superheated gas and debris, drawing ever upward, angry red light sneering from between black cumulous clouds of ash and soot.

Eight warheads. Eight nuclear detonations.

All of them across the southern half of Greeley, where the population of infected had been strongest.

His eyes glanced furtively to the scribbled location he'd written on the back of his hand. Then he looked to Paige, who met his gaze with a surreptitious nod, turned, and began jogging away.

Griffin handed the datapad to Colonel Donahue. "Thank you for the assistance, colonel," he said, oddly formal. But it felt like a moment when formality was needed to stave off the worst of the sensation that the entire world had suddenly become a place without rules. "If you'll excuse me, I have some other business to attend to."

Then he turned away from Colonel Donahue's frown of confusion, and followed after Paige.

***

It was somehow worse that they hadn't been instantly incinerated. A great, unified cringe had taken them, stomachs tightened to breathlessness, eyes squinting as though preparing to receive a massive blow. The tunnel felt like it was bucking and rolling, like they were at the epicenter of faultlines ramming into each other, and every time a crack appeared in the concrete and dust silted down over their heads, Lee thought *This is it. This is when the tunnel comes down.*

He prayed in those interminable moments, that it would be quick, that the tunnel would collapse in one big rumble of death, and instantly crush them under its weight. He prayed that it would not come apart piecemeal around them, that he would not have to watch his friends get battered to death by rubble.

The shaking reached a crescendo, more and more violent, to the point that Lee clenched his eye shut, and with each second, as the shaking got worse and worse, he kept thinking that same thought: *This has to be it. No. This is definitely it. THIS is definitely the moment when it comes down...*

And then the rumbling, bucking earth started to quiet.

What was this? The last cruel joke of the universe? The eye of the storm? The calm before one final detonation? *The* final detonation? The one they'd been waiting the last terrible minute of their life for?

Aftershocks vibrated their bones. Each less convincing than the last, until Lee finally pried his eyelid open and saw what he did not expect to see: Four friends, still sitting in a rough circle, none of them crushed by rubble, all of them still looking like they were expecting it to happen at any second.

"Come on, already," Jones seethed at the ceiling, as though willing it to come down and end the torment of this ghastly suspense.

The earth trembled one last time, as though in a death throe. And then everything was oddly, preternaturally still. In the wake of it all, the cold silence of their tomb rang in Lee's ears. Hyper-attuned with adrenaline-fueled expectation, his ears seemed to be searching for some threatening noise, and coming up with nothing.

"Guys," Sam said, his voice pitched high with stress, his eyes scouring the concrete all around them. "I don't think the tunnel's going to collapse."

And then a worse thought occurred to Lee: They'd assumed that a nuke dropped right on their heads would be enough to collapse the tunnel and possibly vaporize them. But what if it had only buried them alive? What if they were trapped in this tunnel now, in the middle of a dead city that no one would ever venture into again?

What if they weren't going to get a quick death? What if they were going to live for weeks or months down here, slowly starving or dehydrating? Slowly watching each other waste away?

It was clear to Lee that he wasn't the only one that had this thought, because Abe immediately shot to his feet and snatched up his discarded rifle. "I'm going to go see."

"What?" Jones stood up, just as quick. "See what?"

Abe was already jogging down the tunnel, back towards the entrance. "To see if we're buried down here."

There was no way that Lee—or any of them—were going to wait in tense silence for Abe to return with news. As one, Lee and Marie and Sam stood up. Jones glanced at them, then spun and ran after Abe, and the rest of them followed.

Lee, naturally, lagged behind. Marie stayed with him. Maybe for solidarity. Maybe because she didn't actually *want* to know the truth. Neither of them spoke. Hell, none of them did. What could be said? There would be words enough to say if they found themselves trapped. For now, there was only the need to see, to witness, to ascertain how exactly their endpoint would come to them.

The tunnel seemed to go on forever—longer than it had been when Lee had run down it, trying to save his friends.

Abe didn't wait up, and Sam and Jones stayed with him, disappearing into the gloomy redness ahead.

Lee spared a look at Marie. Her troubled eyes met his. Enough was said in that look. More than words could do for them.

The first inkling that maybe they weren't buried alive, was when they reached the ladder and saw no sign of the others. So they must have gone up. So the exit must not be blocked.

Seeming to read his mind, Marie laid a hand on the first rung. "Doesn't mean we can get out of the basement."

And Lee knew that was true. But he also knew that if a five-kiloton warhead had been dropped on this location, there was no way the exit from the tunnel should be clear. It was within the realm of reason to believe that the tunnel and bunker had been constructed heartily enough to withstand a direct blast. But the basement of a house? That didn't seem likely to Lee.

So, what the hell had happened? Had Griffin misjudged the location? It wasn't like Lee had given him a direct coordinate. He'd only given him a general description and a road name. Maybe the nuke had impacted nearby, but not enough to crush the house and basement.

He climbed the ladder after Marie. Watched as she clambered out and disappeared. And then he was at the top. He thrust his head through the opening, and saw all of them, stacked up on the stairs, waiting for him.

His eye went to Abe, who was the first on the stairs, pointing his rifle up. "Looks clear," Abe said, with a flavor of giddy disbelief.

Lee didn't know what to feel in that moment. He'd been up and down so many times in the last hour, he didn't even want to come to a conclusion. He just wanted to take the next step without getting mired in hopes and doubts. He needed to just…level off.

He said nothing as he climbed out of the hole in the ground and joined the others. Marie and Sam gave him a hopeful look that he did not return. Neither did he give them doubt. No need for either. They would see for themselves soon enough.

With all five of them gathered, Abe started up the stairs, moving with a steady caution. At the top, they found that an odd, artificial dawn had been created. A dull, umber light was coming through the windows, casting the world into a strange glow. Lee knew that the source of it must have been the superfires burning, but somehow, he found it beautiful. Maybe just because when you live past the point that you were certain you were going to die, things have the tendency to be beautiful. Everything perceived with newborn eyes.

Lee couldn't tell if the house was any different, because he'd stumbled through it in blackness. But it certainly didn't seem like it was any worse than it had been. A strange smell permeated everything—a hot, ashy scent that hadn't been there before, mixed with the clear, pungent odor of electrical sparks.

They made it to the entryway before Abe held up, shying away from the open door.

"Christ," he said, pulling his head away and stepping back. "It feels like an oven out there."

Lee felt the heat radiating in at them. Hard to say how hot it was outside—worse than any blazing summer day he'd experienced, and impossibly dry, like all the moisture had been burned out of the air.

"Hold up," Lee said, though none of them looked too willing to step outside. "There's a bunker below us. I didn't catch everything Briggs said." He looked to Sam, because Abe was still focused on the weird afterglow outside. "Did he say it was a Project Hometown bunker?"

Sam nodded. "There's a lot we need to fill you in on."

"There's a lot I'd like to know," Lee said. "But right now, we should check if he had any equipment for nuclear contamination. MOPP suits. Iodide pills. Hell, even just an NBC mask would be better than nothing."

Jones stepped away from the open door. "Lee's right. No point in going out in that shit unprotected. Sam, you wanna run down with me and check the bunker?"

Sam nodded, tearing his eyes away from the door and turning.

"Look at this," Abe breathed, drawing their attention back to the outside world.

A small pack of primals were stumbling along on the street, no more than a hundred yards from the house. Their skin was blackened in places, sloughing off of them as they staggered mindlessly about. Whatever skin wasn't black and falling off was lobster-red. Lee heard their rattling wheezes as they tried to breathe through scorched lungs.

Abe lifted his rifle, but didn't aim it. Just stood there watching the creatures.

One of them stopped in the middle of the street. The other four paused, looking back at it. Issued a few hoarse hoots, and then continued on. The one that had stopped seemed like it could go no further. It bent, going to its hands and knees, but didn't seem to want to go further to the ground. Lee thought that the concrete must be hundreds of degrees—burning its palms as it crouched there, swaying. It let out a mournful moan, tried to crawl, but then keeled over. As the rest of its body hit the burning concrete it writhed weakly, mewled, shuddered, and then lay still.

Jones shook himself as though to clear his head. Or maybe it was an involuntary chill. He turned, then unslung his rifle and held it out to Lee.

"Here. If more of them come along while we're down there."

Lee accepted the rifle. Checked the mag and chamber. Slung into it.

Sam and Jones hustled back through the wreckage of the house, and Lee backed up further from the entryway. "Abe. Marie. Let's hold in the stairwell. There's gonna be contaminants in the air. We should breathe it as little as possible."

They moved back to the stairwell, Abe posting just inside the kitchen while Lee and Marie stood on the first and second treads. They pulled their shirts up over their faces to filter out what they could.

They stood there in silence for a long time. Ten minutes, maybe more, had passed before Lee heard Jones and Sam's voices coming up from the hole in the basement, getting clearer as they ascended. Lee watched the stairwell until he saw the two of them clamber back over the couch. No MOPP suits or gas masks in hand. Sam was only carrying a few blister packets that Lee instantly recognized as potassium iodide pills.

"It's all we could find," Sam said. "He actually didn't have much down there."

Sam broke the packaging open, read the directions printed on the front, took the prescribed number of pills, and then passed it on. As they each swallowed the pills dry, Lee spoke.

"The pills will block the worst of it. I say we make a go for the MATV. It should still be working. If so, we can haul ass out of here, get out of the contamination zone, and reassess."

Abe nodded his assent.

Jones smacked his mouth against the bitter pills. "I'll go. Y'all stay here. If the truck's there, I'll drive it over here and pick y'all up."

"Hey," Lee said, touching his arm as he squeezed past. "Don't touch the metal with your bare hands."

"Good tip," Jones nodded in appreciation.

They followed him out, but held up in the entryway. Jones was about one foot out the door when the sound of a diesel engine reached their ears. He paused. Backpedaled into the entryway again, then looked over his shoulder. "Y'all hear that?"

"I hear it," Abe said, snugging into his rifle.

It was close, and they didn't have long to wait. The roar of the engine reached its peak, and then a MATV came hurtling around the corner at the end of the street, charging down the lane at them. For a second, Lee thought it might be *their* MATV, but then realized this one had the assault configuration, which theirs didn't.

"Hold fire," Lee commanded, stepping forward. He was responsible for these people. And he was responsible for the order to hold fire. If shit broke loose, as it was wont to do, he wanted to be standing up front.

The MATV skidded to a stop in the center of the cul-de-sac. An insectoid figure hunched in the turret, and Lee realized he was looking at a soldier in full MOPP gear. The soldier lifted both of his arms into the air and shouted out, his voice muffled and tinny through the mask.

"Hold fire!"

Again, Lee prevented himself from feeling any relief, or any suspicion. If shit went sideways, he'd know it when it happened. Until then, he was just waiting to see what developed.

Lee couldn't see the backend of the vehicle because it was facing them, but he saw the hatch-style double doors open, and another soldier in MOPP gear came around the side. This one had a rifle, but it was slung to his chest, and he too held both of his arms in the air.

"Lee Harden!" the soldier shouted out, now waving at them to approach. "Come on! All of you! Come on!"

The others turned their eyes to Lee.

Lee only took a moment to consider it. But what was he going to do? Run back into the bunker? Start a firefight with a squad of better-armed soldiers? And besides, he'd made a promise. He'd given his word. He intended to keep it.

He lowered his rifle to his left side, held his hand over his face, pinching the shirt over his nose, and, hunching as though he were about to run into a rainstorm, jogged out of the house, down the steps, and towards the waiting MATV.

The others held back, unsure if they should follow.

Lee reached the backend and looked inside. There were four more soldiers inside, all of them in MOPP gear. One of them stood up from the jumpseats posted on the interior of the sidewalls, and took two limping steps to the back so that he stood over Lee, looking down at him through the bug-eyed viewports of his mask.

Lee saw his eyes through those viewports, remembered the limp, and instantly knew him.

"It's Griffin," the figure said with a nod, seeing the recognition on Lee's face. "You have the others with you?"

Lee stood there, again pausing to consider. He was already starting to sweat in the terrible heat.

It felt like the interior of a black car after it's been left in the summer sun all day. He didn't want to ponder too long—every minute out in these elements was poisoning him.

"Yes," Lee finally answered. "But they weren't a part of the deal."

Griffin simply nodded. "I'm aware of that. I'm not here to capture them." A pause. Griffin's masked head tilted to the side. "I give you my word."

Lee nodded, an understanding passing between them. Then he sidestepped to see around the open doors, and waved to the others. "It's clear! Come on!"

Immediately the other four broke out of the house, sprinting through the baking air. Lee turned back to Griffin, who held out a gloved hand to him. Lee accepted it, and let himself be hauled up into the back of the MATV. The others clambered in after him and the soldier that had first exited backed his way in and slammed the doors shut.

Lee looked at the faces of his friends. They all looked a pinch worried and lot relieved.

Griffin sidled through the interior and spoke to the driver up front. "Take us out of here. You know where to go."

"Roger that."

The MATV immediately started moving, cutting a wide circle around the cul-de-sac, and then accelerating out.

Lee collapsed into one of the available jumpseats.

"Alright," Jones spoke up, looking at Lee and jerking a thumb towards Griffin. "Who are these guys?"

Griffin took two swaying steps to the center of them, favoring his left leg, and pulled his mask up and over his head. He looked at Lee's four friends, taking them in as though judging their mettle. "I'm Captain Griffin."

Jones balked, mouth dropping open. He glanced towards the doors as though he might try to make a break for it.

Lee held up a hand. "Just chill," he said, before anyone could get the wrong idea. "This isn't about y'all. He came for me. We had an arrangement. I gave him my word, and he gave me his that you won't be fucked with." A glance at Griffin. "Isn't that right?"

Griffin nodded. "That's right."

Abe was staring at Lee, hard. "You had an arrangement," he echoed, his voice brittle. "What's that mean?"

Lee leaned back in his seat, all the tension going out of him. "I agreed to—"

"We agreed," Griffin cut in. "That he could go and try to save you, provided that he give me a chance to speak with him afterwards."

Lee frowned. Speak with him? Speak with him about what, exactly? That hadn't been the deal that Lee recalled. He searched Griffin's face, and the other man gave him a shaded look, as though to tell him to keep their original arrangement to himself.

"You didn't drop a nuke on us," Lee said.

Griffin didn't respond. Instead, he lowered himself to one knee in the center of them. He took a moment, staring at the metal floor, wincing as he gently massaged his left thigh. He seemed to be choosing his words. Without looking at any of them, he finally spoke. "No, I didn't. I was going to. I was absolutely going to."

"But you changed your mind," Lee said, carefully. "Why?"

Griffin pursed his lips. Turned his gaze to Lee. "Things change. Things *are* changing. Everything is currently in a state of flux. And one of those fluctuating things is: who the hell's going to run shit now?" He raised a gloved hand and rubbed his chin. "As of right now, it looks like that's going to be me. Canada and the United Kingdom have decided to put their support behind me as the current…" he made a face. "I don't even know what the hell to call it. But essentially, they want a period of martial law, administered by me, in order to reclaim and stabilize the United States. Once everything has been stabilized, we'll continue the democratic processes."

Abe stared at Griffin, and Lee remembered as he watched his old friend, that Abe and Griffin knew each other quite well. Not just from being fellow Coordinators, but because they'd both worked for Briggs before Abe jumped ship.

"Yeah," Abe said, his voice bitter with sarcasm. "That's what Briggs said too."

Griffin accepted it with a nod. "That is what Briggs said. I won't deny it. All I can tell you is the one key difference between me and Briggs: I don't want this shit. He did."

Jones chuffed. "Bro, you don't know the half of it."

Griffin's eyes narrowed at Abe, and then Lee. "Which, by the way…"

Lee nodded. "He's dead."

Griffin held his gaze. "Dead as in…?"

"Dead as in I shot him in the head," Abe stated, coolly.

"Hm." Griffin didn't seem surprised or dismayed. "Well, that's *one* theory."

Abe glared at him. "I'm pretty sure—"

Griffin held up a hand for silence. "Let me explain to you what *actually* happened tonight." He paused for a length, staring each of them in the eyes, ending on Lee. "During the final hours of your occupation of Greeley, you, Lee, sent your team to track down Briggs. They successfully located him, captured him, and brought him to FOB Hampton. Lee and Briggs were both confirmed as being inside the penthouse of FOB Hampton when it was struck by one of eight nuclear warheads at 10:19 p.m. The entire structure, and everyone remaining inside of it, including Lee Harden and Erwin Briggs, were instantly vaporized. Their irradiated particles are now wafting about the stratosphere, where they will eventually fallout, somewhere in Colorado. A fitting end to two terrible tyrants."

Griffin took a breath and looked to Abe. "You were also killed in the blast." And then to the others. "I don't know your names, but you were all also killed in the blast. As of right now, anyone that gives a shit about what's going on in our corner of the world knows that Erwin Briggs, Lee Harden, and Abe Darabie—and three of their fellow 'terrorists'—are dead."

Silence.

Lee sat there, parsing through what he'd just been told. But why? To what end? Why this sudden reversal? Why would Griffin cover for them, when hours before he'd wanted them dead?

Lee glanced at the other soldiers in the back of the MATV with them. Griffin spied his inspection of them and waved away his obvious concern. "These are *my* men. Don't worry about them."

"So…" Lee leaned forward onto his elbows. "What? You're going to just…" he couldn't even put it into a logical framework. "What?"

Griffin grunted and stood, then angled himself into the jump-seat beside Lee. Directly across from Abe, Jones, Marie, and Sam. Griffin looked at them all. "Not a bad team, I guess, huh?" He motioned to Jones, Marie, and Sam. "I don't know about y'all, but Lee and Abe seem to think you got what it takes. Is that right?"

The three of them traded a few glances, then looked to Abe and Lee as though they weren't sure if they deserved that dubious honor.

"They're here, aren't they?" Abe growled.

Griffin gave him a wan smile. "Yes, they are." He clasped his hands together between his knees and stared at them. "You want to know what I'm doing. Why I changed my mind. And it's because of what you said to me, Lee. See, you were just pouring out your heart, thinking this was the end for you, admitting all your wrongdoings. But what I heard was that you weren't a madman after all. What I heard was that…you weren't really any different than me. I'm not cut out to be the leader of this nation. And neither were you, Lee. And yet we both had it thrust upon us—you with your United Eastern States, and me with…whatever the hell all this is now. We'll just keep calling it the United States. Hopefully someday it will live up to the name."

He sighed with pure exhaustion. "We're not meant to lead civilians, just like you said, Lee. We're fighters. And fighters *fight*. We don't build good governments. We tear down corrupt ones. We don't hold votes. We do what needs to be done. We don't *rescue the good guys*. We kill the bad ones. And sometimes that helps the good ones survive.

We don't *heal*. We cut out the cancer so that the body can heal itself."

Lee let out an impatient noise and opened his mouth, but Griffin held up his hand again, and looked earnestly at Lee. "Please. Just let me finish."

Lee narrowed his eye, but remained silent.

Griffin straightened up in his seat. More of the commander now, when a moment before he'd just been a man talking philosophy. "Canada and the UK want me to run this martial government. Fine. I agree with their terms. I agree that stability comes first, and then democracy. However, it occurred to me, as I was traveling back to my camp to launch those…" he grimaced. "…Fucking warheads…it occurred to me that they're going to have their fingers so far up my ass, I won't be able to chew gum without them complaining it's getting stuck in their fingernails. I'm under no illusions. They want me because they think that a lowly captain launched into the upper echelons will be easy for them to control. They want me because they know that I'll follow orders and do what I'm told. They want me because they view me as their puppet, and God knows they're not in this out of the goodness of their heart. They'll want me to do things that benefit them more than us. And I'll go along with it, because that's what we need right now. We need powerful allies, even if that means we have to give a bit of ourselves away.

"However…" His eyes got serious and dark. "I'm also under no illusions that I will want certain things done that my *handlers* will not allow me to do. At the very least, they will want…insulation. They will want to have plausible deniability. As the saying goes, what they don't know can't hurt them."

Realization dawned on Lee. And that mad laughter came bucking up to his chest again. Some things were just so outside of what you expected, that all you can do is laugh in disbelief. "You want us to be your black ops."

Griffin held up a finger. "First, let me say: Yes and no. Second, I can already detect some resistance." He was looking at Abe who bore an expression like someone had just pissed in his canteen. "Third—and not to put too fine a point on it—but here's the truth: Every one of you owes me their life. Lee, I let you go on your word that you would return and—these are your words—cooperate with me. Abe, I let Lee go so he could warn you and your team. And then, as I had all of these realizations, following my conversation with Lee, I made the decision *not* to drop a nuclear warhead right on your heads. So, let's just be plain with each other. You're welcome. And yes, your fresh leases on life do come with strings attached."

Of all of them, Jones seemed to be the least resistant. He had a thoughtful look on his face as Griffin spoke, and now looked up at him with appreciation in his eyes. "Seriously," he said. "Thank you. I really didn't want to die in a nuclear blast."

Griffin gave him a slight bow of the head. "Well, we all have strings attached to us, don't we? I saved your lives. Now you're going to help me save this country. I don't want you to be my black ops, per se. I'm not asking you to run around the country assassinating whoever I deem to be a rival. But the United States is not the United States without the west coast and the eastern seaboard, and all the places in between. Contrary to popular belief, there are still people surviving in California, in

Washington, in New York and Massachusetts. There are settlements of survivors out there in places that haven't heard from us in a long time. Places we won't *get to* for another long time still."

The MATV slowed to a stop. They all glanced around, but there were no windows. They had no idea what was outside. It might've been the middle of nowhere. Or it might have been in the middle of Griffin's entire army.

Griffin made a circle in the air with his finger, incorporating all of them. "You five…you'll go. You'll go out into this American wasteland, into the places that have been abandoned, and you will bring them a gospel, of sorts. You will bring them the good news that this country is pulling itself back together. And, as a show of good faith, you'll handle their problems." Griffin raised his brow and looked at Lee pointedly. "And there will be problems. There will be gangs, and warlords, and criminal elements, and infected—God knows those bastards aren't going away any time soon. Slowly, bit by bit, settlement by settlement, Lee, you and your team are going to pave the way. All of this will be done in secret, because you are all dead. You will not reveal to them who you actually are. You will just do what needs to be done, and then move on to whoever needs you next."

Over the course of the last minute, the expressions on the faces of Lee's team had changed. He saw that they'd begun to internalize the picture that Griffin was painting. They'd begun to actually consider it as a possible future, rather than some strange, half-cocked plan spewed at them from a man they barely knew.

Lee had begun to consider it as well. There was the ever-present part of him that wanted to stubbornly tell Griffin to go fuck himself, of course. But then, what were the other options? Where would they go? What would they do?

It was a strange situation to find himself in. He'd spent so long fighting this war and simultaneously dreaming of some fantastical future of peace. That moment in the sun that he'd craved for so long. But there was a certain truth to Lee that he had somehow admitted to Griffin before he'd even been able to admit it to himself: This was what he did. This was who he was. He was a fighter, and fighters *fought*.

There would never be peace. There never had been, and it was folly to believe that it would miraculously come about with the world in the shambles that it was. If peace was even possible, it wouldn't happen in Lee's lifetime. So, what was he going to do with the rest of his life? There would be no porch and rocker for him. Even if he refused to do what Griffin was asking, he wouldn't find that peace, because the world that he lived in wasn't capable of it. If he didn't go out and fight, the fight would inevitably find him. And even if by some miracle, he did manage to find some enclave where men's problems couldn't reach him, what would he do with himself? Learn to farm? Spend his days growing crops and staring off into the sunset?

He'd dreamed of it once. But now he saw it with fresh eyes. He saw it with the new perspective that had been granted him in the moments after he had accepted his death, and all the realizations of his true nature that had led up to that moment.

He was simply not a man capable of living in peace. That didn't mean he would throw away the lessons that he'd learned—he understood now that he could not fix the world by fighting it. He knew that with a fullness so complete that it seemed he'd always known it and simply been lying to himself.

He *could not fix the world.*

But he could cut the cancer out, so that it could fix itself.

He was not the doctor or the healer. But he *was* the scalpel. And knowing what he was, finally, truly, fully embracing it, he knew that that porch and rocker would only be another form of lying to himself about who he was. That fabled moment in the sun would be wonderful…for a very short time. And then it would become a prison.

In that moment, in the back of the MATV, Lee knew what his decision would be. But he could not make that decision for others. He'd made his peace with who he was, and knew for the first time how he truly fit into this world, but he could not assume that the others felt the same.

"And if we decide that we don't want to do it?" Lee said, quickly glancing at his team, curious to see who might seem relieved by him saying that.

Interestingly, none of them did. Their faces were rather blank. Still thinking hard in their own heads, but now listening, passingly curious as to how Griffin would respond.

Griffin pointed out the back doors. "Just outside, there is a truck. It has an auxiliary tank, and I've taken the liberty of filling it up. I've also packed it with…many other things you might need." He paused for a beat. Raised steepled fingers to his chin. "I thought long and hard about what I would do if you all wouldn't agree to it. Should I take you back to my army and place you under arrest? That's what the Canadians and the Brits would expect me to do. But it would undermine me. Because, you see, I've already told them that you're all dead. So that's not really an option. Do I let you just take the truck and run off wherever you please? I suppose I couldn't stop you from doing it. And therein lies the crux of the issue. Yes, you all owe me your lives, and I'd love for that to be enough to motivate you to take this on. But this won't ever work if you're forced into it. You have to *want* to do it. Or, in Lee's case, at the very least, consider it a penance for all the shit you stirred up."

Griffin spread his hands and let them flop. "So…this is where we part ways. Whether you accept what I'm offering or not, you're going to get out of this vehicle and take the one I've given you, and we are not going to speak to each other ever again. Because you are dead. And I don't talk to dead people."

Lee frowned at him. "And what if we *do* decide to do it? How will we contact you?"

Griffin shook his head. "You won't contact me. Ever. I need to maintain that insulation from you. I need that plausible deniability. However, there is a certain lady with a paralyzed daughter who has agreed to be my point of contact with you from here on out. If you need anything from us, you can use the satphone I've left in the truck to contact her, and we will see what we can do to accommodate your requests."

Lee put a hand on Griffin's knee and squeezed. "You're taking care of Abby?"

Griffin looked at him earnestly. "I'm giving her everything I have, Lee. Once Canada and the UK put their resources behind me, I'll have even more to give her. We will do our best for her. You've got my word on that."

Slowly, Lee released his grip. Withdrew his hand.

They all looked at each other. No one really knew what everyone was thinking, except for maybe Abe and Lee. They shared one of their looks, and Lee knew, and Abe knew. They were cut from the same cloth. They'd already made their decision.

Griffin made a sweeping gesture towards the rear of the vehicle. "Time to go, folks."

"My dog," Lee said suddenly.

The soldier at the back of the MATV kicked open one of the rear doors, and at the same instant that Griffin pointed out and said, "In the truck," Lee heard the muted sound of raucous barking coming from outside.

He leaned forward, looking through the open door. It was still pitch-black outside, but the brake lights of the MATV illuminated the side of a big, white pickup truck, and a pale canine face, yammering incessantly and covering the inside of the driver side window with drool and fog from his breath.

Deuce did not look happy to have been left in the truck, but when he spotted Lee looking at him, he stopped, panted, seemed to wag his tail a few times...and then kept on barking.

Lee felt a wash of relief. *Good boy.*

Slowly, as though they didn't quite believe it, or suspected that they might get gunned down in the back, Lee rose first, followed by Abe, and then Sam, Marie, and Jones, and they shuffled their way through the narrow confines of the MATV, stooped over to clear the ceiling, and then trundled their way onto a section of dusty, washed-out road.

Lee stood there in the brake lights, looking one way down the road and then the other. The road seemed to have no end, and no beginning, but rather just existed right there in the middle of nothingness.

The five of them turned back to face the MATV. Griffin was kneeling at the back door with his hand on it, ready to swing it shut.

"Whatever you decide to do," Griffin said, speaking loudly to be heard over the MATV's exhaust and Deuce's barking. "For the love of God, at least do me this one favor to show your appreciation for living another day: Remember that you're dead, and *you don't know me*." He started to swing the door shut, but then paused, looking right at Lee. "Just…do the right thing."

And then the door slammed shut, and the MATV sped away, a dusty halo encircling its retreating taillights until it was swallowed by the night.

THIRTY-EIGHT

REBIRTH

THEY SAT IN THE TRUCK, silent for several minutes.

Lee was in the driver's seat. Abe in the passenger's seat. Deuce had finally settled down after giving Lee a requisite amount of slobber, and seated himself between them in the front.

Lee glanced in the rearview, and saw Marie sitting in the center. Jones to her right. Sam to her left. The only light to see by was the from the dashboard lights. The engine quietly thrummed, but Lee had turned the exterior lights off. The horde that had taken Greeley weren't the only primals in Colorado, and it wouldn't do to make a beacon of themselves.

"I think me and Abe are going to do it," Lee said, breaking the long silence. "That doesn't mean any of you have to. If you don't want it, just say so. We'll take you…" he paused, trying to think where the hell any of them might want to be dropped off at.

Marie's face twisted up. "Where, Lee?"

He shrugged. "Wherever you want."

"Will you take me to Disneyworld?" Jones asked, pushing his way into the center.

Lee couldn't help but smirk. Tiredly. "No. I won't take you to Disneyworld."

"Why not? You said wherever I wanted. I want Disneyworld."

"It's in Florida."

Sam sighed. "You haven't been working with Jones as long as we have, Lee. It's best not to let him suck you in."

Jones snorted and leaned back. When he spoke next, his voice wasn't the needling one he used for getting on people's nerves, but a shockingly serious one. "What I'm trying to say, Lee, in my own special way, is that we don't have anywhere to go."

"That doesn't mean you have to do *this*."

"No," Jones replied, quiet. "I suppose it doesn't. But you know…maybe it was all those wonderful nights in our little plywood box in FOB Hampton. Or maybe it was when I decided I was okay with dying with you fuckers in a tunnel. Or maybe I'm just emotional because it's…" His voice cracked. "…It's been a *helluva* day. Been a helluva week."

"Been a helluva three years," Abe said, and they all nodded at that.

"But…" Jones said, manfully strangling his emotions. "Whether you like it or not, y'all have become my family. There. I said it."

"God help us," Marie whispered.

"That's mean, Mom," Jones immediately said back. Shuffled around in his seat, as though all the feelings were making him uncomfortable. Lee could sympathize. "What I'm saying is that, for better or worse, I go where you guys go."

And they all nodded again.

And just by that, in that silent consent, in the blue dashboard glow, sitting in a truck in the middle of nowhere with the only four people he had left in the world, Lee knew what lay ahead of him now. He still couldn't see the road, but he knew it was there, and he knew he'd get another tomorrow. And when tomorrow came, the road ahead would be clearer, even though there was no way to know where it would lead.

Sometimes you just have to follow the road to see where it ends.

Lee's road had led him into the darkest parts of himself, and sometimes, in the darkness, it seems like there's no more road. He'd made his peace with his endpoint, as had every one of the others on that road with him, and in a way, they had all died in that tunnel. But the universe had other plans, and somehow, despite everything, they had been reborn. The same flesh and blood that had gone into that tunnel had come out of it, but what lay inside of those bodies had been irrevocably changed.

Lee had been granted another tomorrow. As for the night that would come after that, and whether or not he would get a second tomorrow, there was no telling. Because the future is unknowable.

So, you take it mile by mile. Day by day. You can only navigate what you can see.

Lee reached forward and turned on the headlights. They speared out into the night, illuminating a small section of road in front of them. And that small section of the road was clear. Beyond that? No way to know. He'd have to drive forward to find out.

He pulled the shifter into drive, but kept his foot on the brakes. "Well. Team. Where to? Sunny California? Rainy Washington? Primal-infested New York?"

"California's got Disney*land*," Sam pointed out.

Jones sighed, petulant. "I guess I'll settle for Disneyland."

"Mmm," Marie leaned back. "Sun, beaches, sand. Drought. Warlords. Cartel. Massive numbers of primals. What's not to love?"

Lee looked to his right, past Deuce's lolling tongue, to Abe's bearded face, and raised his brow in question.

Abe waved a hand forward. "After sweating my balls off in the Gulf for months, I could do with some drought. Plus, we're already facing west."

Lee shrugged and took his foot off the brake. "Suppose we gotta start somewhere. California it is."

EPILOGUE

ARCHANGEL

"Almost there," Angela said between breaths that she was trying to disguise as not gasping. Her thighs and calves burned from the hike, and from the extra load she was pushing up the trail. Her forearms ached, her grip slipping on the handles of the wheelchair.

"Mush," Abby commanded, pointing forward. "God, Mom, you sound like you're dying."

Guess her attempts at disguising the gasping weren't working. So, she went ahead and gasped for the air her lungs were starved for. "It's no joke…" she said, panting. "…about the air…this high up…there's just…not enough of it."

The wheelchair was made for rougher terrain—not the spindly kinds you'd find in hospitals, with tires like those on a road bicycle. This was the mountain bike of wheelchairs. And it was a heavy bastard. Still, the right tire caught on a stone—the "trails" were pretty much just the path that Angela herself had beaten down on her daily hikes. Angela stopped, gathered herself, and heaved the tire over, then continued up.

Sweaty grip. Breathless lungs. Aching muscles.

All of these things had somehow become good. For so long, they had only occurred when terrible things were happening to her. Living so many years with only horrible things happening to get your heartrate up, she'd forgotten what it was like to experience the sensations of hard exercise without the accompanying terror.

Over the course of the last three months, she'd steadily reminded her body—and her mind—that these sensations could be good things.

She took the last slope to the top of the ridge at something like a jog. It was the final push, and she meant to "leave it all out on the field," so to speak. As she churned for the top, everything in her burning, the sweat whisking cold in the chilly breeze, she watched the sunlight dance in her daughter's hair, watched the tendrils of it twist in the breeze.

Watched Abby lean back with her eyes closed, the sun on her face, feeling life.

And it was good.

At the top, Angela nearly doubled over, wheezing. Yes, exercise was good, but pushing that last length always made her feel like she was dying for a minute until her body could regulate itself. Three months, and she still wasn't quite used to the thin air this high up in the Rockies.

Sweating and heaving, Angela raised her head again and watched as Abby checked her wristwatch. "Nineteen minutes and thirty-seven seconds," Abby noted. "You're getting faster."

"I'd hope so."

Once she could manage it, she stood upright and saw what she'd come to see. All around them the vista of the mountain range spread out around her. It still seemed so vast, even though she knew it was only a valley and the peaks that surrounded it. There was so much more out beyond those peaks. So much that it made her feel tiny, but not in a particularly bad way. She felt tiny in a way that forced the perspective. Forced her to see her life as it was: Both intrinsically, monumentally important, and blissfully insignificant, all at once.

Where she stood was just one small ridge in the miles-long valley that made up Aspen, Colorado. To the north of her, the Aspen-Pitkin County Airport bustled with activity, people just dark spots hurrying about like amoebas under a microscope. Helicopters roaring in and out at all hours, and sometimes the thunderous rumble of the massive, gray cargo planes descending and taking off.

Griffin—now with the tongue-tiring moniker of "Interim Commander of American Operations"—had chosen this location because of the narrow valley. A perfectly defensible location against anything that moved along the ground. And they'd learned long ago that the infected, and their evolutionary progeny, the primals, didn't care to cross mountain ranges. A constant reminder to her burning lungs that the rarified air was one of the many things that kept her safe.

Safe. Was she safe? Was anybody every truly safe? Or was it simply relative?

She didn't think that she'd ever feel as safe as she once did, before the world had gone upside down. But she hadn't been safe then either, had she? Safety was simply an illusion that people felt when they didn't have to worry about dying all the time. And by that standard, Angela thought that she was about as safe as she would ever be in this life.

She turned and looked to the other side of the ridge. Nestled there in a little gorge between this ridge and the glistening, rocky waters of the Roaring Fork River, sat a small community of quaint houses, built in a time when quaintness was a desirable attribute, and people moved here not to escape the perils of the flatlands, but to enjoy the picturesque scenery. In among that small collection of streets, people walked along sidewalks, just as normal people used to do in their normal evenings, in their normal lives, in their normal neighborhoods, probably having normal conversations.

Angela could still recall a time when normalcy meant *boring*. A time when people would bemoan the banality of their suburban existences, or judge others for theirs, because they lived "exciting" lives, or yearned for them. Lives not lived by the clock, lives lived with a sense of danger, lives lived not knowing what would come next.

None of them had known what the fuck they were talking about.

Angela had actually lived a life of danger—not the prosaic danger of yesteryear, like being "brave" enough to pursue a dream, or "courageous" enough to protest things you didn't like, or being "fearless" with your opinions in the face of social castigation. No, Angela had lived the skin-tingling, gut-twisting, mind-altering reality of knowing that you lived every second of your life clinging to a narrow handhold over an abyss of violent death.

She'd lived the type of life that her past self would not have even been able to comprehend. And she had survived it.

If any of those other people that bemoaned their boring existences were still alive today, they would likely agree with Angela: Normalcy was beautiful. She wouldn't trade the rest of her boring life for a single second of the dangerous one she'd somehow survived.

It was in an evening hike. It was in the morning sun coming through windows. It was in a fried egg. It was in a conversation. It was in her bed, in the quaint little house down there, and in her living room, and in her kitchen.

Because the evening hike did not require her to constantly listen for the presence of danger. Because the sun came through windows that weren't shattered by bullet holes. Because the egg had not required her to fight for it, or deprive someone else in order to feed her daughter. Because the conversation could be passed with no mention of perilous decisions and lives hanging in the balance. Because she *had* a bed, and a house, and a living room, and a kitchen.

Normalcy.

Beautiful, boring, *incredible* normalcy.

"It's four-thirty," Abby said, looking again at her wristwatch. "You'll miss your meeting."

Right.

Well, not *everything* could be normal. But Angela didn't begrudge the one final tie she still had to that old life. She would have done far more than that to keep what she had now. And what she had was a *life*. And her daughter had a life. And they had friends—most of them military, but Angela was fairly used to that by now. And Abby had some kids her age.

She'd clawed her way through hell to get to this place, and there was no chance she was going to do anything to upset it, so she dutifully spun Abby's wheelchair around, and started back down the ridge, going slower this time, but not so slow that she wouldn't make it back by five.

As they spun off the trail and onto blessedly-smooth concrete sidewalk, the air cold now in the shadow of the mountains, the wind teasing her senses with the coming of autumn, Abby spoke up.

"I think I want to try the walker again."

Angela stopped. Spun the chair so she could look at her daughter. She felt both electrified, and also hesitant not to show too much eagerness, in case she scared her daughter away from her decision.

"Oh?" was what she cautiously answered.

The walker wasn't really a walker. It was a rig on four wheels, designed to help people learn how to walk again. They'd had it for two months now. Abby had tried it, failed miserably, and then pretty much thrown a fit and sworn she'd never touch it again. Fuck the walker, she'd said. Fuck her legs. She'd just be a paraplegic her whole life.

Angela hadn't said anything about it at the time. Didn't know what to say. Didn't know if she should push with some tough love, or just let the girl figure it out on her own. But she'd folded up the device and put it in the downstairs coat closet, where it had remained to this day.

Abby stared sternly at her fingers as they wrestled with each other. "Well. You know. I can't have you pushing me around for the rest of my life."

"I don't mind," Angela said, and part of her regretted saying so—again, wondering if the right thing to do was to push, or let Abby find her own way.

Abby glanced guiltily up at her. "Well. It's not just that."

Angela let her take the lead. Abby could get prickly sometimes. Moody. Quiet. Depressed. Could anyone blame her? As Angela had so accurately observed once: They were all fucked up in the head. She seemed on the verge of going into one of those moods now. And Angela had learned a difficult lesson: There was no amount of motherly advice or sage aphorisms that could yank her out of it.

Abby had to find her own way. Everyone did.

Finally, Abby just shrugged and sighed, seeming exasperated. "When I said that I don't want you to push me around for the rest of my life, that was just me trying to turn myself into a martyr."

Angela lifted an eyebrow. There was another thing about Abby: She'd become brutally honest, both with herself and with others. Sometimes it could be off-putting. But sometimes it was good.

"What I *really* should have said, is that trying the walker the first time made me feel hopeless. But I've thought about it, and I understand that it's something I'm going to have to work really hard on. I didn't want to work hard. But now I do. I want to try to walk again." Abby frowned at her fingers again. Gave Angela a miniscule glance. "And also, I'm sorry for freaking out about it in the first place."

Angela just smiled, turned the wheelchair around, and kept pushing. It was only a few minutes to five. "Well, if you're ready to try again, I'll bring it out. I can help. Or you can do it on your own. Whichever you prefer."

She hoped that Abby would let her help, but there was no telling. If Angela were being realistic with herself—and, inspired by Abby's scalding honesty, she was trying to be—she knew there would be more tears, more tantrums, and more depression. Realistically, the chances of Abby learning to walk again were extremely small. She knew it, and Abby knew it.

But at least this was a move in the right direction. And that's all you could ever really do:

Just move in the right direction. Sometimes life was a hurricane, and you had to hunker down for a bit. But the sky always eventually cleared. There was always another opportunity, no matter how short-lived, to take a few more steps forward. It wasn't about getting to a destination. It was about having the courage to move your feet when you could.

She pushed Abby into the front door of their home at 4:59 p.m., and let Abby take control of the wheelchair, which she was getting better at. She mounted the steps to the second level, her thighs complaining after their brief reprieve of mostly-level sidewalk.

At the top of the stairs, she hung a left, away from her and Abby's bedrooms, and into a small, spare room. In this room, there was only a utilitarian metal desk, and a single office chair. She did not go into this room on any other occasions. She did not prefer to live in the past, or to think about the thread that continued to connect her to it. But, again, she sure as shit wasn't going to ruin what she had, so she took a deep breath, and sat in the office chair, as she did every day at five o'clock.

She pulled her chair in under the desk. Pulled a notepad and pen to her. And only then did she open the desk drawer and take out the satphone inside. She laid this next to her notepad and then leaned back in her chair, glancing at the analog clock on the wall, right in front of her.

It was 5:00 on the dot.

Sometimes it would ring. Sometimes it wouldn't.

Sometimes it wouldn't ring until almost six o'clock. That was fine. She only had one duty: Be at the desk, with the satphone, between 5:00 and 6:00, every evening. A small price to pay for beautiful, boring, incredible normalcy.

She picked up her pen and began to doodle on the notepad, as she would often do while waiting. Stars, and arrows, and random geometric patterns created a jagged framework around lines of hastily-scrawled notes that wouldn't mean much to the average person.

Things like,

Where the fuck is Escondido? 2 cases 556. AA bats.

And,

<u>Gwendolyn???</u> Former CHP?? Amox. Food/water/ammo for 50+?

And,

Can we drop a guntruck?

She was drawing her fifth iteration of a perfectly-imperfect arrow when the satphone buzzed. She glanced up at the clock. 5:07. Punctual today.

She took up the phone and put it to her ear, always bracing herself to hear something God-awful on the other line, but this time there was no shouting and gunfire, just the gentle murmur of laughter in the background.

Hearing that, she felt a momentary wash of relief. Perhaps some nostalgia for the slim moments of human closeness that they'd shared, spun and woven into the tapestry of madness and fear that had been her old life.

"Evening," she said, all business, even as her chest radiated uncomfortable emotions. They always kept it brief and business-like. But so much was said between the words. "What are you thinking about today, Archangel?"

"Oh, lots of stuff," he replied. His voice was meditative, and she recognized its tone instantly from a thousand moments of her past life. She could picture him just as clear as if he were in the room with her: Arms crossed over his chest, frowning at a map or a sand-table, one intense eye ranging over some slim-chanced plan or another. Trying to figure out how to be a good man on the one hand, while he dealt death with the other.

"Been thinking about hardened targets," he said after a moment's contemplative silence. "So, let's talk about the M141 Bunker Defeat Munition, and how many of them you can get me."

And Angela started writing.

ABOUT THE AUTHOR

D.J. Molles is the New York Times bestselling author of *The Remaining Series*, which was originally self-published in 2012 and quickly became an Internet bestseller. Since then, he has expanded *The Remaining* universe to include the *Lee Harden Series*, and each of the six books in that series have been bestsellers in the Military Thriller genre. The final installment of the *Lee Harden Series* was released in January 2022. With over 20 titles under his belt, and more ideas stewing, there is always something else to come!

When he's not writing, he's taking steps to make his North Carolina property self-sustainable, and training to be at least half as hard to kill as Lee Harden. He also enjoys playing his guitar and drums, drawing and creating things, loving on his dogs, and spending time with his wife and three children.

Find more at:
https://djmolles.com

And sign up for the monthly newsletter here:
https://djmolles.com/newsletter

Would you consider reviewing this book?

Reviews help others find my work, which then allows me to keep writing full time. Without them, it just wouldn't be possible to do what I love. So, would you take a minute to share your thoughts?

I'd greatly appreciate it.

-Molles

Review Terminus Amazon US
http://www.amazon.com/review/create-review?&asin=B09PHTHMS5

Review Terminus Amazon UK
http://www.amazon.co.uk/review/create-review?&asin=B09PHTHMS5

Review Terminus Amazon CA
http://www.amazon.ca/review/create-review?&asin=B09PHTHMS5

Printed in Great Britain
by Amazon